A Passion
Redeemed

A PASSION REDEEMED

JULIE LESSMAN

Revell

a division of Baker Publishing Group
Grand Rapids, Michigan

© 2008 by Julie Lessman

Published by Revell
a division of Baker Publishing Group
P.O. Box 6287, Grand Rapids, MI 49516-6287
www.revellbooks.com

Second printing, November 2008

Printed in the United States of America

Library of Congress Cataloging-in-Publication Data
Lessman, Julie, 1950–
    A passion redeemed / Julie Lessman.
       p.   cm. — (Daughters of Boston ; 2)
    ISBN 978-0-8007-3212-7 (pbk.)
    1. Irish American families—Fiction. 2. Daughters—Fiction. 3. Boston
(Mass.)—Fiction. 4. Ireland—Fiction. 5. United States—History—1913–
1921—Fiction. 6. Ireland—History—1910–1921—Fiction. I. Title.
PS3612.E8189P375 2008
813′.6—dc22   2008021681

Unless otherwise indicated, Scripture is taken from the King James Version of the Bible.

Scripture marked TNIV is taken from the Holy Bible, Today's New International Version™ Copyright © 2001 by International Bible Society. All rights reserved.

To my husband and best friend, Keith—
the greatest evidence of God's love for me,
aside from His Son.
Before we even met, you were the longing of my heart,
and I will love you forever.

Make them like tumbleweed, my God,
  like chaff before the wind.
    As fire consumes the forest
  or a flame sets the mountains ablaze,
  so pursue them with your tempest
  and terrify them with your storm.
  Cover their faces with shame, Lord
  so that they will seek your name.

—Psalm 83:13–16 TNIV

Prologue

Patrick O'Connor stirred from a deep sleep at the feather touch of his wife's breath, warm against his neck.

"Patrick, I need you . . ."

Her words tingled through him and he slowly turned, gathering her into his arms with a sleepy smile. He ran his hand up the side of her body, all senses effectively roused.

"No, Patrick," she whispered, shooing his hand from her waist, "I *need* you to go downstairs—now! There's someone in the kitchen."

Patrick groaned and plopped back on his pillow. "Marcy, there's no one in the kitchen. Go back to sleep, darlin'."

She sat up and shook his shoulder. "Yes, there is—I heard it. The back door opened and closed."

"It's probably Sean after a late night with his friends. He hasn't seen them since before the war, remember?"

"No, he came home hours ago, and it's the middle of the night. I'm telling you, someone's in the kitchen."

Marcy jerked the cover from his body. Icy air prickled his skin. Both of her size 6 feet butted hard against his side and began to push.

He groaned and fisted her ankle, his stubborn streak surfacing along with goose bumps. "So help me, woman, I'll not be shoved out of my own bed . . ."

She leaned across his chest. "Patrick, I'm afraid. Can't you at least go downstairs and check?"

Her tone disarmed him. "It's probably just Faith, digging into Thanksgiving leftovers. She didn't eat much at dinner, you know."

"I know, and that's what I thought too, but I just peeked in her room, and I'm sure she was under the covers."

"One of the others, then—"

"No, they're all sleeping. I checked. Please, Patrick? For my peace of mind? Won't you go down and see?"

He sighed and swung his legs over the side of the bed. "Yes, Marcy, I will go down and see. For your peace of mind." He swiped his slippers off the floor and yanked them on his feet. "*And* for mine." He started for the door.

"Wait! Take something with you. A shoe, a belt—something for protection."

He turned and propped his hands low on the sides of his tie-string pajamas. "Shoes. Yes, that should do the trick. Newspaper editor bludgeons intruder with wing tips."

Marcy tossed the covers aside and hopped out of bed. "Wait! My iron. You can take my iron. It weighs a ton." She padded to the wardrobe and hefted a cast-iron appliance off the shelf. She lugged it to where he stood watching her, a half smile twitching on his lips. "Here, take it. And hurry, will you? He could be gone by now."

He snatched the iron from her hands. "And that would be a good thing, right?" He turned on his heel and lumbered down the hall, stifling a yawn as he descended the steps.

"Be careful," Marcy whispered from the top of the stairs,

looking more like a little girl than a mother of six. Her golden hair spilled down the front of her flannel nightgown as she stood, barefoot and shivering. He waved her back and moved into the parlor, noting that Blarney wasn't curled up on his usual spot in the foyer.

Patrick stopped. Was that a noise? A chair scraping? He tightened his hold on the iron while the hairs bristled on the back of his neck. He spied the shaft of light seeping through the bottom of the kitchen door and sucked in a deep breath. Heart pounding in his chest, he tiptoed to the swinging door and pushed just enough to peek inside.

A husky laugh bubbled in his throat. He heaved the door wide, pinning it open with the iron. "I trust this means you've made up your mind?"

"Father!" Faith jerked out of Collin's embrace while Blarney darted to the door and speared a wet nose into Patrick's free hand. His daughter faltered back several steps and pressed a palm to her cheek. Her face was as crimson as the bowl of cranberries on the table. "I . . . I was just giving Collin Thanksgiving leftovers."

Patrick smiled. "Yes, I can see . . . starting with dessert, were you?"

"Patrick, who is it?" Marcy's frantic whisper carried from the top of the stairs and he grinned, turning to call over his shoulder. "It's Faith, Marcy, getting a bite to eat. Go back to bed. I'll be right up."

Collin took a step forward. His face was ruddy with embarrassment despite the grin on his lips. "Mr. O'Connor, I can't tell you how happy I am to see you again. When I'd heard you were killed in the war . . ." His voice broke and he quickly cleared it, his eyes moist. He straightened his shoulders. "Well, when my mother told me you were alive, I hitched a ride any way I could just to get here from New York." He took another step and held out his hand. "Sir, despite the fact that you could take me to task for kissing your daughter, I thank God you're alive."

Patrick grinned and pulled him into a tight hug. He closed his eyes to ward off tears of his own at holding this man who was more like a son. He pulled away and waved the iron at Collin's chest. "So, the chest wound all healed up? Good as new, despite the war?"

Collin smiled and tucked an arm around Faith. "Better than new, Mr. O'Connor. You might say I'm a new man."

"So I've heard," Patrick said, scratching his forehead with Marcy's iron.

Collin stifled a grin. "Uh, sir, did we wake you up . . . or were you catching up on your ironing?"

Patrick chuckled and set the iron on the table. "Marcy's idea, I'm afraid. She's a light sleeper." He reached over and popped a piece of turkey in his mouth. "So, Collin, you haven't answered my question. Have you made up your mind?"

Collin glanced down at Faith and swallowed hard. "Yes, sir, I have. I'm in love with Faith. I want to marry her."

Patrick assessed the soft blush on his daughter's cheeks as she gazed up at the man who had once been engaged to her sister. Her eyes shimmered with joy, and Patrick had never seen her so happy. He snatched another piece of turkey. "And Charity? You've discussed all of this with her, I suppose? As your former fiancée, she has a right to know of your intentions with her sister."

"Yes, sir, I agree. I wrote her immediately before I came home from the war."

"And she's fine with it? No heartbreak?" Patrick chewed slowly, studying the pair through cautious eyes.

"No, sir, no heartbreak, I can assure you. Actually, she was more than fine with it. As I told Faith, it seems she has a new love interest."

Patrick stopped chewing. "A new love interest? Who in blazes could that be?"

Collin and Faith exchanged looks before Faith took a deep breath. "Father, we think she's after Mitch."

Patrick blinked. "Your Mitch?"

Collin's lips pulled into a scowl, and Faith squeezed his hand. "Father, please, we're not engaged anymore, so he's no longer 'my' Mitch. And yes, we think he's the one Charity's after."

"Saints alive, the man is practically old enough to be her father! And after the stunt she pulled in Dublin, trying to break you and Mitch up, does he even like her?"

Faith bit her lip and glanced up at Collin. "I don't think so. But you know Charity. Once she gets an idea in her head, it's there to stay."

"Yes, yes, I know Charity." Patrick exhaled a weary breath. "Faith, put some coffee on, will you? Then you let that man sit down and eat. I suspect your mother won't be able to sleep any more than I will, so we may as well talk. We've got a lot of praying to do—about your plans for the future, your wedding, and your wayward sister in Dublin."

Faith grinned and scooted to the stove to make coffee. "Yes, sir. Want a sandwich too?"

"May as well. Looks to be a long day, and I'm going to need all the energy I can get." Patrick started to leave, then turned with his hand braced on the door. He squinted at Collin. "You're home to stay, I hope? No more New York?"

Collin shot him a grin and reached for a hefty drumstick. "Yes, sir, home to stay. I hope that's good news. Except for your grocery bill."

Patrick chuckled and pushed through the kitchen door. *Thank you, Lord, for bringing that boy home safe and sound.* With a bounce in his step, he mounted the stairs, anxious to share the good news with Marcy. His thoughts suddenly returned to Charity, and his pace slowed considerably. She was the daughter who puzzled him the most. Beautiful, stubborn, wild—and so hard to reach. He fought a smile and made his way down the dark hall, shaking his head as he entered his room. *God help Mitch Dennehy!*

1

DUBLIN, IRELAND, OCTOBER 1919

*Poor, unsuspecting Mitch. The dear boy—well, hardly a boy—
doesn't stand a chance.*

The thought coaxed a smile to Charity O'Connor's lips as
she entered the smoky confines of Duffy's Bar & Grille. The
aroma of boxty cakes and sausage bangers sizzling on the
griddle reminded her she'd been too nervous to eat. Her escort
held the heavy wooden door while she stepped in. The brisk
night air collided with the warmth of the cozy pub. Her eyes
scanned the room, past the long, serpentine bar crowded with
patrons, to the glazed mahogany booths lining the mirror-
laden walls. Disappointment squeezed in her stomach like
hunger pangs.

He isn't here!

With a lift of her chin, her gaze shifted to the sea of tables
occupied by lovely lasses and well-to-do gentlemen who appeared to be enjoying each other more than the food. In a
cozy corner, a flute and concertina harmonized, the sound of
their lively reel laced with laughter, off-key singing, and the
murmur of intimate conversations.

"Charity, if this is too crowded, I know a quiet place we
can go—"

She whirled around. "No, *please*. I see a table in the back."

Her breathy tone and eager smile produced the desired effect on Rigan Gallagher. His hazel eyes softened. Slacking a hip, he notched his straw boater up with one thumb to reveal an errant strand of dark hair, giving him a boyish look despite his thirty years. His lips pulled into a wicked grin. "Aye, Duffy's it is. But it's fair to warn you, Miss O'Connor, you can't avoid being alone with me forever." He pressed his hand firmly against the small of her back and guided her to the one unoccupied table at the rear of the room.

Every nerve in her body tingled with electricity, but not from Rigan's touch. Charity took the seat he offered and draped her shawl over the back. Her eyes flitted to the booth she had shared with Mitch Dennehy over a year ago. The memory washed over her like the candlelight flickering across the crisp, white tablecloth before her, its flame dancing high and hot.

A tall, gangly waiter approached, and Charity looked up, fixing him with a radiant smile. He must be new, she thought; she hadn't seen him before. A lump the size of a persimmon bobbed in his throat while two pink splotches stained his cheeks. He handed them each a menu. His bony fingers fumbled the parchment sheets. "G'day, miss . . . sir. What can I get for your pleasure?"

Rigan opened the menu. "I daresay the most important thing would be a liter of your best wine, my good man."

"Yes, sir, very good, sir." The waiter wagged his head and darted away.

Rigan perused his menu, absently reaching across the table to twine Charity's hand in his. "Suddenly I find myself quite ravenous." He looked up, a twinkle lighting his eyes. "But then you always whet my appetite, Miss O'Connor."

Charity bit back a smile and slipped her hand from his. "Rigan, you are incorrigible. Behave . . . or I shall never accompany you again."

He leaned back in the chair with a low, throaty laugh. His

gaze assessed her from head to waist, finally lingering on her mouth. "Oh, I think you will. I've been told I'm irresistible."

"Mmmm . . . to the right woman, I suppose." She studied her menu and decided on the shepherd's pie. She looked up, eyes blinking wide in innocence. "Tell me, Rigan, did they happen to mention anything about being a rogue?"

He clutched at his chest with a pained expression. "Charity, you wound me. The moment I stepped into Shaw's Emporium, I've only had eyes for you." He leaned forward, his manner suddenly serious. "Charity O'Connor—you, only you—take my breath away."

She fidgeted with the filmy sleeve of her lavender blouse to deflect the intensity of his gaze. For the hundredth time, she thought what a pity it was she was in love with Mitch Dennehy. With money, looks, and reckless notoriety, Rigan was a catch for any girl. But alas, for her, that's all he was. A catch—the perfect man to "catch" the eye of a certain editor from the *Times*.

Rigan removed his hat and placed it on the table. He returned to his menu, his manner confident as he relaxed in the chair. That maverick strand of ebony hair fell across his forehead in unruly fashion—like the man himself—providing a mesmerizing contrast to the hazel hue of his eyes. His nose, no doubt once straight and strong, now sported the slightest of bumps, as if broken in a brawl. Probably over a woman, Charity mused, given what her friend, Emma, had told her about Rigan Gallagher III.

"Too handsome for his own good, that one," Emma had whispered on the fateful day he entered the shop where Charity worked. "And too handsome for the good of any lass, if you ask me." Dear Emma had rolled her eyes in such a comical way, Charity had to stifle a giggle. "Aye, and too rich as well. But that won't be stopping Mr. High-and-Mighty once he sets his eyes on the likes of you, I'll bet me firstborn."

The waiter returned with a bottle and two glasses. His hands were quivering as he poured the wine. Suddenly a stream of port splashed over the edge into Rigan's hat. Rigan jumped up with a shout. He snatched his hat from the table and shook it out. "You clumsy oaf! It would take two months of your wages to replace this hat!"

Charity shot to her feet. "Rigan, please, it was just an accident, and it's only a dribble of wine." She blotted the table with her napkin, chancing a peek at the waiter. The poor fellow appeared to be having trouble breathing as he gasped for air. Charity chewed on her lip. Oh my—she had never seen a redder face! She laid a gentle hand on his arm. "Don't mind him," she whispered. "It could happen to anyone. Why, my first week on the job, I broke an expensive bottle of perfume and the shop reeked for days." She patted his hand and smiled. "But after that, the place smelled rather nice."

The fear faded from his eyes and he nodded. "Thank ye, miss, you're a kind lady, ye are." He turned to Rigan and clicked his heels. "Forgive me, sir, for my clumsiness. Please allow me to tidy your hat . . ."

Rigan waved him away. "No, the lady's right. It's only a dribble of wine." He glanced at Charity with a sheepish grin. "Although I'd prefer it dribbled down my throat rather than my hat."

"Yes, sir," the waiter said with another blush. "I can bring a fresh bottle if you wish—"

"No, no, just see to our food, my good man, and we'll call it even."

"Yes, sir, thank you, sir."

Rigan ordered their food and dismissed the waiter. Charity watched as he poured their wine and put the bottle down. He propped both arms on the table and leaned forward, slowly twiddling his glass. He fixed her with a probing stare. "So, Charity, tell me. Why are we slumming in Duffy's *again* when there are nicer places I could take you?"

Her cheeks grew warm. "No reason. I came here once and liked it, that's all."

Rigan eyed her with frank curiosity. "With Dennehy?"

Charity drew a quick breath. It lodged in her lungs, refusing to budge.

Rigan's laugh was harsh. He grabbed his wine and downed it. "Really, Charity, how big of a fool do you think I am? The moment you discovered my father owned the *Irish Times*, you were more than willing to go out with me. Of course, that was fine with me—you certainly wouldn't be the first woman after my money."

"Rigan, you're being ridiculous. I couldn't care less about your money—"

"Or me."

"Well, no, not when you behave like a fool."

He poured himself more wine and lifted his glass in a toast. "To the 'fool'—a part I suspect I will play more than once when it comes to you." He took a drink and settled back in his chair. "So . . . what is Mitch Dennehy to you?"

She fingered the silk ruffle of her V-necked blouse, careful to avoid his eyes. "I already told you. He was my sister's fiancé. He's like a member of the family."

Rigan snorted, idly tracing the rim of his glass with his finger. "How is it that I don't get a 'brotherly' feeling?"

Another rush of warmth invaded her cheeks, stiffening her jaw. "What you 'get' or don't get is no concern of mine. Nor are my relationships any concern of yours."

He slanted forward with a low growl. "They are if I intend to go on seeing you."

Charity pushed her wine glass away and reached for her shawl. "Very well, perhaps you'd better take me home." She stood in a rush and swiped a strand of hair from her eyes. *Take that, Mr. Gallagher!*

He rose and blocked her exit, straw boater in hand and a smile on his lips. His thumbs stroked the nubby rim of his hat. "I can do that, but I don't think that's what you want. I think you would much rather stay and enjoy a plate of Dublin coddle with a charming—albeit notorious—scoundrel." He bowed slightly, his boater clutched to his chest. "Especially a scoundrel with a knack for boiling the blood of Mr. Mitch Dennehy."

Charity drew in a quick breath. "What do you mean?"

Rigan pressed close, his low laugh warming her ear. "I mean, who better to enlist in turning the head of the man you love than the one he can't abide?"

"Oh, Rigan, you're utterly impossible. I'm not in love with anyone."

He cocked a brow. "Maybe not, but for some reason I have yet to ascertain, you desperately want to catch his eye. Of course, I hoped you were interested in me. But regrettably, I do believe I detected an increase in your ardor once you learned of my connection with the *Times*. Tell me, Charity, did you think I wouldn't notice your subtle queries about him? And now this—" he waved his hat toward the pub, "your curious obstinance to continually have dinner in a middle-class bar frequented by *Times* employees?"

Charity thrust her chin out. "Are you suggesting I'm using you?"

Rigan lifted a curl fallen loose from her topknot. He fondled it with his fingers as he studied her. A hint of a smile played on his lips. "I am . . . and most happily so. I must admit I was disappointed it wasn't my charm that wooed you. But alas, I will take you, Charity O'Connor, any way I can. If I am to be the bait to entice some hapless suitor, so be it."

Charity sank to her chair. "You would do that? Whatever for?"

Rigan returned to his seat. "Call me a hopeless romantic. Or maybe I'm counting on you falling in love with me in the process. Either way, I'm willing to play the fool—for a price."

Her gaze narrowed. "What price?"

The waiter interrupted with steaming plates of shepherd's

pie and Dublin coddle before dashing off again. Charity felt her stomach rumble. She picked up her fork. "What price?" she repeated, stabbing into her food.

Rigan sipped his wine. He took his time while he watched her over the rim of his glass. He finally set it down and relaxed back in the chair, assessing her through hooded eyes. "The taste of your lips—anytime, anywhere."

Charity's fork clattered to her plate. Her hand flew to her mouth to stop the nervous laughter from bubbling up. Impossible! Giggles rolled from her lips in unrestrained hilarity, bringing tears to her eyes and discomfort to her cheeks. *The rogue! He couldn't be serious!* She dabbed at the wetness with her napkin and took a deep breath, a shaky hand pressed to her chest. "Really, Rigan, I have a mind to leave right now and never see you again. You can't be serious."

He never blinked. "Quite."

Charity quickly reached for her wine, desperate to diffuse her shock. Her lips rested on the edge before sipping it while thoughts of Mitch Dennehy clouded her mind. She stared at the scarlet liquid glazing the glass and fought back the hint of impropriety that nettled her nerves. No! She couldn't do this . . . could she? She swallowed hard and slowly looked up, careful to place the glass back on the table with steady fingers. Her chin lifted with resolve. "My lips? And nothing more?"

She could feel the heat of his gaze from across the table.

"Nothing . . . until you beg."

Heat flooded her cheeks. *Dear Lord, what am I doing?* She picked up her fork and forced a smile she didn't feel. At least the tantalizing smell of the food, if not Rigan, had her salivating. She took a deep breath to dispel her discomfort and strove for a show of confidence. "Not a likely scenario, but I won't ruin your fun."

She closed her eyes for her first taste of the pie, fighting the urge to emit a soft moan as she rolled it across her tongue. Opening her eyes once again, she hoisted her glass with a nervous grin. "Absolutely delicious . . . and far, far better than the taste of my lips, I assure you. Nonetheless, feed me, kiss me, and turn a head in the process, and we, my good man, shall have a deal. After all, I'm a woman who usually gets what she wants—a trait I also admire in others."

Rigan tipped his glass in a toast. "Well then, my dear Charity, I daresay, if admiration were love, we'd be well on our way."

❦ ❦

Mitch Dennehy glanced at the clock and groaned. He plowed his fingers through his short, cropped hair, then stood from his desk to stretch. "Come on, Bridie, I'll buy you supper. It's the least I can do after keeping you so late."

Bridie O'Halloran looked up, and her gold-brown eyes reflected the fatigue of a long day. She slumped back in the chair and blew a wisp of silver hair out of her face. "Sweet angels in heaven, I thought you'd never ask! I'm no good dead from starvation, you know." She held up the latest edition of the *Times* and wagged it in the air. "Read all about it. Fifty-year-old Galway woman perishes at the *Irish Times*."

Mitch laughed and reached for his coat. "And I'll do better than Brody's. How does Guinness stew and fresh-baked soda bread sound, hot out of the oven?"

Bridie rolled her eyes in obvious ecstasy. "Like the gates of heaven itself . . . or further south if you'll throw in a pint of ale."

Mitch retrieved her coat and held it while she slipped it on. "Well then, Duffy's it is. Nothing but the best for my slave labor."

Bridie grunted. "Keep that up and I'll be ordering scones and lemon curd as well."

Mitch laughed and ushered her through the newsroom and into the lobby, nodding at those who worked the second shift. He opened the door, and a rush of cold air assaulted their faces. With it came the fumes of the city, from its gas lamps and motor lorries and faint whiff of manure. Bridie shivered as he led her around the corner to Duffy's, a favorite haunt he'd once frequented. Shouldering open the heavy, oak-carved door, Mitch allowed Bridie to enter before him. One foot on the threshold, and the onslaught of boisterous laughter and tempting aromas assailed his senses. The reaction in his gut was immediate. Everything—from the pungent smell of spiced beef and crubeens simmering on the stove, to the scent of lemon oil gleaming the bar and booths to a high sheen—all of it, dredged up memories he'd rather forget.

Mitch slammed the door behind him. His lips stiffened in a frown as he surveyed the room, hunting for an empty booth or table, to no avail. *What? They giving food away now?*

"Saints above, has it always been this busy?" Bridie asked, searching the room for some sign of an empty chair.

"Didn't used to be. But I haven't been here in a while."

Bridie wheeled to face him. "Aw, Mitch, I'm so sorry. I completely forgot—this is the place you and Faith—"

Mitch pushed past her, hooking her elbow on his way to the bar. "Yes, it is, but it doesn't matter. It's been over a year and by thunder, if I want to eat in Duffy's again, I will." He glanced behind the bar, catching the eye of a portly, red-haired waitress toting a tray of foaming ales. At the sight of him, her mouth tilted into a toothy grin. She passed the tray off to another waitress and hurried over. Her blue eyes sparkled.

"Well, as I live and breathe, if it isn't the man of me dreams." Clutching fleshy arms around Mitch's waist, she squeezed with a teasing groan. "Where on this fair isle of ours have you been keeping yourself, Mitch Dennehy? We've missed you! The rest of us thought maybe Duffy poisoned you." She grinned at Bridie. "Nice to see you too, Bridie."

Mitch laughed and returned the woman's hug with one of his own. He chucked her double chin with his thumb and grinned. "Truth be told, Duffy told me ol' Harry finally proposed. Near broke my heart, it did. Enough to stay away and nurse my wounds."

Sally blushed. The folds of her full cheeks dimpled in delight. "Aw, go on with you now, you silver-tongued rake." Her smile faded. "We heard about Faith, Mitch. No tight lips in a place like this, you know. I kinda wondered if maybe that was why we hadn't seen ya. You okay?"

Mitch sighed and shoved his hands into his pockets. "Yeah, Sal, I'm okay." He leaned forward, ducking his head. "But I'd be a sight better if we had a booth."

Sally tossed her head back in a giggle, causing her short, puffy curls to bob. "Well now, I can't toss customers out, even for a heartbreaker like you." She inclined her head with a saucy sway. "But I'm not without my influence. Why don't you and Bridie sit at the bar and get yourselves a pint. I'll see you get the very next one."

Mitch planted a kiss on Sally's glowing cheek. "You're the best, Sal. Tell ol' Harry to treat you right or I'll hunt him down."

Mitch steered Bridie to the nearest empty stool where she sank against the bar with a low groan. "Never again will you talk me into working this late. I'm starving. Hope you brought lots of cash."

He gave her a wry grin. "I always bring lots of cash when I feed you. What's your pleasure?"

She perked up and squinted at the rows of bottles behind the bar. "I believe I'll have an extra stout porter."

Mitch signaled the bartender and ordered a Guinness for Bridie and a ginger ale for himself. He turned and leaned back to survey the action.

She swiveled on the stool and puckered her brow. "Ginger ale? You're reduced to ginger ale?"

He frowned. "Lay off, Bridie."

The bartender delivered their drinks. He gulped his like it was pure corn liquor, then wiped his mouth with his sleeve.

Bridie shook her head. "I'll lay off when you get back to normal." She took a swig of her beer, eyeing him over her mug. "When you gonna get on with your life?"

"Leave it be, I said." His lips cemented into a hard line as a clear warning.

"No, I won't leave it be. You're miserable. When are you going to move on?"

He shot up from his stool and loomed over her like a tree about to fall. A muscle twitched in his jaw. "I said, lay off! As your manager, my personal life is none of your business."

She bristled. Her chin slanted up. "Yeah, but as your 'friend,' it's getting on my bloomin' nerves. It's been a year. Have you seen anyone else? Even taken another woman out to dinner?"

Mitch turned away, a sour feeling in his stomach. "Not interested."

She lifted her porter in a mock salute. "Mmmm . . . not interested in drinking, not interested in women. Sounds like the old Mitch left when Faith did." She whirled to face the bar, two-fisting her beer like it was her long-lost mother.

Mitch cuffed the back of his neck. He released a noisy sigh, fraught with frustration. "So help me, Bridie, I knew you'd give me trouble tonight. You have no talent whatsoever for minding your own business." He exhaled again, then turned to face her, his muscles fatigued from trying to fake it. "I've given up drinking because . . . ," he closed his eyes and massaged the bridge of his nose with his fingers, ". . . once she left, it got harder to stop." He leaned heavily against the bar and stared straight ahead. "And I gave up women because . . . not one could even come close."

Bridie rested her hand on his arm. "Let her go, Mitch. Faith wasn't for you. But someone is. Find her. Get out there and do what you do best—break a few hearts. Trust me, it will all make sense when you find the right one." She tilted her head and grinned. "Where's that annoying confidence of yours when you need it? Your faith in God?"

A smile tugged at his lips. "Yeah, it did get me through the last year without losing my mind." He downed the rest of the ginger ale. "But I suppose you're right. Maybe it's time."

"Kathleen might be a good place to start, you know. You two used to have a lot of fun before Faith. And you know she still cares for you, Mitch."

He nodded, his gaze fixed on the empty glass in his hand. "I know."

"Ready for a booth?" Sally flitted by, gesturing for them to follow.

Bridie slipped off her stool. "The saints be praised! Another minute and I'd be but a faint heap on the floor. Get your wallet out, Mr. Dennehy. This is going to cost ya dearly."

"It already cost me dearly," he mumbled. He followed the bounce of Sally's head as she led them across the room, menus in hand. He breathed a sigh of relief when she passed the front-corner booth where he and Faith had often sat.

She slapped the menus down on a booth at the back of the smoky pub. "How's this?" she asked with a perky smile. "And Duffy told me to go ahead and wait on you myself, even though I'm working the bar tonight."

Bridie grinned. "Oh, that's a great big tip for sure, Sally girl." She winked at Mitch. "Very dearly, my friend."

"Thanks, Sally," Mitch said, cutting Bridie a searing look. "I'll take another ginger ale, then we should be ready to order." Sally toddled away and he leaned back, stretching his legs. He picked up the menu, hoping he could assess it without drooling. "I swear, Bridie, I'm so blasted hungry, I could order one of everything."

"The shepherd's pie is quite good and, I might add, quite filling."

The sound of a familiar voice froze his fingers to the paper. Looking up, shock nipped at the heels of his hunger.

"Charity . . ." Her name solidified on his tongue, refusing to let another word pass. It was seconds before he realized his mouth hung open, allowing painful silence to fill the air. He cleared his throat and stood to his feet, angered at the heat she generated. "Charity . . ."

"You said that," she whispered, her smile almost shy.

His jaw hardened in self-defense. "You're looking well." Well? She was heart-stoppingly beautiful and nothing less. "How's your grandmother doing?" he asked. He could feel his hands sweat.

The smile faded from her full lips. "She's doing all right, I suppose, despite the fact that my great-grandmother is not." Her clear, blue eyes darkened with worry. She pushed a strand of honey blond hair away from her face. "Mima seems to get weaker every day. Grandmother and I are both concerned."

"I'm sorry to hear that. Is there anything I can do?"

Charity blinked, the depths of her eyes drawing him in. "Mima would love to see you, Mitch. We all would."

Something cramped in his gut, and he suspected it wasn't hunger.

Bridie cleared her throat and held out her hand. "Hello, I'm Bridie O'Halloran. I work with Mitch at the *Times*."

Charity smiled and extended her hand. "I'm Charity O'Connor. Nice to meet you."

"Faith's sister?"

A blush crept into Charity's cheeks. Her gaze fluttered to Mitch and back. "Yes."

"It's good to meet some of Faith's family. We loved her at the *Times*, you know."

The color in Charity's cheeks deepened. "Thank you," she whispered. Her smile faltered as she withdrew her hand and turned to Mitch. "It's wonderful seeing you again, but we have to be going . . ."

"We?"

"My gentleman friend and I. We have tickets to the theater."

She glanced over her shoulder, then returned her gaze to his. "Do come by, Mitch. We would love to catch up."

"Ready, darling?" Rigan appeared behind her. He rested his hands on her shoulders and gave Mitch a cool smile. "Hello, Mitch."

The blood drained from Mitch's face as his jaw calcified to stone. "Hello, Rigan. It's been a long time."

Charity's hand floated to the flounce of silk on her chest. A pretty blush stained her cheeks. "Goodness, you two know each other?"

"Yes, Mitch works for me." Rigan's hands slid to Charity's waist, resting comfortably. "Or should I say, my father?"

Mitch ground his teeth behind a tight-lipped expression, biting back insults that lingered on the tip of his tongue. He forced a smile. "Definitely not you."

Rigan laughed and swung his arm around Charity's shoulders, pulling her close. "No, not at the present, certainly. But perhaps the future?" With maddening ease, his fingers casually traced at the base of Charity's throat, sending another wash of color into her face. "Shall we be on our way, Charity? It wouldn't do to miss the first act. Good night, Mitch." He nodded his head at Bridie. "Ma'am."

"Good night, Mitch," Charity whispered. "Stop by anytime, please." She extended her arm to shake Bridie's hand. "Bridie, it was a pleasure. I hope we meet again."

Mitch watched while Rigan whisked her away. Heads turned as they made their way to the door. Mitch scowled. *Nothing but trouble for any woman. Humph—a perfect match.*

Bridie's voice jarred him back. "My, oh my. So *that's* the infamous Charity O'Connor? Goodness, Boss, rumors don't do her justice. That one could turn the head of the Pope."

Mitch frowned. "Where the blazes is Sally?" he bellowed, ignoring Bridie's remark.

Her eyes narrowed. "And dangerous, too, from the look

of that vein twitching in your head. Who's the guy? He looks familiar."

"Rigan Gallagher III." Mitch all but bit the words out.

Bridie's eyes popped. "No joke? So that's Old Man Gallagher's black-sheep son? Sweet saints above—handsome as the devil and all that money too."

"He's no good."

"For you? Or for Charity?"

Mitch sneered. "He's nothing but heartbreak for any woman."

Bridie paused, then took a deep breath. "But she's not just any woman, is she, Mitch?"

Sally descended upon the table, her cheeks puffing with heat. "Sorry about the wait. There's some sort of company meeting in the back slamming away kegs of ale like it was sarsaparilla. Ready to order?"

"Just bring me another ginger ale, Sally. I'm not hungry."

Bridie looked up. "Sally, bring us two plates of crubeens, a side of champ, and some of your best brown soda bread. And I'll have another Guinness."

"Sit tight; I'll dish it right up for ye." She scooted away, disappearing through the maze of tables into the kitchen.

Bridie crossed her arms and rested them on the table. "She's not, is she?"

He looked up, the whites of his eyes burning. "Not what?"

"Just any woman?"

He leaned in. "She's a spoiled brat who uses her beauty to get what she wants. She ruined my life once. It won't happen again." He fairly spit the words in Bridie's face.

"And you had nothing to do with it, I suppose."

He slammed his fist on the table, causing her to jump. "So help me, Bridie, I'd fire you right now if I didn't think Michael would cinch me up."

The burn in her eyes matched what he felt in his gut. "All

I'm saying is, don't be laying all the blame on her for hanging you up. You're the fool who gave her the rope."

"Stay out of it, Bridie; I'm warning you."

"I will not. At least not until you admit she's under your skin."

"You're out of your mind. No one's under my skin."

"She was once. Enough to change the course of your life."

"She's a kid."

Bridie cocked a brow. "Not from where I was sitting. How old?"

He glared. "Almost twenty . . . going on sixteen."

Her forehead puckered. "Oooh . . . that is rather young. What are you again? Thirty-five, almost thirty-six?"

Mitch looked up with a glare meant to singe.

Bridie ignored it. "Faith was twenty when you fell in love with her."

"She's nothing like Faith."

Bridie reached across the table to take his hand in hers, her voice a near whisper. "Nobody is. But there's a reason it didn't work out."

He grunted. "Yeah, there's a reason, all right. A golden-haired vixen, five foot four."

"No, I mean 'a reason,' like maybe Faith wasn't the one."

Mitch rubbed his jaw with the side of his hand. "Yeah, well, apparently not." He looked up, his eyes shooting her a warning. "Don't get any ideas. That woman gives me cold chills."

Bridie pulled her hand away and leaned back against the booth, a smile hovering on her lips. "So I noticed." She grinned. "I haven't seen you that off-guard since Faith took a potshot at you on her first day of work."

The memory brought a faint smile to Mitch's lips. "Yeah, she was something." He saw Sally heading their way with a tray piled high with food and drinks.

Bridie shook out her napkin. "Yes, she was. And so is her sister, evidently."

Sally plopped two steaming plates of crubeens on the table with a thud. The smell of spicy pork caused his juices to flow. When Sally finished unloading plate after plate, she stood back and grinned, hands propped on her ample hips. "Hope you're hungry. Ready to dive in?"

Bridie smiled at Sally and picked up her fork. She winked at Mitch. "You know, Sally, I think he just might be."

⋘ ⋙

"You've been awfully quiet all night, at least since we left Duffy's. Honestly, Charity, I'm a bit dismayed. I thought you would be feeling quite victorious. You had him eating out of your hand, you know."

Charity continued to stare out the window of Rigan's Rolls Royce as they pulled up in front of her grandmother's house. Moonlight flooded the garden, casting distorted shadows of fuchsia and larkspur across the cobblestone walk.

He turned the ignition off and shifted to face her. "Charity, look at me."

She glanced over, one hand hovering on the door handle. "What is it, Rigan?"

He scrutinized her, head cocked as if trying to decipher the mystery of her mood. "What's wrong?"

She expelled a weighty sigh and leaned back, eyes fixed straight ahead. "I don't know."

"You got your wish. You turned his head. You should be happy."

"I know," she muttered, her tone quiet. *I should be. But what if he still blames me . . .*

"Charity, you effectively reduced the man to moronic monosyllables and clenched teeth."

Mischief twitched on her lips. She *had* caught Mitch by surprise. His clear, blue eyes had stared in bold appraisal, taking her in from head to foot without even being aware. At six foot four, he towered over her, a mountain of a man with unruly blond hair and a petulant gaze, adept at turning heads as well as she. She grinned, peering at Rigan out of the corner of her eye. "I did, didn't I?"

Rigan's smile matched her own. "*We* did, my dear. You and yours truly—your partner in crime."

She giggled and twirled a lock of hair around her finger. "It *was* glorious, wasn't it? And yes, Rigan, I couldn't have done it without you." Her finger suddenly stilled, causing the curl to spring free and spiral to her shoulder. She tilted her head to study him through narrowed eyes. "Why does he dislike you?"

Rigan laughed and reached for her hand, warming it between his fingers. "I could ask you the same thing."

Her rib cage suddenly felt too tight. A sick feeling settled in her stomach. She tugged her hand free and hefted her chin a notch. "He doesn't dislike me."

"Oh, he dislikes you, all right. It was as clear as his stony stare and the humorous tic in his jaw. A thin, cold thread of disgust tightly twined with a scarlet strand of lust. What did you do, Charity? Why does he hate you?"

Fear constricted her throat. *He doesn't hate me—he wanted me!* She sat up, her eyes burning with heat. "I think this conversation has come to an end. Thank you for a wonderful evening. Now, if you'll walk me to the door . . ."

She fumbled with the door latch, finally swinging it open. He reached across and slammed it closed. The heat of his breath was hot on her face. "No, this conversation is not over. Tell me, Charity. Why does a beautiful woman like you need the assistance of a rogue like me to snare another man's heart?"

Her pulse pounded in her throat. She didn't answer.

He jerked her close. "All right. I'll tell you. I think somehow, someway, you're the reason he's no longer engaged to your sister. Lies, perchance. Or perhaps you exposed him, something dark and sinister from his past. Or maybe, just maybe, seduction . . ." He traced his finger along the curve of her jaw, pausing beneath her lips. "That would be my personal favorite, of course. A temptress." He lifted her chin with his finger, his gaze upon her mouth. "I'm quite partial to temptresses, you know." He leaned to kiss her.

Charity pushed him away. "Rigan, stop! What are you doing?"

"Extracting payment," he whispered. The warmth of his words feathered her cheek.

"Oh," she breathed, swallowing hard. He leaned in to nuzzle her neck, and the heat of his lips burned like fire. She twisted away. "*Lips*, Rigan, only lips. Our bargain, remember?" She stared, wide-eyed, her chest rising and falling with ragged breaths.

He grinned. "So it was, Charity, so it was." He stroked her cheek with his fingers. "I see our 'temptress' is nowhere in sight. Pity." He sighed and took her hand in his. "But temptress or innocent makes little difference to me. Either way, payment is long overdue."

Cupping her chin in his hand, Rigan brushed her lips with his own, a gentle sway of his mouth against hers before pressing in. A shiver of heat traveled her spine as he pulled away, and her hand fluttered to her chest. She blinked, surprised he'd left her breathless.

"I'll walk you in." He opened his door, swung out, and circled the car to open hers on the other side. He extended his arm. "I do believe, Miss O'Connor, we've struck a bargain that will serve us well."

Charity blinked and took his hand. "I do believe . . . ," she whispered and clung to his arm for the trembling of her legs on the final few steps to the porch.

"How's it going, Jimmy?" Mitch scrounged in the pocket

of his woolen suit coat. He tossed a punt into a battered can next to a tall pile of newspapers on the street in front of the *Irish Times*. He took a paper off the top, the stack taller than the toothless man hawking them.

"Oh, not too bad, I suppose." Jimmy squatted, warming stubby fingers over a pitiful firepot at his feet. He cocked his head and looked up with a grin. "Let's just say me and the missus won't be going on a seaside holiday anytime soon."

Mitch dug back in the coat. He tossed another punt in the can. "Give Mary my love."

"I will at that, but I'll wager she'd rather have it from you."

Mitch attempted a smile and shoved the newspaper under his arm, yawning as he headed to his Model T. He should kick himself for coming back to work after taking Bridie home. What had possessed him? The work could wait. He reached down to rotate the crank. After several tries, the engine sputtered to life. He clenched his jacket closer and got in the car, slowly weaving into the flow of traffic. A weighty bloke on a bike darted in front of him, forcing him to skid to a stop. Mitch blew through his teeth. *You're testing my limits, mister. I'm in the perfect mood to run somebody down.*

His foul disposition stayed with him all the way home. He parked the car and got out, flinging the door shut before shuffling up the steps to his grey-stone flat on Cork Street. The window flowerboxes spilled over with leggy impatiens and trailing ivy, stubborn survivors of Dublin's temperate October nights. Mitch yanked on the curve-handled knob and opened the heavy Georgian door with its arched window and sunny yellow paint. It slammed behind him with a noisy thud. He mounted the gleaming wood staircase and noted that Mrs. Lynch had been busy—the warm maple flooring was buffed to a sheen. Where in the world did the woman get her energy? She was almost eighty, but her vitality left him in the dust.

Mitch jammed the key in his door and jimmied the lock with

too much agitation. It might as well have been a fortress. He rammed the door with his knee. "Open up, you blasted thing." He jangled the knob until the wall vibrated.

"Easy does it, Mitch." Mrs. Lynch peeped around the corner of her door across the hall, silver tresses trailing beneath a lavender sleep kerchief. Her cornflower-blue eyes sparkled. "It's just like a woman—the gentler, the better."

Mitch hung his head in exhaustion. "Sorry, Mrs. Lynch. I didn't mean to waken you."

"Bad day at the paper?"

He breathed in some air, then blew it out with the last of his energy. His frustration drifted out along with it. "No, not really. I'm just tired."

"Well, I already took Runt for his constitutional, so no need to worry about that. Looks like you should go straight to bed." She squinted, her blue eyes obscured by paper-thin crinkles of skin. "You're home late. Out with a lady?"

He turned back to the door, rotating the key with painstaking ease. "No." The lock clicked and the door swung open. Mitch managed a stiff smile over his shoulder. "Thank you, Mrs. Lynch. Good night."

He closed the door and flipped the bolt, adjusting his eyes to the moonlit room. He flung his coat on the wrought-iron rack as his golden retriever greeted him, tail thudding against the wall while he burrowed his cold nose into Mitch's hand. His lovesick squeals helped to soften Mitch's mood. Tapping his chest with his hands, Mitch chuckled when Runt jumped up, forepaws planted firmly against his shirt. "Hello, big guy, how's my buddy today? Did you have a nice walk with Mrs. Lynch?"

Runt strained and groaned while Mitch rubbed the side of his snout, his tail flapping in ecstasy. Mitch leaned in and nuzzled him, scrubbing his neck with a forceful motion. "I don't know what I'd do without you, big guy. You keep me sane, you know that?"

Runt woofed, jumped down, and commenced dancing in circles.

"All right, all right. Dinner's coming. Give me a minute to get my bearings." Mitch struck a match and reached up to light the oil wick of a pewter wall sconce. The light flickered, then filtered into his parlor with a soft, steady glow. He stooped to pick up a piece of lavender-scented stationery off a stack of freshly laundered clothes. He held the note to the light, its edge scalloped with a lacey effect.

Mitch—Runt has been fed and walked. I still have a few of your shirts to press. You can pick them up tomorrow. Mrs. Lynch

He lifted the sheet to his nose, doubting the lavender fragrance would have any effect in calming his nerves. *God bless her. More like a mother than a landlady.* A niggling guilt settled in. *Great.* Perfect company for the irritability that throbbed inside like a splinter of glass. He should take her on an outing. Lunch and the art museum, maybe. She would like that.

Runt continued to bounce, his tail reaching new heights of aerial flight. Mitch propped a hand loosely on his hip. "Don't try to con me with that pitiful 'I haven't eaten in twenty-four-hours' act. I'm wise to you, buddy-boy. I have it on the best authority you've already been fed and watered, and quite well, no doubt." Runt let out a gruff bark and sank to the floor, extending his forepaws in a long stretch.

Mitch loosened his tie and tossed it on the chair. He lit the Tiffany oil lamp beside his cordovan sofa, then bent to rekindle the remains of a fire he'd started that morning. Warmth seeped into the room, along with the pungent smell of burning peat, but it did little for the cold feeling in his chest. He reached for the newspaper and stretched out on the sofa.

What was wrong with him? His muscles twitched like he'd just sprinted a mile. The clock on the mantle chimed and he looked up, fatigue and edginess warring within. Eleven o'clock, but sleep was nowhere in sight. Mitch sighed and pitched the paper to the other side of the couch. He reached down to scratch Runt, who had sprawled along the foot of the sofa. Mitch exhaled a hefty sigh. His thoughts strayed to their favorite topic.

Faith.

His stomach no longer clutched at the memory of her, but a dull sadness still remained. There had been times when he'd been like this with her, his nerves volatile as if raw and pasted on the outside of his skin. She could always sense it, feel it. And always knew what to do. How to calm him down, soothe him, love him.

Mitch closed his eyes and kneaded his forehead. Usually she'd put her arms around him and hold him, whispering words of love and encouragement and prayer. Always prayer.

Mitch jumped up to dispel the thought and tripped over Runt. A swear word got as far as the edge of his tongue before he bit it back. Runt looked up with liquid-brown eyes. Mitch sighed.

"It's not your fault, buddy," he muttered. Runt's eyes followed him as he paced the room. He stopped and rubbed the back of his neck. He had been doing better lately, hadn't he? More like himself? Going for days at a time without even thinking of her. Even weeks without missing her. She was across the ocean, for pity's sake, engaged to someone else. How much farther out of his life could she possibly be?

And then, tonight. *Charity.* Those hypnotic eyes, staking through his heart with bitter regret and deadly allure.

Just like before.

Mitch slapped the newspaper out of his way and sat back down, hunching on the far edge of the sofa, opposite Runt. He put his head in his hands. She was poison, pure and fatal, even toxic to his mood. Like a spider spinning a light, breezy web, beckoning . . . *"Mima would love to see you, Mitch. We all would."*

He sat up and burrowed his fingers through his hair, cursing the attraction he felt, even now. That had always been the problem. Loving Faith and avoiding Charity. Ignoring the fascination she seemed to have with him.

Until he gave in.

Mitch jumped up, shaking it off. The guilt, the regret, the attraction. He fumbled through his desk drawer for the Bible Faith had given him. He uncovered it beneath a stack of coffee-stained galley sheets. Clutching it to his chest, he sank back on the sofa, calm finally settling in.

He wanted to avoid Charity completely, but something in his gut told him no. He had to see her again, if only to warn her about Rigan. His jaw hardened. She needed to know.

Mitch leaned his head back on the sofa and closed his eyes. It would be good to see her grandmother and great-grandmother again. In the eight months he courted Faith, he'd grown fond of Bridget Murphy and her mother, Mima. They had been like family. Then the war ended, and Faith's family had returned to Boston, leaving Charity behind. To help take care of Mima, she said. Somehow Mitch suspected she had other motives. She always did.

He sat up and opened his eyes, flipping the pages of the Bible at random. He settled on 2 Corinthians, and his eyes widened as he scanned the page. *Be ye not unequally yoked together with unbelievers: for what fellowship hath righteousness with unrighteousness? And what communion hath light with darkness?*

A ghost of a smile flitted across his lips. So much for Bridie's implication that he pursue Charity O'Connor. *"As far as the east is from the west,"* so is Charity from her God. Mitch sighed. It was a real pity. She was an amazingly beautiful woman who drew him like a magnet. Once, he would have gladly explored the bounds of her generosity without compunction. But Faith had changed everything. Attraction, lust, and beauty had been enough before. Not anymore. Now he craved the beauty of the Spirit, the touch of God in his soul. His love for Faith had been pure, God-directed, exhilarating. Never again would he settle for less.

Mitch continued to read, the power of the words warming his body like the fire had been unable to do. He yawned, realizing his tension had finally dissipated, slinking away like the dusk at the end of day. He placed the Bible on the table and stood, stretching to release the kinks.

Thoughts of Charity suddenly flashed in his mind, and he stiffened his jaw. By the grace of God, he could do this. He would warn her and be done with it. And then he'd get on with his life.

He looked up to the ceiling, brows arched in expectation. "I'm gonna need your grace to do it, you know." He stifled a yawn and blew out the lamp. "A boatload should do."

2

Charity yawned, still clad in her pink chenille robe and slippers. She ruffled a hand through the loose curls trailing her back and scratched her head. The smell of sizzling bacon made her mouth water. She shuffled to where her grandmother stood and wrapped her in a sleepy hug.

"Good morning! How was the theater last night?" Bridget Murphy asked, glancing up from the bacon she was frying.

"Very nice, Grandmother, although I don't know what all the dither is about with Shakespeare. Personally, I find the language a bit tedious. Why not just speak in the dialect of the day? As far as I'm concerned, it's 'much ado about nothing.'"

Her grandmother flipped the bacon over with a chuckle. "Dear me, heaven forbid you should get any culture."

Charity thumped into the chair and propped her chin in her hand. "I know, I know, every young woman needs to be refined and cultured. But it all seems such a fuss."

"Culture? A fuss?" Bridget turned, fork in hand. "Goodness, Charity, you never cease to jar my senses. Culture is sustenance for the heart and the mind."

She scrunched her nose. "I'd rather have sustenance of another kind, thank you. I want to feel things, Grandmother, like the racing of my heart. You know, the admiring gaze of someone you love, the sound of his warm whisper in your ear." Charity arched her brows and jutted her chin. "Romance, plain and simple. And methinks it will not come hither with Shakespeare."

Grinning, Bridget shook her head and drained the bacon grease into a can. She cracked several eggs and dropped them into the hot skillet. They crackled and spit while she reached for a mug from the cupboard. She poured coffee from the pot perched on the warming plate. With a wry smile, she placed the steaming cup in front of Charity.

"Methinks you need good, strong coffee to clear the excess sleep from your mind, young lady. It's about time you got up. I fed Mima hours ago." She reached to give Charity a quick squeeze before returning to check on the eggs. "And how was your time with Mr. Gallagher III?"

"Thanks, this is good." Charity sipped slowly, ignoring her grandmother's question.

Bridget dusted the eggs with seasoning, then glanced over her shoulder. "Well?"

A silent sigh drifted from Charity's lips. "Fine. It was fine."

"Only fine?"

"I like Rigan. We have fun."

"But no palpitations?"

She studied her grandmother over the rim of her cup, wondering how much to divulge. There was no use trying to fool her. They were too much alike. She noted the sheen of Bridget's snow-white hair coiled at the nape of her neck. Even at sixty-five, her grandmother was a beautiful woman. And like her granddaughter, not one to dally. She turned, eyeing Charity with the same striking blue eyes she'd inherited. Charity sighed. "He's no Collin, if that's what you mean."

Bridget plopped the eggs on a platter along with the bacon. Not saying a word, she retrieved the toast from the oven. She placed everything on the table, along with plates and utensils, then settled in her chair and bowed her head. "Dear Lord, bless the bounty of our table and the steps of our day. Amen." She reached for a piece of bacon. Her eyes gentled. "I thought you were over Collin."

Charity stabbed at her eggs. "Well, I hardly have a choice now, do I, since he's to marry Faith in less than three months?"

"Might I remind you, young lady, you were the one who sent him packing."

She sighed. "I know, at least the second time around, I suppose. I guess it was inevitable I'd lose interest when he put our engagement on hold before the war. It just hurts, that's all . . . to see Faith and Collin in love back in Boston while I'm here all alone."

One silver brow raised as Bridget stared, her cheeks puffy with eggs. She quickly swallowed. "I'd hardly call dating a small army of men being 'alone.' Not the least of which is one of Dublin's most eligible bachelors."

"I suppose. But it still feels that way."

With a quick swipe of her mouth, Bridget jumped up. "Oh, speaking of Boston, we received a letter from your mother yesterday." She hurried to the counter and plucked an envelope from the windowsill. She placed it on the table with a chuckle. "Poor Marcy, sounds like she has more wedding jitters than Faith and Collin."

The fork all but dropped out of Charity's hand in her haste to pick up the letter. Without thinking, she lifted it to her nose, as if to breathe in the scent of home. She pressed the cool parchment against her cheek, suddenly overcome with longing for her mother. She blinked to clear her eyes, then put the envelope aside. Her fingers lingered to caress her mother's graceful script. "Is she all right?"

"Yes, of course, other than missing you."

Charity smiled. "I miss her too. Terribly. So why the 'wedding jitters'?"

"Well, it seems she's rather fit to be tied with all the preparations. Apparently Katie, the most stubborn flower girl on God's green earth, according to Marcy, is refusing to walk down the aisle with Collin's ten-year-old cousin, the ring-bearer."

Charity grinned. "Father always thought I was the difficult daughter. I suspect he's met his match with Katie."

"So it seems. When he's home to discipline her, that is. Marcy says he's been working longer hours since his promotion to editor, and that doesn't set well with her, either. And then there's Faith and Collin . . ."

Charity took a quick sip of her coffee. "And what's the problem with the lovebirds?"

"Wedding jitters, I suspect. Evidently they're sparring like siblings, Marcy says. Claims Collin wants Faith to quit her job after they get married, and Faith is none too happy about it."

Charity chuckled. "I think Faith traded in the most stubborn fiancé in the world for the second most stubborn. With her temper, it should be interesting to watch." She popped up to refill coffee, her tone suddenly buoyant. "And speaking of stubborn, guess who I saw at Duffy's last night?"

Bridget stopped chewing. "Not Mitch Dennehy, for mercy's sake?"

Charity giggled and shimmied into her seat like a little girl with a big secret. "One and the same!"

"Goodness, don't just sit there grinning like a monkey, how is he?"

"Handsome as ever, of course, but still holding a grudge, I suspect."

Bridget puckered her lips while buttering her bread. She placed her knife on the plate. "Mmmm, I don't wonder."

"Well, it's water under the bridge now, Grandmother; he needs to get over it." Charity chomped on a piece of toast and brushed the crumbs from her lips. "So I suggested you and Mima would love to see him."

Bridget jagged a brow. "And you?"

Charity frowned and shoved a piece of bacon into her mouth. "And me, yes, of course. Why not? We're all family."

Bridget chuckled. "Or would have been."

"Grandmother!"

"Like you said, dear, water under the bridge. We can certainly laugh about it now, can't we? So . . . do you think he'll come?"

Charity polished off the last of her eggs with a smug smile on her face. She drained her coffee and leaned back in her chair, crossing her arms with a definite degree of confidence. "Do I think he will come?" She nodded and grinned. "Whether he wants to or not."

❦　❧

"Tonight? He's coming *tonight*? Saints alive, Grandmother, why didn't you tell me?" Charity all but ripped her black, woolen shawl off her back. Her insides quivered while her arms hung limp at her sides. The shawl dangled to the floor, puddling in a pile at her feet.

Her grandmother blinked. "Well, for mercy's sake, Charity, I just found out myself this afternoon. He came by on his lunch hour."

Charity's heart took a nosedive. "Mitch was here? This afternoon? *Grandmother!*"

Bridget crossed her arms. Her blue eyes bristled. "I believe that's what I said, and I don't appreciate your tenor, young lady."

Charity expelled a calming breath and adjusted her tone. "I'm sorry. You just took me by surprise, and I'm . . ." She pressed a hand to her chest, feeling faint. "I'm not ready!"

"Charity, you look lovely—"

"No! I'll have to take a quick sponge bath, fix my hair, and . . ." Her breath came in short, raspy gasps. She clutched at the front of her gray voile blouse. "And change my clothes."

Bridget rested a thin, veined hand on Charity's arm. "Saints above, Charity, you're white as a ghost. You're not going to throw up, are you? I know what worry does to your stomach. Besides, it's only Mitch. Why are you so nervous?"

Charity felt the color drain from her cheeks and put a shaky palm to her middle, hoping her lunch would stay put.

Bridget stepped back. A hand fluttered to her chest. "Oh, no, please tell me you're not setting your cap for Mitch? Mercy me, Charity, the man's old enough to be your father!"

Charity's jaw ascended the slightest degree. "He wasn't too old for my sister."

Bridget huffed. "He most certainly was! And if it wasn't for that headstrong mother of yours disregarding my opinion, he would have never gotten through that door." She folded her arms, gumming her lips in annoyance. "Just plain stubbornness," she muttered, "inherited from her father, no doubt." She made the sign of the cross. "Bless his soul."

Charity swallowed hard to dispel the sour taste on her tongue, suppressing a tiny burp with a hand to her mouth. "Well, it's too late to argue about it now. When is he coming?"

Bridget glanced at the clock on the parlor mantle. "Six. You've got an hour."

Charity groaned and ran her fingers over the topknot she'd worn to work. She tossed her shawl on the coatrack and raced for the stairs, scaling them two at a time.

"I'll need help with the vegetables and the table, you know," Bridget called after her.

"I will, Grandmother," Charity promised, shooting a smile over her shoulder. "Twenty minutes. I'll be down in twenty minutes—you have my word."

"Humph," Bridget said on her way to the kitchen, "I'd rather have your help."

Charity grinned. A giggle bubbled in her chest that rivaled the nausea in her stomach.

He's coming!

She hurried to her closet and flung it open. She stared at the arsenal of dresses purchased with her wages and discount from Shaw's Emporium. She had to look perfect. She snatched an armload of clothing from the rack and heaved it onto the bed, then kicked off her shoes and shimmied out of her skirt. Her fingers flew over the buttons of her blouse until it opened, allowing her to strip it off and hurl it across the room. She took a deep breath and pressed her hands to her stomach. *Please don't let me throw up.* Why did he make her feel this way? No man had ever reduced her to this, not even Collin.

She plucked a pale green frock from the heap and posed in the mirror, assessing with a critical eye. With a grunt, she launched it across the room to join the blouse. Maybe the pink organdy. No, too dressy, too obvious. *Why is this so difficult?* A skirt and blouse? Yes! Definitely more "Why hello, Mitch, I didn't know you were here . . ." She tunneled through the pile, her breathing erratic. She dragged out a lemon yellow silk blouse that had garnered a number of compliments from male customers at the store. *Yes!* She draped it across her chemise, pleased at how the color brought out the blue of her eyes. She looked at her alarm clock and bit her lip. Oh, fiddle. No time to take a sponge bath. She dressed in the blouse, fumbling with the buttons, then backtracked to the closet. She honed in on a pale blue hobble skirt, guaranteed to show off her figure. Posing, she smiled into the mirror. The smile died on her lips. *Her hair!*

Topknots may be the style, but if she had learned anything from men, it was that they liked a woman's hair free, unfettered, pure seduction in its flow.

With frantic hands, she ripped the pins from her hair. All at once, she doubled over in pain as her frantic nerves churned the soda bread and kippers she'd had for lunch into pure acid. She shot a hand to her stomach and closed her eyes, biting hard on her lip to stop the wretched contents from rising to her throat. With a groan of defeat, she ran down the hall and flung herself over the washbowl in the bathroom and spewed, dislodging any sustenance she'd consumed that day. Slowly she straightened, feeling somewhat better. She brushed her teeth, then moistened a towel and wiped her face before proceeding to gargle with lilac water. She spit it out in the washbowl and sighed. As a child, she hadn't minded when her nerves had worked their way into bouts of easy vomiting. It had won her mother's sympathy on more occasions than one, often alleviating her of going to school or hated chores. It had become, in fact, a talent she had perfected. But sweet saints alive, she had no time for it now when she needed every precious moment to get ready!

Wasting no time, she ran back to her room and grabbed the hairbrush, stroking until her scalp ached. She flipped her hair back and brushed some more until it fell in loose, gleaming curls down the front of her blouse. She reached for the rouge on her dresser and applied the tiniest amount to her ashen cheeks, then cheated and rubbed a bit on her lips. She blotted them with a pucker that resounded with a soft pop and glanced at the clock. 5:19. A mischievous grin worked its way across her rosy lips. How about that? Time to spare.

❧ ☙

Mitch turned the car off and sat, staring blankly at the cottage-style home where he'd once spent happy times. Returning to this house was more difficult than he thought. He had hoped to get his visit over with easily, quickly, during the full light of day. But he'd forgotten Charity would be at work, and Bridget had begged him to return for dinner. As much as he dreaded coming back, he didn't want to disappoint Bridget and Mima. He released a quiet sigh. He missed them.

In slow motion, Mitch pocketed the switch key and climbed out of the car, feeling like a bloke on death row going to his last meal. With the onset of autumn, the days were getting shorter, casting the pale pink glow of dusk over the houses along Ambrose Lane. Despite the coolness of October evenings,

Bridget's garden seemed to thrive, pink mounds of sedum lining the cobblestone walk. Tufts of purple fuchsia stood guard, swaying in the breeze.

He took a deep breath and made his way to the porch. Sagging a bit from age, it still invited him with its rustic bogwood swing and flowerpots burgeoning with impatiens not yet nipped by frost. A mix of smells assaulted him, taking him back to better days: the scent of viburnum, wood fires, and chicken frying on a stove. His stomach growled, and instantly he made up his mind to enjoy the evening. These were people he knew, cared about, despite their relation to the woman whose memory had stolen a year of his life. He lifted his fist to knock on the door. Tonight he would move on, he decided with a rush of resolve. He would put Faith O'Connor out of his mind and his life, once and for all. A wry smile curled his lips. And hopefully keep her beautiful sister at arm's length.

The door swung open. Bridget stood smiling, reminding him so much of Faith's mother Marcy that he felt a twinge of regret she wouldn't be here tonight.

"Mitch! Thank you for coming. I just knew Charity wouldn't want to miss your visit. Come in, come in. Can I take your jacket?"

"Thanks, Mrs. Murphy." He sniffed the air as he handed her his coat. "Something smells awfully good. Fried chicken?"

Bridget giggled and closed the door behind him. "Yes, with colcannon, glazed carrots, and fresh-baked soda bread. And do call me Bridget, will you please? We're old friends now, aren't we?"

She hung his coat up and ushered him to her kitchen at the back of the house, a large, open room with a wood fire crackling in an oversized fireplace. Windows covered in cheery yellow chintz peeked out on a vegetable garden in between seasons, the shimmer of dusk lending an ethereal air. A large wooden table stood in the center of the room draped with a crocheted tablecloth. Yellowed with age, it was charming nonetheless, accented by sparkling china and Irish-lace napkins. A crystal bud vase in the center sported sprigs of fuchsia, a nice complement to two crystal candlesticks glowing with flame.

"Mitch, you don't mind if we eat in the kitchen, I hope. Mima chills so easily these days that we've taken to having our meals in here by the fire."

"Of course not, Mrs. . . . *Bridget*. How is Mima?"

Bridget's smile faltered for the briefest of seconds, then returned. "Oh, she's been better, I'm afraid, but we're muddling along." She glanced out the back window, squinting. "Oh, good, here she comes. I sent Charity to the neighbors to borrow a touch of cream for the coffee. I'm afraid I used all mine for the trifle we're having for dessert."

Mitch glanced out the window just as Charity breezed in. Her cheeks were pink from the chill of the night. A smile lit up her face, and her full lips were the color of berries. She pushed soft strands of shimmering gold over her shoulder.

"Mitch, hello! It's good of you to come. I'm so glad we ran into you the other night."

The muscle in his jaw tightened. She'd caught him off-guard at Duffy's, but never again. He knew how to read women— women like her, anyway. And she was an open book—from the sway of her silk-spun hair to the mesmerizing eyes fringed with heavy lashes. The smooth fold of her silk blouse draped a body no decent woman should have. He nodded. "Hello, Charity. Did you enjoy the theater?"

A spray of pink, which he suspected had nothing to do with the cold, painted her cheeks. She turned away to store the cream in the icebox and fumbled with the latch before finally pulling it open. Her hands were shaking, but her voice was as smooth as the silk of her blouse. "Yes, of course, it was wonderful. But then, I always enjoy Rigan's company." She turned, her composure flawless once again. "I understand you two are old friends."

The smile stiffened on his lips. "Acquaintances. Never friends."

"Really? Well, he speaks quite highly of you."

Mitch scowled. "I doubt that." He turned to Bridget. "Mrs. Mur . . . Bridget . . . I couldn't help but notice your garden. Have you planted your winter vegetables yet?"

Bridget nodded, her eyes sparkling, obviously delighted to discuss gardening with Mitch while Charity poured the wine. Someone knocked on the glass pane of the kitchen door and Charity jumped, spilling the port. Bridget hurried over to let her neighbor in, a tiny woman with flame-red hair and watery eyes to match.

"Oh, Bridge, I sorely need your help. My youngest, Davy, poured some salt in the stew, and I don't know how to fix it. I swear he'll be the death of me yet. Can you be a dear and save me neck? My Johnny's bringing 'is boss home for supper, wouldn't ya know, and it'll be me in a stew if ye don't help me out."

Bridget put an arm around her shoulder. "Sure, and Johnny'll never know once I'm done with it, I can tell ya that." She reached for her shawl and gave Mitch a penitent look. "Make yourself at home and have a sip of wine while I run over to help Maggie. Charity, would you mind bringing Mima to the table? I'll be back, fast as you please." The door slammed behind her.

Mitch glanced at Charity. "Can I help?"

"No, you heard Grandmother. Sit down and make yourself at home. Mima's no problem whatsoever." She hurried out with a smile.

He stood in the middle of the room, feeling lost. He certainly wasn't at home in this house. Not anymore. Rubbing the back of his neck, he ambled to the table and sat down. He eyed the glass of wine. It would take the edge off, but the aftertaste was too bitter to suit him. He pushed it away.

He cleared his throat, drumming his fingers on the table in

a staccato fashion. He crossed his legs, uncrossed them, then crossed them once again. He jumped up, stifling a swear word at the back of his throat. Surely he could help! He marched out of the kitchen and down the hall to Mima's room. He peeked in the door, poised to speak. The breath stilled in his lungs.

At eighty years old, Mima was little more than skin and bones, a tiny Dresden china doll with long, snowy hair fanned across her pillow. Charity stood over her, sponging her pale, translucent cheek with a wet cloth, her voice soft and tender.

"There you are, Mima, your skin is as glowing as a newborn babe's. How pretty you look! Now just a dab of color . . ." Charity rubbed her finger across her own lips and applied a hint of blush to her great-grandmother's cheeks. She leaned back with hands on her hips. "Goodness, Mima, I'll bet if Great-Grandfather could see you now, he'd fall in love all over again."

A weak chuckle rasped from Mima's throat, followed by a harsh cough. Charity soothed her with a gentle touch. "Now let's twist your hair into a pretty topknot, all right?"

Mitch stepped away from the room. He turned and made his way back to the kitchen. Before long, Bridget bounded through the door.

"Goodness, it's nippy out there, isn't it?" She slipped her shawl on the coatrack, then looked at Mitch and smiled. "Ol' Johnny'll be none the wiser tonight, I can tell you that. The stew will go down well enough. But"—her smile broke into a grin—"not as well as the fried chicken, I'll wager."

Mitch laughed. "As I recall, there are few who can rival the cooking skills of Bridget Murphy. Although Mrs. O'Connor does come close."

Bridget chuckled and began to chat until Charity appeared in the doorway, arms firmly around Mima's waist.

Mitch stood up. He observed Charity, patient and tender as she held the frail woman upright with each fragile step she took. Mima wore a thick chenille robe that swam to her feet.

Her hair, pulled back in a knot, emphasized the gaunt curve of her cheeks. The same blue eyes as Bridget and Charity assessed him with a glimmer. "Hello, Mitch," she whispered, allowing her great-granddaughter to settle her into a chair at the head of the table.

"Mima, it's good to see you again. You're looking well."

She grunted. "No, I'm not. But it's kind of you to say."

Charity gently pushed Mima's chair in and leaned to buss her cheek with a kiss. "You do too, Mima, so you might as well face it. You're gorgeous and you know it."

Mima patted Charity's hand with a faint chuckle. "Such a good girl. And speaking of gorgeous. Wouldn't you say, Mitch?"

Mitch smiled, but his mouth went dry. "Absolutely."

Charity giggled. "Mima, you're embarrassing me! Drink your wine."

The evening proceeded pleasantly enough with Mitch enjoying the meal despite the memories it provoked. They chatted on, catching up on Mitch's job at the *Times*, Mima's health, Bridget's garden, and Charity's job at Shaw's, among a host of other amiable subjects.

And then the conversation steered a deadly course.

"It's hard to believe it's been a year since we've seen you, Mitch, and now it's passed so quickly. Why, Christmas is just around the corner . . ." Bridget's voice broke. Her eyes filled with tears, causing Charity to lean and touch her hand.

"Grandmother, please don't," she whispered, her voice suddenly hoarse.

Mitch watched the scene, dread crawling inside like a swarm of spiders.

Bridget straightened in the chair and patted Charity's hand. "I'm sorry, dear, I suppose it's the wine making me a bit melancholy. I'll be all right."

Mitch sipped his coffee, working hard to sound casual. "Not looking forward to Christmas?"

Bridget rose to clear dishes from the table, and Charity followed suit. "Oh, I love Christmas. Just not this year."

"Why not?" he ventured, holding his breath for her answer.

She and Charity exchanged glances. "Well, you see, Mitch, Charity will be going home."

He blinked. "Home?"

"To Boston."

Without thinking, he grabbed his glass of wine and swallowed a sip. "For Christmas?"

"For good, I'm afraid."

He tasted the alcohol on his tongue and scowled, pushing the glass away once again. He turned to Charity, striving for nonchalance. "After all this time and help you've been to your Grandmother and Mima, I just thought you intended to stay."

She watched him, as if studying his face for the slightest expression. "I was. But I'm afraid my father has other ideas. It's important to him we all be together."

He nodded, as if he understood completely. "Of course, for Christmas."

Charity looked at her grandmother, who suddenly shifted her attention to a boiling pot of pump water on the stove. Charity sighed. With the slightest hitch of her chin, she turned to stare at him head-on. "Yes . . . and for the wedding."

He might as well have been gut-punched.

It was the first reference all evening to her family in Boston. The same family that had become his own in the brief time they'd been here during the war. He swallowed hard, remembering with painful clarity everything about them. Everything that should have been.

His family. His wife. *His* wedding.

She was watching him. They were all watching him, and he suddenly realized they'd been avoiding this as much as he. On pins and needles, just like him. He cleared his throat and stood, pushing back his chair. "I really should be going. I have a long day tomorrow."

Bridget approached, her brows knitted with concern. She rested her hand on his arm. "Mitch, please don't feel like you have to run off. You haven't even had dessert."

He patted his stomach and forced a smile to his lips. "Blame it on the sixth piece of chicken or the triple portion of potatoes. Honestly, I couldn't eat another bite. I'm sorry."

"I'm sorry too. We enjoyed visiting with you. Will you come again? Mima and I live a pretty sheltered life. After Charity leaves, it will be mighty dull. We'd love the company."

He nodded and reached to take Mima's frail hand in his. "Mima, it was wonderful visiting with you again. I pray you stay well."

"You, too, Mitch. I'll gladly take those prayers." An impish smile tilted her cracked lips. "And give you some of my own."

He smiled and stood, extending his hand to Bridget. "I can't tell you when I've enjoyed such a delicious meal. Thank you for your warm hospitality."

"Oh, go on with you. It was my pleasure," she said, squeezing his hand. She glanced at Charity. "I'll see to Mima while you walk Mitch to the door." She leveled her gaze on Mitch, a glint of steel in her sparkling blue eyes. "Don't be a stranger. You promise?"

He laughed. "I promise." He followed Charity down the hall, his chest tight from the onslaught of emotions wrenching inside. She opened the door and leaned against it, her hand on the knob. "You don't have to leave, you know. We can talk."

He assessed her striking blue eyes, devoid of any guile he'd seen in the past. They stared back in complete openness, soft and concerned. Gone was the seductive tilt of her head, the calculated pose of her body that had always put him on edge. He smiled. "Thanks, but I really need to get home."

Her disappointment was palpable, changing her demeanor.

"I understand. Rigan says it's been a madhouse at the *Times*, what with the British proclaiming the Irish Republic illegal."

He scowled. Two of his least favorite subjects: the British and Rigan Gallagher. He turned. "Speaking of Gallagher, I've got something you need to hear."

She grinned, and the saucy tilt of her head was back in play. "Oh, now you want to talk."

"Don't turn on the charm, Charity. It won't work."

"It worked once," she said, strolling into the parlor, hands clasped behind her back.

He closed the door hard. "That was a lifetime ago."

She spun around, eyes twinkling. "No, only a year, remember? That night in the car? You said you were attracted to me. That I might have a chance with you if I got a little older." She grinned and dipped in a playful curtsy. "Wish me happy birthday, Mitch, I'm almost twenty."

He leaned against the parlor entryway, trying not to smile. He crossed his arms. "I also told you to shape up and fly straight."

She clutched her hands behind her back, like a little girl about to misbehave. "Most men think I have," she whispered. "I know Rigan does."

His smile dissolved into a scowl. Her blue eyes widened when he pulled her to the sofa and pushed her down. "Sit . . . and listen. Spending time with a lowlife like Gallagher is hardly flying straight. He's nothing but trouble." He slacked his stance, hands braced on his hips. "Although I could say the same for you."

She perched on the edge of the sofa, hugging her knees. "Maybe you're just jealous."

He muttered under his breath and yanked her back up. He turned her to face him, his hands tight on her arms. "I'm not playing here, Charity. Rigan Gallagher is dangerous. I don't want you seeing him."

Her smile faded. "You're hardly my father, Mitch. I'll see whomever I please."

He softened his hold. "Not him. Trust me. He has a reputation."

She pulled out of his grasp and sank to the sofa, rubbing her arms where he'd gripped her. "So do you," she whispered, looking up with hurt in her eyes. "Especially with me."

He drew in a long breath and exhaled. He sat down beside her, his voice quiet. "You're right. I haven't exactly proven my virtue where you're concerned. I'm not excusing what you did, but I'm the one who gave in. I won't deny you were the temptation, but my actions . . . ," he rubbed his palms over his face, "they were wrong." He looked up, his eyes heavy with remorse. "Will you forgive me?"

She blinked. "It's no crime to be attracted to someone, Mitch. It was just a kiss. There's no sin in that."

He stood. "There is when you're in love with someone else."

She jumped up and restrained him with a hand on his arm. Her eyes were naked with pain. "I've died a thousand deaths over what I did to my sister, Mitch. And to you. But she's gone, and I'm still here." A glimmer of hope flickered across her face. "Attraction is the first step to falling in love, you know."

He stared for a long moment, then quietly removed her hand from his coat. "Not for me, Charity. I want more."

She moved away and turned, her eyes chilling him to the bone. "What more could there possibly be?"

He studied her. A little girl with the look of a woman, bent on a track that would destroy her soul. His smile was sad. "I only hope and pray you find out."

She stood stock-still for a full moment after the door closed behind him. Nothing but the cold click of the lock, a rush of frigid air, and the heat of her anger. She pressed a finger to her temple, her gaze singeing the paisley swirl of the worn parlor rug. She straightened her shoulders and moved down the hall, head high and fists clenched. Stopping briefly outside the kitchen door, she drew in a deep breath, heavy with the aroma of Bridget's boiled coffee. She flexed her fingers and practiced a smile, wide and relaxed. There was no need to worry Grandmother.

"Dinner was wonderful," she said, breezing into the room with a warm smile.

Bridget looked up with worry lines etched between her brows. "Is Mitch all right?"

Charity rounded the table to collect the dishes. She blew out the candles. "Of course."

Bridget hesitated. "Are you?"

Charity laughed as she unloaded the dishes onto the counter. "Yes, dear one, I am. It was a lovely evening." She turned. "Mima in bed?"

Bridget nodded.

"Well, you need to head that way too. I'll take care of the dishes."

"We'll do them together." Bridget moved to the sink.

Charity squeezed an arm around her grandmother's shoulder. "No, ma'am. You look as exhausted as Mima. I'm doing them, no argument." She pulled away to rub the sleeves of her blouse. "But I do believe I'll change into something warm first. You might just lose those impatiens tonight, Grandmother."

A sad smile curved Bridget's lips. "It's time, I suppose. Unto everything there is a season . . ."

Charity kissed her grandmother's forehead. "One season ending just means another is beginning." She gently stroked her grandmother's cheek, staring long and hard into her eyes. "I love you so much. I hope you know that."

"I do, dear. And I feel exactly the same way." She patted Charity's face, a glimmer of wetness in her eyes. She put a finger to her lips. "Shhh . . . you're my favorite granddaughter, you know. But mum's the word. Don't stay up too late, my dear."

Bridget shuffled from the kitchen, leaving Charity alone to clear the few remaining dishes. She lifted Mitch's full glass of wine in her hand and held it aloft. Trailing her finger on the rim, she dipped it in the wine, then closed her eyes and touched it to her lips. The taste was warm and strong. Like her feelings for him.

She set the glass on the counter and headed upstairs to her room. She leaned to light the oil lamp by her bed before stirring up the peat fire in the small pot-bellied stove. Her fingers felt numb while she worked with the buttons of her blouse, barely aware when it slithered to the floor. In a daze, she stood before the mirror and unfastened her skirt. Its pale blue folds dropped in a pool at her feet.

Her focus sharpened on the girl in the mirror . . . the one with the tragic eyes.

Sky blue eyes a man could get lost in. Full, ripe lips demanding his gaze. A lush body to quicken his pulse. Every man's dream. So she'd been told.

"Not for me, Charity. I want more."

She shivered and picked up her robe from the chair, tying the sash with a jerk.

More. He wanted more. Anger knotted in her stomach. He wanted virtue and God and a weak-minded woman. One with the icy milk of human kindness in her veins.

She looked in the mirror, her eyes steeped in pain. He wanted Faith. They all wanted Faith—Collin, Mitch. And even her father, preferring her sister as the daughter of his heart.

Charity dropped on the bed. A mix of anger and guilt shuddered through her like the chill of the room. She couldn't escape it. She'd betrayed her sister. Now regret shadowed her in shame, never allowing her to forget.

She grappled her fingers through her hair. If only she could be free. A clear conscience. A forgiven heart. The love of the man she longed for. Her fist trembled to her mouth as an involuntary cry escaped her lips. *Oh, Faith, I'm sorry. When did I start hating you?*

Charity pressed her fingers to her temple and squeezed her eyes shut. Hadn't she, Charity, always been the beauty in the family? The younger sister who turned the heads? The apple of her father's eye? *Yes.* Until the 1907 Massachusetts polio epidemic changed everything. God stood by while it stole the life of her older sister, Hope—Faith's twin. Overnight, the family's focus shifted to Faith, the eight-year-old fighting for her life in a hospital far away.

Charity brushed at the wetness springing to her eyes. Even at the tender age of six, her memories were as sharp as the pain in her throat. No more tea parties with big sisters, no more center of attention, no more "Daddy's girl." No, that role belonged to Faith, along with stacks of pretty books, handmade dolls, and homemade fudge. As if she had a fairy godmother. Someone watching over her.

God?

Charity stood, staring in the mirror over her dresser. The line of her jaw hardened.

God. Some invisible being pandered to by her sister and parents. A lover of men, supposedly, good and kind. But not to her. Never to her. She squared her shoulders, clenching her fists at her sides. Nothing more than a demanding deity, thriving on partiality.

Just like her father.

She lifted her chin. Let her sister have her God. She didn't need him. She would make Mitch Dennehy fall in love with her, and it wouldn't take prayer to do it. She turned and kicked her skirt across the room, then slumped on the edge of her bed. In the flickering shadows of her dark, cold room, she put her head in her hands. And cried.

3

Charity cricked her neck staring up at the ominous red-bricked front of the *Irish Times*. Her lips tightened into a flat line. *Here goes nothing.*

Rigan offered her his arm. "Are you quite sure you want to do this? It seems a bit more obvious than just slumming at Duffy's."

Charity sucked in a deep breath and wrapped her arm around his, hoping to bluff him with her most confident smile. "Absolutely. Since Mr. Dennehy isn't in a hurry to see me again, perhaps you and I need to jog his memory as to what he's missing."

Rigan grinned, hazel eyes glinting as he assessed her head to foot. "Oh, I'm quite sure he knows what he's missing. Trust me, any man who looks at you knows what he's missing."

A rush of heat flooded her cheeks and he laughed, the sound of it grating her nerves. She pulled away with her chin erect. "I don't appreciate your coarse humor, Rigan."

His teeth gleamed white. "Perhaps not my coarse humor, but certainly my coarse conspiracy."

Charity pulled away and shivered. He made her feel dirty, as if she were one of the vulgar women from Mountgomery Street who lured men for a price. She wasn't! She was a woman in love and nothing more. "Your tone, your words, they make me feel as if I'm doing something wrong. I don't like it."

Rigan cocked a hip and smiled, his face contrite. "It comes with the territory, Charity. You can't play the game of seduction without snagging other men in the process, myself included."

Charity fought a faint wave of nausea. "But I'm not a seductress. That sounds so . . . so cheap, so tawdry . . ."

Rigan's eyes softened the slightest bit. "No, you're not, actually. Oh, you certainly look the part and act it at times, but you'll never make the grade, my dear. Deep down, beneath that voluptuous body and those deadly eyes, I detect a frail echo of a conscience."

Charity released a slow breath, her nausea abating . . . or maybe it was her conscience. "Sorry, Rigan. I'm nervous, I suppose. I'll try not to let my scruples get in the way."

He grinned and bowed, offering his arm once again. She took it. "See that you don't. The stakes are too high—for both of us."

Charity leaned close as Rigan escorted her into the building, her mind suddenly far away. The image of an irate *Times* editor invaded her thoughts, causing the churning in her stomach to return, along with an ache in her heart. For pity's sake, she didn't want to deceive Mitch Dennehy, but what choice did she have?

"Good morning, Mr. Gallagher." The crisp tone of the *Times'* receptionist startled Charity out of her thoughts.

"Good morning, Miss Boyle. It's good to see you again. Is Michael treating you well?"

The young woman batted her nondescript eyes. Her professional demeanor was lost in a sea of pink flooding her cheeks. "Oh, yes, sir. Mr. Reardon is fine. He's a wonderful editor." Her lips trembled into a shaky smile. "A wee bit cranky, perhaps, because of the Brits, but fine."

Rigan smiled, sending more color into Miss Boyle's full

cheeks. "Good. I'm here to give Miss O'Connor a tour. Is Michael in? And Mitch Dennehy?"

She bobbed her head, her gaze flitting to Charity's face. "Yes, sir, both of them. May I announce you, Mr. Gallagher?"

"No, that won't be necessary." He glided past, ignoring the receptionist's curious stare as he guided Charity through a set of double doors.

It was another world altogether. Miles away from the calm of her grandmother's cozy kitchen or even the busy pace of Shaw's Emporium. It was a dizzy whirl of action where rock-jawed editors loomed over cowed copywriters and wide-eyed errand boys. Charity swallowed hard. Sounds and scents assailed her senses—the clicking of linotype machines and the tapping of typewriters shrouded in the smell of pungent ink and stale cigar smoke. A harried pace that spoke of import and deadlines and purpose. Charity paused, ignoring the tug of Rigan's arm.

What am I doing here?

"I've changed my mind," she whispered, backing toward the door.

"What?" Rigan turned, his eyes scanning her face. "Charity, you're white as a sheet." He jerked an empty chair from a nearby desk. "Here, sit down. Are you all right?"

"I've changed my mind. It's not the time nor place for this, Rigan." She pressed a shaky hand to her stomach, willing its contents to stay put. It took everything in her to stifle a burp.

He squatted to stare in her face. A slow curve formed on his lips. "Oh, no you don't. You're not sick. You're scared."

Charity hurled his hand away, her tone clipped. "Of Mitch Dennehy? Don't be ridiculous. I just don't think this is the time or place. This is a business, not a battleground."

Rigan's eyes narrowed. "Yes, it is a business. *My* business." He stood and stretched his arms down his side, adjusting the sleeves of his suit coat. "And my battleground." He pulled her up from the chair and hooked her arm over his with a firm grip.

Charity blinked. "What do you mean 'your battleground'?"

"It's simple. You want his heart. I want his head." He leaned close. "And your heart in the process, my dear."

Charity stared. "Rigan, you know my heart is set. Why are you doing this?"

"Short-term? To humiliate him and lord it over the man." He studied her through shrewd eyes. "Long-term? To be waiting with open arms when you tire of him turning you away."

Charity angled her chin. "And what makes you think he'll keep turning me away?"

A low laugh rumbled from Rigan's throat. "Experience, my dear. Cold, hard experience. He's not a forgiving man."

Charity gave Rigan a sideways glance. Challenge rose up in her like a feather caught in a breeze, buoying her resolve. "But . . . he is a man. When it comes to forgiving, I suppose I don't have much experience. But when it comes to men, I like to think I'm somewhat qualified."

Rigan chuckled. He pulled her toward Michael Reardon's office with a definite air of authority. "Yes, Miss O'Connor, I would certainly concur with that." He gave her a wicked grin and swung Michael Reardon's door wide open, not even bothering to knock.

꿍 ꙮ

"Forget it, Michael, I won't do it!" Mitch slammed the cup on his desk. Plops of cold coffee skittered across a haphazard pile of galley sheets. He swore under his breath and reached in his pocket for a handkerchief to mop it up.

Michael appeared to wait patiently while Mitch continued to mumble. Mitch glanced up at his editor, noting the thick arms folded across his barreled chest. A sheen of perspiration began right above Michael's thunderous brows, spanning up and over a bald spot. Mitch swore again.

"You don't have a choice, Mitch. He requested you. And his name is on your paycheck."

Mitch emitted a sound dangerously close to a growl. He crashed a fist on his oak desk. The force of the blow upset the coffee once again, spilling more of its contents across yesterday's news. With a snarl, Mitch righted the cup. "To the devil with my paycheck. He wouldn't recognize a hard day's pay if it bit him in the backside. He's nothing but a leech with a silver spoon in his mouth."

Michael moved in, slapping his meaty hands on top of Mitch's desk. "Keep your voice down, or he'll have your carcass tossed clear across Abby Street. I can't afford to lose my best editor while the presses are hot keeping up with the Brits." The heat in Michael's eyes tempered. He stood and exhaled a hefty breath while his stubby fingers massaged his temple. "Just do it for me, will ya, Mitch? To the devil with Gallagher; do it for me. I can't afford to lose you."

Mitch leaned hard against his knotted fist. He looked up at Michael, biting back the colorful commentary lodged deep in his throat. God help him, how he wanted to hurt Gallagher!

"What d'ya say? Just tighten your lip and give him twenty minutes of your time. Will you do it? For me?" Michael's eyes seemed to plead, pools of weariness begging for mercy.

Mitch slashed his fingers through the cropped curls on his head. "So help me, Michael, I have the mind to shove these galley sheets right down your throat and leave you high and dry." He sat up, aiming his finger within inches of his editor's nose. "You, my friend, are taking advantage of our friendship."

The stress lines in Michael's forehead eased while a semblance of a grin shadowed his lips. "Not friendship, Mitch. More like a son."

Mitch groaned and flipped the galley sheets over. "Yeah?

Well, you owe me, Pop. Double time, and then some. Where is the royal prince?"

"Waiting in my office. He and a lady friend."

Mitch glared at Michael, the muscles in his neck straining tight. "His next victim, I presume?"

Michael pressed his lips tight, draining them of color. "Forget the past, Mitch," he whispered. "Gallagher's not worth the emotion. Twenty minutes of your time. Get it over with and move on."

Mitch stared, his eyes burning in his head. He snatched his handkerchief to sop up the spilled coffee. "Fine. Do what you have to do. Send Little Lord Fauntleroy in."

"No need, Dennehy. He's here."

Mitch froze, the stained handkerchief dangling in his hand. He looked up into the stone face of Gallagher, standing at the door with a lady on his arm. The breath died in his lungs.

Charity.

"Hello, Mitch." Her voice was soft and breathy, impacting his heart with the force of a Big Bertha cannon. The full lips parted ever so slightly with just a hint of a smile. He gaped at her, a vision in lavender crepe, its silky fit far too seductive for the light of day. Strands of pale gold hair peeked beneath a close-fitting cloche hat, making her blue eyes appear all the larger, all the more innocent. The muscles in his cheek tightened. He knew better.

Rigan draped his arm around Charity's shoulder. "So, I understand you'll be showing us around today."

Mitch looked up through slitted eyes, his hand clenched on his desk. "I'm busy, Gallagher. We have a paper to run."

Rigan's smile was cold. "Yes, I know. *My* paper." His fingers caressed Charity's arm. "But Miss O'Connor's been quite anxious to see the inner workings of the *Times*, and who better to show her than an old family friend?"

Michael cleared his throat, a hoarse chuckle cutting the silence. "An old family friend?"

Mitch's eyes never strayed from Rigan's face. "Faith's sister."

His editor began to wheeze uncontrollably, his ruddy face turning scarlet.

Mitch handed him the last of the coffee. Michael lunged for the cup and bolted it down, sputtering out a few final coughs. "Er . . . my apologies, Miss O'Connor."

Charity smiled. "Call me Charity, please, Mr. Reardon. My sister spoke highly of you."

The color in Michael's cheeks heightened and he nodded, the sweat on his brow glittering in the light. "We loved her around here. You can be sure of that."

Her blue eyes widened the slightest bit, barely noticeable, except, perhaps, by Mitch, long familiar with every nuance of her face. She nodded, and her eyes shifted to meet his searing gaze. "Yes, I'm quite sure of that."

"Well, shall we begin the tour? I know your time is valuable, and Charity and I have luncheon plans." Rigan slipped a hand neatly around Charity's waist.

Michael glanced at Mitch and then hurried to the door, stopping to offer Charity his hand. "It's a pleasure to meet you. I trust Faith is doing well?"

A pretty blush skimmed into her cheeks. "Yes, Mr. Reardon. Quite well, thank you."

Michael cleared his throat. "I'm glad to hear that. Rigan, stop by before you leave and I'll have those reports for your father. Enjoy the tour, Miss O'Connor." He hurried out.

Rigan faced Mitch, his tone akin to an arctic chill. "Step outside for a moment. I'd like some privacy with Charity before we begin."

Heat like a horde of fire ants crawled up the back of Mitch's neck. He stood, his jaw clamped as tightly as frozen steel. He headed for the door, fists clenched at his sides.

"And close the door."

Mitch slammed it hard on its hinges, causing Bridie and

Kathleen to jump at their desks. Mitch whirled around, almost knocking his associate editor off his feet.

"Sorry, Boss," Jamie mumbled, jumping back to get out of Mitch's way. Jamie cocked a curious look in Bridie's direction.

Bridie leaned over her typewriter and smiled, nodding toward Mitch. "It seems Mr. Dennehy is playing tour guide today, Jamie. To Mr. Rigan Gallagher III, no less."

A spasm twitched in Mitch's cheek as he stormed past her desk. "Yeah, I'll give him a tour, all right. A tour of my fist." He kept going, making a beeline for the double doors.

Bridie stood up, her mouth hanging open. "Mitch, wait! Where are you going?"

He shot her a withering look over his shoulder. "Tell Michael I suddenly took ill. Just plain sick to my stomach."

"But what about Gallagher?"

Mitch slapped his palm hard against the glass door, flinging it open with a force that rattled the hinges. "Tell him I left to protect his health."

Bridie looked at Kathleen and Jamie, her shock mirroring their own. "Oh, this is not good," she muttered, "not good at all." Bridie sighed and straightened her shoulders. She glanced in the direction of Michael's office and absently made the sign of the cross. "Dear Lord above, let him be stocked up on aspirin."

⋙ ⋘

Bridie tossed a stack of proofs on Mitch's desk. Her lips cemented in a stiff line. "Michael left right after you did. Something about a migraine." She frosted him with a cold gaze before turning on her heel to head out the door.

"Bridie, wait. Was Michael mad?"

She spun around, her hazel eyes glittering like topaz. "Mad? I haven't seen that many shades of red since my Wesley fell asleep on the Dingle seashore." She launched fleshy arms on ample hips. "He took a bullet for you, Mitch. Gallagher was all over him like summer blight on soggy spuds, screaming he'd have your job and Michael's too."

Mitch sank lower in his chair, his anger warping into guilt. "Okay, okay, I lost my temper. I'll make it up to him."

"I hope you get the chance."

Mitch glanced up. "What do you mean?"

"I mean Gallagher's gunning for you, Mitch. He made it crystal clear to Michael—and everybody in earshot—that your days are numbered. He'd like nothing better than to see your name in the obits. Swears he's gonna talk to the old man about sending you packing."

Mitch leaned forward, sweat licking the inside of his collar. "Do you think he means it?"

Bridie regarded him through narrowed eyes, casually lifting one hand to study her nails. Her lips twitched enough for him to notice. "Could be," she said. "All I know is Michael wants *me* to write the eulogy."

Mitch sagged back in the chair with a grin easing across his lips. He fanned his fingers through his hair. "So help me, Bridie, you had my pulse going there for a moment."

Bridie approached his desk and propped her hands on the smooth oak. "Mitch, it's nothing to let your guard down about. Gallagher hates you."

"He's always hated me." He wadded a paper and tossed it in the can. "What's new?"

Bridie straightened. "Charity's new. You made a fool of him."

"So we're even." He shuffled through a stack of papers, giving Bridie a clear dismissal he knew she'd ignore.

"Yeah, you're even, all right. Both hypocrites to the core."

That got his attention. He jolted to his feet, heat sizzling his glare. "What the devil are you talking about? Don't ever put me in the same category with that lowlife."

Bridie notched her chin, her smile conspicuously absent. "My mistake, Boss. You belong in a category all your own. The one with people who profess to live for God, then do whatever they blimey well please."

She might as well have tossed cold coffee in his face. He wavered, shock rippling through his veins at the truth of her statement. His pride surged. She would *not* get the last word.

"You're out of your mind, old woman. I answer to God, not you."

Bridie sucked in a deep breath, releasing it slow and easy as she set her jaw. "Yeah, I know. Wonder what God thinks when he says 'forgive' and you tell him no."

Bridie O'Halloran might be his subordinate in the workplace, but Mitch knew when it came to having the final say, she owned the place, lock, stock, and barrel. She spun on her heel and marched for the door, the last word safely tucked in her pocket. The door slammed behind her and Mitch ground his jaw. He knew she would do it—have the final say—she always did. He blinked. He hated being right.

≈ ≈

Charity propped a finger against her cheek and tilted her head, squinting to study the elderly gentleman before her.

He repositioned a black bowler on his head and turned. His kind, gray eyes lit with a twinkle. "Well?"

She pursed her lips and stepped forward, then reached to tug the derby a bit lower. Leaning back to assess, she finally grinned. "Why, Mr. Hargrove, I do believe you bring new meaning to the word 'dapper.'"

Her playful tone elicited a chuckle from his weathered lips. "It's not too young for a man my age?" His eyes darted back to the looking glass, a crease hovering above snow-white brows.

Charity joined him at the mirror, impressed with the striking image he cut for someone in his eighties. She smiled and patted his arm. "Maybe for a man your age," she teased, "but not for a man who looks twenty years younger."

He laughed, a ruddy color lighting his cheeks. He lifted the derby from his head and held it to his striped silk vest, bowing slightly. Silver hair gleamed in the afternoon sun that shafted through the front window of Shaw's Emporium. "My dear Miss O'Connor, I'm not sure if it's the derby or the young woman selling it that puts a spring in my step. But either way, you've made yourself a sale."

Charity plucked the hat from his hand and giggled. "Shall I wrap it up along with the double-breasted suit, the incredibly elegant morning coat, and the tweed Norfolk jacket?" She cocked her head and dangled the derby in the air. "Or do you want to wear it home to watch the ladies swoon?"

The sound of his rich, throaty laughter turned several heads their way. He snatched the bowler from her fingers and slapped it on his head with two firm taps. He extended his arm to escort her to the front desk. "Charity, my girl, you alone are worth the obscene amount of money I spend in this place."

Charity slipped her arm into his and released a contented sigh. "Why, thank you, Mr. Hargrove. And customers like you are worth the long, long hours I put in."

He stopped abruptly, his brows bunched in a frown. "Does Mrs. Shaw realize what she has in you, young lady?"

Charity laughed. "I believe she realizes she has a loyal employee with a fondness for some of her favorite customers." She took a step toward the register. He tugged her back.

"No, my dear, I mean does she realize what a gold mine you are? That you're the reason that many a customer, myself included, comes into her humble mercantile?"

Charity swallowed. "Why, Mr. Hargrove, that's so very kind—"

"Poppycock, young woman, there's nothing kind about it. It's the raw, unadulterated truth. Why, you're a natural-born merchant, Charity, and I, for one, would like to see you reap the rewards." He leaned close to her ear. "I hear tell Mrs. Shaw is looking to sell. You would make an excellent proprietor, you know."

Charity peeked at the register where Mrs. Shaw was attending to a customer. She touched Mr. Hargrove's arm, shocked at the mistiness that suddenly sprang to her eyes. "Goodness, Mr. Hargrove, you'll have me tearing up any moment if I let you go on. What a wonderful compliment. Thank you so much. I would love to have my own store, of course, but that's a dream for someone other than a poor shop girl."

"Why?"

She blinked. "Why, because I can't afford to buy this shop or any other."

The abundance of wrinkles on Horatio Hargrove's face parted into a mischievous grin. "No, but I can."

Charity felt the blood in her cheeks course all the way to her toes. What was he saying?

He laughed and chucked a withered finger to her chin. "Think about it, Charity. I'm an old man with more money than years left to spend it. I could lend you the money to buy Mrs. Shaw out, and you could pay me back a little each month until the shop is yours. With your knack for business, you'll own it in no time. Until then, I'll reap a percentage of the profits from your extraordinary talent for making old men feel young again."

Her mouth hung open like a simpleton, but she was too stunned to close it.

Mr. Hargrove laughed again. "Really, Charity, it's the ideal business venture for both of us. Will you at least consider it?"

"No, I . . . I can't, Mr. Hargrove, as much as I would love to, I really can't. You see, I'll be returning home to Boston at Christmas—for good."

One of his shaggy, white brows launched a full half inch. "Boston? You're leaving?"

Charity attempted a smile. "Regrettably, I am. But Emma will still be here."

Mr. Hargrove released a weighty sigh and put his arm around Charity's shoulder, continuing toward the register. "Ah, yes, Emma. I do like that young woman, as well. But I'm afraid I've gotten rather attached to you, my dear."

"Good afternoon, Mr. Hargrove. Have you found everything you need?" Mrs. Shaw lighted on her best customer like a heavy mist on an early-morning bog.

Charity slipped from beneath his arm and scurried around the register to box up his purchases. Mr. Hargrove planted one hand on the counter and tapped his derby with the other. "More than I need, Mrs. Shaw, thanks to the outstanding efforts of Miss O'Connor."

Mrs. Shaw beamed, revealing oversized teeth the shade of pale butterscotch. "Yes, Charity has been our top sales clerk for a while now. We're quite proud of her."

Mr. Hargrove displayed some teeth of his own. "I hope that pride is attached to a hefty raise, Mrs. Shaw, because this young woman certainly deserves it."

Pink splotches in her cheeks and a raspy titter quickly replaced the butterscotch smile. "Why, yes, yes, she certainly does, Mr. Hargrove." She shot a nervous look at Charity. "I need to run in back for a moment. Will you finish with Mr. Hargrove, please?"

"Yes, ma'am."

"Good, good." She spun around, her carrot-red topknot all afrizz as she bolted for the back room. One stubby arm flailed in the air. "Have a good day, Mr. Hargrove. Always a pleasure."

Charity giggled. "Goodness, I haven't seen her move that quickly since Emma let a street urchin use the privy. Would you like me to add a pound of your favorite pipe tobacco to the bill?"

He chuckled. "Yes, please. You always seem to know when I'm running low." He paused. "Speaking of Emma, how are things?"

Charity looked up. Her smile faded into a frown. "Not good, but she refuses to leave."

The soft gray of Mr. Hargrove's eyes darkened to pewter. "How can a woman stay with a monster who would scar her like that?"

Charity forced herself to concentrate on folding the charcoal-colored morning coat. She blinked several times to dispel a sting of wetness in her eyes, remembering the day she'd learned Emma's drunken husband had thrown hot grease in her face. "I don't know, sir. She claims she loves him. Swears he didn't mean it. That it was the bottle and not 'her Rory' who was to blame." She shivered.

Mr. Hargrove placed a gnarled hand on top of hers. "Emma told me what you did, my dear. How you saved her job, threatening to quit if she lost hers."

Charity whirled around to scoop tobacco into a bag, heat flooding her cheeks. The sweet, rich scent of maple rum drifted in the air. "Goodness, Emma and I are a team. I can't keep this shop running by myself, you know."

"You're a good friend, Charity O'Connor. Putting your job on the line to save hers." He released a quiet sigh. "What a tragedy. One so young and lovely . . . now so disfigured. I pray God watches over her."

Charity tugged a string tightly around the bag of tobacco and plopped it on the counter, a stiff smile on her lips. "Well, I don't know about God, Mr. Hargrove, but I certainly know an angel who can watch over her."

He pursed his lips and arched his brows. "And who, pray tell, might that be?"

Charity glanced toward the back room before leaning over the counter with a conspiratorial smile. "Why, a silver-tongued angel who holds our own Mrs. Shaw in the palm of his prosperous hand."

Mr. Hargrove grinned and pressed in. "And how may I be of assistance, young lady?"

Charity tallied his bill and presented it to him with a flourish. "I fear Mrs. Shaw finds Emma's scars offensive. I worry about when I leave." She handed him an ink pen with a smile. "But wouldn't it be lovely if Emma were top sales clerk once again? You know, as if she had an angel with pockets deeper than the depth of Mrs. Shaw's greed?"

Mr. Hargrove chuckled. He penned his name with a bold stroke. "Not even I aspire to that level of angelic host, my dear, not even I." He winked. "But we shall certainly try."

"Don't forget to put the new shipment out tonight before you leave." Mrs. Shaw turned at the door to adjust the felt hat on her head. The wilted spray of silk flowers adorning it looked as limp as she did.

"Yes, ma'am. Emma and I will see to it before we lock up. Now, get some rest, Mrs. Shaw. I hope you're not catching a cold."

As if on cue, Mrs. Shaw sneezed. The poppies on her hat flapped in the breeze. She nodded and hurried out, waving a hand in the air. "It's after six. Bolt the door behind me."

"Yes, ma'am."

The door slammed with a jolt. Charity rushed to the window and peeked out. She scanned the street to make sure Mrs. Shaw was well on her way before she nodded to a little boy leaning against the lamppost. He turned and entered the store, the tinkle of the bell as merry as his gap-toothed grin.

"G'day, Miss Charity, I see the ol' queen has left her throne."

Charity's heart softened at the sight of her favorite street urchin. She doubted there was a poorer—or dirtier—boy in all of Dublin than Dooley O'Shea. Although he was ten years old, he was small for his age, with a generous spray of freckles beneath a layer of soot.

"Hello, Dooley, she has at that. So what wares have you brought me today?"

He heaved a dirty sack onto the counter with a grunt, giving Charity a whiff of something that made her want to wrinkle her nose. She fought the urge and folded her arms, her lips twitching with tease. "I hope it's not alive this time."

Dooley grinned. Greasy strands of hair fell over chocolate brown eyes as he dug into the sack. "No, ma'am, I left me pet lizard at home today. This here is a gift from me mum."

With an air of pride, he squared his shoulders and pulled out a knitted gray scarf—or maybe it was just dirty white—riddled with lumps of yarn, puckered and bunched. Charity picked it up and looped it around her neck. "Oh, Dooley, it's beautiful! But your mother shouldn't have done this. She has her hands full with the new baby."

Dooley lifted his chin and wiped his nose with his sleeve. "Mum says a lady like you needs a proper scarf to keep her warm on cold nights. She made it herself. Do you like it?"

Fighting the sting of tears in her eyes, Charity gave him a bright smile. "You tell your mother I absolutely adore it. How much does she want for it?"

The firm set of his jaw tugged at her heart. "No, ma'am, it's a gift, pure and true."

Charity leaned to peer into the bag. "Well, then, what do you have for sale today?"

He pulled a crudely wrapped block from the burlap sack. "Your favorite—raisin bread."

"Your mother is a wonder. Eight children and a newborn, and she still finds time to bake my favorite bread?" She flipped the loose end of the scarf over her shoulder and smiled. "Well, that settles it. Nothing less than a pound will do. Wait right here."

Emma was working on inventory when Charity slipped into the back room. She looked up as Charity pulled her purse from the cupboard. "So, what's on the menu this week?"

Charity grinned. "Raisin bread."

"God love her. I suppose with that many mouths to feed, the poor woman doesn't have time to learn how to bake properly. Did you even finish the last loaf you bought?"

Charity scrunched her nose. "Not after the first taste. I was afraid I'd chip my teeth."

A soft chuckle floated from Emma's lips. "Grab a few punts from my purse, then. I can't let you support them all by yourself, now can I? We'll split the loaf. Less chance of damaging your smile."

Charity shook her head. "No, ma'am. Your money is your sole support. Mine just provides a portion of our larder. Besides, he brought the loaf for me, not you."

Twirling the loose end of the scarf in the air, Charity sashayed through the curtain divider with a flourish, money in hand. On a whim, she sauntered over to a children's display and selected a warm infant bunting before returning to the counter. "All right, young man, tell your mother that if a lady needs to stay warm, a newborn babe does as well." Charity reached for a piece of paper to wrap the bunting in.

Dooley's eyes grew as big as saucers. "No, miss, me mum told me I wasn't to bring anything home but the price for the bread."

Charity arched a brow and put the package in a bag. "Are you arguing with me, Dooley O'Shea?"

A lump bobbed in his throat. "Oh, no, miss, it's just we have no money for—"

Charity propped her hands on the counter. "Are you saying that I can't give a gift to your new baby sister?"

He swallowed. "No, ma'am, if that's what you want. It's just that—"

Charity reached over and plucked a peppermint stick from a glass jar. She held it out. "It's a gift, Dooley, like the beautiful scarf your momma gave me and like this peppermint stick I'm giving you. Take it home and tell your mother 'no more gifts,' understood?"

Dooley stared at the candy. She started to push it into his grimy hand and hesitated. With a wink, she reached beneath the counter for a clean piece of paper to wrap it in. She handed it to him along with the bunting bag. "Here, take this home to your mother. The money for the bread is inside, all right?" She glanced out the window. "You better hurry, now, it's getting late."

Dooley nodded and clutched the bag in one hand and the peppermint stick in the other. His grin was ear to ear. "Thank you, Miss Charity. Me mum's right. You are an angel from above."

"There are some who would argue that point, Dooley," she said with a chuckle. She walked him to the door. "See you next week."

"Yes, ma'am. Good night."

Charity closed the door softly and flipped the bolt. Humming to herself, she strolled back to the register to record the cost of the bunting and peppermint stick on her personal charge. She glanced at the dirty burlap on the counter and sighed. She didn't have high hopes for the raisin bread, but she'd take it home nonetheless. The neighbor's dog seemed genuinely fond of it.

With an armload of merchandise in hand, Emma sailed through the curtain. She stopped in her tracks and lifted her chin, squinting at Charity for several seconds. "What's that on your back?"

Charity glanced over her shoulder in alarm. "My back? What do you mean?"

Emma plopped the clothing on a table. She began to fold a pair of knickers while she shot her a silly grin. "Our Dooley may be right. I think you're sprouting wings."

"Very funny. It's just too bad other men in my life don't share his opinion."

Emma chuckled. "I suppose you mean Mitch Dennehy. He might, you know, if you didn't give him such a devil of a time."

Charity grunted, then looked up from the register. "By the way, Mr. Hargrove was in yesterday. He asked about you."

A smile lit Emma's face as she folded a child's pinafore. The pretty tilt of the left corner of her lips contrasted sharply with the mottled scar on the right. "How is the old gentleman?"

Charity chuckled and dipped a pen into the inkwell to record the day's totals. "As spry as ever. I'll tell you what, if he were a few decades younger, I'd set my cap for him."

It was Emma's turn to giggle. The melodious sound floated through the empty boutique, as warm and welcoming as the tinkling bell over Mrs. Shaw's door.

"If he were a few decades younger, he'd still be married to his dear, sweet wife, God rest her soul. Mrs. Shaw said she was a lovely woman." Emma folded another pinafore and stacked it neatly on the pile before her. "And quite loose with the gentleman's money, I understand."

Charity laughed. "Which is why Mrs. Shaw thought she was lovely, no doubt." She slammed the register drawer shut. "All done. Are you about ready to go?"

A faint shadow flickered across Emma's features. Fear prickled in Charity's stomach as she joined her in arranging the merchandise. She reached for a pair of rumpled knickers and began folding. "Is Rory in one of his moods?" she asked quietly.

Emma nodded. A smocked dress trembled in her hands.

Charity's fear fused into anger. She wadded the knickers into a ball without realizing it. "Then come home with me. He'll be too drunk to miss you."

With shaking fingers, Emma folded the dress, carefully smoothing out the wrinkles. "No, but thank you for the offer. I need to go home."

A grandfather clock at the back of the shop chimed the half hour. Charity glanced up—six thirty. Maybe, just maybe, if she kept Emma long enough, Rory would be passed out already, blessedly harmless after a day at the bar. She bit her lip and circled the table, trailing her hand across several stacks of cashmere sweaters. "Well, the truth is, I was hoping we could talk."

Emma looked up, her one shapely brow puckered in concern. The other, half seared from scalding grease, raised only slightly, lifting a welt along with it. "What about?"

"What do you think?" Charity asked, glancing up beneath a sweep of lashes that perfectly framed the mischief in her eyes.

Her friend shook her head and laughed. "Mmmm, now what might that be?" She peaked her good brow. "Perhaps more diabolical plans to win the heart of an editor at the *Times*?"

Charity grabbed Emma's hand and pulled her toward the back room, giggling like a schoolgirl. "Why, of course. Am I obsessed by anything else?"

Emma curled an arm around Charity's waist. "Yes, as a matter of fact. You are relentless in your quest to knock me out of top sales clerk each month."

"I'm sorry, but you know how competitive I am." Charity bit her lip and gave her friend a squeeze. "Besides, you were the reigning queen for years before I came."

"But not since, your majesty." Emma smiled. "Not to worry. Your arrival brought me the dearest friend I've ever known."

Charity released her arm and fetched a teapot. "And who might that be?"

Emma groaned and plopped in a chair at the scarred oak table where they ate their lunch. She reached for the oil lamp and warmed her hands over its globe. "Well, certainly not

Mrs. Shaw, who keeps this back room as icy as a cave in the Mountains of Mourne."

Charity pumped water into the pot and set it to boil, then opened the stove door to stoke the dwindling peat inside. A bit of flame began to stir. Satisfied, she hurried to join Emma at the table, crossing her arms to tuck her fingers into their warmth. "That she does. But I suppose we should be grateful she provides any heat at all, as tight-fisted as she is with a pound."

"Mmmm, I suppose." Emma inched the oil lamp toward Charity. "Here, warm your fingers while you tell me what's on your mind."

A tired smile pulled at Charity's lips. "The same thing that's always on my mind, I'm afraid." She sighed. "If I didn't know better, I'd swear the man has put me under a spell."

Emma laughed. "More than likely it's just that stubborn streak of yours trading in one obsession for another."

Charity squinted over the flickering globe. "What obsession?"

"Your vendetta against your sister. Seducing her fiancé like she did yours."

"How does that factor into my obsession for Mitch?" Charity sat up.

Emma cocked her head in a pensive manner. "Oh, I don't know. Maybe your passion for revenge fueled you for so long that when the deed was done, it naturally channeled into something new."

Charity blinked, her voice a whisper. "Mitch."

"Yes, Mitch," Emma repeated.

Charity pushed the oil lamp back toward Emma, her gaze fixed on a gouge in the table. "Maybe, but I think I was falling in love with him long before that. For eight lonely months I watched the way he treated my sister, like she was the world to him. I wanted that." She looked up, misty eyes belying the determined cut of her jaw. "I wanted him."

Emma's lips twisted into a sad smile while her gaze faded into a faraway stare. "An attraction driven by hate for your sister, the very woman you stole from him. It certainly explains why he's so gun-shy where you're concerned."

Charity's brow slashed high. "I don't need any reminding on that score, Emma. What I do need are ideas to make him fall in love with me."

Emma blinked, bringing her attention back to Charity. "Sorry. I know you've had your share of pain over this ordeal with your sister." She paused. A gleam suddenly lit in her eyes. "But maybe your sister is the key."

"The key," Charity said as she folded her arms.

Emma chewed on her lower lip, deep in thought. "Yes . . . the key." She glanced up, and her lips parted in a soft *oh.* "I can't believe we didn't think of this before."

"Think of what?" Charity hovered on the edge of her chair, a definite note of impatience in her tone.

Emma plunked her arms on the table and leaned in, her voice almost breathless. "Mitch was desperately in love with Faith, right?"

Charity frosted her with a chilly look. "Yes."

"And him a confirmed bachelor? A different beautiful woman every night?"

A noisy sigh huffed from Charity's lips. "So I've heard."

Emma leaned forward, her eyes glowing softly. "Well, then, give him what he wants."

She blew a strand of hair from her eyes to diffuse the heat she felt in her cheeks. "Believe me, I've tried."

Emma giggled and reached for Charity's hand. "No, you goose. I mean, give him *Faith.*"

A shiver skittered through her. *Give him Faith?*

The teapot began to whistle, and Emma popped up, bustling to the stove. She poured the tea and placed a steaming cup in front of Charity, who ignored it, eyes riveted on Emma's face.

Sinking into the chair beside her, Emma leisurely sipped her brew.

"Out with it! What do you mean?"

Emma grinned. "Well, what was it that made Faith so different anyway? Why did Mitch Dennehy say yes to her and no to dozens of other beautiful women, including you?"

Lips parted in surprise, Charity thumped back against the chair. She closed her eyes, recalling her ill-fated conversation with Mitch the night of his visit.

"Attraction is the first step to falling in love, you know," she had told him.

"Not for me, Charity. I want more."

A breath caught at the hollow of her throat. Her eyes sprang open. "He . . . he once said something, something about . . . God." She shuddered.

Emma leaned in, her hand resting on Charity's shoulder. "So give it to him, Charity. Get on your knees before the Almighty and pray."

Fury prickled the back of her neck. She pushed Emma's hand aside and stood. "Never. I don't need God to lift a finger on my behalf." She picked up her untouched tea and carried it to the sink, ready to dump it out.

"Charity, what's wrong? Why are you so annoyed?"

Charity spun around, her jaw taut with anger. "Because I'm not weak like my sister. I refuse to pay homage to some power-hungry god who may or may not choose to strike me down at any given moment."

The scars on Emma's face faded to white. "Charity, don't talk like that. God is to be feared."

Her tone hardened. "Yes, Emma, I fear him. I fear that given the chance, he will steal everything I've ever loved. I don't want a god who chooses favorites. He chose Faith as the beloved recipient of all his blessings, including my father's love. Well, I can choose too—to live without him."

Emma's fingers trembled as they lighted upon Charity's arm.

"Charity, no. That makes me afraid. No one can live without him."

Her gentle touch sapped the anger from Charity's soul. She stared into the troubled eyes of the only friend she had ever really known. "Don't be afraid, Emma. I've lived this long without a bolt from Heaven striking me dead. I'm sure I'll be fine. After all, he took the life of my sister, the love of my father, and the marriage I had hoped to have. What more can he do?"

Her friend's dark eyes were shadowed with worry. "Oh, Charity, I'm so sorry, sorry for bringing it up. I never meant to upset you."

Charity swallowed hard, determined not to give in to the hot wetness springing to her eyes. "Don't be sorry, Emma. I love you. And you had no way of knowing." She lifted her chin and moved toward the table, taking a seat. "Besides, you've actually given me an idea."

"What?"

She cocked her head. "He wants my sister? I'll give him my sister."

"How?" Emma scurried to sit beside her. The soft flicker of the oil lamp danced across the marred table. It cast shadows over the grooves and pock marks dominating its surface.

An impish smile settled on Charity's lips. "How? Well, Mrs. Malloy, it was your idea, after all. Perhaps the two of us just need to put our heads together and figure that out."

4

What was he doing here? Again? Mitch sucked in a deep breath, thick with the loamy scent of wet leaves and burning peat, and turned the ignition off. The car sputtered to silence. He sagged back in the seat, surrounded by stillness except for drizzle on the roof of his Model T, the distant yapping of a dog, and the pounding of his pulse in his ears.

Chin stiff and face straight ahead, he glanced at Charity's grandmother's house out of the corner of his eye as if it were a forbidden zone, dangerous to his health, toxic to his life. He exhaled, suddenly aware he'd been holding his breath. The cheery light spilling through chintz-curtained windows winked back at him, beckoning. He flung the door wide, slowly unfolding from the vehicle to stand and face the cottage head-on. He grunted. To face his fear head-on. Not fear of losing his heart to Bridget or Mima. No, not that. Fear of losing his heart to her. A woman who was a feast to his eyes but a drought to his soul. He sighed and slammed the car door shut, bobbling a small gift-wrapped box in his hand. What was he doing here?

With great hesitation, he approached the wraparound porch. He stared at its layers of weathered paint and its rustic bogwood swing and wondered if he should have declined Bridget's invitation. He lifted his fist to knock on the door. Mima's eighty-second birthday.

"Can you come?" Bridget had asked in that little-girl voice of hers.

No. I'm busy. For the rest of my life.

"I wouldn't miss it," he had responded. But he would have liked to. In a heartbeat. He knocked again. The door wheeled open to a shaft of lamplight and heavenly smells from the kitchen. His stomach rumbled.

"Mitch, thank you for coming!" Bridget's eyes twinkled with genuine fondness, her face flushed the slightest shade of pink. She ushered him in, tugging him forward as if she thought he might bolt. "It means so much to Mima and me."

He smiled, his eyes inadvertently scanning the room. *And Charity.*

Her gaze lit on the box in his hands. "And what's this?"

"For Mima. Chocolates." He handed it to her and slipped out of his coat, tossing it over the rack in the hall. He turned, his smile dimming. "She *can* have chocolate, can't she?"

Bridget chuckled, the sound of it warming his soul. "Yes, of course. It's her favorite. Although I have to limit her to special occasions." She looped her arm through his and looked up. Her blue eyes were identical to Charity's except for the abundance of fine lines around their almond shape. "She'll love it."

They entered the kitchen with its crackling fire and flickering candles, the room aglow with expectation. Charity turned at the sink, her smile wide and welcoming. "We're having Mima's favorite—pot roast and dumplings. Hope you're hungry."

Mitch's throat went dry. He stared and swallowed. He was. But not for pot roast.

Charity bounded over, her skin luminous in the radiance of the firelight. She surprised him with a gentle hug, and a trace of lilacs teased his senses. She pulled away. "Can I get you a glass of wine, cider . . . milk?" A glimmer of mischief danced in her eyes.

"Cider sounds good," he said, eyeing her with a faint smile.

Bridget patted his arm. "Mitch, you sit down at the table while I bring Mima in."

"Let me help," he said.

Bridget shook her head. "Absolutely not. This is our usual routine and I will handle it." She led him to the chair at the head of the table and gently pushed him down. "Now, sit!" She disappeared down the hall, humming and leaving him to Charity.

He turned and watched as Charity moved to the icebox, chattering about Bridget's cider being the best in all of Dublin. She poured him a glass, and he couldn't help but notice she seemed different. Softer. He scrunched his brows, trying to decipher what it was. The hair? Possibly. The flaxen tresses that normally swayed about her shoulders now gathered into a loose topknot at the back of her head. A few loose tendrils strayed, feathering her neck with soft curls of spun gold. He liked it, he decided. More schoolmarm than temptress. Even her dress bespoke a more subdued Charity. Although her maroon tweed pencil skirt revealed curves no fabric could hide, the cream blouse was cotton rather than silk, its wide bib obscuring the full shape of her breasts.

She handed him the cider, a fragile smile gracing her lips. Her perfectly shaped brows knitted into a frown, sloping as she looked up. "Mitch, I apologize for coming to the *Times*."

Heat cuffed the back of his neck. He took a gulp of the cider. "Forget it," he said, trying to clear the gruffness from his throat.

She swiped a curl from her face. "No, it was wrong of us . . . of me . . . to come." She turned away to occupy herself with the pot roast on the stove. When she lifted the lid, the steam whirled up, enveloping her in a cloud of wonderful smells. She returned the lid with a thud, her fingers lingering there as she kept her back to him. "I . . . I wasn't thinking clearly . . . I was . . . being selfish . . . thinking of myself. I wanted your attention."

Mitch stared, his gaze fixed on the nape of her neck, the curve of her hips. Her words suddenly registered. Honesty? From Charity O'Connor? His eyes narrowed. "Why?" he asked, regretting the word the moment it left his lips. He already knew why.

She turned, her expression as pure and open as a child's. "Because I think I may be in love with you, and I want a chance to find out."

His heart constricted, and his breathing shallowed. "You're not in love with me, Charity."

"How will I know . . . unless you give me the chance to see?" She leaned back, supporting herself with hands that gripped white on the counter. There was a hint of pleading in her eyes. "I think about you, Mitch, dream about you . . ."

He gripped the cider, draining it dry, then slapped the glass on the table. "I can't love you."

She blinked, the luminous eyes jolted with hurt. She lifted her chin. "Can't? Or won't?"

He expelled a breath of frustration, his eyes fixed hard on hers. "Won't."

"Because of Faith?"

"Because of you. We don't believe the same way."

A thin veneer settled over her. "You mean like Faith."

He eyed her, his jaw stiff. "Yes, I mean like Faith."

She inhaled a deep breath, as if drawing in strength. Her chin notched higher. "Then I guess I'll have to settle for friendship. I care about you, Mitch. I want you in my life."

Friends. He studied the strong line of her jaw, the lush, full lips so ripe for tasting, the graceful curve of her neck plunging toward a body that took his breath away. Friends?

Not likely.

"Well, here's the birthday girl." Bridget stood in the doorway, her arm braced around Mima's waist. "Look, Mother, Mitch came to celebrate with us."

Mitch jumped to his feet and pulled out a chair. "Happy

birthday, Mima. Heard a rumor you're eighty-two, but that's impossible. You don't look a day over sixty."

She cackled, a surprisingly deep chuckle for so tiny a woman. "An Irishman to the core, you are, Mitch Dennehy, oozing more blarney than the blessed stone itself."

He laughed, and the tension eased in his neck. "Maybe a wee bit, but not by much. You look very pretty tonight."

She lifted a frail hand to pat her snow-white topknot, looking quite pleased. "Do I? Well, the credit goes to my great-granddaughter who fusses over me like a favorite doll."

Charity adjusted the scalloped collar of Mima's navy blue dress before helping her into the chair. "You are my favorite doll, Mima, the perfect size to primp and pamper."

Mima's faded blue eyes quirked in Mitch's direction while her lips twisted in a smile. "See what I mean?"

He grinned and glanced at Charity. "Some little girls never grow up, I guess."

Charity's brows lifted in surprise. "And some do, but nobody notices." With an air of refinement, she elevated her chin as if to turn away, then stuck her tongue out instead.

Mitch blinked, then burst out laughing. "Thanks for proving my point." He sat down in the chair and shifted to converse with Mima, keenly aware of Charity as she and Bridget chatted and prepared food for the table.

Mitch felt Mima's soft touch on his hand and blinked up in surprise. A serene smile hovered on the old woman's lips.

"She's beautiful, isn't she?" she whispered, her voice so soft and low he had to lean forward to catch it.

Heat roared to his cheeks.

She chuckled. "Inside and out, you know. But few people realize that."

Mitch swallowed, pressing his lips tight.

She tilted her head, her gaze penetrating his. "You don't, do you?"

Mitch jumped when Charity plopped a steaming bowl of

dumplings on the table. "Almost ready." She darted back to help Bridget with the pot roast. Mitch's stomach growled.

He looked over to see Mima studying him once again, her nose wrinkled in thought. She smiled and leaned close, her voice barely a whisper. "She's an enigma, our Charity. A real puzzlement. She begrudges fiercely and loves fiercely. Seems to be no in between with her. Have you noticed that?"

A smile tugged at his lips. "Maybe."

Charity groaned as she hefted a heavy platter to the table. Mitch shot up to take it from her, setting it down with a thump. "Sweet saints above, Mrs. Murphy, who else is coming? You have enough here to feed the whole block."

Bridget turned at the sink with a grin on her face. "I know. I seem to get carried away on special occasions. And it's Bridget, not Mrs. Murphy." She wagged a wooden spoon at him. "And don't make me tell you again, young man."

Charity giggled and leaned close to pour more cider. She scrunched her nose at Mima. "Did she say 'young' man?"

Mitch stifled a smile and fixed her with what he hoped was a threatening glare. "I suppose anything seems old to someone your age . . . little girl."

Charity smirked.

Bridget hurried to the table with a bottle of wine and corkscrew in her hand. "Will you do us the honors, Mitch? We have to have a birthday toast, after all."

He poured Mima's first, then Bridget's, bypassing his glass to move toward Charity's.

Bridget scowled. "Mitch Dennehy, this is a celebration and we must *all* clink on Mima's birthday. Is that understood?"

He hesitated before relenting with a smile. "Maybe just this once. In honor of Mima."

He poured wine for himself, then let the bottle hover over Charity's empty glass. He glanced at Bridget. "Are you sure she's old enough?"

Charity flicked the cuff of his sleeve, causing a dribble of scarlet to splash into her crystal goblet. "Grandmother, make him behave."

He grinned, his eyes challenging hers to a truce. "I will if you will."

Her smile softened into serious resolve. "I will, Mitch."

The hope in her face plucked at his heart. Friends. She wanted to be friends. He smiled and poured her wine. So be it.

❧ ❧

Charity eased back in the chair, legs comfortably tucked beneath her skirt. She studied the man who made her stomach flutter. She wasn't sure if it was the effect of the wine or Mitch regaling them with stories of his dear, old landlady, but either way, she was sure she was glowing. Her gaze drifted to Mima and Bridget, both rapt with attention and giggling like schoolgirls, then back to Mitch with his teasing eyes and heart-melting grin. She released a quiet sigh. Here she was, head over heels, and the man wouldn't reciprocate to save his soul. Instead, they would be friends. She took another sip of wine and smiled. For now.

She entertained the prospect. Gruff, solid Mitch Dennehy, a friend in need, a shoulder to cry on, a stabilizing force. A man who quelled her nerves by just walking into the room. A safety net, a father figure.

Charity silently gasped, startled by the thought. She observed his massive shoulders hunkered down, brawny arms planted firmly on the table, and a hard-chiseled chin shadowed by a day's growth of beard. Fatherly? She smiled. Hardly.

"What are you grinning about, young lady?" he asked.

She blinked, staring at three sets of blue eyes focused on her. A hot flush warmed her cheeks. "Why, your comments about your landlady, of course."

His left brow jagged high. "Which one? The fact she's been widowed for fifteen years or the one about her dog dying?"

Her cheeks scorched hot. "Oh, goodness, Mitch, I suppose I missed that. I apologize."

He chuckled and settled back in his chair. "Well, at least your grandmother and Mima find my company interesting, even if you don't."

"I think someone's just feeling the effects of the wine," Bridget said, stifling a yawn. "I know it certainly has relaxed me." She lifted the watch pinned to the lacey lapel of her best blouse. "Goodness, Mother, you must be exhausted. It's half past ten."

Mima chuckled, her paper-thin eyelids drooping noticeably. "So that's why I'm weaving in my chair. Thank you all for a wonderful birthday. And thank you for coming, Mitch, and for the lovely chocolates. Bridge, Charity—dinner was delicious."

"You're welcome, Mother. Now let's get you to bed before you fall asleep at the table."

Charity jumped up. "Grandmother, I'll do it."

Bridget leaned down to clasp an arm around Mima's shoulders, worry lines bunching her brow. "No, Charity, I'd like to, if you don't mind. I just hope we haven't overdone it tonight. Do you think you can stand, Mother?"

Mima nodded slowly, but it was Mitch who supported her as she rose, his strong arm fastened beneath her elbow. He glanced at Bridget. "May I?"

Bridget's smile was as drawn and tired as Mima's. "No, Mitch, I can manage." She patted his arm. "But I'm sure Charity would love help with the dishes, if you're so inclined. I doubt I'll be much good to her once I get Mima undressed and into bed."

Mitch nodded, glancing at Charity before putting his hand on Mima's shoulder. He leaned to press a kiss to her forehead. "Good night, Mima." He squeezed Bridget's arm. "Good night, Bridget. Dinner was wonderful. Thank you for inviting me."

"My pleasure. So good to see you again, Mitch. Please come back."

Taking her cue from Mima and Bridget's departure, Charity gathered dishes from the table while Mitch followed suit. His towering frame seemed out of place as he carried a lopsided pile of dirty plates to the sink. He stacked them on the counter and turned, pushing his hands deep in his pockets as if not sure what to do next. A crooked grin surfaced on his lips. "You're not going to make me wash, are you?"

She laughed, the warmth of his presence oozing through her like thick, hot molasses. He appeared blissfully relaxed, and she silently thanked Bridget for plying him with wine despite his objections. She cocked her head. "Not if I want you to come back."

She ratcheted the pump, and water spilled into an old, dented pot. She rolled the sleeves of her blouse. "Mind lugging that to the fire? I like my dishwater hot."

He lifted the pot with ease, transferring it to the stove while she reached for two more, filling each half full. She sensed him watching her while she scraped plate after plate, and the thought made her giddy and flustered at the same time. When the dirty dishes were stacked high, she glanced over her shoulder and smiled. "Why don't you pour us more wine? We have to wait for the water to boil anyway."

He cocked a brow. "Don't you think you've had enough?"

Enough? Of this glorious warmth? She turned and smiled a secret smile, her back to him once again. "Might as well finish the bottle."

He cleared his throat, and she knew she'd won when she heard the gentle glug of the wine being poured. She pushed the stacked dishes aside for the moment and whirled around to retrieve her glass. He handed it to her, filled to the brim, while his remained noticeably empty. Her fingers trembled as she took it, keenly aware of his overpowering presence. Desperate for some semblance of calm, she took a careful sip, studying him over the rim of her glass. "You didn't keep any for yourself."

He watched her, his eyes unreadable as he set the empty bottle on the table. "Gave it up. Till tonight. But just for Mima." He turned abruptly to check on the pot. "It's steaming. Where do you want it?"

She set her wine down and hurried to the sink, snatching a dishtowel from a hook. She slung it over her shoulder. "Here . . . half in the wash pot, half in the rinse." She stepped back, allowing him just enough room to pour. Vapor rose like a cloud of mist, delivering the faint scent of Bay Rum to her nostrils. His powerful back strained as he poured, his jacket pulling tightly across broad shoulders. He turned, pot in hand, dwarfing her with his height. "More?"

She swallowed hard. Her chin tilted up to meet his eyes. "More?"

A faint smile flickered at the edge of his lips. "Water. You said you like it hot."

Blood surged to her cheeks. "I . . . no, that's fine. Just fine." She staggered back, lightheaded. Her hands were shaking when she reached for her wine. She gulped it too quickly. *Settle down, Charity. He's just a man.*

She took a deep breath and turned, patting the back of the nearest chair. "Why don't you just sit and keep me company while I do the dishes?"

He leaned against the counter and crossed his arms, assessing her through hooded eyes. "Why? Too close for comfort?"

She blinked, and her lips parted in surprise. Ignoring the heat in her cheeks, she jutted her chin. "No. Is it for you?"

He grinned. A reckless gleam shone in his eyes. "You wash, I'll dry."

Charity took a deep breath and moved toward the sink, confusion and euphoria battling in her brain. She tried to focus on the task at hand, but her thoughts were tripping faster than the beat of her heart. What was he doing? It was as if a few glasses of wine had unleashed the rogue in him. He was baiting her, teasing her . . . disarming her.

This is his idea of friends?

She drew in a deep breath and sliced her hands into the warm water, scouring plates like a madwoman before plunging them into the rinse. Fishing them out once again, she didn't bother shaking them off, just slapped one on top of another in a sloppy clatter, water sluicing onto the counter. After several silent moments, she tilted her head to chance a peek out of the corner of her eye. "You're not drying."

He gauged her through half-lidded eyes. "And you're not washing; you're drowning."

Her chuckle cleaved to her throat when he lowered his gaze to her mouth. The breath in her lungs shallowed, drifting out in short, raspy breaths. "You're still not drying," she whispered.

He moistened his lips, then slowly lifted his eyes to hers. "I need this." His fingers skimmed across the towel on her shoulder, causing the air to still in her throat.

Dear God, what was happening? It was as if he had no control over his hand as it strayed from the towel to the soft curve of her neck. A tilt of her head, the blush of her cheeks, and suddenly he was two different men. One whose every muscle, thought, and desire strained toward wanting her. The other, a distant voice of conscience and memory, quickly fading with every throb of his renegade pulse. Curse the effect of the wine! What else could explain this driving insanity pulsing through him right now? His fingers burned as they lingered, slowly tracing to the hollow of her throat. Against his will, Mitch fixated on her lips, lush and full, staggered at the heat they generated. What was he doing? He didn't want this.

Yes . . . he did.

All night he'd felt it mounting, a desire in his belly that grew tight at the sound of her laughter, the lift of her chin, the light in her eyes. A woman with cool confidence around everyone but him. Call it the wine. Or the fact he hadn't been this close to a woman for well over a year. Or the intoxicating awareness that his very presence seemed to unnerve her. Whatever name it bore, it had him by the throat, taking him places he'd vowed he'd never go.

She blinked up at him, eyes wide and wondering. He was taking her by surprise and knew it. But no more so than him. He stared at her lips, feeling the draw and unwilling to fight it. His fingers moved up her throat to gently cup her chin, his eyes burning with intent. Slowly, carefully, he leaned forward, his mouth finally reaching hers, his breathing ragged as he tasted her lips.

A soft mew left her throat, and the sound ignited him. He pulled her close, his mouth demanding hers. She moaned while he pressed her to the counter, holding her there as he deepened the kiss. With a deep groan, his arms swallowed her up, drawing her small frame tightly against his. He pressed his lips to her hair, allowing her scent to flood his senses . . . to consume him.

Just like before.

His heart seized. What was he doing? The more he touched, the more he wanted. But she had ruined his life. Dashed his hopes. Destroyed his dreams. Dear God in heaven, he wanted her . . . but he didn't want *her.*

Charity stood in a daze, eyes closed and chin raised, every nerve in her body quivering. The sound of her own breathing vibrated in her ears, rasping through parted lips as she waited for more. She felt the heat of his fingers as he clutched her arms, and the silence between them overflowed with the pounding of blood in her brain. Joy surged inside like an adrenaline rush. Dear Lord, how she loved him!

All at once he dropped his hold. Her eyes fluttered open, and his look chilled her more than the absence of his touch.

The heat in his eyes cooled to guarded, and his jaw turned

to stone as he backed away. "Charity . . . I . . . please forgive me."

Fear squeezed in her stomach. "There's nothing to forgive. I love you—"

He groaned and began to pace, muttering under his breath. When he spoke out loud, his voice was a near growl. "You don't love me. I took advantage of you, plain and simple."

"No, you didn't. I want you, Mitch." She took a step forward. "And you want me. Because you love me."

He turned, his eyes piercing hers. "Lust isn't love."

"It's a start."

"Not for me."

She angled a brow.

He glared. "Yes, this was my fault, all right? I can't hang this one on you. But I can see to it that it never happens again."

She honed in, standing before him with heat in her eyes. "Prove it. Take me in your arms and tell me it will never happen again."

A muscle jerked in his jaw, and she could hear his uneven breathing. Taking a chance, she reached to stroke the inside of his palm with her thumb, her smoky gaze fused to his.

Swearing under his breath, he hurled her hand away and stormed toward the door. "I'm leaving."

"Wait, please!" The crack in her voice made him stop.

She had no choice but a change of tactics. Drawing in a deep breath, she shuddered and sagged into a chair. "You owe me, Mitch. You know how I feel about you, but you toyed with my emotions anyway."

The guilt hit dead on. She heard him suck in air before his lips leveled in a tight line. He threaded his fingers through his hair, his breath hissing through clenched teeth. "I know, Charity. I'm sorry."

She stared hard at the floor. "Sorry's not enough. Kind of like lust, I guess."

"It's all I have."

She looked up. "No, it's not all you have. You have feelings for me, Mitch. Virtuous or not, they're there. Give me a chance to make them grow. Please!"

He exhaled loudly before dropping into a chair across the table. "Yes, I do have feelings for you. I care about you . . . as a friend."

Her lips barely formed a smile. "Oh, I see. You kiss all your friends the way you just kissed me?"

He didn't back down. "No, only you." He squared his jaw and stared at his hand, clenching it, flexing it. "Look, Charity, it's no secret to either of us that as a woman . . . ," he looked up, meeting her gaze head-on, ". . . you drive me wild. But as a woman I could spend the rest of my life with . . . it just won't work. The past won't let it."

She released a shaky sigh, turning so he couldn't see the moisture in her eyes. "So we're reduced to friendship, then."

He paused. "We both know that won't work."

She spun to face him, her eyes wet with alarm. "It can!"

He softened. "No, it can't. I couldn't handle it and neither could you." He rose from the chair. "I need to go."

She jumped up, blinking back the tears. "Tell me we'll be friends, Mitch. Tell me I'll see you again."

"I can't, Charity. We both need to move on. If you need me, you can call. But we can't do this again." He glanced at the hallway. "Will you explain to Mima and Bridget for me, please?"

She nodded, no longer fighting the tears that streamed her face.

"Thanks for dinner." He hesitated, his voice low. "I wish you well, Charity."

She squared her shoulders, no recourse but one. "Don't go, Mitch. I need you. I'm afraid of Rigan."

His expression froze before coagulating into rage. He slammed the chair out of his way and rounded the table, gripping her by the arms. "What did he do?"

"N-nothing yet," she said, "but he . . ."

He shook her. "Tell me! Has he hurt you?"

"Mitch, you're scaring me!"

"Has he?"

"No, nothing like that. It's just . . ."

He sucked in a breath. "Just what?"

She rubbed her arm, avoiding his gaze. "Well, he . . . he pressures me . . ."

His face paled. The blue of his eyes darkened. "Are you sleeping with him?"

A hot flush shot to her cheeks. She stumbled back. "No, never! How dare you? How can you even think that? That would be wrong! And I don't love him."

"Because I know Gallagher. And your reputation with me hasn't exactly been pristine."

Anger stung her eyes. "Nor yours with me."

He grabbed her arm and pushed her in the chair, then yanked out another to sit beside her. "We've already established that. What we haven't settled is why you're still seeing him. He's no good, Charity. You're a fool."

She glared. "Apparently. Although Rigan hardly bears the blame for that."

Mitch groaned, scouring his face with his hand. "You see this? This is exactly why it wouldn't work between us. I have no room in my life for a stubborn, calculating woman who I can't trust. Not to mention one with questionable moral values."

"You can trust me."

He dropped his hand on the table with a thud, studying her with a wary eye. "Prove it. Stop seeing Rigan."

She matched his gaze. "Done. If we remain friends. Dinners and all."

She watched the tight press of his lips, the slight movement of his jaw, and waited, breath suspended in her lungs.

He forced out a noisy sigh as his eyes stared her down. "I want your solemn promise you'll never see him again."

She nodded, joy pumping in her chest.

He leveled his finger at her, not a trace of a smile to be found on his face. "Friends. The first time either of us steps over that line, you'll never see me again."

She took a deep breath, releasing it with a shiver. "Done."

He stood and strode to the foyer, retrieving his coat from the rack by the door. He slipped it on and reached for the knob, not even bothering to turn around. "Thanks for dinner."

She trailed behind, sweet satisfaction pervading her soul. "My pleasure. It was fun."

He turned, a wary look in his eye. "Yeah. Fun." And lifting his collar to brace against the cold, he stepped out into the night.

She watched until his car disappeared down the street, then quietly closed the door, sagging against it with eyes weighted closed.

Friends. Better than "never," she supposed. She smiled. And almost "forever."

⋦ ⋧

Mitch was in a sour mood when he stormed across the threshold of Duffy's. He bulldozed through the crowd and the smoke to make his way to the bar. Looming over an empty stool, he pressed his lips into a tight scowl and scoured the pub. Where the blazes was Sally?

She suddenly came into view, red curls bobbing as she delivered a hefty tray of ales to the end of the bar. He stared at her back, willing her to turn around while he huffed out an impatient sigh. She turned and saw him, and a broad grin lit her face. She bustled to where he stood, fuming. "Why, Mr. Dennehy, you look fit to be tied. Are you alone tonight?"

He glared. The daggers that shot from his eyes would've strewn bodies on the floor. "Quite alone. Give me a bottle of your best whiskey."

The pink, freckled skin between Sally's auburn brows puckered in a frown. "I thought you were off the stuff."

He seared her with a look meant to make her flinch. She didn't budge. "Blast it, Sally, not tonight. Wrap it up. I'm taking it with me."

Her lower lip protruded. "It didn't help before, Mitch. It won't help now."

He slapped both palms on the bar and leaned in, his breath hissing through his nostrils. "Don't argue with me, Sally, just give me the blasted bottle!"

She blinked and backed down, her eyes never leaving his. "All right, Mitch. If that's what you want. I'm just trying to do what you asked me to do, keep you accountable." She took her time reaching for a bottle of Bushmill Malt under the counter before thudding it on the bar. "So much for accountability. And so much for your future."

He reached in his jacket and hurled a wad of bills on the bar. "To the devil with my future. It might as well burn with the past."

He wheeled around and bludgeoned his way through the crowd, riling customers on his way out. Outside, the bitter cold assailed him, tinged with the smells of burning peat and the slight whiff of horses. He could hear the faint sound of laughter and singing drifting from the various pubs tucked along the cobblestone road. His anger swelled.

He hurled his car door open and tossed the bottle on the passenger seat. Mumbling under his breath, he rounded the vehicle to rotate the crank, gyrating the lever with such ferocity that it rattled unmercifully. The engine growled to life, its vicious roar rivaling the angst in his gut. He got in the car and slammed the door, slapping the headlights on with a grunt. With a hard swipe of the steering wheel, he jerked the car away from the curb and exhaled a loud breath.

It was happening again. He was finally past the pain of one sister and now it was beginning with the other. He gunned the vehicle down Lower Abbey Street, nearly hitting a pedestrian who probably wouldn't have felt a thing, given the near-empty bottle in his hand. Mitch gritted his teeth. That's what women did to you—drove you to the bottom of a bottle where you drowned in your own liquid travail. He yanked his tie off, loosening his shirt to let the frigid air cool the heat of his anger. Thoughts of Charity suddenly surfaced, and a heat of another kind surged through his body. He swore out loud, the coarse sound foreign to his ears. He turned the corner on a squeal. The bottle careened across the seat and slammed into his leg.

He'd been without a woman way too long. Once, his appetite had been voracious. But Faith had changed all that. Her sincerity, her purity, her honesty. She had ruined him for other women. Since she'd left, he'd had no inclination, no interest. No desire.

Until now.

He pulled up in front of his apartment building and silenced the engine, closing his eyes while he slumped over the wheel. Why her, God? Why Charity? She was poison. *Just like Anna.* And nothing like Faith. Faith had been the first woman he'd trusted in a long, long time. He snorted. The only woman he'd trusted. Other than Kathleen and Mrs. Lynch. And the line was a long one, circling several blocks for sure, beginning at his mother's door.

Mitch grabbed the bottle and climbed out of the car, taking extreme care to press the door closed quietly. The last thing he wanted was to encounter Mrs. Lynch. Not like this. Not now. He lumbered up the steps like a man twice his age, praying she would be asleep. He let himself in as gingerly as possible, tiptoeing up those polished maple stairs she was so proud of. For once the lock to his apartment complied, and the door swung open with ease. Tucking the bottle under his arm, he carefully closed it again, flipping the lock with a satisfying click.

He didn't bother to light a lamp. Moonlight shafted through the window, illuminating Runt's jubilant motions as he pressed his snout and jiggled his tail. Mitch squatted, allowing him to lick his face. Runt's warm tongue lathered against his scruffy jaw.

"Hi, big guy. Yeah, I missed you too."

He stood, massaging the dog's ear with one hand while the bottle of whiskey hung limp in the other. He was grateful Mrs. Lynch had already taken Runt out. He moved like a sleepwalker to the kitchen to hunt for a glass in the near-empty pantry, knocking over cups as his hand fumbled in the dark. When he found one, he filled it with whiskey and downed it before replenishing it and heading for the parlor. He took a swig as he walked to the fireplace. With one hand, he stirred the embers of the peat fire he'd made before leaving, then took another drink. It felt good going down, burning his throat with a warm, rich tingle that he hadn't tasted in a long time. He wiped his mouth with the side of his hand and moved toward the couch. He stopped. His Bible lay open on the table where he'd left it. Even in the dark, the open page burned in his memory.

"Watch and pray, that ye enter not into temptation: the spirit indeed is willing, but the flesh is weak." Matthew 26:41

Mitch growled and flipped the Bible closed, shoving it to the edge of the table where it toppled over and landed on the floor with a clunk. It usually brought him such solace and peace, but not tonight. He had purposely chosen that Scripture earlier, before he'd left, to guide him, strengthen him. So much for guidance. So much for strength. He guzzled another drink. Tonight he had, indeed, found out—for a second time—that his flesh was weak. Particularly when it came to Charity O'Connor.

He dropped onto the couch and laid his head back, closing his eyes. *Why, God? After a year of hell getting over Faith, why draw me to the woman who took it all away? The woman who lied, cheated, and deceived with one goal in mind: tempting me so she could destroy her sister.*

He poured more whiskey into his mouth, licking the excess

from his lips. A haze settled over his mind, inviting his thoughts to drift. Why not Kathleen instead? He pictured the woman who'd been his ready companion before Faith, devoted to him despite his insatiable appetite for other women. A loyal employee whose only goal was to please him. Safe, warm, honest Kathleen, always there, always waiting.

He felt the whiskey dulling his senses and took another swig, his body relaxing into the sofa. All at once, Kathleen's sweet face distorted into Charity's sensual body. Heat jolted through him that had nothing to do with the alcohol in his bloodstream. A curse slurred from his lips. Just one flash of a thought, and the want was so strong it made him dizzier than the drink in his hand. He drained the whiskey and dropped the empty glass by his side, his hand falling limp on the couch. Images swam in his mind: the loving granddaughter, the hard-working clerk, the innocent little girl, the flirt. Sometimes shy, often nervous, always seductive.

"She's an enigma, our Charity. A real puzzlement," Mima had said.

Mitch groaned through the fog in his brain. She was, indeed. A puzzle he had no inclination to solve. Friendship or no.

꿍 꿍

A knock startled him. He jolted on the sofa. Where was he? It sounded again, and Mitch stared at the door, his body sluggish and heavy. He put his hand to his head, as if to still the buzzing in his brain. Where was Runt? The third knock sounded, and the door swung wide in surreal motion.

She stood on the threshold, a vision in blue, the golden curls rippling over her shoulders. "May I come in?"

"What are you doing here, Charity?"

She brushed past him, the scent of lilacs drifting in the air. "I came to say goodbye."

His eyes traveled the length of her, from the blue of her eyes to the curve of her hips. Against his will, heat infused him, and the buzz in his brain droned louder. She turned away, and he rose, moving to stand behind her. He hesitated for only a moment before lifting her flaxen tresses to expose her graceful neck. He pressed his lips to the softness of her skin while his other hand slipped to her waist. "Why?" he whispered.

"Because I'm in love with Rigan."

His lips stilled on her throat while his pulse throbbed in counterbeat with hers. She turned, and her image distorted into another woman whose hazel eyes gleamed like a wildcat on a kill. Silken curls, black as midnight, dropped from his hands as her name fused to his tongue. "Anna . . ."

Her scarlet lips contorted into a cruel smile. "I'm carrying his child."

"I'll kill him!" His words issued forth in a strangled rasp, spewing from lips as parched as his tongue, which cleaved to his throat like adhesive. He attempted to swallow, his eyes sealed with paste.

"Not before he'd fire you, I'm afraid."

Mitch jerked and sucked in a breath, jolting upright. His eyes flew open to see Mrs. Lynch hovering over him, her silver hair pulled in a lopsided knot on the top of her head. Her thin lips bowed in an impish smile, but her usually twinkling eyes held more concern than luster.

"What?" His utterance of that single word caused a slash of pain so severe, it forced him to collapse against the sofa once again. He closed his eyes and groaned, the tips of his fingers thick and clumsy as they attempted to massage the bridge of his nose.

"Mr. Reardon. He called, you know. Said that if you didn't—and this is a direct quote, mind you—if you didn't get your sorry backside into work before one o'clock, he would—I believe he said 'boot' . . . yes, I'm quite sure that's the word he used—'boot' you straight to the nightshift." Her tinkling chuckle was soft, but it still hurt his ears. "I've brewed you some coffee," she whispered.

He tried to get up again but only accomplished sagging to one side, his elbow connecting with something hard. He opened his eyes. The whiskey glass. It lay horizontally, sticky droplets of alcohol spattering his plush leather sofa. He picked up the glass, the smell causing him to heave. Mrs. Lynch gently tugged it from his hand and replaced it with a steaming cup of coffee.

"What time is it?" he croaked. The smell of the coffee produced a second wave of nausea, but he sipped it anyway, grateful for the warm liquid coating his throat.

"Noon. Bridie called at nine, Kathleen at ten, and now Mr. Reardon just a few moments ago." She leaned in to pat his cheek, her fingers cool against his skin. "They're worried."

His eyelids lifted just enough to allow a glimpse of the worry lines etched in his landlady's face. "And you're not, I suppose."

She laid a tiny, blue-veined hand on top of his. "You're like a son, Mitchell. And you haven't done this in a long, long time. What brought it on?"

He set the coffee on the table and hunched over, elbows draped on his knees and eyes staring at the floor. "It was a one-time thing, Mrs. Lynch. It won't happen again."

He felt the sofa give as she perched beside him. She patted his back, the gentle tapping providing a comfort that quelled his spirit. "I know it won't, Mitch, because I know the caliber of man you are. What reduced you to this?"

He sighed and scrubbed his face with his hands. He didn't want to talk about Charity. Not to anyone. Especially Mrs. Lynch. But she cared. And she was relentless. Two factors that convinced him he needed to tell her something. Anything. "I dreamt about Anna," he whispered.

The hand on his back paused. "It's been a long time since that troubled you. Why now?"

He stood, wincing from the pain in his head. "Who knows?

Gallagher actually found his way to the *Times* last week. Maybe that's what put me in a funk."

"He was at the *Times*? Whatever for? I didn't think he even knew where it was. He's never done a day's work in his life."

Mitch moaned while stooping to retrieve the Bible from the floor. "To ride me, as usual. So help me, I'd smash his face in if I wasn't a God-fearing man."

Mrs. Lynch chuckled. "Or needed to eat." She shot up from the sofa, as spry as any youngster. "Well, get cleaned up and ready to go in. I don't want you losing your job." She grinned, giving her delicately wrinkled face an endearing elfin quality. "I need the rent."

It pained him to smile, but he did. "Thank you. You're better than any mother."

She tossed her head, shaking the disheveled knot further off-center. "You mean, grandmother. And yes, I believe I am. I always told Mr. Lynch that we needed to have more than our Betsy because one daughter couldn't possibly supply me with all the grandchildren I'd require." She sighed. "But, alas, it wasn't meant to be. And now with Betsy halfway around the world . . ." Her blue eyes dimmed, suddenly glazed with a faraway look.

"How is Betsy, by the way?"

She snapped back from her reverie. "Oh, that British husband of hers has her falling in love with India, I'm afraid. India, of all places, for heaven's sake. But she claims to love it . . . and him, which is good, I suppose, albeit lonely for me." She paused at the door. "She won't be home for Christmas."

He swallowed, his throat so dry the saliva congealed on his tongue. "Actually, we've been issued an invitation for Christmas this year, the both of us. At Faith's grandmother's."

She blinked. "Why, that sounds lovely. But how did that come about? I had no idea you kept in touch with Faith's family."

He gulped the rest of his coffee. "It's a long story, but if you'd rather not go—"

"Oh, no! I would be delighted to go . . . thrilled to go. It will be good to see them again. I can hardly wait." The excitement in her eyes made her look all of twelve, despite her age.

He smiled, absently rubbing his head. "You won't have to. We're invited to a Thanksgiving celebration next Saturday. In honor of Faith's sister. She's returning to Boston for good before Christmas. It's an American holiday celebrated the following Thursday. But Charity wanted to have it this weekend so she would be off work to help with preparations."

Her eyes glowed. "Ohhhh! That sounds wonderful. What shall I bring?"

His smile was sheepish. "I'm afraid you'll have to bring your apple duff. I bragged on it."

She tossed her head to the side and giggled. "Did you, now? And I suppose I'll have to make an extra for your pantry, to pay for the compliment." She glanced at the watch pinned to her sleeve. "You've no time to waste, Mitchell, you best hurry." She turned to go, then wheeled around, pursing her lips. "One more thing. Before you face that irate editor of yours, promise you'll eat the hot breakfast I made. It's keeping warm on the stove."

He managed another smile. "What would I do without you, Mrs. Lynch?"

She lifted an almost invisible silver brow. "Starve, no doubt." She wagged her fingers in the air and disappeared through the door, closing it with a loud slam that shook him to the core.

He glanced at the clock on the mantle. The motion jarred his brain. 12:10. He plodded to the bathroom and scowled, squinting at the blinding sunlight streaming through the window. He stared in the mirror, nose to nose with a man haunted by his past: sunken eyes, pasty skin, bloodless lips. He rubbed the itchy growth of beard darkening his jaw and wondered if he would ever feel better than he looked right now. He splashed cool water in his face, lathered with soap, and reached for the razor. Skimming it across his skin, he thought of Charity. The blade nicked. He winced, staring at the blood pooling on his cheek.

This wasn't going to happen. Not again. He'd promised they'd be friends, but he'd been wrong. They could never be friends. It would be lovers or nothing. And he chose "nothing." He was through loving women he couldn't trust. A woman without God. He'd die of loneliness first.

Rinsing the blood from his face, he stared in the mirror, the weight of his burden forcing his eyelids closed. Thoughts of Charity invaded his mind and body like a warm venom pulsing in his bloodstream. He sagged over the sink, fatigue sapping his resolve.

One more month. Surely he could tolerate friendship for one more month. And then she'd be gone forever, along with the temptation. And at least he would have kept her from Gallagher.

Hate gurgled in his stomach like acid. The thought of Rigan's lips on Charity's mouth, his filthy hands touching her soft skin, strangled his throat like a fist of rage. His knuckles strained white on the grip of the razor. Never had he wanted to kill a man more. To slit his throat. To watch him bleed. *Just like Anna.*

Mitch positioned the razor against his jaw and looked in the mirror. What he saw chilled him to the bone: the eyes of a murderer, dark with hate and fury.

The razor slipped from his hands and clattered into the sink.

Thou shalt not kill; and whosoever shall kill shall be in danger of the judgment: but I say unto you, that every one who is angry with his brother shall be in danger of the judgment.

Mitch hunched over, his fingers gripping the sink. He struggled to inhale, suffocated by hate. His head lurched up and his teeth clenched in his jaw. "No! You can't expect me not to hate him. I have a right."

Who, being in very nature God, did not consider equality with God something to be grasped, but . . . humbled himself and became obedient to death—

Mitch pressed his palms to his face and drew in a ragged breath. Jesus had laid down his right to be God. Could he lay down his right to hate? When had it resurrected? The hate, the pain? All these years, he'd thought it was over, long buried and gone.

Until Charity.

As if conjured up, her image appeared in his mind, ensnaring him with thoughts of last night. Touching her. Kissing her. Exploring her. He shivered, heat licking inside like a thousand raging fires on the verge of blazing out of control. She'd destroyed his life once. And now, when he'd been ready to move on, she was back, poisoning him with desire and rekindling his malice.

How could he fight it . . . fight her?

All at once, the memory of Faith lighted upon his mind, as gently and softly as if she stood before him, her emerald eyes awash with hope. She had wrestled with her own betrayal, her own hate over what he and Charity had done to her. But in the end, she'd remained true to her beliefs, choosing life over death, forgiveness over hate. She had shown him what it was to live for God's desires rather than her own. To delight in him.

Delight thyself also in the Lord; and he shall give thee the desires of thine heart.

Mitch hung his head over the sink, wetness stinging his eyes. He was truly happy for her, he was. Soon she would be Collin's wife. She had her heart's desire . . . while his was buried beneath a mountain of lust and hate.

A quiet thought slowly drifted through his brain, as inconspicuous as the tiny wisps of whiskers scattered in the sink. He could have it. That quiet strength, that solid peace, a true commitment to a Being who shouldered burdens and carried you through. That's what he needed. A depth of faith that was more than a pass through a Bible, a visit to a church. A living, breathing relationship with a living, breathing God.

His eyes blurred as he stared in the mirror. He blinked once, and everything shifted into focus. He released a draining breath. "All right, God, I'm done. Done keeping you at arm's length. Done doing it on my own. I'm ready to give you everything—my life, my hopes, my desires. Help me. Guide me. Show me what to do."

Forgive.

His jaw tightened and then released. Slowly, he expelled a weighted breath, like fingers being pried away and letting go. "Okay, I'll try. But not on my own. Help me."

Pray for him.

The concept was clear, but the application was as foreign as the Greek in which the apostle Matthew had penned it: *love your enemies . . . bless those who curse you . . . pray for those who persecute you.*

Mitch closed his eyes, unable to imagine ever uttering a prayer for Rigan. "I can't."

Pray.

His fists balled on the edge of the sink. Faith had once told him, when you can't pray, pray that you can. He opened his eyes to glare upward. "All right . . . help me to *want* to pray."

His fists relaxed. The tension eased from his face. Hope overtook him like a flash flood. Mitch exhaled, aware that his hands were trembling. He looked up at the ceiling. "Dear God in heaven, where have you been all my life?"

Sucking in a deep breath, he carefully tested his mind, edging toward thoughts of Charity. A surge of heat rolled over his body like a hot summer breeze off the coast of Donegal. Mitch sobered considerably. He doused cool water on his face and reached for the razor, then put the blade to his throat. He exercised extreme caution while his lips flattened into a hard line.

Charity.

Obviously an area that still needed some work.

5

Bridie sauntered to the threshold of Mitch's nearly closed door and peeked in. She grinned. The poor guy looked like he'd just been poured out of the very bottle he'd drained the night before. Rumpled clothes, bleary eyes, pasty skin tinged the color of the amber liquid that, no doubt, still traveled his bloodstream. His hulk of a body sagged pathetically over his desk, elbows planted on piles of disheveled galley sheets while he cradled his head in his hands.

She tiptoed in with the utmost care, then slammed the door with a resounding bang.

Mitch's body jerked in the chair like a marionette on elastic strings. A salty word from his former vocabulary peppered the air, eliciting another grin from Bridie's lips.

"What the devil are you doing?" he growled, jumping to his feet. His hand went immediately to his head with a groan. "Blast it, Bridie, when this pain is gone, I'm going to make your life so miserable."

She strolled over and tossed her article on his desk, letting loose with a deep chuckle. "Well, you're certainly the king of miserable. Practicing on yourself, are ya?"

He lowered himself into the chair slowly, his hand grafted to his head. He massaged his forehead with his fingers, a pained expression on his face.

Bridie plopped into the chair in front of his desk and folded her hands in her lap. "So, what pushed you off the wagon this time?"

He looked up from under swollen lids. "Go pester someone else."

"Can't. You're the only one who's any fun. The only one I can get a rise out of." She adjusted the sleeve of her blouse and grinned. "The only one who hasn't gone home."

Mitch sank deeper in the chair and closed his eyes. "Leave me in peace, will ya?"

She sat up and leaned in, arms flat on his desk. Her smile shifted into serious concern. "That's what I'm trying to do, Mitch, leave you in peace instead of this wretched misery you've drunk yourself into. What did it this time? I'm guessing a woman's involved because that's the only time you go on these benders. So who is it? Charity?"

A groan trailed from his lips. "Go home, Bridie."

Bridie settled back in the chair and shimmied into a position of comfort. "Can't do it, Boss. You might as well start talking because I'm not leaving until you do." She propped her feet up on the trash can for good measure.

He managed an exasperated sigh before dropping his head back against the chair, eyes still closed. There was a half-day's growth of beard beginning to shadow his jaw. "I need a woman bad, Bridie."

Her feet fell off the can. Heat steamed her cheeks. "Well, sweet saints above, that might just be the one thing you could say to get me to go home."

Mitch's eyes, usually a clear and penetrating blue, slowly lumbered open, now glassy and spidered with red. "I mean it, Bridie. I need a wife."

Bridie swallowed the chuckle tickling her throat. "Well . . . I can certainly understand how a man of your age and . . . experience . . . would feel the need to . . . commit, but who exactly did you have in mind?"

"Kathleen."

Bridie sat up. "Kathleen?"

Mitch reached for a half-empty cup of cold coffee. "Yes, Kathleen. She's always been in love with me. You said so yourself." He opened his drawer and grappled for aspirin.

"I . . . I know, but, Mitch, you don't love her. You've never loved her. To be honest, you used her and broke her heart. Would you risk doing that again?"

He scowled, then popped the aspirin in his mouth and gulped the coffee, wincing as it went down. "I wouldn't hurt her this time. I'd learn to love her. She's a woman I can trust. A woman who only wants the best for me."

Bridie sighed. "Yes, but I remember the agony you put her through, gallivanting with other women while you took the best of her. And then there was the heartbreak of Faith . . ."

Mitch leaned back in the chair again and slammed the drawer shut with his foot. "That was the old me. I do things by the book now. I need a woman, so I'll marry one."

Bridie twisted her lips in a wry smile. "Mmmm . . . lucky Kathleen."

"Look, Bridie, I don't need your grief right now. I care about Kathleen, you know that. I'll go to my death protecting her and taking care of her. Who knows? Maybe her love will stir mine and we'll live happily ever after."

"That's nothing but a line from a fairy tale, Mitch, and you know it."

"Yeah? Well maybe I want a fairy tale right about now. I'm getting pretty sick of the real thing." His mouth settled into a mulish press and he closed his eyes, this time squeezing them hard as if to shut her out.

Bridie clicked her tongue against the roof of her mouth as she studied him through squinted eyes. The confirmed bachelor who had it all—looks, brains, talent, a comfortable living. Everything but the right woman. She folded her arms and jutted her chin. "What are you running away from, Mitch? Or should I say whom?"

His eyes flashed open and he leaned forward, jutting a massive finger into her face. "Look, Bridie, I've had just about enough of your flip responses. If I want to marry Kathleen, I'll bleedin' well marry Kathleen."

Bridie studied the flare of his nostrils and the muscle throbbing in his chiseled cheek and took a quick gamble. "Even if you're falling in love with Charity?"

His steeled jaw went white.

Bingo!

"What the devil are you talking about?" He snatched his cup off the desk and chugged the rest of the coffee.

She was smart enough not to smile. "You've been seeing her, haven't you? I tell ya, Mitch, when it comes to women, you're the front page of the *Times*."

He slapped the cup down on the disheveled pile of papers. Splotches of coffee splattered everywhere. "Blast it all, woman, it has nothing to do with her."

This time Bridie grinned. "So she is involved."

He jumped up from the chair and stormed to the door. In a huff, he wrenched his black woolen coat from the hook. The loop tag inside the collar snagged. Bridie heard the fabric tear and bit back a chuckle. Mitch muttered something under his breath. She was pretty sure it was another colorful word from his vocabulary of old.

She followed him out. "What is your problem? Wait, she doesn't love you, is that it? Is that why you're such a crank?"

Mitch pushed her out of the way and barreled for the door. She stayed glued to his heels, sprinting to keep up with his long legs. Spurting around him, she beat him to the double doors, flinging herself in front with arms pasted to either side to block his way. He slammed to a stop like a locomotive screeching on its rails. Any moment, she expected to see smoke billowing out of the crop of blond curls on his head. She was breathing hard. "You love her and she doesn't love you. That's it, isn't it?"

His lips were white, his eyes red, and a vein in his temple throbbed a dangerous blue. Not a good color combination. The few employees on the nightshift were gawking, but Mitch didn't seem to care. He glared at her, the fire in his eyes all but cauterizing her to the door. "Get out of my way," he said through clenched teeth.

Bridie revamped her strategy. "Mitch, I'm worried sick about you. Talk to me, please."

Not the slightest chink in his armor. "So help me, I will rip you from that door—"

"It's not good to stay bottled up like you do. Didn't you prove that last night?"

He sucked in a deep breath, then huffed it out. Some of the fight must have drifted out as well. His shoulders suddenly sagged while he scoured his face with his hands. "What do you want to know?"

"Does she love you?"

"Yes."

"And you love her?"

He turned around and slogged back to his office. She followed, closing the door behind. He dropped into his chair with a thud and stared, eyes resigned. She returned to her chair and perched on the edge, her hands cupping the edge of his desk. "You love her, don't you?"

"I don't love her, Bridie. I'm in lust with her." He sighed and snatched a pencil from his desk, staring at it as he twirled it in his fingers. He continued, his voice low. "There was a time— before Faith—when I would have enjoyed this, toying with her affections, carefully leading her down the path where I could satisfy every urge she provoked in me. And God knows she provokes. When I'm around her, it's . . . it's like . . ." He shuddered. "Like she possesses me. I lose control. I crave her lips, her body, her soul . . ."

"Why is that bad? Why does that scare you if she's in love with you?"

He tossed the pencil on the desk. It ricocheted off and skittered to the floor. "Because she's no good for me. She's nothing like Faith. No faith in God, a minimal sense of right and wrong. She lies, she manipulates, she coaxes. Anything to get what she wants."

Bridie leaned forward. "You can teach her. Like Faith taught you."

He shook his head. "No, it's not just that. I don't trust her, not one golden strand on that beautiful head of hers. Every time I think of her, I get this heat, this desire. And then right on its heels slithers this cold, paralyzing fear so strong, my stomach turns."

Bridie expelled a deep breath and slumped back in the chair. "Anna really inflicted some damage, didn't she?"

A bitter laugh escaped his lips. "Yeah. She kind of picked right up where my beloved mother left off."

"I'm sorry, Mitch." She hesitated. "But Charity may not be Anna."

"True. But you know, Bridie, I'm just a bit skittish about going down that road to find out for sure."

"So, what are you going to do? Even the best Irish whiskey won't dull the effect she obviously has on you."

"No, but she's leaving Ireland before Christmas, thank God, so I'll just have to keep my emotions in check until then."

"You weren't serious about marrying Kathleen, were you?"

He released a weighty breath. "I think I am. I'm a thirty-five-year-old man with needs and a conscience. A wife will do me good. And Kathleen will make one of the best."

"Don't hurt her, Mitch."

He glanced up, his gaze locking with hers. "I won't, Bridie. Once I commit to Kathleen, there will be no turning back."

"It might be wise to wait till Charity's out of the picture."

He nodded. "Yeah, I thought of that. I'll wait till Charity's just a speck on the horizon, sailing home. And then I'll court Kathleen like I should have years ago."

Bridie stood up. "You'll make her the happiest woman in the world, you know."

He nodded, a shadow of a smile lifting his lips. "Yeah. That's something, anyway."

❧ ❧

The bell over the door jangled, delivering a blast of cold air and another shivering patron into the cozy confines of Shaw's Emporium. Emma glanced up and elbowed Charity. "Don't look now, but our favorite customer is here."

Charity peeked out of the corner of her eye and spotted Rigan chatting with Mrs. Shaw. She groaned under her breath. "Not *my* favorite customer—Mrs. Shaw's." She kept her gaze glued to the receipts in her hand, tallying numbers she no longer saw.

Emma chuckled softly. "That's what I meant. But we all know he's not here for Mrs. Shaw, now don't we?"

Charity swallowed. Yes, she knew. All too well. She'd been dreading the encounter for days. Since she'd promised Mitch she wouldn't see him again. Emma patted her arm. "Why, Mr. Gallagher, so nice to see you."

Charity looked up, feigning surprise. "Rigan! What are you doing here? Out slumming?"

Rigan propped his arms on the counter and leaned in, a lazy smile on his handsome face. "Hello, Emma, Charity. I'm in dire need of a new suit." He winked at Emma before giving Charity a seductive grin. "I want to look my best when I take a particular lady to the theater on Saturday night."

Charity chewed at her lip. "Rigan, I . . . I'm sorry, but I won't be able to accompany you."

The smile died on his face. "Charity, I've had tickets for

❧ 115 ❧

months. It's Shaw's *Pygmalion*, a limited engagement at the Abbey Theater."

Emma quietly slipped away while Charity drew in a tight breath. "I know. Everyone's been talking about it, but I can't go. Please forgive me." She attempted a teasing smile. "Now you can ask one of the scores of other women vying for your attention."

He stood to his full height, his umber eyes deepening to brown. "Why?"

She fidgeted with the receipts in her hand. "I . . . I'd rather not go into it here . . ."

A muscle twitched in the hard line of his jaw. "You better go into it here."

Charity glanced around. "Rigan, I'm working."

She felt the heat of his stare before he turned. "Mrs. Shaw? Would you mind if I spoke with Charity privately in the back room?"

Mrs. Shaw looked up from another customer, a hesitant smile on her lips. "Why, no, Mr. Gallagher, not at all. Charity, you may take your break now."

Rigan's gaze shifted back. He arched a brow and extended his hand. "Shall we?"

Charity nodded and made her way to the back. Rigan followed, yanking the curtain closed behind him. She turned. "Rigan, I'm truly sorry."

He ambled to a chair and kicked it out with the tip of his shoe, his eyes never straying from hers. He sat and hiked his leg up, the heel of his boot propped on the lower rung of another chair. His voice was calm, almost matter-of-fact. "I want to know why."

She took a deep breath and exhaled slowly. His bold eyes penetrated hers like gold fire. A muscle flickered somewhere in that swarthy complexion of his that always reminded her of a pirate. She stared at the deep cleft in his chin, already shadowed with a midday growth of dark beard, and swallowed hard. If it weren't for Mitch Dennehy, she might have very well fallen in love with this man. Every other woman certainly did.

He cleared his throat. "Why, Charity?"

She sighed and sank into a seat, twiddling her thumbs on the table. "Well, you see, our plan worked." She looked up and forced a bright smile. "We were quite successful in getting Mitch's attention."

Rigan never blinked. "If it's working, why quit?"

She hesitated, then steeled her jaw. "Because I promised I wouldn't see you again."

"I see. Well, I suppose congratulations are in order. Have you set a date?"

She could feel the heat in her cheeks clear down to her toes. "No. It's nothing like that."

The chair scraped as he shifted forward. He cocked a brow. "Then what, exactly?"

She bit her lip. "Friends."

He threw back his head and laughed, the husky rumble inflaming her cheeks even further. "Friends? And he dictates whom you may see?"

"Rigan—"

"Charity, you're a fool."

She stood and squared her shoulders. "Thank you for the unsolicited opinion."

He grinned. "You're welcome. Now sit down and hear me out."

She crossed her arms in defiance. "No, thank you, Mr. Gallagher. I believe my break is almost spent."

He rose to his feet and rounded the table. He gently pushed her back into the chair and squatted before her, his eyes earnest. "Charity, now is the time to turn up the heat, to go for the kill."

She glanced up through narrowed lids. "What do you mean?"

"I mean, he obviously cares enough to rid you of me, so let's put it to the test. Marry me."

Charity gasped. "What?"

He laughed and pulled her to her feet, skimming his hands up the sides of her arms. "Make him crazy. Marry me. Or at least say you will."

She tried to swallow, but her throat was too dry. "You're joking."

He lifted her chin with his finger. "I wish I were. But, alas, you've stolen my senses, Miss O'Connor, leaving me little recourse of the heart."

"Rigan, I—"

He drew her in his arms and pressed his mouth against her cheek, his breath hot on her skin. "I need you, Charity."

She pulled away. "I . . . I can't. I don't love you."

"I can remedy that if you allow me more than bargained kisses."

She sighed and sank into her chair. "Rigan, you have no idea how many times I've wished I'd fallen in love with you instead. But I didn't. You've known all along how I feel about Mitch." She glanced up. "For your sake as well as mine, I think it's best we end it now."

He studied her. "You're serious."

"Yes."

He moved to stoop beside her, taking her hand in his. "I can't accept that. I knew when we struck our bargain that I was taking a risk, so I accept that I've lost. But I can't accept losing your friendship. I care about you."

"I care about you too, Rigan, but I'm leaving Dublin in a month anyway."

"Then what's the harm of friendship till you leave?"

She bit her lip. "I promised."

He stroked the knuckles of her hand with his fingers. His voice was low. "And you promised me you'd go to the theater on Saturday night."

"I know. But I was hoping you'd be a gentleman and understand."

He stood. "I do. You're a woman of your word. So keep yours to me."

She assessed the seriousness of his manner and sighed. "All right. You win. I'll accompany you on Saturday night. But our bargain is over. We go as friends."

"Agreed. I'll pick you up at six for dinner." He moved to the door and turned. "As *friends*." Bending at the waist, he bowed and flashed a grin before disappearing through the curtain.

She shook her head, realizing she would probably miss his ardent attention when it was all over. She bit her lip. One night at the theater. Surely there was no harm in that. She stood and adjusted her skirt, her fingers as cold as the apprehension that slithered her spine. No harm, indeed. As long as Dennehy the Tyrant never found out.

❦ ❧

"But you promised you would stay the night." Charity paused, her fingers buried deep in the golden curls piled high atop her head. Her brow wrinkled as she peered in the mirror at Emma, perched on the bed behind her.

"I promised I would *try* to stay, Charity. But Rory—"

Charity jabbed several hairpins into her hair and spun around. "I don't want to hear it, Emma. It's always Rory this, Rory that. The man does nothing but abuse you."

"He's my husband, Charity."

Charity slapped a stray curl out of her eyes. "Then let him act like it instead of drinking your paycheck and sleeping around. He's no good. Can't you see that?"

Emma sighed and slumped against the headboard. Her voice was barely a whisper. "Yes, I can see that." She looked up, the soft gray of her eyes as gentle as doves. "But it doesn't change the vows I took."

"Oh, Emma, I don't understand you." Charity plopped down beside her friend. "Rory's not concerned about his vows. Why are you?"

A quiet sigh drifted from Emma's lips. "I answer to a higher power than Rory. Besides, he was a good man before the drink poisoned him."

Charity glanced at her out of the corner of her eye, her lids slanted in warning. "You're not going to start spouting God stuff again, are you?"

Emma actually smiled. She looped an arm around Charity's shoulders. "It's who I am, Charity, and well you know it. But, no, I think you need to finish getting ready, and I need to see if Bridget needs my help. What time is Mitch coming?"

"Saints alive, he'll be here in fifteen minutes," Charity said with a glance at the clock. She bolted up from the bed. "Emma, tell Grandmother I'll be down as soon as I finish my hair. Oh . . . it would be so much easier to leave my hair down. But no, saintly Mr. Dennehy seems to prefer this overly modest, holier-than-thou type of woman, so I'm forced to fiddle with pinning it up."

"It worked last time, didn't it?"

Charity smiled over her shoulder. "Like a charm."

"Well, then, you best get busy pinning, and I'll get busy praying. Between the two of us, Mr. Dennehy should end up more lovesick than you."

"Not possible, but oh, I'd give anything to make it so."

Emma turned at the door. "Anything?"

Charity pinned a curl in place and grinned at Emma's reflection in the mirror. "Anything."

Her friend chuckled and nodded her head toward the ceiling. "Good. He's listening."

∽ ❧

It irked him beyond belief that he didn't want the night to

end. He watched from across the candlelit parlor as Charity took her turn at charades. Full lips pressed into a beautiful pout and eyes squinted with determination, she looked like a little girl pretending to pry a lid from a jar. His gaze strayed to the shapely curve of her fitted cotton blouse tucked into a dark tweed skirt that hugged her body. All thoughts of a little girl suddenly bolted from his mind. He swallowed hard. She was too beautiful for her own good.

And his.

"Twist! Oliver Twist!" Emma flew up from the faded flame-stitch sofa, gesturing wildly in the air. Charity shook her head, and more golden strands dislodged from the knot of curls pinned at the back of her head. She tugged on her ear.

"Sounds like . . ." Mima edged precariously close to the edge of her seat.

Balling her fists to her eyes, Charity pretended to cry.

"Cry . . ."

She tapped her index finger on her nose and pointed to Mima before continuing to twist a lid from a make-believe jar.

"Pry. *Pride and Prejudice!*" Emma shouted.

Charity squealed. "We win, we win! Losers have to serve dessert, as agreed." She shot a cocky look in Mitch's direction. "An ample piece of Mrs. Lynch's apple duff, if you please, Mr. Dennehy. And don't skimp on the cream in my coffee."

He seared her with a half-lidded gaze and a smug smile of his own, noting with satisfaction that her cheeks tinged pink. "At your service, Miss O'Connor." He scanned the parlor. "Mima, Emma, would you like coffee with your dessert?"

"Oh, no, Mitch, thank you. I need to be getting home, so I'll pass." Emma stood.

Charity whirled around. "No, Emma, not before dessert! Please stay."

"I wish I could, but Rory's expecting me home, and I have a long walk."

"Mitch will run you home right after dessert, won't you, Mitch?"

"Absolutely. Besides, Emma, you can't be walking home alone in the dark and the cold."

Emma smiled. "I do it all the time, Mitch. Shaw's Emporium is about the same distance from my flat as Charity's grandmother's house. No, I refuse to disrupt your evening. I'll be fine."

Mitch angled a brow in Emma's direction. "I'm not arguing with you, Emma. I'll drive you home after dessert, and that's the way it will be."

"Very well, if you insist. I don't suppose I'd have much success arguing with the likes of you, anyway. I hear you possess all the stubbornness of a small clan of Irishmen."

He chuckled, his gaze roving to Charity's face, which now sported a lovely shade of rose. "Really? And would the clan's name be O'Connor, by chance?"

Emma giggled. "I think it just might be."

"I can certainly vouch for that," Mima chimed in. "At least the O'Connors I know are inclined toward a mulish bent. Inherited, no doubt, from their grandmother."

"Mother! That's certainly the sot calling the lush tipsy." Bridget laughed and grabbed Mitch by the arm. "Come, Mrs. Lynch, Mitch. I believe we have dessert to serve."

"And mouths to stuff with something other than cocky comments," Mitch mumbled.

Bridget giggled as she led the trio to the kitchen. "Oh, dear me, yes."

❧ ☙

Mitch glanced over his shoulder before easing into the thin stream of traffic outside of Emma's ramshackle apartment building. He shifted and glanced at Charity. "What happened to Emma's face?" He caught the stiff set of Charity's jaw before he returned his gaze to the road.

"Rory happened to Emma's face. Like a fatal disease."

"He beat her?"

A hoarse laugh erupted from her throat, thick with scorn. "If only that were all."

"What do you mean?"

Charity stared out the window, emotion trembling in her voice. "He tried to kill her."

Mitch clenched his teeth. "How?"

"Tried to strangle her. Right before he threw hot grease in her face."

A curse parted from his lips before he could stifle it. "Sorry. For the love of God, why does she stay?"

Charity turned her gaze to his, her face distorted by the headlight glare of a passing vehicle. "For that very reason."

"What reason?"

"The love of God."

He drew in a deep breath and shifted to turn a corner.

Her tone was flat as she continued. "You know, for better or worse, till death do us part? Though he scars her, beats her, carouses with women, and drinks what little profit she manages to bring in, Emma refuses to break her wedding vows and leave. She takes 'till death do us part' very seriously. And I worry every night that it will . . . while God looks on."

Mitch exhaled slowly, quietly, the silence between them as telling as the bitterness in her tone. He turned onto Ambrose Lane, not sure how to respond. The car slowed in front of her house. He turned the engine off. "Charity," he began.

She swiveled in the seat. "No, Mitch, I don't want to hear it."

He studied the curve of her face, shadowed by the streetlight, and noticed the firm press of her lips. "Don't want to hear what?"

"Your defense of God. That's what you were about to utter, weren't you? That's what Faith would say, and Emma—"

"But not you."

"No. Why should I? God has never done anything for me. He's only taken—first the life of my favorite sister, then my father's love, and now the beauty and joy of my best friend. And the ultimate irony is that by my very disdain for him, he's robbed me of any chance I might have at winning your love."

Mitch remained silent. The pain in her voice eclipsed all questions whirling in his brain.

"Well, I'm right, aren't I? You deny your feelings for me because I'm not a woman of faith. Don't you?"

He released a weighty breath and sank against the seat, his eyes closed. She was right, of course. He did have feelings for her, urges almost too strong to resist. But he would have to. He didn't trust her. How could you trust someone who lived to please themselves rather than God?

"Yes. I want a woman of faith. A woman I can trust."

"See? See what your God has done for me?"

He opened his eyes and leaned forward, his gaze intent. "My God has done amazing things for you, Charity, only you're too stubborn and blinded by bitterness to see it. He's blessed you with great beauty, intelligence, wit . . . and a family who loves you more than you can comprehend."

A sheen of tears glimmered in her eyes. He cupped her chin firmly in his hand. "Let it go, Charity. Unload all that painful bitterness and hurt from your past. It's time to experience the joy and peace of God."

She pulled away, forcing tears to spill. "I can't. You don't understand. You haven't been rejected by a parent you adored."

He smiled the faintest of smiles. "You're wrong."

Charity paused, her eyes fixed on his. "Who?"

He exhaled and sifted his fingers through his hair. "My

mother. Unfortunately, I was never quite as important as the legions of men in her life."

Charity gasped. "What do you mean?"

"I mean she cheated on my father and she rejected me, over and over again."

"No! How could she do that?"

"She was a woman without faith, Charity, without morals, without conviction. She only believed in herself and the plea-sure she sought."

Charity collapsed against the seat, hand clutched to her chest. "Oh, Mitch, how horrible. What did your father do?"

Mitch closed his eyes and swallowed hard. "He died. Because of a broken heart, I say, but the doctors said his health was compromised by a love affair with the bottle."

"How old were you?"

"Nine, going on ancient. I had to grow up pretty fast. I sold papers in front of the *Irish Times*. It was all that kept us going. That and an occasional handout from one of the long line of suitors that made their way to my mother's bed."

Charity scooted closer to rest her hand on his arm. "Mitch, I'm so sorry. I had no idea. Have you . . . have you forgiven her?"

He opened one eye to squint down at her. "Working on it."

She smiled and snuggled close until he finally curled an arm around her shoulder. "Do you ever see her? Ever try and talk it out?"

"No, a few years back she remarried and moved to England, so I don't get much opportunity. We exchange letters at all the appropriate holidays, of course, but there's not much depth to it. One day I hope to remedy that."

Charity sighed. "I'm glad. That's a horrible burden to bear."

"You should know."

She pulled away and sat up. Her eyes searched his for several seconds. "How are you even able to entertain the notion of forgiving after such pain? I can't imagine . . . can't fathom how it's even possible . . ."

He wrapped his fingers around her small hand, holding it tightly. "It's something your sister taught me, something I've struggled to apply."

"What?"

"First you acknowledge your anger and bitterness as sin and tell God you're sorry. Then you pray for the person who caused it."

"I can't do that."

Without thinking, he lifted her hand to his lips and kissed it. "Yes, you can. That's something else your sister taught me. If you can't pray for the person who hurt you, start where you can: pray to be able to pray. It's the one place everyone can start, no matter the hurt. And it works. I've tried it."

She stared at him, her lips parted in surprise as he kissed her hand again. Their eyes met and held. "I suppose . . . I could start there. But I can't imagine God would listen to me."

He smiled. "He'll listen. You're the apple of his eye."

"What?"

"The apple of his eye. That's what the Bible says we are to him. The gleam in his eye. His pride, his joy. That's you . . . and that's me."

Tears brimmed in her eyes. She shuddered.

He pulled her close. "Cold?"

"No," she whispered. "Just a bit shaken. My father used to call me that. The apple of his eye. Before Hope died and Faith got sick."

"And so you are. He's never stopped loving you, Charity, and neither has Faith."

She shivered again. He wound both arms tightly around her small frame, resting his face against the top of her head. "What do you say we get this taken care of, once and for all?"

She pulled away to look up at him, eyes wide. "Now?"

He grinned. "Of course, now."

She blinked. "How?"

"You open your mouth and talk."

"To you?"

"No, to him, you goose."

Her mouth snapped shut. He watched her lower lip protrude the slightest bit.

"Charity?"

"What?"

"You can't go on like this forever, hurting inside, hating. You have a choice to make: turmoil or peace, life or death, blessing or curse. What's it going to be?"

She stared at him, lips pressed tight and eyes narrowed in thought. A soft huff of air finally escaped her lips, signaling surrender. She nodded and flopped against his chest again while her fingers gripped the lapel of his coat.

Minutes passed before he heard her voice, halting and quiet. "God, I'm angry at you, angry that you let Hope die, angry that Faith was crippled. That you took Father's attention away from me, his love. I'm not sure I can forgive you for that . . . all the hurt, the pain. But I want to be free from it. Help me, please. Bring me to the point where I'm able to forgive—first you, and then Father . . ." She released a heavy sigh. "And then Faith. Amen."

He gave her a squeeze. "Good girl. Feel better?"

She nodded. "I do. But I'm not sure if it's the prayer that's done it or being in your arms."

He pushed her hair away from her face and kissed her forehead. "We best get inside before the ladies think we're lost."

A shadow of a smile played on her lips. "I am lost. Deep in my thoughts."

"And what might those be?"

Her smile teased. "Dear God, that my forehead were my lips."

He grinned. His gaze settled on her mouth, and a rush of

heat chased the smile from his face. His heart began to pound. *Friends. Only friends.*

"Does it matter, Mitch? Does it change anything at all that I've taken steps toward God?"

He swallowed, forcing his gaze from her lips to her eyes. "I don't know, Charity."

"Oh, I hope so," she breathed. She lifted her face to brush her lips to his cheek, then pulled away to slowly scoot to her side of the seat, poised to open the door.

His hand clamped her arm. "No."

She turned. Shock flickered across her features. "No? It doesn't make a difference?"

His throat worked as his eyes settled on her mouth once again. "No, don't go. Stay. Please." He hooked his arm around her waist and pulled her across the seat, his breathing quickening. His pulse took off as he lowered his mouth to hers and caressed her lips gently, softly, feeling her astonishment in the kiss, her mouth open in surprise. She moaned softly and clutched his chest with her fingers. He deepened the kiss, groaning at the sheer joy of tasting her.

Lord, help me, please, the want is so strong . . .

With every force of his will, he pushed her away and snapped the car door open. He jumped out and gulped in a deep breath, grateful for the cool night air filling his lungs and brain with reason. She waited patiently while he leaned against the car, his fingers dragging through the cropped curls on his head. No woman had ever affected him this way. Was it just her or was he sorely in need of a wife? Exhaling, he slammed the car door shut and made his way to her side of the car. He yanked the door open and extended a hand. She slid to the edge of the seat and peeked up at him with wide eyes and the barest of smiles.

"You can wipe that smug smile off your face, Charity. We both know the disastrous effect you have on me. Let's just get inside and steer clear of temptation. And any mention of this."

"Whatever you say, Mitch." She tilted her head, her lips sporting a shy smile. "But one thing. Are we still friends? Or more?"

His jaw twitched as he studied her, irritated at the way his pulse raced. "Inside. Now."

She popped up out of the car and grinned. "We are more, aren't we?"

He kicked the door closed with the heel of his shoe before literally dragging her toward the front porch. "Maybe."

She giggled. "You're falling in love with me, aren't you, Mitch Dennehy? And I'm hoping there's not a thing you can do about it."

He nudged her through the door, following close behind. "Oh, yes there is. I can stay far away until you're on that ship. And I will if given the slightest provocation. Understood?"

She whirled around to bestow a quick peck on his cheek. "Yes, Mr. Dennehy," she said with a laugh. She unbuttoned her coat and slung it on the coatrack. "Grandmother, we're home."

He took his coat off and hurled it on top of hers, following her every move as she sashayed into the parlor. She stopped and shot him a teasing look over her shoulder. He shook his head and laughed, wondering what in the world he had just gotten himself into.

"Goodness, you're back already? I've just begun to show Margaret my latest stitches."

Mitch eyed the spools of yarn littering the coffee table and gave them a wry smile. "It's nice to be missed."

Mrs. Lynch glanced from Mitch to Charity, obviously taking in the pink glow in Charity's cheeks. She chuckled, her silver brows arched in a display of innocence. "And it certainly appears you missed us in much the same manner."

A bit of heat crept up the back of his neck. He grinned to

deflect it. "I suggest you be nice, Mrs. Lynch, or we'll be heading home before Bridget can knit and purl."

"Oh, my, we certainly don't want that. Why, we have a number of techniques yet to discuss, don't we, Bridge?"

Bridget looked up. "Absolutely. Charity, why don't you and Mitch occupy yourselves while Margaret and I finish up here?"

"We'll do dishes—" Charity began.

"Already done. Margaret is faster in the kitchen than the three of us put together. And Mima was so tired, I put her to bed just before you came in. But I would appreciate you taking a quick peek out the window to see if there's any light on at Maggie's. Johnny stopped by earlier to tell me the poor thing's been at the hospital all day with Davy. Seems the little dickens fancied himself a whittler with Johnny's woodcarving knife. Cut the tip of his finger clean off."

Charity pressed a hand to her mouth. "Oh, poor Davy!"

"Yes, and poor Maggie too. They'll all be exhausted and starving when they finally get home. I told Johnny to just knock on the door and I'd keep supper warm. But you and Mitch help yourself to the checkers in the desk drawer, or I believe there's an old chess set in the hutch."

Charity glanced at Mitch. "Feeling brave enough to take me on in a game of chess?"

He laughed. "Personally, I think you could do with a bit of chastening."

She hiked a brow. "Oh, you think so? I'll enjoy watching you beg for mercy. My father happens to be one of the best chess players in Boston, a skill he required of each of his children."

Mitch grinned and rolled up his sleeves. "So, you going to stand there bragging all night? Set up the board."

Charity laughed on her way to the kitchen to see if Maggie was home. She quickly returned to the parlor to proclaim all was still dark. She dug through Bridget's hutch, then carried a wooden box to a small table by the hearth. Mitch hoisted two of Bridget's needlepoint chairs to either side, then squatted to stoke the fire while Charity set up the board. He stood and turned.

"All ready, Mr. Dennehy. Prepare to die." Challenge gleamed in her eyes. She sat perched on the edge of her seat, primed for victory with arms crossed and a smug smile on her face.

"Prepare to die?" He let loose a husky laugh and seated himself across from her, his eyes locked on hers. "This will be your funeral march, Miss O'Connor, not mine. Even with your unfair advantage of being white."

Charity scrunched her nose and moved her king's pawn two spaces. "Black just seems to suit you so much better, don't you think, Mr. Dennehy?"

A knock sounded at the door. Bridget popped up. "Stay put, Charity, I'll get it. Excuse me, Margaret, I'll just be a moment to get Johnny his supper."

Charity could hardly contain herself. She propped her elbows on the table and rested her chin on her hands, tightly clasped to dispel any shaking. She could feel the breath hitching in her chest and forced herself to breathe . . . calmly, quietly, working hard to display a composure she didn't feel. Inside she was all awhirl, tipsy with joy over the prospect that Mitch was finally returning her affection. She studied him from across the table, the slight pucker of a frown wedged between his brows as he contemplated his first move. Her heart wanted to burst. He was everything she had ever wanted in a man: smart, tough, no nonsense, yet a heart as soft as fresh-churned butter. She stifled a sigh. And more handsome than the law allowed. How in the world had he managed to steer clear of the altar all these years? She suddenly thought of Faith and felt a rush of heat to her cheeks.

He moved his pawn and settled back in the chair. The corners of his lips twitched. "I suggest you focus on your game if you hope to win this match, Miss O'Connor."

Her face burned hot as she fumbled to pick up her pawn.

"Charity . . ." Bridget's voice drifted from the foyer.

"Yes, Grandmother?" Charity craned her neck to see Bridget standing at the front door.

Bridget shot a worried glance over her shoulder. "You have a visitor."

"Good evening, Charity." Rigan stepped around her grandmother into the foyer. "You left your glove in my car the other night, and I thought you might need it."

Charity's hand froze on her pawn, her fingers white and pinched. Not unlike her face, she was sure. She tried to breathe, but the air only fused to the back of her throat.

Rigan waggled the glove in the air. "I truly apologize for barging in like this, but the weather has been frightful. I didn't want you to be without it." He nodded curtly toward Mrs. Lynch and then Mitch. "Good evening. Please forgive the disruption."

Charity dislodged the painful lump in her throat and sucked in a deep breath, dropping her pawn on the board. She dared not glance at Mitch, but stood to face Rigan head-on. Even with her back to him, she felt Mitch's tension as if heat were singeing the hair on her arms.

"Rigan . . . I . . . thank you. I've been hunting for that glove for well over a month." Her eyes entreated his cooperation.

Rigan smiled. "Perhaps another. But I believe this particular glove was the one you lost last Saturday night when we went to the theater."

All the blood that had drained from her face returned in a whoosh. She began to cough.

"Charity, are you all right?" Bridget moved toward her granddaughter, leaving the door in the foyer wide open.

She gasped for air. "Yes, Grandmother, I'm fine. Just a tickle in my throat." She squared her shoulders and glared at Rigan, her tone clipped and cold. "Since that was our final night out together, I appreciate your courtesy in returning it. Good night, Rigan."

She took immense satisfaction in the blotch of red that crept into his swarthy cheeks. His eyes flickered with anger while he bowed slightly at the waist. He tossed the glove on a nearby table and nodded before turning to leave. Bridget clicked the door closed behind him, the sound as menacing as the click of a revolver.

Charity turned. Her stomach plunged. Mitch stood, face immobile except for a muscle throbbing in his temple. His eyes glittered like splintered turquoise, full of cold heat and fury.

"Mitch, I—"

"Bridget, forgive me for cutting the evening short, but I've suddenly taken ill." He strode to the foyer and plucked his and Mrs. Lynch's coats off the rack.

Mrs. Lynch stood by the sofa with worry in her eyes. "Mitch, I know you're upset, but please settle down. Don't let Rigan ruin the evening for you."

His jaw was hard and cold, as if etched in marble. Without a word, he moved to where she stood, holding her coat while she slipped inside.

Charity was barely able to breathe. "Mitch, please don't leave. Let me explain—"

"Bridget, thank you for a wonderful dinner. Ready, Mrs. Lynch?" He commandeered her arm, steering her quickly toward the door.

She shot a look of apology over her shoulder. "Bridge, thank you so much for having me. I'll return the favor soon."

The door slammed shut, its finality reverberating in the air like the sealing of a tomb.

Bridget sat on the sofa, a pale statue with yarn in her lap and needles limp in her hands. Her mouth hung open as she blinked several times. "What in the world just happened?"

Charity slumped in the chair, too stunned to speak.

"Charity, answer me." Bridget discarded her needles and hurried to her granddaughter's side. "Why was Mitch so angry?"

"Because I lied to him," she whispered.

Bridget pulled a chair close and sat down, resting her hand on Charity's arm. "What do you mean, you lied to him?"

"He hates Rigan." Her head sagged into her hands. "He made me promise I wouldn't see him again."

"I see. And he was just starting to trust you, care for you, wasn't he?"

Charity looked up and nodded, a single tear trailing her cheek.

"Well, he'll get over it. He cares for you. I can see it in his eyes."

She shook her head, the motion weighted with regret. "No, he won't, Grandmother. Mitch has this obsession with trust. It started with his mother. Now he doesn't trust any woman who lies to him." She choked back a sob. "Or cheats on him."

Bridget gently stroked Charity's hair. "Trust is not an obsession, darling, it's an extension of love. When we truly love someone, we give them our heart to hold in their hands. And when that love is returned, that very trust is balm to our souls."

A sob convulsed in Charity's throat. She grabbed her grandmother's hand and held it to her lips. "Oh, Grandmother, I love him so much, but now he'll never trust me."

Her grandmother's fingers feathered through the loose strands of Charity's hair. "But then, he never has, now has he?"

She opened her eyes. "It's not funny, Grandmother."

Bridget smiled. "No, but it's not life and death, either." She patted Charity's hand. "Earn his trust, Charity. Don't lie. Don't deceive. Be true to him . . . and yourself."

"I am being true to myself, Grandmother. I love him. If I didn't bend the truth a little and plot my strategy, I would have never gotten this far with the man. He's as guarded and unapproachable as a fortress of steel."

"Yes, but once your love is tucked securely inside, I suspect you'll be assured of its safekeeping, now won't you?" Bridget stood.

"You talk in riddles, Grandmother. All I know is I love him and I'll do whatever it takes."

Bridget sighed. "That's what I'm afraid of."

Rising to her feet, Charity flipped a strand of hair from her eyes. She crossed her arms. "What's that supposed to mean?"

Bridget bundled her knitting into her arms and dropped it into a wicker basket by the side of the sofa. She stretched, pressing her hands to the back of her hips. She eyed Charity through tired eyes. "It means I worry that 'whatever it takes' may be exactly what it takes to lose a man like Mitch Dennehy."

Charity turned her back, hands shaking as she picked up the chessboard and slanted it hard. The pieces plunged into the wooden box with a jarring clatter. "Don't underestimate me, Grandmother, I won't lose him. Whatever it takes—" She pivoted slowly, arms stiff and fingers taut as she gripped the wooden box. Her left brow angled dangerously high. "And I do mean 'whatever'—I will become Mrs. Mitch Dennehy, mark my words." She arched her back with an air of defiance seldom displayed to her grandmother. "And when I'm done, it'll all be worth it."

Bridget sighed, apparently too tired to argue. "It will never be worth it, Charity. I only hope and pray you find that out before it's too late. Good night, dear. Douse the lights before you retire. And leave the back door open with a note for Johnny, will you? His supper is in the oven."

Without awaiting her reply, Bridget departed the room, leaving Charity with nothing but the taste of bitter regret in her mouth.

Turmoil and unrest. Mitch stared at the headline of Monday evening's *Irish Times*, and his anger resurfaced all over again. It began when he'd stormed out of Charity's parlor Saturday night and had only mounted throughout the wee hours of Sunday morning. That's when he'd learned that the Irish Republican Brotherhood, a group favoring armed revolt against the United Kingdom to secure Ireland's independence, had had a particularly busy night.

Mitch tossed the paper on his desk and rubbed the back of his neck. The last twenty-four hours had been—for both Ireland and him—a nightmare of turmoil and unrest. As if it wasn't bad enough having Dublin turned inside out, he was still seething over Charity's broken promise—a deception that had robbed him of a decent night's sleep up until Michael's frantic call at six in the morning. His stomach growled, reminding him he hadn't eaten since lunch. He glanced at his watch. Near midnight. Thank God for Mrs. Lynch. She took such good care of Runt. Now if he could just find someone to do the same for him.

He rubbed his hand over his scratchy jaw and yawned. He hadn't been home in almost forty-eight hours, and he was pretty sure his hygiene was questionable. He was grateful that most everyone else had gone.

Michael popped his head in the door of Mitch's office. "You best get your carcass out of here. I want you fresh in the morning. The earlier, the better."

A wry smile twisted on Mitch's lips. "I can guarantee early. Can't do much about fresh."

"It's been a devil of a couple of days, hasn't it, though? I thought I was going to have to carry Bridie out of here, she was so exhausted."

Mitch stood and stretched. "Don't think you're off the hook yet. You may have to carry me. I haven't had a decent wink of sleep since Friday night."

Michael whistled. "So the old Mitch is finally back, eh, burning the candle at both ends?"

"Nope, no candles." Mitch shoved his desk drawer closed

and plucked his coat off the back of his chair. "But fire was involved, and I definitely got burned."

"You care to explain that?" Michael leaned against the doorframe and crossed his arms, appearing intrigued.

"Nope. Good night, Michael."

Michael waited till he was almost to the double doors. "Bridie tells me you're thinking of picking up where you left off with Kathleen."

Mitch stopped, his back to Michael. Anger pushed his fatigue aside. "Bridie's got a big mouth."

"That's a given. But she also has a big heart. And she cares about Kathleen. We all do."

Mitch spun around, his jaw clenched tight for the hundredth time in the last two days. "I'm not going to hurt Kathleen. I'm looking for more this time."

"Bridie says you're in love with Faith's sister."

He swore under his breath. "Bridie needs a lip lock. I'm not in love with anyone."

Michael squinted and scratched his bald head. "That's good. She appeared to be real cozy with Gallagher, you know? And I don't want you ruffling his feathers. Or hurting Kathleen."

Heat broiled the back of Mitch's neck. He took a step toward Michael and jammed a finger under his nose. "Look, Michael, you may be my editor, but get this and get it good. My life is none of your blinkin' business, nor Bridie's . . . nor Kathleen's, for that matter. So butt out."

Michael yanked on his trousers to pull them up around his ample stomach and leaned in, rising to his full five-foot-two height. He prodded a stubby finger right back into Mitch's chest. "You bet your blasted backside it's my business when it affects the welfare of this paper and its employees. You've hurt Kathleen once. You make bloomin' sure you don't do it again. And as far as Faith's sister is concerned, if there's any brain in that thick head of yours, you'll stay as far away from her as you can get. I can't afford to lose you if Gallagher wants your head. Although God knows I'd love to give it to him right about now."

Mitch blasted out a loud breath of frustration and leaned in, standing his ground. "Trust me, Michael, we're in tight agreement on one thing. I have no intention of going anywhere near Faith's sister ever again. And as far as Kathleen goes? If and when I pick up where we left off, it will be with a ring on her finger. Is that bloomin' sure enough for you?"

His editor readjusted his pants one more time. "Good." He expelled a heavy sigh, releasing all the bluster along with it. His eyes softened. "We just care about you, Mitch. Is that a crime?"

Mitch scrubbed his face with his hands. "Good night, Michael."

"Good night, Mitch. Get some beauty sleep, will ya? You need it bad."

6

Bridget looked up from her plate piled high with turkey and stopped chewing, watching Charity pick at her stuffing. She and Mima exchanged glances. "Charity, I know it's left over from Saturday, but you seemed to enjoy it then. And you haven't even touched the cranberries."

Charity shot her a mournful gaze. "I'm sorry, Grandmother, it's not the food—it's delicious. It's just that my appetite isn't what it was on Saturday."

Bridget put her fork down. "Apparently nothing's what it was on Saturday: your appetite, your mood, your sleep. Have you tried to call and straighten this all out?"

Charity prodded at a piece of turkey. "Of course. I've left messages everywhere—the *Times*, Mrs. Lynch's, even Duffy's, because Mrs. Lynch says that lately, he practically lives there for his meals. But he won't return my calls. She says he's been working long hours, trying to keep up with all the turmoil going on right now."

Mima put a frail hand on Charity's arm. "Give him time, Charity. He'll come around."

Charity dropped her fork on the table to grab Mima's hand. There was desperation in her tone. "But I don't have time, Mima! I'm leaving for Boston in less than a month. My time is dwindling." She closed her eyes and hung her head, massaging her forehead with her hand. "I can't believe it. Here it is, Thanksgiving, and the very thing I'd be the most thankful for is slipping away."

Bridget softened her voice. "Charity, maybe it's not God's will—"

Her eyes flew open and her head snapped up. "It's *my* will, Grandmother, and it will be me who wins Mitch's heart, not God." She pushed her chair back and stood. "Dinner was wonderful. Please leave the dishes for me. I'll do them when I get back."

Bridget's eyes widened. "But where are you going at this late hour? It's almost eight."

"I'm going to confront him, whether he likes it or not. He has no difficulty ignoring my messages, but he can't ignore me in the flesh." Charity leaned to give Mima a tight squeeze, then rounded the table and planted a quick kiss on Bridget's cheek.

"What are you going to do?"

"Don't worry, Grandmother, I won't do anything that offends your moral sensibilities. When it comes to sins of the flesh, I'm afraid our Mr. Dennehy is too devoted to God for that. But I do happen to know, firsthand, that sins of the flesh are a particular weakness of his. And since all is fair in love and war, I'm going to put on my most tempting dress, unpin my hair, and pay him a visit."

Bridget jumped to her feet. Her napkin floated to the floor. "Charity, no!"

Charity smiled over her shoulder. "Good night, Grandmother, Mima. I'm warning you—don't touch those dishes." She stopped at the door to pose against the frame, suddenly delirious with the feeling of a little girl about to misbehave. Bridget made the sign of the cross while Mima's lips gummed in disapproval.

Charity blew them a kiss. "I love you both, you know that. But don't wait up."

Mitch yawned and leaned against the door of his office to watch Bridie and Kathleen at their desks. Bridie's usually disheveled topknot sagged lower on her head than usual. Several long strands of silver hair escaped to flutter down the back of her neck. Even at this late hour, her fingers flew over her typewriter keys, pounding out yet another article on the latest upheaval in Ireland's struggle for independence.

His eyes flicked over to Kathleen at the next desk, her long, lithe body poised and calm while she typed the reams of chicken scratch Mitch had tossed at her earlier. Her rich, chestnut hair was piled high on her head, exposing the graceful beauty of her long neck, feathered with soft ringlets of stray curls. He assessed the way she sat straight and strong, as if fatigue couldn't affect her focus. And, as he had done more than once in the past week, he compared her to Charity. Where Kathleen seemed almost prim, Charity was definitely not proper. Where Charity was flirtatious and sensual, Kathleen was soft and shy, exuding an air of innocence despite giving her all to Mitch years before. His jaw tightened. He should marry her. He owed her that. Besides, where Charity was bold and defiant, Kathleen was quiet-spoken and compliant.

The perfect wife.

He cleared his throat and both women looked up. "I'm ravenous. Who feels like eating?"

Bridie cocked her head and narrowed her eyes. "Who's buying?"

He grabbed his coat off the hook and gave her a droll smile. "Who do you think?"

"In that case, I'm ravenous too." She chuckled. "How 'bout you, Kathleen?"

Kathleen smiled as her cheeks tinted a pretty shade of pink. She peeked up at Mitch with liquid-brown eyes that brimmed with adoration. "I suppose I could eat a bite."

"Humph, a bird's bite, if I know you. And all to spare this slave driver the expense of a high-priced supper. Not me. I take great pleasure in spending his money. He can afford it."

Mitch tugged Kathleen's coat off the rack and held it while she slipped it on, fixing Bridie with a narrowed gaze. "Can't afford not to. You'd make me pay, one way or another." He started for the door.

Bridie chuckled. "Ah, yes, one of my greatest pleasures in life, making you pay." She stood up and waggled her brows. "Hey, what about my coat?"

Mitch kept walking. "I'm providing dinner, not chivalry. Get your own coat."

He heard her mumbling as she snatched her wrap and wrestled to put it on. She hurried to the door. "You did it for Kathleen," she muttered with a pout.

Mitch grinned and held the door as they scurried past. "Kathleen doesn't give me grief."

"Yeah, that's her problem," Bridie said under her breath.

"Be good, Mrs. O'Halloran, or you'll be buying your own pint to go with the meal I provide."

"Yes, sir," she said, bundling her coat tighter to ward off the cold. "My lips are sealed."

"When pigs fly," he said.

Their laughter carried on the night breeze as they hustled around the corner to the welcoming sounds and smells of Duffy's. He held the heavy oak door as the women hurried in and waved to get Sally's attention.

She hurried over and ushered them to a booth in the back. "So, you have the whole gang with ya tonight. Working them to the bone, I suppose, with all that's going on. Where's Jamie?"

"Sick," Mitch said, perusing his menu.

"Of working for him," Bridie whispered, pointing to Mitch behind hers.

Sally and Kathleen giggled while Mitch handed the menu

back. He settled in, rested his head on the back of the booth, and closed his eyes. "Ignore her, Sally, she's just mad because I can push her around. I'll take the biggest steak you can rustle up, the rarer the better, a hefty side of colcannon, and a double order of apple fritters."

Sally nodded while she scratched on a pad. She looked up, a tease in her tone. "Another bottle of Bushmill Malt, Mr. Dennehy?"

He opened his eyes halfway, searing her with a nasty look. "Ginger ale. And I swear you two are related."

Sally tossed her head and giggled. She patted Mitch on the arm. "Oh, you know we love you, don't you, you big bully?" She turned to Bridie. "What'll it be, sister dear?"

"The same as him, only throw in an order of crubeens for good measure, a mug of Guinness, and scones and lemon curd all around."

Mitch groaned. "I still have to pay rent for this month, Bridie. Have a heart."

She handed her menu to Sally. "I do, Boss. I'm thinking you can always move in with me . . ." She folded her hands on the table and looked up at the ceiling, the picture of innocence. "Or Kathleen."

Kathleen blushed scarlet and Bridie jumped. "Ouch! Did you just kick me, Mr. Dennehy—"

"Kathleen, what do you want to eat?" Mitch said, ignoring Bridie.

Kathleen studied the menu as if it were the most fascinating thing she'd ever read, her cheeks beet red. She cleared her throat. "An apple tart, please."

Mitch grabbed the menu from her hand, thinking he had never met a more unassuming person. "Kathleen."

She looked up, eyes blinking wide.

"Are you sure you don't want something else?"

She shook her head.

"Then, would you like coffee with that apple tart?"

A gentle smile tugged at her lips as she nodded.

"Two coffees as well, Sally. One for me, and one for the lady."

"Me too," Bridie piped up.

"And one for the troublemaker," Mitch muttered. He leaned back, feeling the heaviness of fatigue settling in his shoulders and neck. He barely listened to Bridie and Kathleen's idle chatter. The lull of sleep pulled at his eyelids until Bridie's voice jolted him back.

"Boss!"

"What?"

"I said you look beat. How much longer do you think we'll keep these hours?"

He straightened up in his seat. "For the next few weeks anyway, until things calm down."

"Do you think the Limey's will ever cut us loose?"

Mitch yawned as Sally unloaded their drinks. He reached for the ginger ale. "If the unrest escalates into bloodshed, I don't see how they can fight it, short of war. But that won't happen."

Bridie grabbed her Guinness, guzzling half of it before finally setting it down again. "No, the Brits are a civilized lot, for all the crick they put in our necks. And they've had their fill of war, that's for sure. I really think we're close, I do."

"Oh, I hope so," Kathleen whispered.

Mitch looked up and studied the soft curve of Kathleen's lips, the shy bent of her head. His eyes roved the length of her from across the table, taking in her full breasts and slim waist. He looked up, catching her gaze. Her cheeks flamed and he smiled. "Kathleen, how's your mother?"

She ducked her head and nodded. "Fine, she's fine. I was actually able to purchase several copies of Braille books for her, so she occupies herself quite well with knitting and reading while my sisters and I are at work. Elise, of course, still stays at home to care for her."

Mitch nodded, ashamed of the times he'd taken Kathleen to his apartment for his own pleasure. Her one request had always been getting home by ten for her shift with her mother.

On impulse, he reached to take her hand. "You're a good person, Kathleen."

Her cheeks tinged pink. He smiled. Other than Faith, he had never met anyone who blushed more. He squeezed her hand. "Your family is lucky to have you."

Sally descended on the table once again, this time with a steaming platter of crubeens. "Okay, the steaks are still sizzling, but here's something to tide you over." She nodded at Kathleen. "You, too, you skinny thing. I'm not delivering your apple tart until you've had your share of these crubeens. Don't let these two have 'em all, ya hear?" She thudded the platter in the center of the table and pushed it toward Kathleen. "You first."

Kathleen giggled and carefully poked the spicy fried meat with her fork, daintily putting a few sparse pieces on her plate. Bridie huffed and grabbed Kathleen's dish to load it high. "Dear Lord above, the poor girl would starve if we didn't intervene."

"Thank you, Bridie," Kathleen whispered and nibbled a piece on her fork.

Mitch let Bridie take her portion, then speared a hunk for himself. His stomach rumbled as the spicy juices rolled across his tongue. He closed his eyes to savor it.

"Hello, Mitch. I thought you just might be here. Good evening, Bridie."

The pork lodged at the back of his throat. He began to choke, his napkin over his mouth. Charity slapped him on the back several times. The pork shot into the cloth.

"Good heavens, you should chew a little more slowly." Charity grinned at Bridie, then nodded at Kathleen. "Don't tell me he made you work until now?"

Bridie chuckled. "Afraid so. Didn't your sister tell you what a terror he was?"

"Wh-what are you doing here?" Mitch said, pushing his napkin aside.

She flashed her killer smile. "Looking for you. We have unfinished business, I believe."

Bridie's brow lifted a notch while Kathleen stared at her plate.

The rapid-fire beating of his heart made him irate. Out of pure self-preservation and a touch of meanness, he reached for Kathleen's hand. She startled and looked up, eyes large with surprise. He tightened his hold. "Any business we may have had is finished." He fixed his gaze on Kathleen's face. "And at the moment, I'm very busy."

He heard Charity's soft intake of breath as he stroked the inside of Kathleen's hand.

Charity touched his arm. "Mitch, I need to talk to you. Alone. *Please*?"

Bridie jumped up and grabbed Kathleen by the sleeve. "Blast it all, I forgot to tell Sally I wanted a bowl of champ on the side. And you said you needed to go to the loo, didn't you? We'll be right back, Mitch."

Mitch ground his teeth while Bridie dragged Kathleen away.

Charity's smile was tentative. "May I sit down?"

He gave her a half-lidded glare. "Like I could stop you?"

The moment she took off her coat and slid into the booth, he started praying for strength. God help him, she had never looked lovelier—pale blue silk blouse cut with a deep V, enough to hint at the fullness of her breasts if she dared to lean over. And, oh, she dared. Resting her elbows on the table, she bent forward and crossed her arms, the deep V causing him deep pain. The only thing that saved him was the cascade of silky hair that fell down the front of her blouse, only slightly obscuring temptation. His cheek twitched as he pinned his gaze to her face.

"What do you want, Charity?" His tone was as stiff as his jaw.

Her fingers fluttered together while her blue eyes flicked up nervously, feathered with dark lashes. "You know what I want, Mitch. What I've always wanted."

"It's no good. My interests are elsewhere."

She bit her lip while a spray of pink fanned her cheeks. "I don't believe that. I know you care for me. And I certainly know you're attracted to me."

He leaned back in the booth, his eyes hard. "Not anymore. You ended that when you lied. I'm not attracted to women who lie."

She pressed her hands on the table and leaned forward. "I told him I couldn't see him anymore, that I had promised you. But he begged. Said I'd promised him first . . . to go to the theater. And he was right—I had. But it was only to be that one last time, Mitch. To keep my promise, that's all. I'll never see him again. You have my solemn word."

He cupped the side of his ginger ale and twirled the glass in his hands. He finally took a drink. "Sorry, Charity, but your word is not worth a whole bloomin' lot."

She caught her breath. Her gaze darted around the room before she leaned in, eyes pleading. "Mitch, let's leave so we can talk . . . alone . . . please?"

The muscles in his gut tensed. "Sorry. There's no way on God's green earth I'll ever be alone with you again. You're like a spider, spinning your web, inflicting your poison whenever we're alone, enticing me, weakening me." He shook his head, guzzling more ginger ale. "I'm done, Charity. Go home."

She straightened her spine, her head high despite tears brimming in her eyes. "All right. I guess you've made yourself perfectly clear. But can I at least trouble you for a ride? I walked."

He studied her through slitted eyes, willing himself to be cold. "We just ordered. It could be awhile. I'll drop you and Bridie off before I take Kathleen home. You're welcome to wait—at another table."

She winced and lifted her chin a notch higher. "Is she the one? Where your interests lie?"

He saw the hurt in her eyes, the fear in her face, and knew he should go easy on her. His jaw tightened as he dropped his gaze to the V-neck blouse. Yeah. Like she went easy on him. "Her name's Kathleen. We were involved before Faith."

Her composure seemed to crumple before his eyes. When she stood to her feet, she wavered like a colt, palms flat on the booth. "Do you love her?"

He stared, sick at what he had to do, but there was no other way. "I'm going to marry her."

Her head lurched up and her eyes blazed with blue fire. "Do you love her?" she rasped, her knuckles clenched white. Several heads turned their way.

The muscles in his jaw strained, and his heart felt like it was pumping in his throat. He swallowed hard to moisten his mouth. He forced the near lie through his lips. "Yes."

She slumped forward, as if the wind had been knocked out of her. Her hands dropped to her sides like dead weights. Only then did she lift her chin and straighten her back, her eyes hard and glossy. Without a word, she picked up her coat and slipped out of the booth.

He grabbed her wrist. "Where are you going? It's late. You need to wait for a ride."

She yanked her arm free and seared him with a look that grieved him to the core. She wrapped her coat loosely over her shoulders. "No thanks. I'd rather walk."

He leapt up and pushed her back in the booth. "You're not walking anywhere. You'll wait till I'm good and ready to take you home."

She jumped back up with hair flying wild and nostrils flaring.

"I hate you!" she cried. She lunged at him with fingernails extended. He clutched her wrists. She started kicking and flailing, her protest drawing attention. His blood began to boil.

With a grunt, he locked her in a vise and bent his mouth hard against her ear. "So help me, Charity, the more you fight, the more it'll hurt."

"Let me go," she said, her words little more than a hiss.

"Are you going to behave if I do?"

She didn't answer.

He tightened his grip, feeling the pounding of her heart as he locked her against his chest.

"Yes, you overgrown ape."

He fought a grin. "Promise. Although we both know your promises aren't worth the air that surrounds them, I'm willing to give you one more chance. Promise you'll settle down and wait for me to take you home."

He felt her resistance dwindle as she slowly relaxed against his chest. "I promise."

He softened his hold. All at once, he was painfully aware of every curve of her body, pressed hard against his. Heat infused him, shooting up the back of his neck and into his face. He flung her away, pushing her into the booth, as if his fingers burned at her touch.

She looked up, almost prone on the seat, her hair and coat splayed behind her. The deep V of that blouse rose and fell with every hard breath she took. The slightest tilt of a smile shadowed her lips as she arched a perfectly shaped brow. "Why, Mr. Dennehy, I do believe you're blushing."

He felt the blood gorge his cheeks once again and shoved her farther into the booth. He yanked her coat from beneath her, rolling her to the other side of the seat. He sat down and crammed it between them as if she were a leper. "Charity, so help me, the happiest day of my life will be when you get on that blasted boat."

She adjusted herself in the seat and picked up a menu,

studying it with practiced nonchalance. "No, it won't, Mitch. It will be when you finally admit you're in love with me."

He put his head in his hands and groaned, massaging his forehead with his fingers. "How many times do I have to tell you that I am *not* in love with you? I don't even know if I like you."

She turned the menu over to study the other side. "Oh, you do. A lot."

He peered at her out of the corner of his eye, his head still in his hands. "*No*, I don't."

She calmly placed the menu on the table and folded her hands. "Your mouth says no, no, no, Mitch, but your body says yes, yes, yes."

He actually laughed, shaking his head. "You are really something, Charity. A little girl with big delusions."

She turned in the seat. Her eyes offered a challenge. "I'll prove it. Take me home last."

"Not on your life."

"You're scared."

He laughed again. "You bet I'm scared. I've seen the damage you can do. I'm no fool."

Her smile faded. "Only when it comes to love—"

"Uh-hum . . . hope you don't mind, Boss, but Kathleen and I ran into some friends by the bar, so we stopped to chat." Bridie descended on the table, allowing Kathleen to scoot in first. She eyed Mitch with a questioning gaze before plopping down. Her eyes flicked from Mitch to Charity and then back again. She leaned forward, her tone a whisper. "I thought you said there wasn't going to be war?"

He paid Bridie no heed and forced a smile at Kathleen. "Kathleen, this is Faith's sister, Charity." He picked up his ginger ale to take a drink, ignoring Charity altogether. "Charity, this is Kathleen Meyer, my proofreader and all-around assistant."

Charity extended her hand. Kathleen took it, offering a shy

smile in return. "Nice to meet you. Faith and I were great friends. I still miss her."

Bridie looked up. "Oh, sweet saints above, we're finally going to eat. Sally, where on earth have you been?"

Sally grunted as she plopped a heavy tray on the table. She scrunched her freckled nose in apology. "Sorry for the wait, but the kitchen's backed up something awful. I keep telling Duffy to turn those blasted men's athletic clubs away, but he's a greedy tyrant, he is. Athletic clubs, my maiden aunt's tush. The only athletics they do is lifting a mug of ale to their traps."

Sally spotted Charity and stopped unloading the tray. "Now where in the sweet bogs of Blarney did you come from? I'll bet me mother's eyeteeth if I sent you back to put in my tickets, I'd get 'em quick enough. You wantin' to order?"

"Yes, please, I'd like a glass of your best wine—"

"No wine. Two more glasses of ginger ale, Sally." Mitch shoved his extra order of apple fritters in front of Charity. He glared, one brow jutted high. "Unless you prefer milk?"

She iced him with a cool gaze. "Ginger ale will be fine, thank you."

"Good. You want anything else?" He cut into his steak, feeling his juices begin to flow.

She sat back in the booth and folded her arms. "Nothing on the menu."

He popped a slab of meat in his mouth and swallowed, barely chewing. "Good. Enjoy."

❧ ☙

"It was very nice meeting you. I hope we see you again." Kathleen turned to smile over her shoulder at Charity, who sat, arms folded, like a deaf mute in the backseat of Mitch's Model T.

He glanced in the rearview mirror and grinned. "How was the ride back there?"

Her lips flattened into a nasty frown. "Wonderful." She wrestled with the back door handle, grunting until it finally swung open. She jumped out and slammed the door hard, rattling the chassis. She leaned in on Kathleen's side with a sour smile on her face. "Thanks for the ride. Kathleen, it was nice meeting you too."

Mitch leaned forward and grinned. "Always a pleasure, Charity."

"I wish I could say the same."

He chuckled. "Give Mima and your grandmother my love, will you?"

If looks were lethal, he'd be dead on the spot.

"I'll do that," she said in a sugary tone. "And I'll be sure to tell Rigan as well."

The smile hardened on his face. "You're a fool, Charity."

Kathleen spun around. "Mitch!"

"No, Kathleen, he's right. I have been a fool. But that's about to change." Her gaze shifted from Mitch to Kathleen. "I understand congratulations are in—"

Mitch jerked forward, the muscles in his jaw tensing. "Charity!"

She stopped midsentence, a flicker of pain in her eyes. She swallowed hard and forced a smile. "What I meant was, Mitch tells me you're a godsend in the office. Congratulations for being one of the few women in the world who can make him happy."

He exhaled slowly, unaware that he'd been holding his breath.

Charity flashed a pretty smile. "And, I suppose, congratulations are in order all around."

He stopped breathing again.

"How's that?" Kathleen asked, her face as innocent as an angel in the lamplight.

Charity's features hardened, belied by an almost imperceptible trembling of her jaw. She bit down on her lip and tossed her head as if she hadn't a care in the world. "Why, I'm getting married."

Kathleen caught her breath.

So did Mitch. Only he was pretty sure his wasn't kicking in anytime soon. It was lost, plunged somewhere between constricted lungs and the pit of his stomach.

"Oh, Charity, that's wonderful news! Who's the lucky man?" Kathleen leaned on the door, her hands clasped like a little girl.

"Why, Rigan Gallagher, of course." She stared straight at Mitch with a lift of her chin. "He's been hounding me for months, you know, but I've been putting him off. Somehow, I've run out of reasons to say no."

Mitch's stomach jerked as if he'd been kicked. He clenched hard, first his teeth and then the steering wheel, desperate to keep himself from leaping out of the car and shaking some sense into her. Instead, he yanked the throttle lever to give the car gas, then spit out the first thing on the tip of his tongue. "Charity, you're a fool. You deserve everything you get."

Kathleen whirled around. "Mitch, what in the world is wrong with you?"

He rammed the floor lever way too fast, grinding the engine. Muttering under his breath, he fixed Charity with a threatening glare. "Nothing's wrong with me, Kathleen. I've never been better. Regrettably, I can't say the same for her." He shot a quick look in the rearview mirror and lurched the car away from the curb. "Don't say I didn't warn you," he shouted.

He slammed hard on the pedal to shift from low to high speed. His jaw ached from pressure all the way down Ambrose Lane until the car screeched around the corner. He swore under his breath and punched the side of the door with his fist. "Brainless woman." He glanced at Kathleen out of the corner of his eye and began massaging the bridge of his nose. "Sorry."

"I already know you have a temper, Mitch. What I don't know is what's going on."

He blew out a loud breath. "Nothing's going on. At least, not anymore."

"She's in love with you, isn't she?"

"It's not important."

"It is to me," she whispered softly.

He sighed. "Yes. Or so she says."

"Bridie guesses you're in love with her."

He muttered under his breath again. He risked a quick look at Kathleen, but shadows hid her face. "Bridie needs a blasted muzzle. And a compass. Her guesses are way off."

Kathleen looked away and remained silent, hands folded in her lap.

Mitch took a deep breath and cleared his throat. "You look very pretty tonight."

She didn't move. "What's going on, Mitch?"

"I already told you, nothing's go—"

She turned. "Between you and me. Why now? Out of the blue?"

He veered onto her street too quickly, the squeal of the tires piercing the sanctity of the still night. He killed the engine and faced her, grateful for the dark. "Kathleen, I . . . well, you know when . . . well, when Faith left, so did my interest in women." He laughed, the sound of it bitter. "In fact, pretty much everything left. My appetite, my sleep . . ." He reached out to take her hand in his. "My passion."

She tugged her hand free and tucked it in her lap. She stared straight ahead while the muscles worked in her throat. "Mitch, I think you know I love you. I've never stopped loving you. But when Faith came, she didn't just change your life, she changed mine too."

He shifted uncomfortably in the seat. "I know I hurt you, Kathleen. I'm sorry—"

"No, that's not what I mean. Yes, you wounded me when you fell in love with Faith, but I always expected it. I knew you never loved me. I was simply convenient."

He reached out to take her hand again, but she pulled it away. He swallowed. "Kathleen, I'm sorry. I didn't know how to love anyone back then. Not until Faith."

She took a deep breath. "Let me finish, please. What I mean is, before . . . when I gave myself to you, it was because I loved you and it felt right. I did it for you . . . and for me. But Faith taught me otherwise. She introduced me to a faith in God that is more than I ever knew before. More than I thought existed. A relationship and devotion that compels me to live for him, following his precepts with all of my heart and soul." She pivoted in the seat to face him dead-on. "What we had before, it was wrong. As much as I loved you—and still do—it was wrong. Hear me, Mitch. Never again will I be a convenient outlet for you or your passion."

He blinked. The eyes were the same gentle brown, the voice still soft and halting, but the spirit inside the woman he thought he'd known was different. He took her hand. This time she didn't pull away. "Kathleen, Faith changed both of us. I can't express how sorry I am for all the times I took advantage of you, hurt you. Believe me, I've sought God's forgiveness, and now I'm seeking yours. Trust me, I have no intention of ever hurting you—or God—like that again."

Even in the dark, he saw tears in her eyes. "Just exactly what are your intentions, Mitch?"

He exhaled and leaned back against the seat. "My intentions are to find a woman I can grow old with, a wife to love and care for all the days of my life. I'm not making any promises, Kathleen, and I still need time to sort things out, but eventually—" he swallowed, squeezing her hand "—soon, I hope to find that woman." He paused, then slowly reached out to reel her into his arms. The glistening wetness in her eyes now coated her cheeks. "Kathleen, I think you may be the woman I need."

She rested her head on his chest, her body trembling. "Oh, Mitch, I may be the woman you need, but am I the woman you *want*?"

He stiffened. Unbidden, thoughts of Charity barraged his brain. He tightened his hold and lifted her chin with his finger. Her tearstained face wrenched his heart, fusing with his anger. With gentle force, he cupped the back of her neck and brought her mouth to his, tasting the salt of her tears. He felt her respond and pressed in, his physical need beginning to kindle.

No, my son.

He jerked back.

"Mitch, what's wrong?"

He stared at her, his chest heaving. In one quick sweep, he pulled her into an embrace and rested his head on top of hers. "Kathleen, you deserve so much. I never want to hurt you again. But I need time . . . time to purge my system . . . to get over . . . things."

Her voice was as soft and frail as a child's. "You mean Charity."

Her words sucked the air from his lungs, crystallizing in his brain.

Bridie guesses you're in love with her.

The muscles in his neck worked furiously. In love with her?

No! Please, God, no!

He crushed Kathleen tighter against his chest. "I don't know. Maybe. But either way, with God's help and every fiber in my being, I'll get past this. I promise . . ."

She stirred. He let her go. She sat up and gently pressed her hand to his heart. "No, Mitch, no promises, please. Not until you can keep them."

She turned to scoot toward her door. He grabbed the handle of his and jumped out, intending to walk her in. She put her hand up. "No, please, we're co-workers only. Not lovers or even courting. Please don't lead me on with anything that even remotely looks like it. Thank you for dinner and the ride home. I'll see you tomorrow."

He swallowed hard. "Yeah. Tomorrow."

She turned and ran up the walk to her house, disappearing inside faster than the clip of his heart. He stood and stared at the humble cottage she called home, as if seeing it for the first time. How in the world had he been so thickheaded all these years not to realize what an amazing woman she was? He lumbered to the front of his vehicle, shaking his head. The same way he'd been too thickheaded to see that his feelings for Charity were more than lust. Stupidity. Pure, unadulterated stupidity. And apparently he was lousy with it.

Fatigue weighted his shoulders as he cranked the car to life. He hopped in and stepped on the pedal, moving the throttle forward before easing down the darkened lane. He released a cleansing breath and shot a quick glance at the canopy of stars overhead. "Thank you, God, that you're the one with the brains, because you definitely have your work cut out for us." Rounding a corner, he headed home—to Runt, sound sleep, and undoubtedly, a serious bout of prayer.

Mrs. Lynch's windows were dark when he parked in front of his building. He dragged himself from the car and shut the door quietly, the strenuous pace of the last week finally catching up. He yawned and glanced at his watch. Almost eleven. Felt like three in the morning. He plodded up the steps and inwardly groaned at the thought of rising early just to satisfy Michael's bloodlust for extended hours.

Runt greeted him at the door, his enthusiasm a stark contrast to his own exhaustion. He closed the door and Runt pounced to give him his customary welcome, paws planted firmly on Mitch's chest. A dry chuckle rattled from Mitch's lips. "Yeah, I love you, too, big guy."

Runt sniffed and pushed his snout against Mitch's coat.

"No, I haven't been with any other dogs. You're the only one for me. And to prove it, I brought you something special."

Runt jumped down, his front paws jiggling in excitement. Mitch reached inside his jacket and held out a crumpled brown package, allowing Runt to get a whiff of the steak bone he'd saved. The dog whimpered and sat while Mitch discarded the paper and handed him the bone. Runt clamped enormous jaws on it and disappeared.

Mitch tossed his coat on the rack and struck a match to read a note on the table.

Mitch—Charity called again this morning. She seems quite upset. I know you'll do what's best. Your clean shirts are hanging in your closet. Mrs. Lynch

He blew out the match and wadded the paper, shooting it across the room to the trashcan, along with the crumpled doggie bag. Yeah, he'd do what's "best." He'd save himself from the throes of death.

He trudged to the fireplace to stoke the peat fire Mrs. Lynch kept burning during his long days at the paper. Energy depleted, he shuffled into the moonlit bathroom to get ready for bed. He wrested the tie from his neck and flung it over the side of the tub, along with his shirt and trousers. Yawning, he pulled his pajama bottoms off the hook on the door and put them on, and leaned over the sink to splash water in his face. He caught a glimpse of his reflection in the mirror. Puffy eyes, scruffy whiskers, sagging jaw. Even his muscled arms and chest slouched with fatigue. He needed sleep bad. He swished some soap and water in his mouth and spit it out. *Lord, let me go right to sleep tonight, please. Don't let me think, or my thoughts wander.*

Like a sleepwalker, he moved to his bedroom, shoving the covers aside to collapse on the bed and tunnel beneath. He moaned and closed his eyes, then stretched his long legs over the edge. Even the icy bedding couldn't daunt the relief that flooded his body as he lay stretched on his back, drained of anything but the desire to sleep.

Charity.

His eyes popped open. The thought of her name chilled him more than the frigid sheets.

Pray.

The silent command unleashed a flood of feelings he'd fought so hard to ignore. Anger flared in his gut. She was going to marry a man who would destroy her. Why should he care?

Because you love her.

He shifted to his side, jabbing the pillow several times till it bunched in a ball. He curled his arms around it, flopping his head on top. She deserves what she gets.

Forgive.

"That's your pat answer to everything, isn't it?" he groused, causing Runt to jump up and thrust his cold nose in Mitch's face. Mitch huffed out a blast of air and scrubbed the side of Runt's snout. "It's not that easy. She deceived me. She lied."

Love suffereth long . . . is kind . . . not easily provoked . . .

He punched his pillow again. "So now you're hounding me with Scriptures, is that it?"

Silence.

He rolled over on his back, arms limp at his sides. "You're not going to let me sleep until I pray for her, are you?" He sighed and closed his eyes, finally allowing his mind to focus on the one thing he'd struggled so hard to avoid.

Charity. The very name inflicted a sharp ache in his heart. Sky blue eyes that teased and tempted, lips that were the curse of his resolve. A wounded little girl, stubborn and strong, defiant in her quest for love. And all the while, a sensual woman, resilient to the core, fiercely devoted to those she opened her heart to. He drew in a deep breath to ward off the longing. No! He may love her and, yes, forgive her, and certainly pray for her, but he would never trust her. Not enough to make her his wife.

The realization lodged in his mind like a thorn, throbbing with both pain and desire. He knew what he would do. What he had to do.

He would choose Kathleen. Faithful and true, a seeker of God, she was rooted in the same faith as he. Together they would be strong, undaunted by any wind that raged. Unlike

Charity, whose faith was little more than stubble or straw or chaff before the wind.

He sat up, straining to remember the Scripture he'd read earlier. Lumbering out of bed, he padded to the parlor where his Bible lay on the table. He picked it up and plopped onto the sofa, the leather emitting a soft whoosh from the bulk of his frame. He struck a match to light an oil lamp. The soft light filtered into the room, dispelling the darkness. His fingers rustled through the pages until they stopped, pressed on the page before him.

Make them like a whirling thing, like stubble before the wind. As fire burneth a forest, and as the flame setteth the mountains on fire, so pursue them with thy tempest, and terrify them with thy whirlwind. Fill their faces with shame, that they may seek thy name . . .

He dropped back against the sofa, his eyes closed and the book open in his lap. There she was, summed up in Psalm 83. A woman whose faith in God was nothing more than chaff blown by her own whims and desires. Mitch shuddered. A woman who consumed him like a fire and set his passions ablaze. There was no question how he needed to pray. God would have his way. He would pursue his wayward child—with terror and shame if need be. Until she sought his name . . .

Mitch drew in a sharp breath. Slowly, he bent over his Bible, his head in his hands. "Lord, I'm baffled by it, but beyond all the heat she generates inside of me, I think I may be falling in love with her. She's so lost, so lonely for you. Bring her to know you, your love, your peace. Let her experience all that Faith taught me. She's so stubborn, so proud, I worry . . . worry that it's going to take more . . . to get her attention." He exhaled slowly. "It's hard to pray this way, God, but I'm asking that you do it. Draw her to you. *Whatever it takes.*"

He opened his eyes, feeling a sense of peace. He smiled and closed the Bible, then glanced up. "Are you going to let me sleep now?"

Kathleen came to mind. He sighed and put the Bible back

on the table. "All right, that's another subject we need to discuss."

Runt ambled into the parlor looking sleepy-eyed. He yawned with a half growl and pushed against Mitch's legs.

Mitch reached down to pet him. "Sorry for waking you up, buddy. Let's head back." He blew out the oil lamp and returned to his room, slipping under the covers. Runt put his chin on the bed. Mitch sighed. "All right, just this once. And only because I robbed you of sleep." He patted the covers and Runt bounded up, snuggling against Mitch's backside. Mitch adjusted his pillow and butted closer to Runt's warm body. He stared in the dark.

"I love Kathleen as a friend, Lord, I always have. The attraction is there, and I know it could grow. But she's not Charity. She doesn't make my pulse race nor invade my thoughts at every turn. She doesn't annoy me or rile me . . . or stir me. Not like Charity. But she's committed to you, she loves me, and I trust her. I think I could grow to love her deeply. But the decision is yours. Show me what to do. I intend to proceed with my plan to court and marry Kathleen after Charity leaves. So if it's not what you want, let me know. Sooner rather than later. Amen."

He blew out one final breath and closed his eyes. Sleep wasn't far behind.

The clock in the parlor chimed eleven. Charity had been home for almost an hour, yet she still sat in the kitchen with her coat on and her head on the table in the dark. The embers from the waning hearth fire occasionally popped, disrupting the silence that surrounded her. She lifted her head and pushed the hair from her eyes, blowing her nose on a handkerchief that now resembled a soggy dishrag. A halting whimper escaped her lips. *He didn't care.*

Why had she thought he had? Because he wanted her? She shivered. A bitter lesson to learn. "Wanting" wasn't "loving," apparently. Yes, she could arouse his body with no problem. But not his heart. She slouched over the table, elbow cocked and head in hand.

She groaned and jolted up, suddenly noticing the clean counter where stacks of dishes should have been waiting. Guilt slithered within. Not only had she made a fool of herself with Mitch, but she had disappointed her grandmother and Mima. Flitted off to do her own bidding, completely flaunting their wishes. And after Grandmother had slaved for hours to make a special Thanksgiving dinner just for her. Charity choked back a sob. She was a miserable creature. An ungrateful granddaughter and a selfish human being. She didn't deserve Mitch's love. Why would God even consider it?

She sniffed and dabbed the cold, wet handkerchief to her nose. Standing to her feet, she put a hand to her head and forced herself to think. Maybe she could turn over a new leaf. Perhaps make it up to her grandmother and Mima in the remaining three weeks. She could prepare all the meals, do all the dishes, let them know how very much she loved them. She stopped. In one halting breath, the reality of leaving Ireland struck hard, forcing fresh tears to her eyes. The sodden handkerchief flew to her mouth at a shocking realization: all her hopes had been pinned on marrying Mitch. On staying. Another broken sob issued forth as she collapsed into the chair, sick at the thought of leaving those she loved—Grandmother, Mima, Emma.

Mitch.

"Why, God? Why do you hate me?"

"You're the apple of his eye."

She shivered. Did she believe it? Mitch did, and certainly Faith, and no doubt everyone else in her family. But did she? She looked up at the ceiling. "I want to believe it, I do. But I don't know if I can." She thought of returning home . . . to a sister she'd betrayed, engaged to the man who'd jilted her, and a father who'd probably spurn her more than ever before. She squeezed her eyes shut. "Please, if you're real, help me. Make me know it . . . that you love me, that I'm special . . . like Faith. *Whatever it takes.*"

She sniffed and opened her eyes. A strange calm settled inside. She cocked her head and looked up. "I know I haven't exactly followed your rules, but . . . on the chance that you're real and I am the apple of your eye like Mitch says, can you— would you—make him fall in love with me? And if not" —she took a deep breath— "please help it not to hurt so much."

She stood and yawned, exhaustion taking its toll. She took off her coat and hooked it on the rack by the door. Three more weeks. How she wished she could return to Ireland after Christmas. But she knew Father would never allow it. Not unless . . .

Rigan.

The thought jarred her awake. She'd lied to Mitch in the heat of her anger, telling him she was marrying Rigan. But what if she did? He had proposed, after all. And maybe, just maybe, it would make Mitch crazy like Rigan said, perhaps even driving him into her arms.

Charity started breathing hard, and adrenaline surged through her body. She paced the kitchen, her thoughts pumping faster than her pulse. What's the worst that could happen? She would be Mrs. Rigan Gallagher, wife of one of the wealthiest men in Dublin. She could buy Shaw's Emporium outright, expand it, grow it. She could stay in Dublin, take care of Grandmother and Mima and Emma. And in the end, Mitch would see what a success she'd become. He would regret ever turning her away.

She clapped her hands together, a throaty giggle gurgling in her chest.

Rigan.

The giggle died as quickly as it had come.

He loved her. If she married him, she would be his wife. In his bed. Surprisingly, the thought wasn't altogether objectionable. She knew for a fact that if Mitch hadn't been in the picture, she would have ended up there anyway. He was charming, fascinating, witty, and his kisses offered a pleasant diversion, almost a tingle, when he didn't try to force more. *And*, she could stay in Ireland!

She closed her eyes and lifted her head, hands clasped to her chest. Yes! A completely workable solution. A situation where she could win, no matter the outcome. She hugged herself tightly in the sanctuary of her grandmother's kitchen, not even feeling the chill of the room from embers long since faded. No, she had a plan to keep her warm. A plan to stay in Ireland. A plan to be married. And at the moment, it didn't really matter to whom.

7

BOSTON, MASSACHUSETTS, THANKSGIVING, 1919

"Collin Timothy McGuire, you're cheating!" Faith arched her brows in a stern manner and tried not to laugh as she wrestled the wishbone from her fiancé.

Fiancé. The word sounded magical to her ears, even after a year to the day. Soon, at the ripe old age of twenty-two, she would be Collin's wife, a thought that never failed to bring a sense of wonder to her soul. The wishbone snapped, leaving nothing but a splintered fragment in her hand. She wrinkled her nose and wagged the pitiful sliver in his handsome face. "Unfair! Your hand's twice the size of mine and took up most of the bone. *And* you're stronger."

He grinned and brandished his piece for all the family to see. "Yes, *I am.*" He placed it in the center of the table with great ceremony and leaned back in his chair, sporting a devilish gleam in his eye. "And don't ever forget it, Little Bit. *Especially* when you're my wife."

"There's still time to change my mind, you know." She pushed her chair in and flashed a smile around the table. "Who wants dessert?"

In the midst of the clamor for pie, Collin stood and pulled

her close, his eyes smoldering. "But you're not going to change your mind, now are you?" he whispered.

Faith stared into the eyes of the man she'd loved since she was a child. The usual rush of warmth seeped through her body, shooting straight to her cheeks.

"Mama, Daddy, make 'em stop," Katie moaned, rolling her blue eyes in disgust as only an eight-year-old can.

"I think it's romantic," Beth said shyly, her cheeks tingeing pink as soon as she uttered the words.

"That's because you're fifteen and all you think about is falling in *looovwe*. I don't want any of that stuff in my life." Katie wrinkled her freckled nose in distaste and puckered her lips in the air, making obnoxious kissing sounds. Beth's cheeks bloomed bright red.

Patrick eyed his youngest daughter. "That's quite enough, Katie. Stop tormenting your sisters—"

"But, Daddy—"

"Or there won't be dessert 'in your life,' either." Patrick shot a weary look at Faith and Collin. "Thank goodness you two have only a month till the wedding. You act like you're married already, with all your sparring and mooning." He leaned back in the chair and unbuttoned his vest, then winked at his wife. "Woman, bring on the pie."

Marcy O'Connor gaped at her husband. "Patrick, you can't be serious. After three helpings of Thanksgiving dinner, you're still ready for more? Don't you think you should wait?"

"I'm ready too, Mama," Katie said. She clutched a fork and spoon tightly in each hand, her tiny elbows propped on the table.

"Me too," ten-year-old Steven echoed, his elfin features scrunched in a smirk.

Patrick grinned at his wife. "It's Thanksgiving, Marcy; we have a lot to be grateful for. Not the least of which are those fresh-baked pies in the kitchen." He picked up his spoon and fork to mimic Katie, a stern look on his ruddy face. His gray eyes narrowed to half closed, issuing a threat that reminded Faith of an older version of Collin. "I suggest you serve up the pie, Marceline, and soon. My gratitude—and my appetite— know no bounds."

"Better do what he says, Mother. I want him in a good mood after dinner when I beat him at chess," Sean said, the tease in his eyes identical to his father's.

Marcy shook her head and laughed while Katie, Steven, and Beth giggled. "We do have a lot to be grateful for." Her smile turned wistful. "I just wish Charity, Mother, and Mima were here. I miss them."

Patrick cleared his throat. His tone softened. "Charity will be here soon enough, Marcy, and our family will be intact once again."

Faith slipped out of Collin's grasp and began to collect dirty dishes. She avoided her father's eyes. "She's definitely coming, then?" She stacked Collin's dirty plate on top of her own, absently working her lip.

"Absolutely," Patrick boomed, reaching for his water. He swallowed a large gulp, then thumped the empty glass on Marcy's lace tablecloth. "I told her in no uncertain terms we wanted her home by Christmas, no ifs, ands, or buts. Christmas—and your wedding—are family affairs. And she's part of this family, whether she likes it or not."

"Pumpkin or apple or both?" Marcy asked, rising to fetch dessert. She glanced at Faith's older brother. "Sean, I assume you want pumpkin with double whipped cream, as usual? And, Beth, apple for you?"

"Perfect, Mother," Sean said while Beth nodded.

Faith reached for her mother's empty plate and piled it on top of the stack in her hands. "Mother, I'll get dessert. You sit. A piece of each for everyone else?"

"I'll help," Collin said, rounding the table to collect dirty utensils.

"Two big pieces of each, if you please," Katie announced with authority.

Patrick's brow angled. "She'll have a sliver of each and save herself a bellyache."

"But, Daddy . . . ," Katie began, her blue eyes prepared to do battle. She slapped a strand of white-blond hair over her shoulder as if to ready her stance.

"Or none at all," Patrick threatened.

Katie's rosebud mouth flattened in a tight line. A noisy sigh made it evident what she thought of her father's intervention.

Collin laughed and tapped Katie on the head as he passed. "If you eat like a pig when you're young, Katie girl, you'll look like a pig when you're old."

Katie's eyes narrowed to slits. "One father is quite enough, thank you very much."

Collin's laughter followed them into the kitchen. Faith unloaded the dishes into the sink while Collin did the same. Standing on tiptoe, she reached to retrieve dessert plates from the cupboard, only to feel his strong arms circling her waist. She whirled around, a shaky smile on her lips. "We're supposed to be getting dessert."

His eyes shone with a dangerous glint. He fixed his gaze on her mouth. "I am," he whispered, then gently pressed her shoulders against the cupboard door.

Her heart skipped a beat while the heat of his touch emanated through her like the warmth of a crackling fire. She swallowed hard, her breathing erratic as he moved closer. "Collin, the wait is almost ov—"

He cut her off with a brush of his lips against hers, gentle at first and then urgent as he gathered her into his arms. A soft moan escaped her lips when he nuzzled her neck. She pushed him away, pasting herself hard against the cupboard. "Collin . . . be good!"

The slow smile turned wayward. "I thought I was."

He leaned in again. She blocked him with knuckle-white palms to rock-hard chest. "We're talking dessert here, and they'll send a posse if they don't get it soon. Now, behave!"

"Waiting for dessert is nothing compared to the wait I've endured." He reached up to trace her lips with his finger, his eyes searing hers.

Heat scalded her cheeks. "Collin Timothy McGuire, hush! You have been so good for almost a year now. What's gotten into you this last month?"

He heaved a heavy sigh and released her, his tone a near growl. "Blast it anyway, Faith, why did we let your father talk us into waiting this long?"

She touched her hand to his cheek. "You wanted to court me properly, if you recall. And get the printing business up and running, remember? Besides, it just made sense to tie it in with the holidays when Charity would be home."

Collin scowled. "But that was before I knew it would be this hard." He folded her into his arms and squeezed her in a tight hug, his cheek against her hair. "I'm a twenty-five-year-old, red-blooded American male. I love you, Faith, and I want all of you. *Now!*"

She shivered in his arms, his words and touch sending dangerous goose bumps over her body. "I know, me too, Collin. I thank God every day I'm going to be your wife." She pulled away to look up at him, her eyes gentle. "But it's because of what God did for us, bringing us together, that we wait . . . *and* wait patiently." She pushed a strand of chestnut hair away from his forehead. A rush of love filled her as she searched the depths of his clear, gray eyes. "Once we're man and wife, I'll be all yours."

The wicked grin resurfaced. "It could be days before we come up for air . . ."

Faith slipped out of his grasp, unnerved at how quickly this man could bring blood to her cheeks. She pulled a serving knife from the drawer and turned her back to him, cutting the pumpkin pie as if it were life-and-death surgery. "Have you given any thought . . . you know, to Charity being home?"

Collin sauntered to the icebox to retrieve the whipped cream before returning to thump the bowl on the counter. "Nope. But I take it you have?"

She looked up at him, working her lip. "Not at all? I mean, you haven't thought about it? What it would be like to see her again?" She looked away, fumbling for a spoon to dollop the cream. Her voice dropped to a whisper. "You were in love with her once."

She heard him sigh before he gently took the spoon out of her hand. He lifted her chin to face him. "Yes, I thought I loved her once, but I was wrong. It was you, Faith—and God—who taught me what true love really is. Charity coming home doesn't change that or what we have. I love you, Faith O'Connor, more than I ever dreamed I'd love any human being on the face of this earth. Charity has no hold on my heart. Only you."

Faith sniffed, blinking to fight the moisture in her eyes.

Collin's gaze reflected concern. "You're afraid, aren't you? Of facing her again?"

She nodded. "I haven't spoken a word to her for almost fifteen months now, since the day I found her with . . ." She swallowed hard, shocked at how much it still hurt after all this time. Her sister's betrayal, the hatred in her eyes despite the fact they were blood. A shiver iced through her. "Maybe I haven't forgiven her."

Collin picked up the spoon and plopped whipped cream on top of each piece of pie. "No, you have. I know you, and that would have been the first thing you did when you finally came to your senses. You're the only person I've ever known bent on pleasing God and following his precepts to every jot and tittle. Trust me. You've forgiven her."

"Then why doesn't it feel like it?"

He picked up two plates of pie, his eyes tender. "Because

sometimes, when you're obeying God, feelings are the last things to follow. You've been true to his Word, Faith. You've forgiven her, you've been praying for her, and soon, somewhere down the road . . . ," he bent to gently graze her cheek with his lips, ". . . you'll feel love for her too. Trust me. Or better yet, trust him."

Faith smiled. "You think?"

He smiled back. "I know."

≈§ ଛ∾

Patrick studied the sheen of Marcy's golden hair as she brushed it, flecked with silver as it tumbled down her back. Except for the slight touch of gray, she didn't look anywhere near forty-one. Giving birth to seven children had only served to round out her once reed-thin body, softening it with curves he loved. Her eyes, though weary at times and etched with the faintest of lines, were still a vibrant cornflower blue, never failing to draw him in. Though her youth was clearly fading, her beauty was not. He sighed, the sound rising from half exhaustion, half grumbling. "You know, Marcy, one night without your one hundred strokes would not change the world as we know it. By the time you get into bed, I'll be long gone."

Marcy turned, brush in hand and a half smile on her lips. "I'm almost done, and I suspect you won't be 'gone' until you can throw your leg over me to relieve that sore hip. Besides, I'm waiting for you to warm up the bed."

"You best make it quick, woman. Much longer, and I won't let your ice-cold body near me." Too tired to smile, Patrick exhaled loudly and closed his eyes. He burrowed deeper under the blankets to stretch his long limbs to the bottom of the bed. His toe stubbed something. "What the . . ." He sat up, reaching beneath the covers to unearth one of Katie's porcelain dolls. He groaned. "That girl will be the death of me yet. You mark my words."

≈§ 171 ଛ∾

Marcy placed her brush on the bureau and laughed, leaning to douse the oil lamp with a quick breath of air. "Not before she extracts every dime from your pocket for an education and a wedding, I'm afraid."

Patrick tossed the doll on the floor, where it landed in the dark with a thump. He pulled the covers back up to his chin. "I don't want to talk about it. We should have had her first, when we still had the energy."

"You'll have to take that up with the Man upstairs, my love," Marcy said, slipping under the sheets. She snuggled close to Patrick's side and rubbed her cold feet along his warm leg.

He jolted to the far side of the bed. "No, ma'am, you warm up first."

"Patrick, please, you're being a baby. I'm freezing and you're warm. It's your husbandly duty." Marcy pressed in closer, a slight pout in her voice.

"It's survival of the fittest, Marcy, and right now you aren't fit to warm anything. Not till you get some heat in your bones."

Giggling, she slid her hand to the muscle of his thigh. "Speaking of 'fit,'" she whispered in his ear, apparently deciding on a different approach, "why don't you just get it over with and warm me up? It's like jumping into a cool lake, Patrick. At first you turn blue, but then you get used to it."

The heat of her breath against his neck countered the chill of her hand on his leg. He turned over on his other side to face her, his fatigue suddenly forgotten. "Marcy O'Connor, you don't play fair one bit." He dragged her body close, his mouth seeking hers.

Marcy screamed and scrunched up against her pillow. "Patrick! There's something at the foot of the bed—I just felt it!"

Patrick sat up, observing a tiny mound tunneling its way up the middle of the covers. He sighed. "Katie Rose, you were supposed to be asleep an hour ago."

Katie popped up, looking more like six years old than eight, her eyes wide in her petite face. She blinked at them in the moonlight. "But, Daddy, I can't sleep without Miss Buford. You know that. Where is she?"

"Right where she shouldn't be, young lady—on the floor."

"But I didn't put her on the floor," Katie protested.

"No, I did because—"

"Mama, Daddy left Miss Buford on the floor. Aren't you going to punish him?"

At Katie's smug tone, Patrick suddenly felt exhausted all over again. He pushed the covers back and snatched his youngest daughter in his arms. Her little legs thrashed against his nightshirt while her giggles echoed in the dark. She squealed in delight, ignoring his whispered warnings as he carried her out.

"What's all the commotion?" Faith asked, standing in the doorway with a sleepy grin.

Patrick jumped, startled by her sudden appearance, which only served to set off another round of Katie's laugher. He grunted and threw Katie over his shoulder like a sack of baby raccoons. "An invader in our midst." He tugged on Katie's toe. "Katie Rose, you best quiet down or I'll give you another tug that won't feel so friendly."

"But, Daddy, Miss Buford! She needs to be in her own room."

Patrick halted midstride with a groan, then backtracked to scoop the doll from the floor. "That's where you both should have been in the first place. Marcy, keep the bed warm," he bellowed, disappearing down the hall.

Marcy patted her side of the bed, eyeing Faith with concern. "Trouble sleeping?"

Faith rounded to her mother's side and plopped down, allowing Marcy to tug her close.

Marcy pulled the blankets up and began to stroke Faith's hair in a slow, calming motion. "Is something bothering you?"

Faith started to shake her head, then stopped. Her quivering sigh drifted in the air.

"Come on, out with it. What is it?"

"What is what?" Patrick demanded, bounding into the room. He slid into the bed next to Marcy. "Warm me up, woman, I'm freezing."

Faith laughed and started to rise. Marcy pulled her back. "Oh, no you don't . . . not till you tell us what's bothering you."

Patrick sat up. "Something's bothering you?"

"No, not really, Father. I'm just tired."

"But not tired enough to sleep," Marcy said, glancing at her husband. She turned back to Faith. "Is it Collin or the wedding or what?" She sat up, blocking Patrick's view.

He tapped her on the shoulder, and Marcy scooted over. "Sorry," she mumbled. "Now, what's this all about?"

Faith lay back against the pillow. "It's nothing, really. I'm just worried about Charity."

"What about Charity?" Patrick asked, realizing his chances for a good night's sleep were slipping away faster than the heat from his bed.

"I'm worried she's holding a grudge . . . that it will ruin my wedding . . . that we'll never be friends. You name it."

Marcy sat up straighter. "Holding a grudge? Over what? It can't be over Collin because Mother says she's set her sights on . . ."

Faith looked up. "Mitch, yes, I know. But, no, it's not about Collin or Mitch. This is about Charity and me. About how she . . ."

Patrick cocked a brow, ignoring the knot in his stomach. "She what?" he whispered.

Silence loomed in the air, as dark and downcast as the shadows distorting his daughter's face. Her lips parted as if the words were fused to her throat. The knot tightened in his gut. "Spit it out, Faith. What are you trying to say?"

Moonlight glinted off the sudden moisture in her eyes. "She hates me. Charity hates me."

Marcy huffed, repositioning herself to sit ramrod straight against the headboard. "That's ridiculous, Faith. Charity doesn't hate you. Sisters fight—"

"No, Mother, Charity does hate me. She's always hated me, from the moment . . ."

Even in the dim light, Patrick could see the steel line of his daughter's jaw, so like his own. Wetness spilled from her eyes, casting a silvery trail down translucent cheeks. He swallowed the fear in his throat. His voice was a strained whisper. "From what moment?"

His daughter turned to stare at him, her eyes deep pools of hurt. "From the moment Hope died instead of me."

Marcy gasped. "Stop it, Faith! That's an awful thing to say. Your sister loves you."

"No, she doesn't, Mother. She loved Hope. But then, who didn't?" Faith closed her eyes, and Patrick sensed a faint shiver traveling her body. "Hope was . . . the kindest, most loving person I knew, always mothering Charity, always defending her, begging me to let her tag along." Faith opened her eyes. "I didn't want to, but I did. Because of Hope. Because I loved her."

"You love Charity too," Marcy cried, her shock echoing in the dark room.

"Maybe deep down inside I do, but I have never felt it, never really shown it. Not until you forced me to read the Bible to Mrs. Gerson when I was sixteen." A faint smile lifted the corners of Faith's mouth. "Who would have thought that a blind woman would be the one to open my eyes? She showed me how to apply God's Word, praying for Charity every time she tried to hurt me, forgiving her. And I did, over and over again." The smile flattened on Faith's lips. "But apparently it was too little too late."

Marcy grasped her daughter's hand. "It's not true. Charity idolized both you and Hope."

"Maybe then. But once Hope died, and I came home after being away for a year in that dreadful hospital, things were different. Charity hated me, Mother, I know it. I could see it in her eyes and the hurtful things she'd say. She resented the attention you and Father gave me."

"That's just your imagination talking. Why, Charity was only six, just a mere child—"

Patrick placed his hand over Marcy's, his eyes locked on their daughter. A slow, painful comprehension prickled through him. "A child too young to realize why her parents focused attention on her sick sister." He closed his eyes and exhaled, massaging the bridge of his nose with his fingers. "Dear God, all these years, how could I have missed it?"

Faith's hand gently touched his arm. "Father, you lost one daughter to polio and were on the verge of losing another. No one can blame you or Mother for not being aware."

Patrick opened his eyes and searched his daughter's face in the pale light, the air thin in his lungs. "I should have known. I should have guessed. You two were always fighting, bickering." He lowered his head. "I thought it would pass."

"So did I," Faith said, her voice barely audible.

Marcy stared, first at her husband, then at her daughter. "This can't be . . ." She swallowed hard. She blinked several times and pressed a hand to her chest. "Faith, we didn't know. Dear Lord, we didn't know! Why didn't you say something?"

"I didn't know myself. Not really. Not until Ireland." Faith looked up, her eyes dark with pain. "You saw it, Mother. She stabbed me through the heart. I knew then that her hate was real, that I hadn't imagined it. It wasn't until I was on the ship home that I started thinking about it, wondering why. And then it all came back. The times she'd accuse me of stealing Father's love, hurtful things uttered when I came home from the hospital. Until I thought about it on the ship—really thought about it—I never fully understood why."

Faith looked up at Patrick. "Father, do you remember what you used to call her?"

Patrick blinked, his mind blank. "No."

"You used to call her 'Daddy's Girl' and 'the apple of your eye.'" The sound of Faith's words pierced the air like the shaft of moonlight streaming across the bed. "She was a beautiful child. Everyone thought so. And none more than you."

"Faith . . ." Patrick's voice stilled in his lungs. He extended his hand.

Faith clutched his fingers. "Daddy, I know you love me. But I know you love Charity too. And because of me, her love was stolen from you . . . and yours from her."

Patrick pulled her into his arms, his heart full of grief. "Oh, Faith, I do love you! The thought of losing you back then nearly destroyed me. I couldn't see anything but you, your welfare, your joy. I had no idea what I'd done to Charity. I only knew Hope's death had snuffed out part of the light in my soul. And as long as I had breath in my body, there was no way I was going to allow your light to die too." He pressed his face hard against his daughter's neck, tears springing to his eyes. "God forgive me, for my weakness and what I did to Charity."

Marcy touched his shoulder. "Patrick, God more than forgives you. But I'm afraid it's our daughter in Ireland who's not so inclined. I think we should pray."

Patrick rubbed the wetness from his eyes and nodded, his heart lighter at the thought. He extended his arm around his wife's shoulder, wrapping both wife and daughter in a tearful embrace. "And that, Marceline O'Connor, among a host of other things," he said with a hitch in his throat, "is exactly why I married you."

❦ ❧

Collin cocked his head and squinted at the flyer in his hand. *Hammond's Christmas Sale: Pig Assortment of Bon Bons and Nuts.* He crushed the sheet into a ball and hurled it across the tiny printing shop, a rare curse hissing from his lips.

Brady looked up from the small offset press he was cleaning. "Last time I heard that word, old buddy, we were side by side in a trench."

Collin glanced at his partner with a wry grin and exhaled loudly. "Sorry. Don't know where that came from. Old habits die hard, I guess." He closed his eyes and kneaded the back of his neck, the grin widening on his face. "I don't suppose Mr. Hammond would agree that a 'pig' assortment is appropriate for his pre-Christmas sale."

Brady laughed and wiped his hands on a ragged cloth, oblivious to a telltale splotch of ink smudged across his tanned cheek. His warm eyes, which matched the thatch of brown hair falling across his forehead, shone with affection. "Although it certainly qualifies as truth in advertising," he remarked dryly, tossing the soiled rag aside and stretching back in his chair with a low groan. He propped his long legs against their prized Bullock web-fed press, careful to avoid scuffing the roller he'd just wiped clean.

He looked over at Collin and swiped his cheek with the side of his hand. The splotch of black smeared clear across his face in a bold streak, striping him ear to jaw. "Speaking of 'truth in advertising,'" he said quietly, "what exactly is bothering you, old buddy?"

Collin expelled a deep breath and closed his eyes, allowing his tired body to cave into his chair. Barbs of irritation nettled through him like always when Brady got too close to the truth. But nothing like it'd been during the war. A hint of a smile creased Collin's lips at the memory of John Morrison Brady, soldier, trench mate, and all-around nice guy. Sweet saints above, how Collin had hated him! Him and his squeaky-clean lifestyle and his Christian philosophy and his sad, tattered

Bible that he'd carried everywhere, even into the trenches. At the thought, gratitude swelled in Collin's chest, and his throat tightened at just how blessed he was to know him. It had been John Brady and his worn Bible that had finished the work that Faith had begun, bringing him to the brink of salvation. Bringing him home. To God . . . and to Faith.

Collin opened his eyes to stare frankly at his good friend. "What's bothering me? I'm not sure," he said, resigned that Brady's relentless probing would not rest until Collin's soul was at peace. "There's an edginess, an underlying nervousness twitching under my skin."

A frown creased Brady's brow. "Anything to do with Faith or the wedding? Second thoughts, maybe?"

Collin laughed out loud, the sound ricocheting through the tiny print shop he and Brady had opened almost a year ago. "No, no, not even close. Faith is . . . amazing. I still can't believe she's going to be my wife."

The furrowed lines around Brady's mouth relaxed into a grin. "Worried about the wedding night, then? Being out of practice?"

Collin shot him a sheepish grin, topped off by a cocky jag of his brow. "Not on your life. But the wait has been tough, I won't lie to you. Kind of like a thoroughbred at the gate, if you know what I mean."

Brady chuckled, scratching the back of his neck. "Knowing you, or the man you used to be . . . yeah, I know what you mean. So what's the problem?"

"I don't know. Might be Charity coming home."

Brady sat up. "You don't still have feelings—"

"No, nothing like that. I mean, I'm not exactly sure how I'll react when I see her again, but right now, the thought of her, memories of her, hold no appeal. I'm in love with Faith."

"Good. Are you worried about her? That maybe she still has feelings for you?"

Collin leaned forward for a moment, entertaining the

question before pushing himself up out of the chair. "Nope, I don't think so. She actually ended it before I even had a chance to tell her it was over. And judging from Faith's grandmother's letters, Charity's got her eye on . . . well, *someone else*."

Brady blinked. "Gee, that was a pretty clipped tone. Sounds like you care."

Collin glanced at the clock and lumbered to the door, flipping the "closed" sign in the window with a flick of his fingers. He slacked a hip and gave Brady a wary look. "Trust me, I don't care. They deserve each other."

"Who?"

"Charity and . . . what's-his-name." He plucked his jacket off the coatrack by the door. "Come on, Brady, let's get out of here. Hammond's flyers can wait till tomorrow."

"What's-his-name?" Brady repeated, rolling his shoulders to clear the kinks. He stood and reached for the ink rag, then arced it into a laundry box at the back of the shop. He turned and fixed Collin with a penetrating stare. "He has a name, Collin. Call me crazy, but it sounds like you're holding a grudge."

The hackles rose on the back of Collin's neck, compliments of John Brady. He glared and enunciated through clenched teeth to make sure Brady knew he'd overstepped his bounds— *again*. "Mitch. His name is Mitch, okay? And back off, Brady. I flat-out don't like the guy."

"Yeah, I can see why. He's a real lowlife. Up and left the fiancée he loved so you could have her."

Collin fisted his jacket in one hand and stabbed a finger in the air with the other. His eyes burned. "So help me, Brady, one more word and I'll lay you out right here, I swear." He slammed his chair against the linotype machine. "What in blazes was I thinking going into business with you?"

The ink smudge on Brady's cheek sagged along with the tired look on his face. "Well, I suspect you were thinking of the truth. Of a friend and partner who'd tell it to you, no matter how much you didn't want to hear it."

The air in Collin's lungs was as thick as the conviction in his heart. He rubbed his face with one hand while his jacket hung limp in the other. "Thanks, Brady, I needed that. And you're right. I have no reason to hate Dennehy."

"Not if you want God's blessings in your life."

Collin heaved a weary sigh. "I know." The line of his jaw stretched tight. "But you know, this 'pray for your enemies' thing really gets on my nerves."

Brady chuckled and extended an arm around Collin's shoulder. "Yeah, I know. But in the end, it's worth it." He ambled toward the door and fished his coat neatly off the rack. "So. Charity and Mitch, huh? Not much can happen if she's moving back home."

Flicks of anxiety nicked at him once again. "Yeah, right. Thanks for the reminder. I wish he'd marry her and stay in Ireland. Just the thought of her returning home has set me on edge this last week, and I'll be hog-tied if I know why."

Brady slipped on his coat and unlooped the key from the hook by the door. He reached for the knob. "What, you don't trust her?"

Collin halted in the middle of putting on his jacket, a grin traveling his lips. "Trust her? Charity?" He laughed, dousing the lights on his way out the door. "Oh, I trust her—completely. To be Charity."

8

DUBLIN, IRELAND

"Nervous?"

Charity nodded, prying her gaze from the vulgar diamond on her finger to smile up at Rigan. "Uh-huh." Her gaze shifted back to the ring. She hadn't been able to look at anything else since they'd left the jeweler. She sighed. "Have you told your family yet?"

He grinned. "Nary a syllable. It may leave my father speechless, which is near impossible. You?"

She stretched her hand out to study the diamond. "Just Emma, of course, because she covered for me when I left early today, but not my grandmother or Mima. I want to surprise them. Oh, and Mr. Hargrove. The dear old gentleman was in today, teasing me about settling down with the right man. I have to admit, it felt pretty good telling him I was spoken for." She spared a quick grin in Rigan's direction. "He was thrilled. He thinks it's about time someone tied you down." She refocused on the ring, admiring the way it shimmered on her finger. "Honestly, Rigan, my nerves have never been in such a jumble, meeting your family like this. But when I look at this, it's all worth it."

Rigan chuckled as his Silver Ghost Rolls-Royce coupe

crawled to a stop in front of his father's estate. He switched off the ignition and turned in the seat to draw her into his arms. He sloped her across his lap with a decadent gleam in his eye. "And what about this?" he asked, then nuzzled her ear before sealing her mouth with an urgent kiss. He pulled away. "Is that worth it?"

Charity swallowed and managed a shaky smile. Her stomach fluttered with an odd mix of excitement and trepidation. "Yes, of course, Rigan, it's all worth it." She shifted in his arms, wiggling to get up.

He pinned her in a hungry embrace while his hands roamed the back of her thin coat, exploring her waist, the curve of her hips. "Charity, you've made me the happiest man alive." He kissed her again, a low moan escaping his lips. She felt the sweep of his hands up the side of her waist to territory that was definitely off-limits.

"Rigan, no!" She clamped her hands hard on his arms. "What will your parents think if they see us like this? I'd be mortified."

He chuckled. "Of course you're right, darling. It's just that now that I'm not limited to bargained kisses, I find I have a voracious appetite for more." He brushed his lips to her cheek and prodded her toward her door, his palm lingering on her thigh.

Charity twined her fingers with his, effectively diverting his hand. "Rigan, be good. I'm not your wife yet."

"A minor point in the throes of passion, my love." He squeezed her hand and got out on his side. He rounded the car to unlatch her door and extended his arm. "Your palace awaits."

"Charity looked up, and the whites of her eyes expanded. "This . . . is where you live?"

"Where 'we' will live, darling, at least in the winter. Come late spring, we'll reside at the summer house on Muckross Lake."

Charity absently took his hand and stood transfixed, her gaze slowly rising to scan the mansion's several stories. Never in all her days had she seen such splendor, not even in the best neighborhoods of Boston. An impressive cascade of marble steps flared wide as they spilled to the cobblestone drive. Gardens of perfectly manicured boxwoods flanked either side, encasing a collection of rose beds, pergola, and rhododendron, tastefully interspersed with fountains and statues. The house itself was a monument of granite and Georgian brick, with castlelike turrets rising to the sky. Graceful arches hovered over endless rows of windows while ivy tunneled between each, blanketing sections of the house with a glossy coat of green.

"Do you like it?"

Charity swallowed hard. "I . . . I had no idea, Rigan. I knew you were wealthy, but I truly had no idea."

He chuckled and took her arm in his, leading her up the steps to massive mahogany doors twice the height of a man. Brass handles, burnished to a gleam, took the shape of roaring lions while the wood of the door peaked to a commanding arch before converging with lustrous white marble.

The polished door swung open, attended by the least lifelike creature Charity had ever seen. Well over six foot five, the man stood ramrod straight to the side, lips pursed and face pinched. His pointy chin was elevated, as if leading the way. "Good evening, Master Rigan."

"Good evening, Robert. This is my fiancée, Charity O'Connor."

"Congratulations, sir, and good evening, Miss Charity."

"Good evening, Robert," Charity said, cheeks flushing.

Rigan allowed her to enter first, then followed, quickly shedding his coat and draping it over Robert's arm. He peeled Charity's wrap from her shoulders and handed it to the butler. "Is the family having cocktails?"

"Yes, sir, in the library. Shall I announce you?"

Rigan planted a kiss on Charity's bare neck, sending another rush of heat to her cheeks. "No, thank you, Robert, that won't be necessary."

"Very good, sir."

Rigan hooked Charity's arm and started toward an extravagant set of burlwood doors. Charity balked, forcing the heels of her new Mary Jane shoes to dig into the plush Oriental rug.

He stopped and arched a brow. "What's wrong?"

She swallowed hard several times as she looked around the foyer, taking in the glittering chandelier, the sweeping marble staircase, the spray of fresh flowers perfectly arranged in an exquisite crystal-cut vase. She began to hyperventilate.

"Darling, what's wrong? Your skin is as pale as that alabaster sculpture."

She opened her mouth. Nothing came out. Her hand flew to her stomach, its contents threatening to rise.

He took her clammy hand in his. A smile tilted his lips. "I can't believe it. The indomitable Charity O'Connor—afraid?"

She nodded, sucking in a deep breath. "Oh, Rigan, I . . . I . . . what if they don't like me?"

He threw his head back and laughed. "They won't be able to help themselves, darling, any more than I can." His gaze roved the length of her, taking in the graceful fit of her pale blue dress, cinched snugly at her small waist before falling into shear jagged layers to the middle of her calf. She didn't miss the smoky look in his eyes as he scanned her V-neck bodice, where just a hint of her breasts could be seen through the gauzy overlay. His finger slowly traced from the nape of her neck to the yoke of her dress, pausing briefly to fondle the wisps of curls that strayed from her loose chignon. The blood warmed in her cheeks. He grinned. "Especially my father who, like his son, has a penchant for beautiful women."

Rigan took her arm and tucked it firmly in his. "Besides, your father is the editor for one of the largest papers in the world. My father will like that. He has an unhealthy fascination with newsmen who work their way to the top."

Charity glanced at Rigan's profile, noting that his tone—along with his jaw—had suddenly hardened.

She had time for only one deep breath before he ushered her into a room that immediately took it away. Two entire walls of floor-to-ceiling cherrywood bookcases gleamed with shelf after shelf of gilded books rivaling those in Boston's prestigious library. A stunning collection of artwork seldom seen outside of a museum graced the other two walls, interspersed with large windows and a set of French doors that led to a lighted courtyard. A crackling fire blazed in a marble fireplace tucked in between two walls of books, and the spitting and popping of the logs were the only sounds Charity heard upon entering the room.

Rigan tugged her forward, his palm shoring up the small of her back. "Good evening, everyone. Mother, Father, I'd like you to meet the woman who's agreed to become my wife, Charity O'Connor."

Charity radiated a confident smile that defied the nausea in her stomach. "Good evening, Mr. and Mrs. Gallagher. It's a pleasure to finally meet you."

The room was a morgue, deafening in its silence. Even the crackling fire resorted to stealth while five pairs of eyes assessed her, measuring her every breath, every quiver of her hand, every hair on her head. The smile grew stale on her lips. She lifted her jaw and stiffened her spine.

A silver-haired version of Rigan stepped forward, clearing his throat. He extended his hand with a disarming smile as his gaze traveled her body. "Charity, please forgive our rude lack of speech. Rigan told us you were lovely, but as usual, it seems he woefully underestimated. I'm Blaine Gallagher, the patriarch of this family. Come, take a seat by the fire while I make the introductions."

He led her to a chair next to a woman who was as plain as he was handsome. Her nondescript eyes flicked up nervously, revealing sweeping lashes offset by too large a nose. Dark hair, the exact shade of Rigan's, was piled high on her head and wisped with gray. She offered a bejeweled hand in stark contrast to the simple gray dress she wore. Her thin lips trembled into a faint smile. "Hello, Charity, I'm Rigan's mother, Olivia. Rigan has spoken of you so often, it was clear he was smitten. And now we see why."

Charity clasped her hand and smiled. "Thank you, Mrs. Gallagher. It's wonderful to be here."

Rigan's father dismissed his wife with a wave of his hand. "Charity, that bored-looking young woman reclining on the settee is Rigan's sister, Fiona, and the gentleman hovering over her is her husband, Bennett."

Charity nodded, her nerves fluttering at the look of disdain on Fiona's face. She appeared to be a replica of her mother, albeit devoid of humility. She simply stared, her eyes mere slits of contempt while she guzzled her drink. Her husband—tall and striking—seemed cut from the same cloth as Rigan and his father, with a confident air and an eye for women. His smile, more than friendly, set her on edge.

Blaine Gallagher turned on his heel. "May I offer you a glass of port?"

She nodded and sat down as he shot a look in Rigan's direction. "Don't just stand there, Rigan, pour your fiancée a glass of wine so we can raise a toast."

Charity observed the tension twitching in Rigan's face when he handed her the glass. She met his eyes and smiled. His jaw softened. He bent to kiss her cheek, then stood and proposed a toast. "To Charity O'Connor, the woman who will soon make me the luckiest man in the world."

Blaine lifted his wine in salute and downed half of it. He licked his lips, then pressed them tight. "Luck certainly seems to play a hand in your good fortune, Rigan, but I would prefer you'd earn some of it as well." He flashed Charity a warm smile. "Rigan tells us your father is the editor of the *Boston Herald*."

Charity took a large sip of wine, hoping it would quell her

nerves. "Yes, Mr. Gallagher, he was promoted to editor shortly after he returned from the war."

Mrs. Gallagher leaned forward. "You mean to tell me your father fought in the war?"

"Yes, ma'am, he did, along with my brother and—" She stopped, aware of their scrutiny. She shifted in the chair. "Actually, we were informed by the military that he'd been killed, but thankfully it was a miscommunication."

Olivia put a slender hand to her chest. "Your poor mother!"

"Yes, but all ended well. My father and brother returned safely, and Mother sailed back to Boston, along with my three sisters and younger brother. I offered to stay behind to help my grandmother care for my great-grandmother."

Rigan smiled and lifted his glass. "And to marry me, of course."

Charity smiled. "Of course."

With a fresh drink in hand, Blaine settled into a plush chair. "Rumor has it that your sister was engaged to one of my best employees."

The port pooled in her mouth. She swallowed hard. "Yes, my sister was engaged to Mitch Dennehy last year, but she broke it off."

He smiled, twiddling the glass in his hand. "Pity. Such an admirable man to be so unlucky in love." He swallowed half of his wine in one sip. His eyes flicked in Rigan's direction, their umber shade darkening to brown. "I suppose you could say he's the son I never had."

"Blaine, please!" Olivia perched on the edge of her chair, her eyes pleading.

Rigan chugged the drink in his hand. "Don't bother, Mother, nothing you say is going to change his mind."

A deep dimple gouged Blaine's chiseled chin as he laughed. "The son I never had in the business sense, of course." He glanced at Charity, his brows arched in question. "Heir to the largest newspaper in Ireland, but does that inspire him? No, I'm afraid our Rigan prefers the good life and plenty of it."

"Blaine, can't we please change the subject?"

"I'll change it, Mother," Fiona said, her boredom obviously forgotten. She leaned forward on the settee. Her eyes suddenly glowed with interest. "I understand you work as a clerk in a shop."

"Not just any shop, Fee, Shaw's Emporium," Rigan said with a frown. "Charity is Mrs. Shaw's top sales clerk."

Her lips twisted in a near sympathetic smile. "But a clerk, nonetheless. That must be dreadful standing on your feet all day, waiting on people who spend more in five minutes than you make in a year."

Charity stiffened in the chair, chin rising. "Not at all. I enjoy my work immensely and find it rewarding—and empowering—to earn my own way."

"Bravo, Charity!" Blaine placed his empty glass on the table and stood to his feet to applaud. "But, alas, I'm afraid your commendable appreciation for work falls on deaf ears with Fiona and Rigan. It seems the silver spoons in their mouths have more metal than their spines."

"Blaine darling, please, must you—"

The mirth in his eyes cooled to contempt. "Yes, *darling*, I must. And it would behoove you to mind your tongue with your husband."

"Really, Father . . ." Fiona rose from the settee in a huff, unloading her empty glass into Bennett's ready hand. "Shouldn't we be heading into dinner? I'm ravenous."

"Yes, shall we?" Blaine turned and strode for the door, leaving his wife little choice but to rise and shadow behind. Rigan alleviated Charity of her glass and offered his arm. She stood and took it, holding on for dear life. He smiled and pressed his lips to her ear. "Ready for dinner?" he whispered.

"Absolutely." She squeezed his arm and managed a tentative smile, although her appetite had long since faded. She sucked in a deep breath as they followed the others from the room. "As long as I'm not the main course."

✎ ✎

Rigan yanked the massive doors closed with a deafening slam. Music to her ears! Charity finally breathed, releasing hours of tension in one cleansing sigh. She filled her lungs with the crisp, night air and turned her attention to the problem at hand.

Rigan.

Bracing him tightly with an arm to his waist, she carefully guided him down one marble step at a time. "I've never seen you drink this much before," she muttered, following it with a grunt as he veered off course.

His bitter laughter echoed in the still night. "Ah, but you've never seen me with my family before, my love. Quite an experience, wouldn't you say?"

Rigan lunged for her car door and opened it wide. "Your carriage, my lady."

"Are you sure you're up to driving? Perhaps we should ask Robert to drive me home."

"Nonsense, I'm perfectly fine." He stumbled to his side of the car to get in and fumbled with the ignition switch. He cursed before managing to push the advance lever down. The Rolls lurched away from the entry and puttered down the cobblestone drive.

"So," he said with an exaggerated drawl, "you survived, even if I didn't."

Charity jolted in the seat. "Rigan, the gate!"

He jerked the wheel. The car swerved wildly, narrowly missing the corner of an imposing granite column embedded with an open iron gate.

He chuckled. "Close call, eh, my love?"

Charity sagged into the leather seat, her heart still thumping in her chest. "A bit too close, Rigan. Please keep your eyes on the road."

"Your wish is my command."

She exhaled slowly, studying his profile out of the corner of her eye. His lean face and angular jaw, so like his father's, were as finely sculpted as one of the marble statues littering the house. She forced herself to relax. "Your father certainly runs the show, doesn't he?"

His deep laugh was menacing, reminiscent of the pirate he so often brought to mind. "Oh, you noticed, did you? Yes, Father is famous for cracking the whip." He afforded a brief glimpse in her direction. "Or the hand, whatever the case may be."

Charity shivered.

"Are you cold?" He extended an arm.

She stiffened, upright once again. "No, Rigan, keep your hand on the wheel, please."

He obliged, gripping both hands to negotiate a turn. The tires squealed.

She folded her arms to her waist, her eyes on the road. "Well, he does appear to be quite driven, which I suppose is understandable for someone who has worked his way to the top."

Rigan appeared to get a good chuckle out of that. "Darling, I think you mean 'wormed' his way to the top."

She shifted, chancing a peek at his face. "I don't understand. He's at the helm of one of the most influential newspapers in the world, affording a lifestyle few have attained."

"Yes, I suppose you could credit him with the success of the *Times*, but that hardly pays the bills for his extravagant tastes."

"What do you mean?"

He grinned. "I mean he married well, darling. Much as you're about to do."

"Rigan!"

His dark brows slanted in contrition. "As am I, I most heartily assure you. You possess the kind of beauty my father has only dreamed about."

"Your mother is a lovely person."

"Yes, she has a good heart. But after tonight, sampling just a taste of the Gallaghers, surely you know why he married her? She was the only child of one of the wealthiest widowers in Britain, who, I might add, has conveniently passed away."

Charity was aghast. "That's heartbreaking!"

He slid her a sideways glance. "Is it? Yes, I suppose it is. But then I'm used to it."

She shivered again and bit her lip. "Fiona doesn't like me."

"Fiona doesn't like anyone. Not even Bennett."

"I can certainly understand that. Bennett gives me the jitters."

Rigan chuckled. "Just see to it he doesn't try to give you anything else. He's notorious for womanizing. He apprenticed under my father."

A chill skittered down her spine. "Do they live there too?"

"Yes, we're all one big, happy family. And never happier than when Bennett and my father get a daily feast of you."

Charity's heart stopped. "Your father . . . he wouldn't . . . well, he wouldn't . . ."

"Make a pass?" Rigan's laughter bounced off the walls of the car with a sickening grate. "I'd be disappointed if he didn't. But then, that's the beauty of our union, my love. Not only do I get to ravage one of the most beautiful women I've ever seen, but my father gets to stand by and watch, knowing his son has finally bested him."

"Rigan, that's sick."

He coasted to a stop in front of her grandmother's house, jerking the advance lever all the way up. He switched the ignition off and turned in the seat with a dangerous glint in his eye. "Yes, it is, darling, but you'll get used to it. We Gallagher men have an insatiable lust for beauty."

Charity reached for the door. "No need to walk me in. Go home and get some sleep. And promise you'll drive slowly."

He chuckled and hauled her into his arms, his breath hot on her face.

She turned her head from the smell of stale whiskey. "Rigan, please! I'm tired and you need to go home."

He ignored her and smothered her neck with kisses while his hands explored her body.

She shoved him away. "No! I will not be familiar with you until the gold band's on my finger."

He jerked her left hand in the air, then pressed the diamond close to her face. "This is on your finger, isn't it, darling? That should afford me more than a few tame kisses, don't you think?"

She hurled his hand away and reached for the door. He wrenched her forward and twisted her arm behind her back. A weak cry escaped her throat.

"You're hurting me. Stop! You're acting just like your father."

His eyes gleamed in the lamplight as he loomed over her. "And in the words of my father, 'It would behoove you to mind your tongue with your husband.'" He gripped the back of her neck and plunged her lips with his own while his fingers gouged her shoulders with pain.

She grew faint, unable to breathe. Pain forced a groan that died in her throat, and panic seized in her chest. His hands, which wandered her body with reckless abandon, seemed distant and removed, as if the body they violated were not her own. A dark dizziness closed in, weighting her lids and her brain with the desire to sleep.

He broke free, and a rush of cool air surged into her lungs. She coughed, and the putrid contents of her partially digested dinner coated her throat. She felt his fingers cutting into her arms, shaking her till she rattled. "Charity, are you all right? Darling, I . . . I lost my head with passion. Forgive me, please."

He bundled her into his arms and attempted to soothe her with a rocking motion. "Darling, my desire for you is so strong, I can hardly control myself from devouring you. But once we're married and I can have you completely, our lovemaking will be more gentle, I promise." He began to button her coat, which he had undone, and propped her upright on the seat like a little girl. "It's time we get you to bed."

He kissed her on the cheek and staggered out of the car, quickly opening her door and helping her out. She continued to draw in deep breaths while he walked her to the porch. He put his hands on her shoulders and brushed a sodden kiss across her lips. "I love you, Charity. I can't wait until I can really take you home. Forever. Good night, darling."

He opened the door and steered her in, quietly closing it behind her. In a daze, she slumped back against the door and pressed her head hard against the wood.

Home. *Forever.*

She thought of the Gallagher Estate and shivered.

Of Boston, and put her hand to her eyes.

Of Ireland, and began to cry.

Home. Forever. There was no such thing.

Charity lifted her head at the sound of a gentle knock on her bedroom door.

"Charity, it's Emma. May I come in?"

"Yes." Charity plopped her head on the pillow.

The door creaked open and Emma peeked in. Her good brow tipped up in concern. "Are you all right? Mrs. Shaw said you called in sick. I was worried. You've never done that before."

Charity rolled on her side and sniffed. "I've been feeling nauseous and achy all day, sore to the touch. I think I'm coming down with something." She glanced at the clock on her nightstand and groaned. "Oh, no, please, I can't do it."

"Do what?"

Charity flopped facedown on her pillow and draped her arm over her head. "See Rigan tonight. It's almost five forty-five, and he's supposed to be here at seven."

"I can call him for you if you want. Tell him you're sick."

The arm shifted and one eye peered out. "You would do that?"

Emma moved to perch on the edge of the bed. "Of course, silly. You're sick, aren't you?"

Charity curled up and bunched the pillow to her chest. She rested her chin on top, avoiding Emma's eyes. "Yes, I haven't been right all day. I think I may have a fever." She looked up. "Was Mrs. Shaw mad?"

Emma giggled and tucked a leg beneath her. "First day of inventory? Absolutely livid."

A grin pulled at Charity's lips. "That's sure to cost me double-time tomorrow."

"Think you'll be well enough to go in?" Emma cocked her head. She reached and pressed a palm to Charity's forehead. "Mmmm. Cool as Mrs. Shaw's back room." She folded her arms and arched her brows. "Are you sure you were sick?"

Charity chewed on her lip and absently fiddled with the silk tie of her flannel nightgown. "I actually feel much better now." She pushed the covers aside and lumbered out of bed. "Can you stay for supper?"

"That would be nice. Rory said not to wait up, which means I won't see him at all."

"That's been happening a lot lately, hasn't it?" Charity glanced over her shoulder, a skirt and blouse bunched in her hands.

Emma looked away. "More than usual."

"Is he seeing someone again?"

"I think so." Emma slumped, her voice barely a whisper.

The bed squeaked as Charity sat beside her. She hooked an arm around her friend's shoulder. "Well, I wish I could say I was sorry, Emma, but I'm not. Because when Rory is occupied elsewhere, he doesn't abuse you physically."

Emma sighed. "No. Just emotionally." Her head suddenly shot up and she grabbed Charity's left hand. "Wait! I can't believe I forgot. Did you get the ring?"

"Yes."

"Well, don't just sit there, let me see it! Did you meet his family too?"

With a stiff nod, Charity stood and reached in the drawer. She hesitated, then slipped the diamond on her finger. A touch of nausea returned. She turned and extended her hand.

"Sweet saints alive, do diamonds really come that big? That had to cost a blimey fortune."

Charity angled her hand, studying the glittering stone. Her lips twisted in a wry smile. "Yes, well, they certainly have a blimey fortune."

A giggle parted from Emma's lips as she plunked back down on the bed and circled her knee with her arms. "So you met his family? What are they like? Did you like them?"

"Not really. They're very strange, not normal at all, which certainly gives me more insight into Rigan." She tossed the blouse and skirt on the bed, then tugged on the silk tie of her nightgown. The flaps fell away from her throat.

"Charity!"

Charity blinked, alarmed by the pallor of her friend's face. "What is it?"

Emma sprang up from the bed. Her finger quivered as she gently touched a purple bruise above Charity's collarbone. Her voice was barely audible. "How did this happen?"

She rushed to the mirror and loosened her gown, dropping it off her shoulders. Air trapped in her throat. "Oh, God, help me . . ."

"What happened? Did you fall?" Emma ran to her side, her face etched in shock.

Charity shook her head, staring at the spattering of ugly

bruises that mottled her shoulders and chest. With quivering fingers, she dropped the gown to the floor.

Emma gasped. "Lord help us, did he beat you?"

Her mouth opened, but nothing came out. Her stomach seized with queasiness. Black-and-blue blotches marred every inch of her torso, causing bile to rise in her throat. She stood like discolored stone while Emma stooped and picked up her nightgown, slowly pulling it up to cover her shoulders. She began to shake. "I've been achy all day, sore to the touch. I didn't realize . . ."

"Charity, did Rigan beat you?"

She struggled to respond, her mind in a fog. "No, he . . . he was kissing me and he . . ." Tears stung her eyes. "He got carried away, he said, overly passionate . . ."

For once, Emma's voice was hard. "This isn't passion, Charity, it's abuse."

She squeezed her eyes shut, not wanting to face the truth of Emma's words. "He told me he was sorry, that his desire for me is so . . . strong, that he couldn't control himself. That once we were married, he'd be more gentle. He promised."

"Look at me, Charity, please."

She opened her eyes.

"This isn't normal. This isn't what love is supposed to be. Something's desperately wrong." Emma reached for Charity's hand. "You can't marry him."

Charity dropped on the bed and put her hand to her head, the diamond weighting her finger like a glittering albatross. Her forehead was suddenly clammy with sweat. "I . . . I know, Emma, but I don't know what to do." She looked up with pleading eyes. "I thought it was an answer, a way to turn Mitch's head. And if Mitch didn't want me, I thought I could learn . . . to love Rigan."

"You have to tell him."

Her stomach squeezed with fear. "I . . . I can't."

Emma sat down and clutched Charity's arm. "You can and

you will. I won't let you stay in a relationship that threatens your safety."

The truth of her statement drew Charity's eyes to hers. "You do."

A sigh quivered from Emma's lips. "Yes, that's how I know. I speak from painful experience."

"Emma, the way you feel right now about Rigan is the way I feel about Rory. I love you, just like you love me. And every time Rory wounds you, it tears away a little piece of my heart."

Realization widened Emma's eyes. "Oh, Charity, I . . . I never thought of it like that. Not until now." She hunched over, her hands limp in her lap.

Charity leaned against her, shoulder to shoulder, her head resting against Emma's. "Maybe my bruises were a means of opening your eyes. I heard my sister say more than once that 'all things worked together for good for those that love God.'"

"You're quoting Scripture now?" Emma gave her a sideways glance.

Charity laughed and squeezed Emma's shoulder. "That is pretty pathetic, isn't it? Shows how low I've sunk. I'm reduced to quoting my sister."

Tears glimmered in Emma's eyes. "Oh, Charity, I thank God every day for you, friend of my heart."

Charity blinked to clear the wetness in her own eyes. "Well, 'friend of my heart,' how about a promise of the heart?"

"What?"

"Your welfare for mine."

"What do you mean?" Emma said, her tone barely audible.

"You leave Rory; I'll leave Rigan."

Emma caught her breath. "I don't know if I can . . ."

"Well, then I don't know if I—" Charity stood, a stubborn bent to her chin.

"All right," Emma whispered harshly, the muscles of her neck working hard.

"All right, what?"

Her friend stared at her a long time before answering. "I'll leave Rory."

"When?"

She looked away, her eyes pools of desperation. "I don't know."

Charity crossed her arms. "Not good enough."

"Next week," Emma said with a shiver.

Charity shook her head. "Tonight. And you'll move in with us like I've been begging you all along."

Wrapping her arms tightly around her torso, Emma rocked slowly back and forth, her brow furrowed in thought. She finally huffed out a shaky sigh. "Oh, all right. Tonight."

Charity giggled and lifted her in a hug. "Oh, Emma, I've waited so long to hear that."

"Now you. Promise." Emma's good brow lifted in challenge.

Sobriety tempered the smile on her face. "I will."

"You will what?"

"Tell Rigan it's over."

"Forever."

"Yes, forever."

"Well, it's a good thing I didn't call him, because you can tell him tonight."

"Not tonight," Charity said. Her nausea returned with a vengeance.

Emma stood. "Yes, tonight. I'll be with you."

"What do you mean?"

"I mean you can ask Rigan to drive us to my flat so I can pack my things. Then just tell him you need to drop me off before you can go out. Only you won't be going back out. You'll give him his ring right then and there, then come inside. Understood?"

Charity nodded, feeling a bit light-headed. Her smile was weak. "Okay."

"But first, we're going to apply some of your sister's sage advice."

Charity stiffened. "What advice?"

"We're going to take God up on his offer to turn things around for good for those who love him." Emma took Charity's hands in hers.

"But that's you, not me."

"Right," Emma said with a grin. "But it's you down the road. Trust me."

"Trust you?" She gave a short snort. "Easier you than him." Charity flipped her hair back in defiance and closed her eyes, waiting.

Emma's soft giggle filled the air. "Dear Lord, if you'd given her half as much brains as beauty, she'd be a force to reckon with."

Charity opened one eye. "I am now."

Emma shook her head and laughed. "And well I know it."

⌘ ⌘

Mitch exhaled. Two more weeks. Fourteen long days. He absently scratched figures on the galley sheet he was supposed to be working on. Three hundred and thirty-six grueling hours. He groaned and launched the pencil on the desk. "A bloomin' lifetime," he muttered.

The pencil skidded across one of the few areas free of clutter and plummeted to the floor. Mitch stretched back in his chair and closed his eyes, kneading the bridge of his nose. How long would it take this time?

He swiveled around to stare out the window, completely oblivious to the usual hurry and scurry of Lower Abbey Street at eight in the morning. It took a year to be free of Faith, a woman he'd loved to the depth of his soul. If "free" was even accurate. How long could it possibly take to get over her sister, a woman with whom he'd barely scratched the surface?

He sighed. But scratch the surface he had, whether he liked it or not. The lust had finally simmered and stewed, thickening into something he'd tasted before. Longing. Missing. Caring. He closed his eyes. Dear Lord, how long would it take this time?

"Excuse me, Mitch . . ."

He jolted in the chair and spun around, his mouth sagging low. He blinked. "Emma, what the devil are you doing here?"

She blushed, making the red welt beneath her eye all the more noticeable. Her gaze dropped to the coat she clutched in her hands. "I'm here for—"

He shoved himself up out of the chair. "If Charity sent you—"

She glanced up, her soft gray eyes as skittish as a fawn's. "No . . . no, Charity doesn't even know I'm here."

He sat and exhaled slowly, idly scratching the back of his head. "Sorry. It's been a rough couple of weeks around here. I tend to get grouchy."

The trepidation in her face diminished, softened by a hint of a smile. "So I've been told."

He peered up and finally let loose with a grin. He waved her toward a chair. "Sit. Tell me why you're here." He stretched back and braced his hands behind his neck.

Emma moved timidly, lighting on the edge of the seat like a firefly ready to flit at the first glimmer of dusk. She folded her hands on top of the coat in her lap and trained her eyes on the front of his desk. "It's Charity," she whispered.

He stiffened. The smile faded from his lips. "I thought you said she didn't send you."

Emma's eyes fluttered up. "She didn't; her grandmother did."

He leaned forward. "Bridget? Why? Is something wrong?"

She nodded, chewing on the scarred edge of her lip. "Charity's been hurt."

Her words registered in slow motion, drifting in his brain until they congealed into a cold heap at the pit of his stomach. His voice was a hoarse croak. "When? How?"

She twitched in the chair. "Two nights ago. We think Rigan beat her."

A spasm jerked in his neck as he stared, his fury rising faster than the bile in his throat. "How badly?"

"One arm broken, a sprained wrist, three bruised ribs, and a broken leg." She looked up, her eyes filled with pain. "Multiple cuts and bruises on her face and body, and judging from a nasty bump on her head, the doctor thinks a possible concussion."

He closed his eyes. Liquid rage pumped through his veins. He bit it back, his breath coming hard. "Did he . . ."

"We don't know. Charity hasn't spoken, not once since she returned home from the hospital. The doctor wanted her to stay longer than one night, but she refused. Since then it's as if she's in a fog, drifting off to sleep whenever we try. The doctor says it's a form of shock." Emma shifted in the chair, then put her hand to her head, shielding her eyes. "When Rigan carried her in that night . . . her clothes were torn. Her blouse . . . and her skirt."

Mitch slammed his fist against the desk. "I'm going to kill that no good—" He jumped up and yanked his coat off the back of his chair. He rammed one arm through a sleeve and then the other. "He had the gall to do this and then carry her in, bold as you please?"

Emma rose, wringing her hands. "Claims he found her like that. Says she jumped out of the car after they fought. He was angry because she broke the engagement, so he didn't follow at first. Swears he heard her screams and found her in Paley Park. A bobby escorted them home."

A nerve twittered in his cheek. "Scum of the earth. Engaged? So she really did it?"

Emma nodded. "A ring the size of Gibraltar and dinner with the family." She lowered her eyes. "She hoped it would bring you around."

He swore under his breath. "Well, it worked. Get your coat on."

Emma jumped up and fumbled with the sleeves. Mitch snatched it from her hands and held it while she slipped it on. "Thank you," she whispered.

He took her arm and steered her out the door. "Bridie, tell Michael I had an emergency and won't be back. I'll call."

Bridie looked up, her mouth slacking in shock. "B-but your meeting with the board? What'll I tell 'em?"

Clamping tighter on Emma's arm, he all but dragged her past Bridie's desk. "Charity's been hurt. Her grandmother needs me." Mitch glanced at Kathleen, and guilt squeezed in his chest.

Her voice was quiet as he passed. "I'll be praying, Mitch."

"Thanks, Kathleen."

He ushered Emma to the double doors, almost yanking her through as she slowed to shoot a backward glance. "Is that the woman you told Charity you were going to marry?"

He scowled. "Does she tell you everything?"

"Pretty much."

With a nod at the receptionist, he picked up their pace on the way to the front door. The woman jumped up and flashed an eager smile. "Goodbye, Mr. Dennehy. Will you be back today?"

"No, Miss Boyle. I have an emergency. Forward my calls to Bridie."

He shoved the glass doors open with one arm and propelled Emma through with the other. "Why did she break the engagement?"

Emma seemed out of breath, running to keep pace. "We made a deal . . . after I saw bruises on her body. To leave Rory if she left Rigan."

Mitch gave her a sideways glance. "You're a good friend, Emma Malloy."

A faint smile softened the harsh bent of her misshapen lip. "So is Charity, if given the chance."

He grimaced and opened the car door, then helped her in. "You sure she didn't send you?"

"No, but I think we both know who did." She looked up with a shy smile. The soft light in her eyes made her almost beautiful.

Mitch hesitated. "You're not talking Bridget, are you?"

She shook her head and smiled, fingering a delicate filigreed cross around her neck.

He slammed the door and clamped his lips tight, rounding the car to grind the crank. "I didn't think so."

❦   ❦

He took one look and knew only God could keep him from snuffing out Gallagher's life. She lay in the bed like a limp rag doll who'd been battered and bruised, then tossed on a trash heap. His jaw felt like rock as he blinked, fighting the wetness that suddenly sprang to his eyes. She seemed smaller, more vulnerable, barely a bump under the covers as she slept, eyes sunken and shadowed. He stared at the bandages on both wrists, his gaze traveling past the soft cast on her arm and up to her throat, mottled with ugly bruises. She barely resembled the beautiful woman he'd known. Her face was pale and drawn, painfully accentuated by purplish swelling on one side, hairline to chin. Pulpy and discolored. Like overripe fruit.

God help me not to kill him.

He swallowed hard and moved forward, desperate to hold her in his arms and comfort her, heal her. He lowered himself into the chair by her bed and hunched over, one hand to his head and the other resting on the bed. Guilt assailed him and he closed his eyes, wishing he'd given her a chance, regretting his cowardice. He could have prevented all of this. Mere assent of his will, that's all it would have taken.

She moved in the bed, and his eyes flicked open. He gently grazed her shoulder with his fingers. She opened her eyes and stared, no spark or light glimmering in their pale depths. "Charity . . . I'm so sorry."

She turned away. The effect was the same as if she'd spit in his face. He drew in a deep breath and rested his hand on her shoulder. "I swear I'll make sure he never does this again."

She turned then, a flash of fire in her eyes. "Like you did this time?"

He blinked, the shock of her words hardening his jaw. "Don't you dare try to hang this on me. I warned you what kind of man he was."

"Yes, you did. But you failed to warn me what kind of man you were. A coward in love, afraid to take a chance."

He stood. "I'm leaving. I don't want to upset you."

"Too late. Again." She turned away and closed her eyes, slumping back into a stupor.

His cheek pulsed as he watched her, a profile in pain. He went downstairs to the kitchen, where he knew Bridget, Mima, and Emma would be waiting. They looked up when he entered, their eyes full of questions.

"Was she glad to see you?" Emma breathed.

He yanked out a chair and flopped down. "Ecstatic."

Bridget leaned forward. "What's wrong?"

He rubbed his hands over his face and sagged in the chair. "She's angry. I think she blames me."

The three women exchanged glances. "It's not your fault," Bridget whispered.

He looked up through lids weighted with guilt. "Then why do I feel like it is?"

Bridget bustled to the counter to pour him a cup of coffee. She set it down and patted his shoulder. "She's angry. We all know she's in love with you, but that's not the only reason this happened."

He paused, his cup pressed against his lips. "What, then?"

"She wants to stay in Ireland." Bridget sighed and pushed a plate of apple muffins in his direction. "She thought marrying Rigan—or you—would accomplish that."

He snatched a muffin from the plate. "Which wraps it up rather neatly that I'm at fault."

Mima cleared her throat. "Nonsense. Charity's misguided actions are not your fault, no matter how much she wants them to be. I told you once that Charity begrudges fiercely and loves fiercely. Congratulations. You're now the proud recipient of both."

His lips twisted in a wry smile. "Thanks for the encouragement, Mima."

She chuckled and took a sip of her coffee, then set it back down and lost the smile. Her lips gummed into a hard line. "That said, I just have one question, young man, and I want a straight answer. Are you in love with my great-granddaughter?"

Mitch choked on his coffee, spitting it out. Bridget handed him a napkin. He swabbed his mouth and took a deep breath. "Respectfully, Mima, that's none of your business."

The fire in Mima's eyes blazed, growing her tiny four-foot-eleven frame to the height of intimidation. "Don't sass me, young man. You best answer me now or so help me, I'll rise from this chair—"

Bridget gasped. "Mother!"

Shuffling her feet, Mima struggled to stand.

Mitch pounded his fist on the table. "Yes. Are you happy?"

Mima's jaw of rock matched his. "No, I'm not happy. I've got a precious great-granddaughter lying upstairs, beat to a bloody pulp because you're too blasted thick to know a good thing when you see it."

"It's not that easy, Mima." Mitch stood to his feet, hands clenched.

"Do you love her or not?"

"Blast it, I told you I did."

"Then marry her."

He groaned and groped his fingers through his hair. "I can't."

"Why? Are you a coward?"

He glared. "It's more complicated than that."

"So is life, but we manage." She wilted against the table, leaning on it for support. "Do you know what I think? I think you've never forgiven her for taking Faith away from you. But Faith was only yours for a season. I think you're missing the whole point, along with the woman that God may actually have for you." She turned. "Bridget, this young man has worn me out. Can you see me back to bed, please?"

Mitch stepped forward. "Mima—"

"Thank you for coming. I'm sorry I lost my temper. Good-bye."

Bridget helped Mima to her feet, casting a contrite look in Mitch's direction. "Come along, Mother. We're all under a lot of stress right now. Mitch, stay where you are. We need to talk." She glanced at Emma who sat quietly at the table, her eyes saucers of shock. "Emma, would you mind brewing another pot of coffee, please? I think we'll need it."

Bridget ushered Mima from the room, and Mitch strode to the coffee pot, wrenching it from the warming plate. "I'll make it, Emma."

She was by his side in a heartbeat, gently wrestling the pot from his hands. "No, please, sit. I've had time to get used to all this. You haven't."

He released the pot, his energy suddenly ebbing away. He nodded and dropped in his chair, staring at the uneaten muffin next to his cup. He took a bite.

Bridget breezed back in the room and sat down next to him. "Good, you're eating. You probably go to work every day with nothing in your stomach, don't you?"

He continued chewing, ignoring her comment.

She laid her hand on his arm. "Mitch, Mima loves you. We

all do. And we're all pretty upset, so don't take her temper to heart. We've got bigger problems to solve."

He swallowed the muffin. "Okay. What do you need me to do?"

She shifted in the chair and glanced up to smile at Emma, who quietly joined them at the table. She returned her focus to Mitch. "Charity needs to go back to Boston. Immediately."

Mitch sat up, his eyes locked on hers. "I couldn't agree more."

"But she's too weak to travel alone, and I can't leave Mima."

"And she needs someone strong. Someone who can assist, carry her around, or I would go," Emma whispered.

Mitch glanced her way, then back at Bridget. "You want me to take her?"

They nodded in unison.

He scowled and jumped up from the table to pluck the boiling coffee off the stove. "Is this some diabolical plan to get the two of us together?"

Emma and Bridget traded looks. Bridget fidgeted with her fingers while Mitch poured her fresh coffee. "Not entirely, Mitch. There is another reason. A more important one."

He put the pot back on the stove and returned to the table, stretching his legs out while he sipped the steaming brew. He eyed her over the rim of his cup. "And what might that be?"

Bridget drew in a deep breath. "She says she won't go. That we can't make her."

He grunted. "Oh, we'll make her all right."

"That's just it. We can't, but you can. She'd have no recourse if you just swept her up in your arms and carried her off to that ship. How can she fight you with a broken arm and leg?"

"And a sprained wrist," Emma said.

Bridget's eyes were hopeful. "She would have no choice."

He sipped his coffee slowly, studying the muffin crumbs

on the table as he listened. "Why doesn't she want to leave? Because of me?"

"Partly, I'm sure, but not all . . ."

He looked up, sensing the hesitation in her tone. "What else?"

Bridget chewed on her lip, flexing her clasped hands on the table. Her voice was so low he had to lean in to hear it. "I have a suspicion that Rigan may have threatened her."

"What?"

Her worried gaze flicked to his face. "When I told her I was sending her home, she panicked, saying she couldn't leave, ever."

He leaned his arms on the table, his gaze glued to hers. "Maybe she meant because she didn't want to leave . . . because of you, Mima, and Emma."

Bridget gnawed on her lip. "Maybe, but I don't think so. When I told her she could just go for the holidays and return later, she seemed frantic, saying she couldn't risk it."

Mitch grabbed his coffee. "She could mean risking her father not letting her return."

Bridget swiveled in the chair to face him. "No, something inside tells me it's more than that. I have this sick feeling that Rigan may have threatened harming Mima or Emma or me if Charity left." She shivered, as if warding off a cold chill. "All I know is that he pushed the ring in my hand that night and told me in no uncertain terms that he and Charity would be married."

Mitch slapped his cup on the table and hissed something under his breath. "Over my dead body," he said. "And his."

Bridget touched his hand. "So you see, Mitch, you're the only one I can ask to see her safely home. Will you do it?"

He stared hard at the cup in his hands several seconds before answering. He finally put it down. "Yes."

Emma jumped up from her chair and threw her arms around

his shoulders from behind. "Oh, Mitch, I was so frightened you wouldn't do it. Thank you so much!"

He grunted. "I'm not the ogre Charity's convinced you I am."

Emma giggled and sat back down. "Ogre? No, I think 'thick-headed' was the word she used, wasn't it, Bridge?"

Bridget smiled and patted his hand. "Several times, as I recall." Her smile faded. "Tell me, Mitch, will it be a problem to get away from the paper with all that's going on in Dublin?"

"It will be for my editor, but he'll get by."

Bridget's brows wedged up in concern. "But I don't want you losing your job."

Mitch gulped the rest of his coffee and shoved the cup away. He slanted back in his chair and sighed, closing his eyes to massage his temples. Several seconds passed before he opened them again. When he did, he flashed them a devious smile. "I wouldn't worry if I were you, Bridget. When I'm done with Rigan Gallagher, I won't have a job to lose."

9

Michael Reardon jerked his desk drawer open and groped for the aspirin. He hurled four to the back of his throat and washed them down with cold coffee.

Mitch gave him a wry smile. "You know, that can't be good for you, all that aspirin."

Beads of sweat started to gleam on Michael's bald spot. "Neither are you, but I keep you around. What the devil do you mean you've got bad news?"

Mitch sailed a piece of paper at him and plopped in a chair. He leaned back, hands hanging limp off the armrests.

"What's this?" Michael snapped the paper up and began to read. His bushy brows bunched up thick and dark, like a threatening thundercloud. "What the devil are you doing? Have you lost your mind?"

"Nope. But I'm about to lose my job, so I figured I'd save you the trouble."

Michael wadded the paper and chucked it in the waste can. "You're an idiot. Consider it denied."

"You can't deny a resignation, Michael. I quit. You have no say in it whatsoever. This is merely a courtesy."

Michael shot up from his chair. He shoved his shirtsleeves up and leveled beefy palms on his desk. Mitch could feel the blast of his ire. "Courtesy? My best editor sashays through that door to quit in the throes of one of the bloodiest times we've seen, and you call it courtesy? I call it courtesy that I don't lunge across this desk and rip the hairs off your chest."

Mitch couldn't help it. He grinned. "Ouch! Come on, Michael, 'sashays'? You can accuse me of a lot of things, but I don't sashay."

A swear word sizzled the air as Michael snatched the pencil tucked behind his ear and hurled it at him.

With a quick duck, Mitch released a low whistle. "You're taking this better than I thought."

"You think this is funny? How about when I drop over from a heart attack? Will that be funny too?"

"I'm sorry, Michael. And, no, I don't think this is funny. It's just that if I don't retain some humor, I'm gonna blow like you've never seen before."

Dropping into his chair, Michael cuffed the back of his fire-red neck with his stubby hand and grunted. "What the devil is going on?"

Mitch blew out his constrained tension in one long, heavy breath and propped his elbows on Michael's desk. He scrubbed his face with his hands. "I'm quitting so you won't have to fire me."

Michael leaned forward and gritted his teeth. "And why would I do that?"

"Because when I leave here today, I am going to hunt Rigan Gallagher down and beat him to a bloody pulp. Literally."

Michael shot up again. "Blast you, Mitch, why do you have to go looking for trouble?"

Mitch stood and stared Michael down. "Because right now, Faith's sister is lying half dead in a bed with a broken arm and leg, a sprained wrist, a possible concussion, and more black bruises than a crate of four-month-old bananas."

His editor blinked and slumped back in the chair. "Curse the swine, is she okay?"

"No, she's not okay. That cowardly lowlife terrorized her.

He beat her silly and God knows what else." Mitch started pacing.

"Is she gonna press charges? Go after the scum?" Michael pawed his sweaty forehead.

Mitch stopped, one brow jerking up. "Press charges? Against a Gallagher? Oh, wouldn't that be rich. A poor shop girl against Gallagher's millions. Do you have any idea how they would crucify her?"

He nodded and reached into his back pocket for his handkerchief. "You're right. I wasn't thinking." He mopped the back of his neck. "But can't you just threaten him? Old man Gallagher likes you. If you just chew Rigan out, you might not lose your job."

"No, Michael. I should have done this a long time ago, but I didn't." Mitch sighed and stared past his editor. "I'm not going to make that mistake again."

"There must be another way. Talk to Mr. Gallagher, tell him what happened. Maybe he'll deal with Rigan on his own."

"No, this is my fight, and I'm going to finish it. Besides, Faith's grandmother asked me to take Charity back to Boston and I agreed. We leave in a few days. I'll be gone at least two weeks. Maybe more."

"Then make it a leave of absence. I'll talk to Mr. Gallagher, try to fix it with him." Michael leaned forward, his eyes pleading. "You're not gonna kill the lowlife, are ya?"

Mitch's lips twisted. "I don't know, Michael. I have a lot of pent-up rage."

"No, you've got more brains than temper, although not by much." Michael exhaled and collapsed in his chair. "So, it's settled. You're on a leave of absence. Period. Make sure you see me the minute you get back in town. In the meantime, think Jamie's up to filling in?"

"Yeah, Jamie's your man." Mitch shifted uncomfortably, his hands propped on the back of the chair. He took a deep breath and pulled an envelope from his suitcoat. "I guess this is it, then. Mind breaking the news to Jamie and Bridie after I leave, and then the rest of my group? And will you give this letter to Kathleen?"

Michael nodded.

"Thanks." Mitch dropped the sealed envelope on the desk and headed toward the door, his stomach in knots. Facing Bridie, Jamie, and Kathleen right now was more than he could handle. He was about to do something rash, and he didn't want them trying to talk him out of it. As for Kathleen, he'd been unfair to her in the past. He wouldn't ask her to wait. The last thing he wanted was to string her along with false hope. But maybe—just maybe—when he came back, they could start fresh.

"Mitch."

He paused and turned, his hand on the knob. "Yeah?"

"Don't let that maggot kick your butt, ya hear? I want to do it myself when ya get back."

He forced a grin. "In your dreams, old man." He closed Michael's door behind him and glanced across the newsroom. Jamie was lounging with his feet on his desk, probably laughing at one of Bridie's off-color remarks. Even from this distance, Mitch could see the blush on Kathleen's face. A spasm jerked in his cheek. This was going to be tough.

He strode by and flicked Jamie's feet off as he passed. "Jamie, there's a list on my desk a mile long of things I need you to do. I'm leaving early." He strode in his office and snatched his coat off the hook.

Bridie glanced at her watch. "But, it's only two. What about that budget for Michael?"

Mitch scooped a stack of papers off his desk and tossed them on Bridie's. "Done. All it needs is your fine-tuning, Mrs. O'Halloran." He wrestled his coat on. "Kathleen, Bridie, Jamie's going to need your help. I'm taking a few days off."

"But where are you going?" Bridie lunged to her feet.

He started for the door, glancing over his shoulder. "None of your business. Good night."

Her voice trailed him out the door. "Well, have fun, you tyrant. We'll be here pounding the keys and carrying your load."

He blasted through the door of the *Times* with a surge of relief, grateful to escape into the cool rush of autumn air. He took a deep breath before pressing his lips into a grim line. Yeah, he'd be doing some pounding of his own. And carrying a load that may well break his back. He flipped up the collar of his jacket and headed to his car. And it would be anything but fun.

Charity surveyed the damage in the mirror. Bile rose to her throat.

Again.

She couldn't get used to her reflection in the glass. The right side of her face was still swollen, its puffiness in stark dissymmetry to the smooth curve of the other, finally healed. She lifted her hand to touch the bluish streak along her cheekbone and flinched. She blinked wide, noting that her right eye, still a bit swollen, sported a fading shiner that rivaled those of a pub brawl on St. Pat's. She shivered and turned away, closing her eyes to block out the image in the mirror Emma held. "Don't let me see until I really start to heal, no matter how I beg."

"As if that's possible. All of your whining and pleading wears me down. What makes you think I'll do better next time?" Emma laid the mirror on the dresser and chuckled.

Charity tried to smile and moaned instead. She put a hand to her head, shielding her bloated eye. "Oh . . . don't make me laugh. It hurts even to smile."

"Not as much as it hurts to cry. Ready for lunch?" Emma

sat in the chair by the bed and leaned in to push a stray curl from Charity's eyes.

"Can I feed myself?"

Emma sighed. "We've been over this time and again. You're right-handed, are you not? With a broken right arm? And a left-wrist sprain? How do you propose to eat?"

Charity squirmed in the bed, wiggling to sit up. "Well, if you'll be kind enough to assist, I can try it left-handed. A most sloppy southpaw, perhaps, but at least feeding myself."

Emma shook her head. "Pure, unadulterated obstinacy. You are truly queen."

"And you, Emma Malloy, are my loyal subject, so stop moaning and give me a boost."

With another sigh, Emma wrapped her arms around Charity's waist and gave her a gentle tug to elevate her to a sitting position. "How does your leg feel?"

"Fine if you like dragging fifty pounds of plaster of paris around."

"Doc Simms just wanted to make sure you didn't sabotage his hard work. Does it hurt?"

Charity wiggled her toes. "Surprisingly, no. But the black-and-blue marks all over my body are really annoying. I never knew a body could ache in so many places."

Her friend's eyes softened. "You're a trooper, my friend. Even Doc Simms thinks so. You've come along faster in four days than any patient he's ever seen. Must be the prayers."

Charity rolled her eyes, then grimaced, hand to head. "No, it must be the boredom. When did the doctor say I could go back to work?"

"He hasn't said." Emma reached for the bowl of stew, then flipped a napkin in Charity's lap. She set the dish on top, avoiding Charity's gaze.

"Well, I certainly intend to ask." She reached for the utensil, but her grasp was precarious at best. She awkwardly buried the spoon in the stew, feeling every bit the invalid. Gritting her teeth, she ignored the pain and ladled the broth into her mouth. "When is he coming back?"

"I don't know," Emma mumbled, settling in the chair once again. "Tell me when you need a drink. Your grandmother sent up apple cider."

"This is good. I'm finally starting to feel like a human being again."

"Charity . . ."

She looked up, the spoon hidden deep in her mouth. "Mmmm?"

Eyes fixed on the cider propped in her lap, Emma shifted in the chair. "I've been . . . well, I've been worried about something . . ."

The spoon plunked back into the bowl. Charity leaned her head back against the pillow while she rested her sore wrist on the blanket. "What?"

Emma hesitated. "Well . . . you haven't spoken one word about what happened that night. At first, we left you alone because we knew you were in shock. But we need to know. Was it Rigan who beat you . . . or did he find you in the park like he said?"

The mention of Rigan's name constricted Charity's throat, narrowing her passage of air. It hurt when she swallowed. "I don't want to talk about it," she whispered.

"You have to tell us the truth."

She closed her eyes and breathed in slowly, desperate to calm the sudden racing of her pulse. Fear shivered through her. Fear for Emma. Fear for herself. Rigan had made it clear. If Charity left Dublin, he'd retaliate against Emma. If she told Emma the truth, Emma would tell Grandmother. And Grandmother would force her to go home. She took another breath, deeper this time, then winced at the soreness it produced. Doc Simms said five to seven weeks before she could walk. There was no way she could travel till then. And Faith's wedding would be over. Done. Maybe Grandmother would let her stay. She shivered. But not if she knew Rigan had hurt her.

She finally spoke, her voice barely a whisper. "Promise me, Emma. Promise you won't tell Grandmother or Mima."

"No, Charity, I can't . . ."

She gripped Emma's hand. "I won't tell you unless you promise."

Pale and biting her lip, Emma finally nodded. "All right. I promise."

Charity sagged against the pillow. Tears stung her eyes. "Yes, it was Rigan."

A shudder rippled through Emma. She wrapped her arms around her middle. "Why didn't you tell the police officer that night?"

She stared straight ahead. "I was afraid. Rigan . . . he . . . said he would do terrible things if I told anyone . . ."

Emma laid a hand on Charity's arm. "Your grandmother and I . . . well, all of us . . . we believed it was him all along, that he was lying." She bit her lip and began to fiddle with the glass in her hands. "There's . . . something else."

"What?"

Emma flushed. "I have to know, Charity. Rigan . . . did he . . ."

The blood siphoned from her face and tension strained in her jaw. "No. He didn't. Not that he didn't have every intention."

"How . . . how did you stop him?"

She hesitated, focusing on the bowl in her lap. "I bit his ear."

Silence.

She looked up. Emma's mouth was gaping.

"You bit his ear?"

Charity nodded, pride swelling in her chest. "Drew blood too. And then I stabbed him with his own umbrella."

Emma gasped. "Oh, dear! Is that when he beat you?"

"No. That didn't happen until I bolted from the car. He was a madman when he finally caught up with me in Paley Park. I was running so hard in the dark that I tripped . . . on a root, I think. All I know is I heard something crack in my leg right before I hit my head on a rock. I screamed. He found me, then, and he was livid, telling me this little jaunt was going to make it 'worth his while.' He began pawing at my blouse and skirt, and when I tried to fight him off, he started beating me, twisting my arms behind my back. I was screaming, and I honestly believe he would have raped me then and there, except for the bobby on his nightly round. Rigan picked me up then, just as the officer approached. He whispered in my ear—threatened me, really—to keep quiet or . . ." A shiver traveled her spine. "The next thing I know, he was carrying me in his arms, telling the officer I'd been mugged."

"Dear Lord, it's the grace of God that blessed bobby arrived."

Charity's lips twisted. "Yeah, well, the 'grace of God' could have come a bit sooner to suit me. And spared me broken bones in the process." She took another taste of stew, scrunched her nose, and tossed the spoon back in the dish. "Suddenly I've lost my appetite."

"Do you want cider?" Emma asked, removing the bowl.

Charity sighed and inched down in the bed. "No, I think I'll get some rest. But tell Grandmother thank you for me, will you?" She glanced up. "I don't know what I'd do without you, Emma. Rory's the biggest fool alive. Has he tried to get in touch with you at all?"

Emma shook her head. "He had one of his drinking buddies drop off a note at Shaw's." She paused to pick up the napkin and adjust the covers.

"And?"

"Well, I believe his exact words were 'Good riddance.' Said not to bother coming home as his new missus-to-be has already moved in." Emma blinked and swiped at her eyes.

Charity's face hardened. "Men. Worthless creations, the lot of 'em." She closed her eyes.

"Not Mitch Dennehy," Emma whispered.

Charity grunted. "Especially Mitch Dennehy. It's his fault I'm in this predicament in the first place."

Emma didn't answer.

Charity opened her lids a slit. "Don't you? I mean think this is his fault, at least partially?"

Clutching the bowl close to her chest, Emma straightened her shoulders and jutted her chin, completely out of character. "No. No, I don't. We make our own decisions, Charity, and you made a bad one. Just like I did with Rory. It isn't Mitch's fault that you fell in love with him. Nor is it his fault if he chooses to marry someone else. That's his right, plain and simple. Just like it was yours to marry Rigan. Moronic as it was."

Charity blinked. "Well, thank you, Emma Malloy. Now if you don't mind, I think I'll lay my moronic head down on this pillow and put us both out of our misery." She plopped back and squeezed her eyes shut, lips clamped in a flat line.

The sound of Emma's chuckle floated in the air, followed by a light squeeze on her shoulder. She ignored it and pinched her eyes tighter.

"I love you, Charity O'Connor. And just for the record? When it comes to being 'thickheaded,' I'm afraid you could teach our Mr. Dennehy a healthy thing or two."

⧼ ⧽

Mitch yawned and glanced at his wristwatch. Four o'clock in the morning. Typical. He propped his head against the headrest of his Model T, parked in the shadowed street of the Gallagher Estate. He scowled. Little Lord Fauntleroy was either somewhere downing his last quarter bottle of booze or lying passed out in some woman's bed. A rush of rage suddenly replaced his fatigue, surging adrenaline through his veins once again.

Gallagher was an animal. Using women for his own selfish pleasure. Like he'd done to Charity. Nothing but pure slime.

And you? Before Faith?

Mitch froze in the seat. Anger burned in his chest. He was nothing like Gallagher.

Love seeketh not its own . . .

Kathleen's face loomed before him, lovesick, anxious to please, giving her all. Mitch heaved his fist on the dash, his breathing shallow. "I cared for her, I did!"

Love seeketh not its own . . .

He groaned and hung his head on the steering wheel, his heart sick with grief. The realization pierced him with brutal force. He had used her. For his own pleasure. And when all was said and done, other than physical abuse, there was really very little difference between Gallagher and him.

The silence of conviction engulfed him. "Forgive me," he whispered. "I'm new at this. Understanding you, understanding your Word. I try to apply it like Faith did, but it's hard. I've prayed for Gallagher; you know I have. But when I think of what he did to Charity . . ."

Vengeance is mine.

Mitch heaved his palm against the steering wheel. "No! This time it's mine. I won't kill him because I fear you, but I won't turn my back. Not again."

The sweep of headlights diverted his attention. A Rolls-Royce squealed onto the street, careening toward him at breakneck speed. Mitch's jaw tightened, and his fingers were itchy on the wheel. The coupe barely slowed as it approached the Gallagher entrance, finally screeching to a stop to avoid slamming into the gate. The gate Mitch had closed.

The driver's door swung open with a jerk, and Rigan Gallagher tumbled out, his slurred expletives rising into the still night air. He stumbled toward the iron bars and rattled the latch as if it were the gates of hell. Curses echoed in the dark. Mitch smiled and opened his door. Apparently Gallagher didn't

like the wire Mitch had wound around the bolt. Too bloomin'
bad.

Mitch moved like a shadow to the front of Rigan's car. He
crossed his arms and eased back against the grill, his muscles
as taut as the skin on his fists. Nerves twitched in his cheek
like skittering drops across a white-hot skillet.

"Guess they finally wised up and locked you out . . . Mr.
Gallagher III." His voice was pure acid.

Rigan spun around, as if Mitch's tone had eaten away at his
drunken stupor. The glaze in his eyes glinted into anger.

"Dennehy? What the devil are you doing here?"

Mitch stood to his full height, dwarfing Rigan by a head. He
took a step forward. "Oh, just the usual. Out slumming. What
about you, Rigan? Beat up any defenseless women tonight?"

"You come any closer, and I'll have your job."

His laughter was chilling as he took a step forward. "I'll make
a deal with you, Mr. Gallagher. You can have my job . . . and
I'll have your head. On a platter."

Sweat beaded on Rigan's brow. "You're way out of bounds
here, Dennehy. Have you been drinking?"

"Oh, yeah. Lots and lots of ginger ale. I wanted to make sure
I was good and sober when I paid my respects to the devil."

Rigan's eyes darted nervously, first to his car, then back to
Mitch's face. He licked his lips. "If this is about Charity, I saved
her life—"

Mitch lunged, silencing him with a powerful thrust against
the gate. His hands squeezed Rigan's throat, pinning him to
the iron bars. He bared his teeth. "Don't do it, Gallagher. I'm
a God-fearing man, but so help me, one more lie out of you,
and I'll be forced to break a commandment."

A choking sound sputtered from Rigan's throat. Mitch tightened his grip and leaned in, his words spitting into Rigan's face.
"Admit it, Gallagher. You beat her and then you raped her."

Rigan's eyes widened. With a fierce grunt, he managed an
upper jab at Mitch's throat.

Mitch reeled back.

Shoulders hunched and feet straddled wide, Rigan clenched his fists up in ready stance. His voice was hoarse as he gasped for air. "Is that what she told you? Well, she lied. She does that, you know."

Mitch pounced, butting him back against the gate. Before Rigan could recover, Mitch whipped his head to the side with a sharp blow of his fist. Blood splattered everywhere. "Throwing stones, Gallagher? You make me sick."

Weaving, Rigan brushed a hand across his bleeding cheek. His eyes were slits of hate. "You're a fool, Dennehy. She's lying to you, like she always does. She gave it willingly, any time I wanted. How does it feel to be in love with a whore?"

Rage exploded inside of Mitch's brain. He delivered an iron-fisted punch to Gallagher's gut, doubling him in half with a sickening groan. "Let me tell you how it feels to want to kill somebody so bad it aches, you worthless sack of dung." He reached down and grabbed Rigan's tie and yanked his body up, slamming him hard against the gate. He let fly with a jaw-breaking bash to his right cheek. Rigan's face twitched to the side. Blood oozed from his nose.

"I'll kill you for this," he sputtered. He stabilized himself with one hand while wiping blood with the other.

Mitch's laugh was savage. "Yeah? Well, you're lucky. I don't have that luxury. I have to turn the other cheek." He back-handed an iron fist against Rigan's left jaw, whirling his head to the other side. "Of course, my scriptural interpretation may be a bit off."

Rigan stumbled back, breathing hard. "I'll make you pay for this, both you and your whore." He spit out a wad of blood and raised his fists. "But then, you always had a penchant for whores. First Anna, now Charity." He grinned, the loathing in his eyes as thick as the blood on his face. "I'll give you this—they're a good time in bed." He grinned like a madman as he flew at Mitch, driving him back against the Rolls' saucer headlights.

Mitch groaned and staggered up, sustaining a blow to his cheek before launching a fist into Rigan's eye. Rigan teetered back with a curse, then crumpled to the ground, legs sprawled. Mitch's laugh pierced the night with an unholy sound. "You know, turning the other cheek is okay, but I prefer an eye for an eye, a tooth for a tooth. Kind of a paraphrase—'an arm for an arm' or 'a wrist for a wrist.'" He drew back to shatter Rigan's kneecap with the blunt sole of his shoe. "Of course, my personal favorite is a leg for a leg—"

What does the Lord require of you, but to do justly and love mercy?

"No!" Mitch shrieked, then bludgeoned the fleshy side of Rigan's leg instead. Rigan wailed and listed to his side. Mitch released a shuddering breath and sagged forward, his breath coming in heavy, ragged gasps. He shoved Rigan all the way over with the tip of his shoe, extracting a garbled groan from Rigan's throat.

Mitch clutched the gate and bent to one knee. "Now you listen to me, you load of human pus. If you so much as breathe near Charity O'Connor ever again, I'll see to it you never hold your head up in this town. I'm personally taking her back to Boston for good, and when I return, I suggest you locate elsewhere. Because if I smell your foul stench anywhere near Dublin, I'll consider it an extreme pleasure to go to the papers and reveal what a bloodsucking lowlife abuser you are. And when I'm done with you, Mr. Rigan Gallagher III, not even a mangy, flea-infested dog will lick your sores, you sorry excuse for a man."

With a grunt, Mitch rose to his feet and unlatched the gate. "Now crawl to your car like the snake you are. You'll want to clean up before Daddy sees you. He might ask questions. Then you'd have to tell him you're better at beating up women than men."

Mitch untethered the wire from the latch and tossed it into the bushes. He hurled the gates open and stepped over Rigan's crumpled body to head to his car. He glanced over his shoulder, noting with satisfaction that Rigan was writhing on his side. "Good night, Mr. Gallagher. Enjoy the rest of your evening. And if you look half as pretty in the morning as Charity did when you were done with her, I'll consider this a most productive night."

჻ ჻

Mitch held his breath, then closed the front door to Mrs. Lynch's apartment building with a careful click. He exhaled and turned to mount the newly waxed staircase, grimacing as each squeak resounded in his brain. Leaning on the banister, he reached the top step, mere feet away from his apartment door and blessed sleep.

"Goodness me, I've been tossing and turning all night, and now I know why." Sleepy eyes peeked out from the door across the hall. Mitch groaned inwardly.

The door opened wider, revealing Mrs. Lynch in all her bedtime glory. She tugged her floral robe tighter and adjusted the matching kerchief on her head. Her eyes expanded at the blood on his shirt and face. "Sweet saints in heaven, are you all right?"

He nodded and inserted the key. "Fine, Mrs. Lynch. Good night."

"But you're bleeding."

"Not as much as the other guy." He pushed his door open, anxious to close it again.

A lavender slipper blocked his way. "Mitch Dennehy, did you hurt Rigan Gallagher tonight?"

"Go back to bed, Mrs. Lynch."

She pushed an arm and a leg through. *Great.* He had a stubborn, silver-haired midget lodged in his door.

"Don't patronize me, young man. Did you hurt Rigan Gallagher?"

He was too tired to fight. He dropped his hold on the knob and trudged inside. He took his coat off and threw it on the sofa. "Yes."

"Mitch Dennehy, I'm ashamed of you." Mrs. Lynch closed the door and folded her arms. "Ashamed it's taken this long to deal with that upstart."

Mitch looked up and blinked. "You're ashamed? That I didn't do it sooner?"

Mrs. Lynch hurried to his side. "Absolutely. That little rich boy has had it coming for a long time." She bullied him toward the sofa and touched a hand to his nose. "Is this your blood or his?"

Mitch yawned. "His."

"Good. How about this?" She feathered a finger across his swollen cheek.

"Oww . . . mine."

"I was afraid of that. The tincture of iodine will sting on that one." She scrunched her nose, eyeing his blood-spattered shirt. "Mmmm . . . that shirt's headed for the rag basket, I think. But we'll see. I'll be right back."

"Mrs. Lynch, wait."

She whirled around.

"I heard something . . . in my head tonight, a thought really, not a sound. A Scripture I'd read. 'Vengeance is mine.'"

Mrs. Lynch cocked her head. "Yes?"

Mitch took a deep breath. "Well, I just thought that maybe . . . maybe I did the wrong thing. You know, let my temper get the best of me." He looked away, guilt weighting him down more than fatigue. "Like maybe I chose my way instead of God's."

Mrs. Lynch pursed her lips. Her blue eyes squinted back at him. "Probably. But God is God. He can use whatever or whomever he pleases—good or evil—to execute justice. Your temper got the best of you tonight, Mitch. But right or wrong, I believe God used it."

He sank back against the sofa and closed his eyes. "Thanks, Mrs. Lynch. I needed that."

"You also need sleep. But not before I take care of that nasty cut on your cheek. What time does the ship sail tomorrow?"

He lifted his arm to glance at his watch, then dropped it like a dead weight, eyes closed. "Four o'clock. I've got a lot to do before then. But at least I can sleep till noon."

"I'm glad. Well, stay right there. I'll get my supplies."

As if he could move.

When she returned, she dressed the wounds in seconds flat, then patted his cheek and headed for the door.

His eyes flipped open. "Mrs. Lynch?"

She turned at the door. "Yes?"

"In case I forget to tell you, thanks for taking care of Runt while I'm gone. And for everything you do."

She laughed. "And thank you for the month's advance on your rent. Are you sure you can afford it?"

He closed his eyes and smiled. "In case it escaped your attention, I haven't exactly been spending my money on wine, women, and song."

She chuckled and opened the door. "So, I've noticed." She slipped out and closed it again, but not before poking her head in one last time. "But those ginger ale bills are going to send you to the poorhouse, my boy." The door banged closed, leaving him with a smile warm on his lips and slumber hot on his heels.

"Grandmother, look!" Charity perched on the edge of the bed, eyeing herself in the hand mirror. "I did it. Broken arm, bum wrist, and all. This chemise is a cinch to put on with the large loop and button you sewed in. You're a genius. And the lace . . . it's so pretty!"

Bridget looked up from her sewing. Her brows sloped high, colliding with the wrinkles on her brow. "Oh no, Charity, that chemise is way too small."

Observing the deep cleft between her full breasts, Charity tilted her head. "It does rather make me look like a vamp, doesn't it?"

"Oh my, it certainly does." Bridget tossed her sewing aside and stood, hand to cheek. "Take it off this instant, and I'll add some material."

Charity laughed and studied herself in the mirror. "Not on your life, Grandmother. For the first time in days, those awful bruises are fading, and I'm finally feeling pretty again. This chemise makes me feel very . . . shall I say . . . womanly? Besides, no one is going to see me in it but you or Emma." She flicked the lacey edging and sighed. "Such a pity."

"Young lady! It's bad enough I've made you look like a tart in that chemise, must you talk like one too? Now take it off and I'll fix it."

Charity snatched her blouse off the bed and quickly lifted it over her shoulders. "Sorry, but I'm already half dressed, thanks to your ingenuity." She slipped the good arm through the wide sleeve, then the broken one. Ignoring the worry on her grandmother's face, she fumbled with the oversized loop Bridget had stitched into her pale pink, double-breasted satin blouse. With a grunt, she managed to hook it over the good-size pearlized button. She took a deep breath. "There. How does it look?"

Bridget bit her lip. "Way too snug."

A giggle escaped Charity's lips. "Good. Now for the skirt." She fished her burgundy and gray plaid tweed skirt off the bed and dropped it over her head. Propping her good arm, she pushed herself to a standing position. She wobbled a bit before stabilizing, then shifted her weight to her strong leg. She tugged the skirt down. "There. That wasn't too bad. Now for the button . . ." She fiddled with another wide loop, finally catching it on the large button at the waist. "The saints be praised. I did it. How do I look?"

Her grandmother eyed her up and down, worry creasing her brow. "A wee bit too 'womanly,' if you ask me."

Charity grinned. "Perfect. This will be the outfit I wear when Dr. Simms says I can go back to work. If I can get a rich louse like Rigan Gallagher to propose, I should be able to land another wealthy suitor soon enough. And let Mr. Heart-of-Stone Dennehy choke on that bit of news when it comes."

She plopped on the bed and grimaced at the jolt to her arm. She rubbed it and looked up. Her grandmother was fussing with the sewing in her lap. Charity squinted, noting her grandmother's nervous habit of rolling her tongue across her front teeth.

"Grandmother?"

Bridget's gaze remained fixed on the sewing in hand. "Mmmm?"

"Is something wrong?"

She didn't look up. Instead, her tongue did another quick glide. "No, nothing, dear. I'm just concentrating hard on getting another blouse sewn for you."

Charity cocked her head. "Is it Father? Are you worried what he'll say when he receives my letter? He can't make me stay in Boston if I don't go home, you know."

Bridget's cheeks burned red.

"You did send it, didn't you? The letter I had Emma write?"

"I forget, dear."

"Well, even if you didn't, there's no way I can be back in time for Christmas and the wedding. Dr. Simms says I won't get full use of my leg for another five to seven weeks. You know I can't travel alone, and besides, I already told you. I don't want to go home. I want to stay here with you and Mima and Emma. Forever."

Sadness ringed her grandmother's eyes. "I know, dear."

Charity exhaled and gave her a tremulous smile. "I love you, Grandmother. You, Mima, and Emma are all the family I need. You've shown me more love and attention than I've ever known before. Making all these special clothes so I can dress myself. Cooking for me, reading to me, washing my hair, even bathing me. I want to always be here for you."

Tears brimmed in Bridget's eyes while her chin trembled. "I love you, Charity. No granddaughter could hold a more special place in my heart. And I want the very best for you. Please . . . always know that."

Charity turned her head. "Did you hear something? Was that a knock downstairs?" She turned back to Bridget, her brows dipping low. "Are you expecting Dr. Simms today?"

Bridget fumbled the sewing in her lap and stood in a hurry. The blouse she'd been working on fluttered to the floor. She stooped to pick it up. "I . . . I don't know. I don't think so. I'll go check." She rushed to the closet to retrieve Charity's shoes and a pair of gray woolen stockings. She laid them on the bed. "Here, practice putting these on, if you can, and we'll see about getting you downstairs like I promised." She whirled around and charged from the room, closing the door behind her.

Charity shook her head and hiked her skirt to her thighs. She snatched a stocking. This wasn't going to be easy. She did her best to push her good hand into the finely knitted wool and rolled it up her forearm. Lying back on the bed, she lifted her good leg in the air and bent it toward her, latching the toe of the stocking on her foot. It caught and she extended her leg, slowly tugging the stocking to her thigh. She sat up, pinned it to her garter and took a deep breath. "One down, one to go."

The second would definitely be more difficult with a cast. Charity reached for the stocking and smiled. Dear, wonderful Grandmother. She'd doctored it with an extra piece of material to accommodate the cast. Charity carefully rolled it up in her good hand and sank back on the bed, bare leg and cast pointed at the ceiling.

A knock sounded. Bridget opened the door and peeked inside. "Are you decent?"

Charity grunted, desperate to flip the stocking over the toe of her broken leg. It missed. For the third blasted time. "Oh, thank God you're here," she groused. "Maybe you can help me with this ridiculous thing."

Bridget bustled into the room and carefully closed the door. "Of course I will, dear. And Mitch is here to help carry you down the stairs."

Her fingers froze to the limp stocking, and heat rolled into her cheeks before her leg plummeted to the bed. "No! I don't want to see him. And I certainly don't need his help to get downstairs."

Bridget hurried to the bed and took the stocking out of Charity's hand. "Settle down, young lady, and swing your legs over the side of the bed. There is no way you can attempt those steps on your own. And you heard Dr. Simms—no crutches until after the first week."

"It's been five days, Grandmother, a few days more or less won't matter. And for the record, other than Rigan Gallagher, Mitch Dennehy is the last person I want to see right now."

Bridget bent to slip the stocking on Charity's leg and tugged it over the cast. "Now hush," she whispered, "he's right outside the door. He took time out of his busy day to help us, so you best mind your tongue and be grateful."

"Grateful?" She jerked the stocking up and pinned it to her garter with trembling hands. She glared at the door and raised her voice several octaves. "To a thickheaded womanizer who's indirectly responsible for the condition I'm in?" She flipped her skirt over her legs and lifted her chin. "When pigs fly! My crutches, please."

Bridget sighed and hurried to the door. She opened it and

poked her head in the hall. "Sorry, Mitch. She's ready now. I'll get her crutches."

Mitch appeared in the doorway, his face a blank except for the faintest twitch of his lips. His eyes narrowed as he slacked a hip against the door jamb, hands in his pockets. "Hello, Charity," he drawled. "It's a beautiful day. Blue skies with lots of clouds, birds . . . *pigs*."

"Get out! I can manage the stairs myself. I wouldn't put it past you to drop me."

"Enough!" Bridget's tone held a warning. "Now, you can't do it yourself, young lady, and that's all there is to it." She glanced down at Charity's stockinged feet. "You don't even have your shoes on."

Charity snatched the shoes off the bed and dropped them on the floor with a loud clunk. She tried to lumber up using her good arm and groaned.

Mitch took a step forward.

Her icy look froze him to the spot. "I don't want him here, Grandmother. Make him leave."

"Hush and slip into your shoes. I'll help you."

Charity shot him another slitted glare, then hobbled up on her good leg and anchored her hand to Bridget's arm. "Make him turn around, then. I don't want him watching me."

His jaw tightened before he rotated slowly, hands loose and low on his hips.

She looked him over and sighed. What a waste of a beautiful man. Broad shoulders, narrow hips, hard muscles everywhere you looked. Especially in his head.

She latched securely onto Bridget's extended arm while she slipped on her shoe, then pressed down until it felt good and snug.

Her grandmother nudged the other shoe toward her.

"Thank you," she muttered, wiggling her toe until it eased inside. "Now, if you'll just hand me the crutches . . ."

"She's ready, Mitch."

Charity glanced up at the waver in her grandmother's voice. "Grandmother, I can tackle the stairs myself, honestly. Just give me the crutches. I don't need him."

Crutches firmly in hand, Bridget started toward the door. "Emma?" she called, and Emma suddenly appeared, her smile as stiff as Charity's fifty-pound cast.

Mitch strode toward the bed, and Charity backed away, feeling the nightstand as it gouged the back of her knees. "What are you doing? Get away!"

He completely ignored her and whisked her off her feet, his tight-lipped expression as rock-hard as the arms that pinned her against his chest.

She tried to scratch him with her good arm, to no avail. "Put me down, you lout! I tell you, I can do it myself."

"Emma, the sling," Mitch shouted.

She nodded and darted to the nightstand to scoop it up.

Charity tried to kick, but her efforts were futile against his hold of clamped steel. She blew out a noisy breath of disgust. "Oh, you people are something else. I tell you, I can do this. Grandmother, please!"

Bridget patted her good arm while Mitch carried her through the door. "Charity, I'd feel much better if you would let Mitch carry you just this once, all right, dear?"

Charity groaned and sagged against his chest of stone, literally and figuratively, she mused, suddenly aware she was in Mitch Dennehy's arms. She glanced up at his clean, chiseled chin and felt her stomach tighten. The scent of Bay Rum drifted to her nostrils, causing her hand—the one pressed hard against his chest—to burn. With a quick intake of breath, she jerked it away and crossed her arms, willing herself to ignore the heat he generated. She sighed. What good would it do?

He strode down the steps with ease, as if she were a mere child instead of a woman. He paused in the foyer and glanced at Bridget. "I put her bags in the car. Are you sure she has everything she needs?"

Charity blinked. "Bags? Grandmother, what's he talking about?"

Tears pooled in Bridget's eyes. "Charity, love, you have to go home. For your own safety."

The air clotted in her throat. She jerked, struggling to get free. "No! Please, no! Don't do this, Grandmother. I love you. I want to stay."

His arms tightened like a vise. "Should I take her to Mima?"

Bridget nodded and wiped her eyes with her apron.

Charity battered his chest with her good arm, thrashing like a crazy person in the midst of a nightmare. "Put me down. I hate you, Mitch Dennehy. I'll never forgive you. Let me go!"

"I'm just following orders."

The sound of Bridget sobbing followed them while he carried her down the hall, his grip like steel. The moment she saw Mima's face, she started to cry. "Mima, don't let them do this. I want to stay. With you and Grandmother and Emma. Make them understand."

Her great-grandmother's cheeks glistened with grief. She shook her head, and her frail lips were wet and trembling.

Charity's heart seized in her chest.

Leaning to hold her close to Mima, Mitch allowed the old woman to press a weak kiss to Charity's cheek. "I love you, Charity. You've brought us much joy."

"No, Mima, please, let me stay. I don't want to leave." She grasped Mima's shoulder with her good arm, clinging with everything in her.

"You have to go, dear. We can't risk letting you stay. As much as we love you, you need to go home."

"This is my home!" she screamed. "My only home."

"Goodbye, darling girl. We will miss you terribly."

"No!" Charity tried to hold tightly to Mima's frail shoulder, her chest heaving with sobs.

Mitch pried her fingers loose and swept her up and away. He hurried down the hall. Bridget and Emma wept at his heels.

"Wire me as soon as you arrive, do you hear?" Bridget blew her nose on a handkerchief and stood at the front door.

Mitch nodded and turned to Emma, the right side of her face mottled and red from crying. She reached out and hugged Charity's side. "I love you, Charity O'Connor. You're the best friend I've ever had. I will miss you so much."

"Emma, why? Why are you all doing this? You're breaking my heart."

"We love you, Charity, that's all we can say." Emma stepped back. "We want you safe. I pray you come back someday."

Bridget opened the door. Her face was haggard as she looked at Mitch. "You better go. I packed her coat like you requested, along with a bit of supper in her smaller bag. There's enough for several days, just in case."

He nodded and strode toward her, halting at the door long enough for Bridget to throw her arms around Charity's neck.

The anguish in her grandmother's sobs pierced Charity's soul. She clutched Bridget hard. "Grandmother, I love you; why are you doing this? I'll never understand. It's not what I want."

"Nor I, darling, but sometimes love requires sacrifice. You're the granddaughter of my heart, Charity. I will miss you more than I can say." She pulled away and backed toward the door, her handkerchief limp against her mouth.

Mitch swept past and out to the porch. "I'll take good care of her."

"We know you will." Bridget wiped her eyes with the handkerchief, then waved it in the air. "Goodbye, Mitch, Charity. We love you both."

Emma came to stand beside Bridget. Her face was swollen with tears. "I'll be praying, Charity. Please write."

Mitch bounded down the steps, moving quickly to his car.

Charity craned over his shoulder for one last look. Her sobs quieted to short, raspy heaves as she stared. Emma and Bridget huddled so close on the porch that they blurred into one. Charity blinked and Bridget stepped forward, a miserable attempt at a smile on her face. "Mitch, don't let her give you any sass, you hear?"

"I won't." He opened Charity's door and carefully set her inside. He reached for a blanket and tucked it around her. He shut the door, then rounded the car to churn the crank.

Charity stared out the window with tears streaming her face. Mitch got in and released the handbrake. The car pulled away from the curb with a lurch that felt like her heart was being ripped from her chest.

She blinked. The people she loved most in the world stood waving goodbye. A fresh wave of sobs choked from her lips. She pressed her head back against the seat and squeezed her eyes shut. Tears spilled with reckless abandon. Mitch nudged a handkerchief against her arm. She snatched it and wiped the wetness from her face. "I hate you, Mitch Dennehy."

She heard his long, weary sigh as the car picked up speed. "I know. So do I."

10

Mitch pulled his Model T into the cobblestone lot in front of the pier, barely noticing the flurry of activity that always ensued on sailing day. The sounds and smells of bleating livestock drifted in the air as drovers and handlers prodded cattle onto cargo ships. The port scurried with activity, not unlike a colony of ants skittering in all directions. Muscled men lumbered up gangplanks with bundles and crates bulging with iron, nails, salt, bricks, glass, and textiles for the westward crossing. Beady-eyed runners rasped their services like barkers at a carnival, hungry to prey upon inexperienced travelers who dreamed of immigrating to America.

Mitch looked up as a string of barges chugged steadily down the Liffey River, heaped high with crates of Guinness. Coal merchants scattered along the quays, bellowing orders to men shoveling coal into ten-stone bags. Gritty-faced stevedores with rippling backs lifted the sacks, hauling them down a single gangplank two feet wide, bouncing with every step.

His lips compressed at the sight of the Black and Tans, special British police created to fight the revolutionist Sinn Feiners. Their khaki uniforms and black hats stood out like silent threats among a throng of sweating dockers, huddled families, and dandied merchants.

Mitch yanked the lever to disengage the drive gears and

turned the engine off. He looked at Charity, her eyelids closed in apparent sleep. Even with her face swollen from crying and a hint of bruising, she was still a beautiful woman. Long lashes swept high above chiseled cheekbones while soft, golden tendrils feathered her face.

He leaned back in the seat. She hated him. He let it sink in, and deep down inside, it made him feel hollow. A mere two weeks ago, she'd been desperate for his attention, lovesick to the core. Now she claimed to hate him, her tone and manner depleted of warmth. The thought left him unsettled, and he didn't know why.

He closed his eyes. Yes, he did. He was in love with her, plain and simple. He'd grown used to her interest, her flirting, the way her eyes softened when his gaze held hers. Suddenly all of it was withdrawn, and it grated on him more than it should. He intended to marry Kathleen. He had no business being concerned whether Charity hated him or not.

He was glad she was asleep. He reached in his coat pocket and pulled out two gold bands. He pushed the larger one on his ring finger and pocketed the other in his trousers. He and Bridget had decided Charity wouldn't go easily. Bridget had given him her old wedding bands, just in case. He pushed the car door open and swung out, firming his resolve. One week on a ship with a woman who hated him was certainly safer than seven days with one who melted his heart at the tilt of a smile. Impassioned love didn't guarantee happiness. His father had been proof of that.

He opened her door and leaned in, shaking her shoulder lightly. She stirred and wrinkled her nose, lids still closed. "Dear Lord, what is that smell?"

"Factories—fertilizer, gasworks, glass—you name it. The aroma of Guinness hops mingling with the delightful smell of raw sewage and animal dung."

Her nose remained scrunched. "It's awful! I may be sick."

Mitch bit his tongue with little success. "After keeping

company with the likes of Gallagher, I'd rather thought you'd be used to it."

Her eyes popped open to reveal a heated blue glare. "I just assumed it was you."

"I washed before I came. Didn't want to offend your delicate sensitivities." He reached in to hoist her in his arms, blanket and all. He stood up carefully to test the cobblestones, then shifted her in his arms. He grunted. "You feel a lot heavier than before, which is odd, given all the tears you spent."

She folded her arms and stared straight ahead. "Good. I hope I'm sheer dead weight."

He bobbled her a bit, pretending to slip on the pavers. She lunged for his neck, her good arm digging into his back. He grinned.

"You can wipe that smirk off your face. There's nothing worse than a cocky kidnapper."

He grunted as he made his way to the docks. "Kidnapper? I prefer the term 'victim.'"

She scalded him with a look. "Excuse me, you barbarian, but I'm the victim here. You're just the baboon they hired to ruin my life."

"Our lives. Keep in mind I may not have a job when I come back."

"Or a fiancée, if she has a brain in her head."

He stopped to adjust his hold, his lips as tight as his grip. "She'll be there," he muttered. He joggled her forward a bit, indicating the ship they would board. "That's our passage. The SS *Hermina*. Takes us through to Boston with stops in Liverpool and New York."

A gasp drifted from her lips. "It's so huge!"

He wended his way up the plank, following a stream of passengers. "Yes, well, unlike you, a lot of people *want* to go to America."

She jerked around. "We're not in steerage—"

"No, ma'am, only the best for a 'victim' like you. We have a first-class cabin."

Her brow angled high. *"We?"*

He glanced down through slitted eyes. "Both of us. *Separately.* It's costing a month's wages, but your reputation will be pristine. At least when it comes to me."

She turned away and jutted her chin high. "I'm sure Kathleen will appreciate that."

"Not as much as me," he mumbled, hauling her through the gangway. He stopped at the end of the line, his breathing noticeably heavy. "Reach inside my coat pocket."

She blinked. "Excuse me?"

"The tickets. They're in my inside pocket."

She stared.

"Unless you want me to drop your carcass on this dirty planking."

"No!" Her hand fumbled inside his jacket, pink tingeing her cheeks.

His lips clamped tight.

She yanked out an envelope and pinched the corner as if it were a snake. "Here."

He inclined his head toward the mustached purser standing before them. "Give it to him . . . darling."

"Good afternoon, Mr. and Mrs. . . . ."

"Dennehy." Mitch bit back a scowl.

Charity stiffened in his arms. She looked up. Her eyes were slivers of heat, but he ignored her. "Give him the tickets, *dear*." He glanced up and down the deck, then turned back to the purser. "B deck. Which way?"

The man's pencil-thin brows bunched in a frown as he waited for Charity to hand over the tickets. She blinked, then suddenly flipped them over her shoulder, smiling as they skittered on the breeze to the brink of the gangway.

"Charity!" Mitch all but dropped her as he lunged to slam

a foot on top, swearing under his breath. Both the tickets and his temper teetered on the edge.

The purser bent to tug them from beneath Mitch's shoe. His eyes flicked up, first to Mitch, then to Charity, taking in the sling on her arm. "Yes, Mr. Dennehy. Your cabins are up that staircase on the starboard side of the ship, 219 and 220." He lifted his chin and handed the tickets back to Charity, then nodded at Mitch. "Adjoining, of course."

Charity flashed him an innocent smile. "Sir, would you be so kind as to call a constable, please? This lout has kidnapped me from my home. He is not my husband, as you will surely see from my name on the ticket. Charity O'Connor, not Dennehy."

The man's gaze flitted to the gold band on Mitch's hand. "I'm sorry, ma'am, but the cabins on this ticket are clearly assigned to Mr. and Mrs. Mitchell Dennehy. I'm afraid it's company policy to refrain from involvement in domestic disputes."

She clutched the purser's arm. "But you've got to believe me. He's not my husband." She wiggled her hand in his face. "Look—no ring. He brought me on this ship for illicit purposes, I assure you. Please, may I speak to the captain?"

Mitch yanked her hard against his chest, then locked her good arm tightly in his grip. "Darling, you asked me to keep your ring in my pocket because your fingers were swollen, remember?" He butted his knee to hold her while he fished in his pants pocket. He held a ring up in his hand. "Here. Do you want to try and put it on?"

Her mouth gaped open. "Of all the low, despicable—"

Mitch leaned close to the purser, man to man. "Sir, I'm afraid my wife is under a bit of a strain. We were married this morning, and I think she's a bit nervous, if you know what I mean."

"He's lying!" Charity shrieked, wriggling to free her arm.

The purser nodded in sympathy. "I understand, sir. It's a big adjustment."

"No, wait, please! This moron is abducting me."

"Thank you, Purser," Mitch muttered, pushing past the crowd that had begun to stare. He barreled toward the steps, clamping onto Charity like a vise.

She thrashed in his arms, attempting to lash her good leg against his thigh. "Stop it," she hissed. "You're hurting me."

"I'm going to hurt you, you little brat, right where it's long overdue."

"My wrist, you're pinching my sprained wrist!"

Instinctively, he released his hold, realizing the lie too late. Her good fist reached up and clipped him on the jaw.

He grunted and pinned her arm to her side, squeezing hard.

She tried to wrench free. "You're going to break it."

He staggered to the top of the stairs and collapsed against the corridor wall. His jaw twitched faster than the pounding of his pulse. "Maybe that's the answer. Break all of your stubborn bones to keep you in line."

"You'll never keep me in line, you thickheaded Neanderthal." Her face and neck strained white as she tried to twist free.

He sucked in a deep breath and continued down the hall, Charity flailing and screaming all the way. Several elderly couples squeezed past with heads turning.

She latched on to one of the men. "Sir, please, you've got to help. He's abducting me!"

Mitch smiled. "Darling, you're just upset. You'll love America, I promise." He smiled at the couples, then dropped his tone to a bare whisper. "Honeymoon jitters."

Understanding flashed in their eyes, causing Charity to whip about all the more. "No, he's lying. Help me, please!"

The gentlemen smiled politely and quickly ushered their wives down the hall, the sound of Charity's accusations echoing behind.

She jerked to face him. Her eyes glinted with fury. "I should have known. First a coward, then a bully, and now a liar. You booked me as your wife? I'd rather starve in steerage."

He gritted his teeth. "Trust me, it can be arranged."

"Trust is the last thing I'd do. I must have been deaf, dumb, and blind to think I was in love with the likes of you."

"You wouldn't know the meaning of the word 'trust' if Daniel Webster personally defined it for you. And as far as love goes, 'deaf, dumb, and blind' describes you perfectly when it comes to knowing anything about it."

He panted while he studied the numbers on each doorway and finally stopped. He shifted a hand and butted his knee while turning the knob. The door squeaked open barely an inch. He used his foot to kick it wide. With a final grunt, he set her on one of the twin beds none too gingerly, barely concerned when she bounced like a spring.

A gasp sputtered from her lips. "Go ahead, break my other leg, why don't you?"

"Don't tempt me," he rasped. He sucked in a deep breath and leaned over, hands on his knees. Apparently three nights a week at Pop Delaney's boxing gym hadn't prepared him for this. He was huffing like a steam engine.

She struggled to rise up on her good arm. If looks could singe, his brows would be aflame. "I despise you, Mitch Dennehy."

He looked up between winded breaths. "So you've said. Best news I've had all day. Give me cold, honest hate over manipulative charm any day."

She dropped back on the bed. "Stop your wheezing, you sissy. You act like I weigh three hundred pounds."

"Yeah? Well, it felt like it."

"The cut on your cheek. Did I do that?"

He absently rubbed his hand to his cheek and winced. "No."

"Who did?"

He lumbered over to a small table against the wall and poured a glass of water from a floral pitcher. He gulped it down. "None of your business."

"Did you fight Rigan?"

He stretched and rolled his neck. "I'm going to get the bags. The toilet facilities are down the hall. Do you need to use them?"

A haze of color washed into her cheeks. "No. Did you fight Rigan?"

He started for the door.

"Yes!"

He turned, his hand on the knob. "You have to use the loo?"

She nodded.

Exhaling loudly, he trudged toward the bed and picked her up. He started for the door.

"No, not really. I just want to know. Did you fight Rigan?"

He whirled around and dumped her back on the bed. "You're relentless, you know that?"

"Did you?"

He propped his hands loosely on his hips. "Yes!"

"Is that why you may not have a job when you come back?"

"Yes."

She averted her gaze, appearing to study the porcelain water pitcher. "Did you hurt him?"

He rubbed a hand over his face. "Black-and-blue marks that would make you proud."

She looked up, her eyes wet. "Thank you."

"You're welcome." He turned to go. "Will you be okay till I get back?"

Barely nodding, she laid her head on the bed, staring at the ceiling.

"Get some rest," he said, noting the shadows under her eyes and the wilt in her face.

He closed the door and headed toward the stairs, his jaw twitching with fatigue.

Rest. Something they both needed desperately, he thought with a tightening in his gut. And probably wouldn't get.

Time to face the music. Charity sighed. Unfortunately, when it came to facing her failings, she never could carry a tune. She rolled over on her side and tried to position her bad leg exactly right. The cabin was completely dark, and she wondered what time it was. Mitch had headed off hours ago, leaving her alone with her thoughts. That hadn't been kind. She had drifted off into periodic bouts of disturbing dreams, always jerking awake with guilt and dread. How could she do this? How could she face them all again?

She licked her lips. But face them she would. For the first time in almost two years for her father. The thought churned in her stomach like a spell of seasickness bubbling in her throat. She put her hand to her mouth to stem the nausea.

They hated her. They had to. After what she'd done to Faith, how could they not? She swallowed, the bitter taste of bile souring her tongue. Soon it would be the same old nightmare all over again. Everyone crazy about Faith.

At least, everyone that mattered. Collin. Father. *Mitch*.

She thought of her mother, and the tension eased in her stomach. Mother loved her, she knew it. Always worrying about her, defending her, showing she cared. And Charity loved her back, fiercely, missing her so much at times it produced a physical ache. In Ireland, they'd been especially close, bonding all the more at the false report of her father's death on the battlefield. In one awful beat of their hearts, they'd exchanged places—Marcy becoming the lost child and Charity the mother with the strong shoulders and tender heart. She'd taken control, becoming the rock everyone leaned on, never allowing her own grief to show. She'd grown up considerably that day, in a way that had birthed a new respect from her mother, grandmother, and Mima.

Charity sighed and stretched out her bad leg. Her mother's welcoming arms were the only beacon in an otherwise dark journey. She hesitated, thinking of Sean, Beth, Steven, and Katie. Well, maybe not the only one. A pang of homesickness took her by surprise as wetness sprang to her eyes. Goodness, she probably wouldn't even recognize Katie. "Eight, going on thirty," her mother would always write. Charity smiled. At least it would be good to see them.

She rolled on her back and peered up in the dark. All at once, her father's face invaded her thoughts, robbing her hope. She swallowed hard. When would it stop? The sick feeling inside? She didn't want to be "Daddy's Girl" anymore. She wanted to be free from it, immune to the fact that her sister was the apple of their father's eye. A warm stream of wetness slid down the side of her face and into her neck, chilling her on impact. All she had ever wanted was his approval. But, no, that had been reserved for Faith. Every crippled step, every measure of progress, had brought a sheen of pride to her father's eyes.

And a tear to her own.

A gentle knock sounded, startling her. The door opened, and a shaft of light spilled across the bed. She propped herself up with her good arm, blinking in the glow of the corridor lamp.

"Are you awake?" he asked, his silhouette looming large in the door.

"Yes."

"Did you sleep?"

Her eyes adjusted to the light, making out the lean curve of his jaw, the firm press of his mouth. "On and off. Mostly off. Dreams."

"Good ones, I hope."

"Some."

"Are you hungry?"

Was she hungry? It shocked her that she hadn't even thought

of it. Breakfast had been a lifetime ago. She pressed a hand to her stomach, feeling it rumble. "I think so."

He shifted in the doorway. "Do you want to eat in your cabin or go to the dining room? Bridget sent food."

She swung her leg carefully over the edge of the bed. "I'm not ready for the dining room." She looked up. "Do you . . . could we . . . eat here?"

A gleam of teeth flashed in the dark. He leaned against the doorframe. "I was hoping you'd say that. The dining room has been crawling with people ever since we set sail."

"We've set sail?" she said weakly.

He straightened. "Hours ago."

A chill shivered through her. She dropped her head in her hand, and a sob wrenched from her throat.

Silently he moved toward the bed, letting the door thud behind him. The bedsprings squeaked as he sat beside her in the dark and bundled her in his arms. She laid her head on his chest and wept, her sobs purging the pain from her soul. He rested his head against hers and rubbed her back, holding her close.

When she'd spent her grief, she stilled in his embrace, calmed by the heat of his body and the rise and fall of his chest. She inhaled deeply, breathing in his scent.

He lifted her chin with his finger. "Are you all done? Can we eat now?"

The corners of her lips tilted in the dark. "What if I'm not?"

She could almost feel the curve of his smile. "Then can we eat first and cry later?"

She sniffed. "I suppose, but can you light the lamp, please? I feel like a mole."

He rose and fumbled in the dark to light a sconce over the table, then struck a match to the wick. A soft glow filled the room.

A gasp parted from her lips. She hadn't noticed before. The

dark hole transformed into a cozy little parlor-boudoir, complete with seascape pictures on the walls, an intricate Persian-style rug, and two delicate Queen Anne–style chairs. "Oh, it's beautiful," she breathed.

He grinned. "It's a cracker-box stateroom, Charity, not the Taj Mahal."

"But it's all mine. You forget I had to share a room with Faith in Boston, with my entire family on the boat over, and with Faith and Emma in Ireland. I didn't expect this."

He glanced around. "Well, it cost enough, even if it isn't much to look at." He squinted at her. "Did you really think I'd book us in steerage?"

With a grunt, she shimmied to the edge of the bed. "I don't know what to think when it comes to you. One minute you infuriate me, the next, you surprise me."

"Does that mean you don't despise me anymore?" He picked up her smaller bag and tossed it on the bed.

She opened the satchel and pulled out the lunch basket Bridget had packed, then looked up in sober consideration. "Maybe."

"Enough to feed me?" He pulled one of the Queen Anne chairs alongside her bed.

With a bare hint of a smile, she placed the basket in her lap and unlatched the lid. She dug in to dole out a slab of cold corned beef and fresh-baked soda bread. She tossed the bread in his lap. He tore off a piece and put it to his lips—

"Wait," she cried, "we've nothing to drink."

He groaned and popped it in his mouth, then laid the rest on the nightstand. He jumped up and headed for the water pitcher.

"Do you think I could have a glass of wine?"

He turned around. "What?"

"You heard me."

A scowl creased his face. "No wine. How 'bout ginger ale?"

"But I don't want ginger ale. Can't I have wine instead? Please?"

His mouth snapped closed. He snatched the pitcher and poured two glasses of water. "You'll drink water or nothing at all." He set the glasses on the nightstand and sat back down.

She squared her shoulders and cradled the basket in her lap. "Fine. No wine, no food."

His jaw shifted back and forth the tiniest bit, a mulish habit she was quickly becoming familiar with. "No wine," he enunciated.

She turned away and closed the basket. "Enjoy the dining hall, then." She felt the heat of his stare and released a deep breath when he finally stormed out. The door slammed behind him.

Minutes later he returned, a scowl on his lips and a bottle in hand. He poured her wine, then set the bottle on the table and handed her the glass. "One per night. Take it or leave it."

"I'll take it, thank you."

He plopped in the chair and reached for his bread once again. He shoved a hunk in his mouth and stared straight ahead, chomping hard.

She smiled. "Now isn't this nice?"

That earned her a half-lidded glare as he continued to chew.

She took a sip of wine, then nibbled on some bread in companiable silence, humming under her breath. She was quiet for a long while, not saying a word until she handed him her glass. "Would you mind setting this on the table please?"

He muttered under his breath and got up to lift the table— water pitcher, wine bottle, and all—to the side of her bed. He snatched several pieces of meat and sat back down.

"Perfect. Thank you so much."

He watched as she picked at the meat in the basket. She

foraged through the pieces, fiercely intent on selecting just the right one. When she found it, she looked up at him with a triumphant smile.

He stopped chewing and swallowed hard. "Are you always this much trouble?"

She took a nibble of the beef. "Not always. But usually. I just know what I want."

"So I've learned. The hard way."

She stuck her nose in the air and reached for her wine. "Don't be so cocky. You're officially off my 'want' list. For all I care, Kathleen can spend the rest of her days with your brow-beating." She took a drink and smiled, staring at him dead-on. "Besides, you're too old."

He choked on a piece of beef.

She handed him a napkin.

His eyes were watering as he coughed into it and wiped his mouth. "Too old?"

"What are you, thirty-eight, thirty-nine?"

His teeth began to grind. "Just turned thirty-six. And in my prime."

"Almost late thirties is the way I see it, pushing forty." Her eyes widened and she grinned, feeling wicked. "Goodness, you could be my father."

He rose in the chair. "You can thank God I'm not, because if I were, I would have—"

She thrust her chin out. "What? You would have what?"

He settled back, a stubborn bent to his mouth. "I would have swatted some sense into you a long time ago. Saved you from being so spoiled."

Another sip of wine and she felt the warmth beginning to seep into her toes. She put it down and picked up some bread. "Spoiled? I'm afraid you've got the wrong sister. That privilege belonged to Faith."

He leaned forward. "Spoiled? Faith? She was the most loving, selfless human being I ever met, more mature than you and I could ever hope to be. There's no woman like her."

His words cut her to the quick. She dropped the bread back into the basket and set it aside, avoiding his eyes. Her hands trembled as she reached for the bottle to refill her glass.

"Charity . . . I'm sorry . . . I shouldn't have said that. It was unkind."

She forced a smile. "Why? It's the truth, isn't it? Everybody knows it. And nobody more than me." She took a large gulp.

His voice gentled. "Take it easy with that, will ya?"

Tears glazed her eyes. "Why? Right now it seems to be the only friend I have."

"That's not true."

"Isn't it? I'm forced away from people who love me, and for what? To live in the shadow of a sister I betrayed, her husband I once loved, and the disappointed father I could never please. And you? Well, you don't even want to be my friend."

"You know why."

She laughed. "Oh, yes, I know why. Because although you may be attracted to me, you're still in love with her. Just like everyone else in Boston." She raised the glass in mock salute and drained it, tilting straight up to catch the last drop. She strained for the bottle, managing to pour more before he could snatch it away.

"You've had enough." He picked up the table and moved it back against the wall, then turned. "And I'm not in love with your sister."

She nodded her head in exaggerated fashion, swaying with the motion. She upended the last of the wine in her glass. "Oh, yes you are. You think you're not, but you are. And both of us—me . . . ," she poked her chest hard several times, then waved a shaky finger in his direction, ". . . and you—are going to see just how very painful Boston can be."

Mitch swore under his breath. *Great.* Bridget would be delighted to know he'd gotten her granddaughter drunk their first night at sea. He should be horsewhipped for allowing her anywhere near alcohol on a near-empty stomach, or otherwise. He took the basket from the bed and set it on the table. He glanced at his watch. "Okay, let's get you to the loo and then to bed."

She fell back, a giggle bubbling from her throat. "What time is it?"

"Almost nine." He retrieved her suitcase by the door and set it next to her.

She sighed and closed her eyes. "Mitch, did you know the room is spinning?"

He pulled her up by her good arm to steady her upright. "Open your eyes; it'll stop."

Her eyes popped open and she giggled again. "Oh, you're right. Much better."

He gave her a glass of water. "Here, drink this."

She took it and sniffed, scrunching her nose. "Why?"

"Because you're drunk, and it will help dilute the alcohol in your system."

"I'm not drunk. I'm tipsy."

"Drink it."

She complied and chugged the entire glass. She handed it back with a hiccup, and a hand flew to her mouth. "Ooops . . . sorry."

"Is there anything you need to take to the bathroom?" He opened her suitcase.

Lifting her chin, she peeked over and yanked out a nightgown.

He eyed it and frowned, uncomfortable with the tiny buttons trailing down the front. "Bridget said she made you a gown you could fasten with one hand. Is this it?"

Her head veered slowly, side to side. "It's at home. I wore

it last night." She thumped back on the bed with a silly smile on her face.

He groaned and set her back up. "Well, let's get you to the bathroom first, then we'll worry about undressing you. Do you have a toothbrush? And a washcloth?"

With an exaggerated nod, she tunneled through a pile of unmentionables to pull both out. She waggled them in the air with a smile. "See? Prepared for anything . . ." Her eyes suddenly expanded and her mouth formed a soft *oh*. Color burnished her cheeks with a telling shade of pink. "D-d-did you say . . . 'undressing' me?"

He stared. At times, she had this endearing quality of innocence that totally disarmed him. A little girl at heart, badly bruised along the way. She blinked at him now, blue eyes wide and soft, and golden hair tumbling in beautiful disarray. He grinned. "Consider it a threat . . . if you don't do what I say."

In the time it took for his heart to pound, she shifted like a chameleon. She gazed up beneath thick lashes. A smile teased on her lips. "What if I don't . . . consider it a threat?"

He shook his head and picked her up. "Always the vamp. When are you going to realize that will only buy you heartbreak?"

Her head dropped back with a giggle. "I don't know." The smile suddenly dissolved on her face. "It certainly brought me heartbreak with you."

He shifted to open the door and then headed to the bathroom. Her satin blouse strained over her breasts, leaving little to the imagination. He swallowed and quickened his pace down the hall. "Well, at least that's over now. I'm off your want list, remember?"

She waved her good arm, then let it drop, completely limp. "Oh . . . that's right."

He knocked on the door. No answer. He carried her in and positioned her in a stall, then waited outside until she was ready, grinning as she sang off-key. He watched her as she brushed her teeth, eyes closed and face intense, and wondered who the real Charity was. He found himself wishing he could find out.

She spit in the sink, then wiped her mouth with the towel. She gave him a lopsided grin. "All done. Time for night-night."

He carried her back and set her on the bed, lunging for her good arm when she started to topple. He straightened her back up, his hands hovering to make sure she stayed put. He let go and snatched the nightgown from the bed, then unbuttoned it halfway down. He put it in her lap and stood straight. "Okay, Bridget says you can get undressed by yourself. I've unbuttoned the nightgown to make it easier to pull over your head. I'll be in the next room with the door cracked if you need anything. Okay?"

"Okay." She smiled and fell over.

"Are you all right?"

"Uh-huh." She lay flat on her back, satin blouse strained and eyes closed.

He shifted his feet. "Charity?"

"Mmmm?"

"You need to undress."

"Okay." She began to snore.

He grinned and shook her. "Charity, wake up. You need to undress."

"Why?"

He rubbed the back of his neck. "I don't know. That's what ladies do. It's more comfortable."

"Pretty comfortable now."

He tugged her up and pulled her toward the edge of the bed, eyes closed and chin drooping. Her feet dangled over the side. With an exasperated sigh, he unlatched the few pearl buttons from her blouse. The folds of satin flopped open. Air locked in his throat. He swallowed hard and shook her arm. "Charity, wake up. You need to do the rest."

Her eyes fluttered open. She looked down at her chemise, her full breasts edged with lace. Two bright splotches of pink popped out on her cheeks. In slow motion, she gasped and splayed a hand across deep cleavage, providing a poor mask for the temptation before him. She avoided his eyes. "Go, please! I'll do the rest."

He spun around and strode to her door, flipping the bolt from the inside. Without a backward glance, he unlatched her adjoining door and left it ajar as he entered his room. He stood behind it, head cocked to listen.

"Charity?"

"What?"

"Are you going to be okay?"

"Yes, thank you. Good night."

He sighed and began to remove his tie, certain he had never been this tired. One thing was for sure. When his head finally hit the pillow, he was going to sleep forever.

"Mitch?"

He dropped a shoe on the floor and raced to the door, leaning close. "Did you call?"

"I think I'm going to be sick."

He hung his head. *If* his head ever hit the pillow.

He flopped over in the narrow bed for the twentieth time, his feet ice-cold as they jutted over the edge by a foot. He jerked the blanket down with his big toe, groaning when it dislodged from his shoulders. A chill skittered down his bare chest. He yanked it back up, opting for cold feet over a shivering torso. He sighed and stared at the ceiling. The sound of whitecaps battering the hull of the ship drummed incessantly in his brain.

There were any number of reasons he couldn't sleep tonight: the cold, the rough sea, the small bed, the countless trips to the bathroom. *The image of Charity in her chemise.*

He drew his legs up a bit, huddling under the blanket. All reasons that had afflicted his body with a vengeance. But only one ravaged his mind. He jabbed the pillow several times and worked his head in, trying to get comfortable.

It was downright unfair. Having to lie here like this for a solid week while the most desirable woman he'd ever known lay in a bed just a few short feet away. Blast Bridget Murphy. And blast her granddaughter. She was the last thing he wanted to think about. He grunted. But one small and lacey chemise had certainly taken care of that.

He shifted and tried to think of something else. Charity bent over the toilet while he held her hair out of her face. Yes, definitely better. Her face white and sunken as he swabbed her with a cool cloth, the full lips drained of all color. His heart stirred with compassion, and he lunged from the bed. No! He didn't want to feel sorry for her. That made him more vulnerable. He couldn't afford that. He buffed his arms with his palms while he padded to the moonlit porthole. He held his wristwatch to the shaft of light streaming in. Almost four o'clock in the morning. He moaned and dropped back into bed. The springs objected with deafening squeaks, paralyzing the muscles in his stomach. Dear God, please don't let her wake up. *Again.*

He held his breath while he waited. Ten seconds. Twenty. Forty. One minute. He slowly released it, his body finally yielding to the curve of the bed. Thank God. She was still asleep.

And he was still awake.

Pray.

The silent directive shivered his skin more than the chill of the room. It had echoed in his brain, but it hadn't come from him. He was dead certain. His lids flipped up, and he stared at the dark ceiling. He forgot the shivers, suddenly aware of a presence that generated warmth and peace to his cold and disrupted soul.

Pray for her.

He nodded. "I will, I will. But what about me? I'm the one in trouble here. I need your strength. I can't stop thinking about her." He shifted on his side and pinched the covers around his shoulders. "Ya gotta help me. I don't want to love her. I want to love Kathleen."

Pray.

His jaw hardened. "That's your solution to everything, isn't it?" He squeezed his eyes shut and exhaled. "Sorry. I know what you want, and I'll do it. Every time I think of her, blasted chemise or no, I'll pray. You have my word on that." He glanced up at the ceiling, a scowl on his lips. "Which will pretty much be all the time, if I don't get some serious grace from your end."

He closed his eyes again and sighed. "Help her, please. Get through that thick skull of hers. Open her heart to you. Heal the hurt. Between Faith and her, and their father." He hesitated, not sure if he wanted to utter the next words. "And help her to forgive me for whatever she thinks I did, rejecting her, denying her love . . ." A smile tilted his lips in the dark. "Kidnapping her."

He drew in chilled air, releasing it in one long, liberating breath. "Use me, Lord, to reach her. To teach her what Faith taught me. To bring her to you."

He rolled over on his side and sank into the pillow, his prayers thickening on his lips. His lids felt heavy. He succumbed, drifting in his mind to thoughts of Kathleen. She was kneeling, bent over her bed, beseeching their God. He closed his mind's eye and she faded, leaving him with profound peace and one last prayer on his lips. "Don't stop. Please."

⌁ ⌁

Rigan slammed her head against the wall with one casual slap. Her father did nothing. Uncle Paul stood beside him, both indifferent, both smoking their pipes. Charity put her hand to her head, barely able to contain the pain. Her fingers were wet and sticky. She stared at them, the shock of blood dulling the throb in her brain.

"Daddy," she screamed, but he only turned away. Rigan jerked her up and set her on his lap, whispering familiar words. "It's all right, Charity. Your daddy left, but I'll take care of you. He doesn't love you like I will. You're my beautiful, beautiful girl."

Charity squirmed to get up, smoke and tears pricking her eyes. "I want my daddy."

Rigan stroked his hand up her leg. "Shhh . . . Your daddy's gone, but I'm still here . . ."

The hand continued to move.

Charity screamed.

"Shhh . . . I don't want to have to spank you, but I will . . ."

He squeezed her shoulder, shaking until she stopped.

"Charity, wake up."

She jolted in the bed and opened her eyes, a horrendous pain in her head. The pounding of her heart began to slow as relief flooded through her.

It was only a dream.

She blinked and gulped a breath of air. A blur of skin loomed over her. Mitch came into full view, bent over and stripped to the waist. His blue eyes were bleary with sleep, and the clean line of his jaw was heavily shadowed with overnight stubble.

"It was just a nightmare. You're okay."

She blinked again and pulled the cover to her chin, the nightmare suddenly forgotten. Blood warmed her cheeks as she stared wide-eyed, taking in his hard, lean muscles and the blond coiled hair matting his chest. She swallowed hard, the warmth in her cheeks apparently contagious—it was spreading through her body like a high-grade fever.

He yawned and dragged his fingers through his short, unruly curls, bicep bulging with the motion. He glanced at his watch. "It's five twenty. You don't plan on getting up, do you?"

She continued to stare, her mouth agape.

He glanced down, then quickly up, a sullen slant to his brows. He jerked his pajama bottoms up a fraction of an inch, then scrubbed a hand across that golden mat of hair. "You dragged me out of bed, what the devil did you expect?"

"I woke you a number of times throughout the night, as I recall, and you were always dressed. Do you sleep that way?"

He slacked a hip and ran a hand over his face. "I put my shirt on every time you called, and yes, I do sleep this way. What business is that of yours?"

"Why didn't you dress this time?"

He groaned, all bleariness gone. "Because I was sleeping! *Finally.* Until your blood-curdling scream shattered the precious little rest I've been able to get."

"Well, hog-tie me and I'll walk the plank. Serves you right for dragging me on this ship. And stop yelling, I have a splitting headache."

"Good." He glowered and spun on his heel, charging toward his cabin.

"Wait, please!"

He stopped at the door, his back to her and fingers taut on the knob. She massaged her forehead, annoyed at the way his powerful back tapered into a low-swung waist. "I have to go to the bathroom," she whispered.

She watched his broad shoulders sag. The tendons of his thick muscles twitched. He jerked the door open and let it bang against the wall. She groaned and put a hand to her eyes. He disappeared for several minutes, finally returning with his shirt hanging out of his pants.

She peeked up from under her hand, a finger and thumb rubbing each temple. "And could you please not yell? I feel awful."

He grunted and swooped her up from the bed. He started for the door.

"Wait, my robe."

He kept moving, balancing her with his knee to unlock the door. "You didn't wear it last night, you don't have to wear it now."

"But it's daytime."

He flipped open the door and tore down the hall. "It's bloomin' five thirty in the morning, Charity. I guarantee, nobody's up but you."

She glanced at his shadowed jaw, stiff and prickly with whiskers. His mouth was clamped tight, and the lower lip protruded in a mulish manner. She grinned. "And you."

His narrowed gaze swept down over the half-buttoned nightgown before flicking up to her smile. His eyes softened just a tad. "You are the biggest little brat I have ever seen."

She leaned her head against his chest and sighed, rubbing the bridge of her nose. "I know. I'm sorry. But you deserve it for kidnapping me."

"So you keep telling me." He stood before the bathroom door and kicked it with his shoe, waiting to see if anybody answered. He pushed the door open and deposited her into a stall. "I'll be outside. Call when you're ready."

"I will. And, Mitch?"

He stopped, hand on the door.

"Thank you for taking care of me last night."

The corners of his mouth shifted. "You're welcome."

The door slammed behind him, and she sighed. He really was a decent sort of fellow. That is, when he wasn't being obnoxious. Which wasn't all that often. She scowled. It was a real shame he was one of the most handsome men she had ever laid eyes on. It made hating him all the more difficult. And she wanted to hate him. The alternative was too frightening. His rejection before had been painful enough. Now that he was bent on marrying Kathleen, if she tried to seduce him, his denial would only destroy her. And she'd already danced that reel one time too many.

"I'm ready," she called, and he was there in a heartbeat, his demeanor considerably improved. He held her at the sink so she could wash her hands, his eyes studying her face in the mirror. She smiled. "How many times did we do this last night?"

His mouth quirked up. "Four. Not counting now."

"I'm sorry. I usually don't get up in the middle of the night. It must have been the wine."

He gave her a half-lidded look. "Must have been."

"I . . . I got sick, I know. Did you . . ."

His lips twitched. "I did. Wasn't too much of a mess, though. Fortunately, we managed to get to the toilet in time. A cool, wet washcloth, and good as new."

She bit her lip and pressed a hand to her head. "Not exactly. My head is killing me."

He shifted her in his arms and opened the door. "Nothing a few hours of sleep and two aspirin won't cure." He fumbled with the latch of her door, finally swinging it open. He laid her on the bed. "I'll get that aspirin." He returned with a glass of water and pills in hand.

With one, long gulp, she drained the water.

His brow shot up. "Thanks. That's another trip to the bathroom."

She giggled and handed him the glass, then snuggled down into the bed until the covers rested at her chin. She sobered. "Mitch . . . about last night, I don't know what went wrong. That's never happened before."

He set the glass down and tucked the covers in on both sides of her bed, giving her a wry smile. "Well, you're not used to drinking all that much, especially on an empty stomach. Add to that some pretty rough whitecaps, and it was bound to happen. It's my fault for getting the wine in the first place. Bridget would string me up."

She grinned. "Yes, she would. Don't let me bamboozle you again."

He stood and propped his hands loosely on his hips, a smile fidgeting on his lips. "I won't. Now get some sleep." He moved toward the door.

"Mitch?"

He turned.

"Can we call a truce? If we're going to be on this boat for six more days, I'd like to get along." She looked down, a lump forming in her throat. "Besides, I could really use a friend."

He didn't respond, and she glanced up to see the muscles working in his throat, his eyes unreadable in the dim morning light. "I'd like that, Charity."

"Real friends, this time. No games. I know you intend to marry Kathleen."

He nodded, lowering his gaze to the floor. "Sounds good. Now get some sleep."

"You mean let *you* get some sleep."

He looked up, and a slow grin spread across his lips. "Exactly."

11

Collin groaned and hurled his last card on the pile. "I can't believe it—you did it again. We went set. Where's your head tonight, Faith?"

Faith blinked, her hands still on top of the few tricks she'd managed to take. She swallowed, aware of everyone's stares. "It's just a card game, Collin. I'm having an off night, that's all."

He shoved his chair back from the table and jumped up, storming toward the kitchen. "Yeah? Well, Pinochle's not all that difficult, you know. I need some milk." He huffed out of the dining room. His muscled arm rammed the swinging kitchen door so hard it swayed and squeaked for a solid fifteen seconds. Faith blew out a noisy breath and stood, her shoulders squared for battle. "Mother, Father, I apologize for Collin. He's not been himself the last few days." Her chin jutted up. "But that's about to change."

Her parents exchanged a look.

She pushed her chair back in and rounded the table to kiss them good night.

Marcy reached up and patted her cheek. "He's just nervous,

Faith. Keep your tongue in check. Men have a tendency to get a bit testy when they're about to lose their independence."

Patrick chuckled. "Your mother's right, darlin'. I wasn't too bad, I don't think, but Collin's a pretty stubborn man—"

"Hah! Don't go putting on airs, Patrick O'Connor, you were one of the worst. Snapping at me at every turn for weeks before the wedding. You and that boy are cut from the same stubborn cloth—prime Longhorn cow leather."

Patrick's brows sloped up. "How can you say that? I'm hurt."

She rose, her lips skewed into a wry smile. "Because it's true, my love. You were every bit as nasty as Collin, right up until the wedding, and don't you deny it."

He pushed away from the table and stretched, a sudden twinkle lighting his eye. "But that all changed on the honeymoon, now didn't it, Marceline?"

She blushed. "Patrick! I can't believe you're saying that in front of your own daughter."

"Really, Mother, the way you two moon over each other, do you think it's a surprise to any of us?"

"Faith!" Marcy's cheeks fused scarlet.

Patrick's laughter rang out as he stood and put an arm around his wife. "Marcy, Faith is a woman about to be married. This will all be common knowledge for her in a few weeks. Come on, woman, I'm tired. Take these old bones of mine to bed."

Marcy wriggled out of his grasp and gave her daughter a kiss. "Don't be too hard on him, Faith. He's a wonderful man, you know. Just a bit scared. Tell him good night for us, will you?"

Faith nodded and stacked the cards in a pile. She glared at the kitchen door, forcing herself to be calm. Taking a deep breath, she approached and pushed it open.

Collin sat at the table, a half-eaten ham sandwich on the plate before him. His eyes bore through her as he stuffed the rest in his bulging cheeks and chewed hard. Faith ambled over to the icebox to pour herself a glass of milk. She strolled over, plunked it on the table, and sat. Locking gazes with him over the rim of her glass, she took a sip. She licked her lips and set the glass back down. "So, are you going to tell me what's really bothering you? Or are you going to sit there and stuff your face like a pig-headed mule?"

He glared and swallowed hard, his gray eyes narrowing to black. "That's the pot calling the kettle black if I ever heard it. What makes you think something's wrong?"

She placed her arms on the table, fingers tightly laced. "Oh, I don't know, maybe it's all the sulking and nasty temper you've been giving me all week. If you don't want to marry me, Collin, just come out and say it."

He shoved the plate away and reached for his milk, upending it until it was all gone. He slammed the glass back down. "Don't tempt me, Faith."

She shot up from the chair with heat scorching her cheeks. She thumped a fist on the table. "Just what exactly is your problem?"

He slanted forward. "You're my problem. My oh-so-honest fiancée, the one who hides things from me."

"What are you talking about?"

He stood up and leaned hard on the table, the thick tendons of his arm protruding below his rolled-up shirtsleeve. "I'm talking about Charity."

"I told you she set sail two days ago. What more is there to know?"

He straightened, slow and deliberate, his gaze unflinching as it pierced her own. "Oh, I don't know, maybe that your *ex-fiancé* is bringing her?" The word sounded like a curse.

The blood drained from her cheeks. She took a shallow breath. "Collin, I was going to tell you, but I didn't want to upset you. You've been on edge these last few weeks."

"So I have to hear it from your mother? Who, by the way,

is just thrilled to see 'dear old Mitch' again." He fairly spit the name in her face. "Not unlike her daughter, I'm sure."

Faith skirted the table to stand before him, her eyes contrite as she stared up. "Collin, look at you. This is why I didn't say anything. You have nothing to worry about."

"You're right I don't because you won't be talking to him."

She stepped back. Her eyes expanded as she put a hand to her chest. "Excuse me?"

"You heard me. Other than hello and goodbye, I forbid you to talk to him."

"You can't do that."

"Yes, I can. A wife has to submit to her husband. It's in the Bible."

Faith planted her hands on her hips and leaned in, the heat in her eyes matching his own. "One minor problem. I'm not your wife—yet. And if this keeps up, it doesn't look promising."

Collin groaned and jerked her into his arms, crushing her to his chest. "What are we doing here, Faith? I love you. I don't want to fight."

She relaxed in his arms. "Me, either, Collin. But you can't bully me into not talking to Mitch."

He picked her up and sat down in the chair, placing her on his lap. He had a dangerous gleam in his eye. "No, but I can make sure you're too breathless to do it . . ."

"Collin, what are you—"

He dipped her back and cradled her neck while his mouth searched hers with a vengeance. Her insides grew weak as the heat began to build, and she moaned when his mouth strayed to the lobe of her ear. Dear Lord, she loved this man! His hands roamed her back. They edged lower to pull her close.

She twisted away, her breathing accelerating. "Collin, stop it . . . now!"

With an evil grin, he pulled her back up and steeled his arms around her, eyes half-lidded as if he'd just fallen out of bed.

His gaze settled on her lips. "You won't be able to stop me in a few weeks," he whispered in a husky tone.

Her breathing quickened. "I know. Whatever will I do?"

He tugged at the corner of her lower lip with his teeth, then slid his mouth across hers. "Give in, of course." His words were warm and low against her mouth. "First this, then whatever I want."

She lurched in his arms, ready to pop him. He laughed, and his deep, throaty chuckle filled the kitchen. "I'm crazy about you, Faith O'Connor, you know that? But I have a feeling you and God will have words about a particular subject."

"And what might that be, you mule-headed Irishman?"

He tapped her nose with his finger, his grin positively annoying. "Submission. Ephesians 5:22. I suggest you read up on it before the wedding."

She slapped his hand away and tried to wriggle free. "And I suggest you read what follows, Mr. McGuire—'husbands, love your wives'—that is, if you want a willing wife in your bed."

He laughed again, hauling her close despite her objections. He dug his lips into the crook of her neck, causing her to giggle and moan at the same time. "Oh, I'll have that, all right, Mrs. McGuire," he whispered in her ear, "and you can empty your purse on that."

❦ ❦

Mitch blinked. Oh. What a surprise. She was stunning.

He worked hard to mask his approval, but it wasn't easy. She sat on the bed, sheer layers of pale blue surrounding her like a cloud. Sweet saints in heaven, he was staring at a blessed angel. His eyes scanned up to the V-neck bodice where a gauzy overlay did little to obscure what lay beneath. He swallowed. Nope, definitely not the pearly gates.

She bit her lip as a hint of color washed into her cheeks. "You . . . said to dress up, and this is all I have. I'm sorry."

He forced his gaze up to her face and smiled. "Don't be. You look beautiful. But I think you're going to have to wear Bridget's ring to fend the men off."

"Are you still wearing yours?"

He looked down at his hand, a faint smile on his lips. "Yeah."

"Then I'll wear mine. Can you get it for me?"

He nodded and left, returning a few moments later with the ring. She held out her hand. "Will you put it on?"

He slipped it on her finger, suddenly realizing he was holding his breath. He released it slowly. "Ready?" He picked her up in his arms. "Our dinner reservations are for seven. We don't want to be late." He stopped. "Don't you need the sling for your arm?"

"I don't think so. I want to feel pretty tonight. And my arm's much better. Really."

She seemed different as he carried her down the corridor, quiet, content, as if she had no need to talk. He was grateful. Seeing her dressed up for him, putting the ring on her finger, had left him undone, confused, moody. Heads turned as they stood at the entrance to the dining room, the sight of a man carrying a woman unusual in itself, but Mitch knew the stares would have been the same had she walked by his side. He saw men gawking at her, and his lips pressed tight. Blasted leches. For pity's sake, she wasn't the only woman in the room.

She was for him.

"Your name, sir?" the maître d' asked.

"Dennehy," he snapped, aware of Charity's gaze.

"Yes, Mr. and Mrs. Dennehy, your table is ready. Follow me, please."

Mitch strode behind him. The maître d' pulled out her chair, and Mitch set her down, carefully pushing it back in.

She adjusted her skirt. "Thank you."

The maître d' handed them menus and returned to his post.

Charity leaned forward with a flush on her cheeks and shielded her face with the menu. "I'm sorry, Mitch. I suppose it's embarrassing carrying a cripple in."

He looked up. Embarrassed? *By her?* He grabbed her hand. "No, it has nothing to do with that. It has everything to do with my temper and the way men ogle you." He released her hand and cleared his throat, heat crawling up the back of his neck. He pretended to study his menu, not comprehending a word on the sheet. "Not the least of which is me. Forgive me, Charity, for all the times I did the same."

"But you were the one I wanted to ogle me, Mitch."

He glanced up, his mouth flat. "I've done my fair share, and I'm not proud of it. Both of our lives would be very different right now if I hadn't."

"I know." She looked away. "I . . . don't think I ever really asked your forgiveness . . . for what happened." She swallowed hard. "I regret it . . . not because it caused me to fall in love with you, but because it caused you so much heartbreak." She looked up and took a deep breath. "And Faith."

"She's forgiven you, Charity. Whatever she did to hurt you, can't you forgive her?"

Her lips parted as if she had difficulty breathing, the gauze of her dress rising and falling.

"She loves you, you know," he whispered.

She nodded and picked at the edge of her napkin. "I know."

He sighed and refocused on the menu. "Let's order. We have all night to talk."

She ordered tenderloin and lobster like a little girl on a holiday, and he couldn't help but think he enjoyed her this way. He offered wine, but she refused, giving him the same warm feeling inside as if he had a glass himself. They talked for hours, over potato puffs and almond green beans and crêpes Suzette, barely pausing long enough to chew. She divulged Mrs. Shaw's deepest secrets and laughed over Emma's gentle wit, and grew melancholy over her own dreams to be a shop owner some day. She plied him with questions about himself and taunted until he answered, making him feel like the most important man in the room. When the waiter presented the check, he fought the inclination to order cordials. He didn't want the night to end.

"I've cost you a small fortune, haven't I?" she asked, a bit of hesitation in her tone.

He smiled. "I can afford it."

"Without a job?"

His gaze narrowed. "The *Times* isn't the only paper in Ireland, you know. I've had offers before; I'll get them again."

"Rigan won't stop you?"

"Rigan won't be around."

"What do you mean?"

He reached inside his coat pocket for his wallet. He didn't answer.

"Mitch, tell me, please. What do you mean?"

He exhaled. "I mean I threatened him. Told him if he was in Dublin when I came back, I was going to the papers."

"To do what?"

He slapped his money on the table. "Expose him for the coward he is. Beating on women, taking advantage of them."

"But with me gone, you won't have proof."

"I don't need proof to sully his reputation. That's all I intend to do. Label him for the abuser he is so Dublin society thumb their noses at him."

"You hate him, don't you? And not just because of me."

He paused, wondering how much to disclose. He held her gaze. "I did hate him, and I'm working on that. But it's hard to forgive scum like Gallagher."

"What did he do to you?"

He pushed his chair back and stood. "You feel like some fresh air?"

Her eyes lit up. "A moonlight stroll?"

He smiled. "More like a moonlight sit, on benches on the deck. Might be pretty cold."

"We have our coats . . . and the blanket you wrapped me in when you abducted me."

He grinned and pulled her chair away from the table. "I thought we weren't going to discuss our prior enmity. We're friends, remember?"

She giggled. "Oh. I forgot. Sorry."

He squatted down. "Look, you stay here, and I'll run up and get the blanket and our coats, okay?"

She nodded, watching as he jumped up and strode toward the door. He turned the head of every woman in the room, annoyingly handsome in his dark suit. Charity took a quick sip of water. Why was this happening? Now that her anger toward him was fading, she was falling in love with him all over again, and the thought terrified her. He'd made himself quite clear. Other than as a friend, he didn't want her. She thought of the way his eyes had raked over her in the cabin. Correction. He wanted her . . . just not as his wife.

She groaned and dropped her head in her hands, reflecting on the last twenty-four hours. How he'd taken care of her when she was sick, his tenderness, his kindness. Her heart ached to belong to him forever. To be the woman he cared for always. And she, him.

"Are you all right, Mrs. . . . ."

She looked up, her eyes growing wide. A debonair man stood before her, devouring her with his eyes. She pressed a hand over the V of her dress. "Yes, I'm fine, thank you."

He smiled and bowed slightly. "Graham Huntington. And you are . . ."

"Charity O'Con—" The name froze on her lips. She swallowed hard. "Dennehy. Charity Dennehy. My husband just left to get our coats for a moonlight stroll."

He smiled again. "A real pity, Charity Dennehy. Married happily, dare I ask?"

"Extremely." The tone was a near growl.

Charity looked up, relieved to see Mitch. He loomed over Huntington by a head, glowering as if he intended to stare him into the floor. Huntington smiled. "I was just admiring your wife's extraordinary beauty, Mr. Dennehy. You're a lucky man."

"So are you, sir, that I arrived when I did. Good night."

Huntington bowed and left. Mitch scowled and helped her on with her wrap. He muttered under his breath.

"What, Mitch?"

He began to button her coat. "I said I pity the man who marries you. Men hovering around the rest of your life, even when you're old, I'll wager. You're too beautiful for your own good, Charity O'Connor."

"Thank you. I think."

He picked her up in his arms. "Don't you get tired of it? Men hounding you?"

She smiled, a hint of sadness in her manner. "Only when the right one doesn't."

He carried her through the doors out onto the deck. The rush of cool air stung her face.

"Too cold?" he asked.

"No, I like it. Clean air, the pungent smell of brine. And the moon—just look at it on the water. Like a ribbon of fire, rippling on the waves. Thank you for bringing me out."

He chuckled and made his way toward a bench at the far end of the stern. "You won't be thanking me if I don't get you bundled up in this blanket." He put her down and sank beside her, wrapping the blanket around them both. He pulled her against his chest, then leaned against the wall. "How's this?"

She sighed and nestled back, contentment swallowing her up like the strong arms of the man who held her. "Perfect."

She burrowed in closer and chuckled softly. "I can't believe I thought I hated you."

"That's when you thought you were in love with me. Now that we're friends, you're right. It is perfect."

"Mmmm." She tilted her head up. "Mitch?"

"Yes?"

"What happened with Rigan? In your past?" His arms stiffened around her, and she laid her head back. "I'm sorry. You don't have to tell me if you don't want to. I was just curious."

"Actually, now that we're friends, I'd like to. It might help you understand why I was so adamant about you not seeing him." He hesitated. "And other things."

"Other things?"

"My lack of trust in women. You, in particular. And why Faith broke through."

She held her breath. "Tell me. Please."

He was quiet for a moment while his eyes focused on the shimmer of moon striping the water. When he finally spoke, his voice was a monotone. "Rigan Gallagher is responsible for the death of my wife."

Charity felt like a wave had slammed over the hull and into her face. "Your . . . wife? You were married?"

"Ten years ago. Her name was Anna."

"Anna . . ," Charity whispered the name, fascinated by it. "Was she . . . beautiful?"

His laugh was harsh. "Incredibly. Hair as black as midnight and eyes like gold flame."

Charity swallowed to moisten her throat. "Did you . . . love her?"

He didn't answer right away, and she could feel the steady beat of his heart against her ear. "I thought I did. I was young and swept away by her beauty. By the time I learned it was skin deep, we'd been married a year."

"Did she love you?"

"I think she did at first, but I was gone so much, working at the paper till the early hours of the morning, that she got resentful. I can't say I really blamed her. She was a new bride, stuck at home all day in a run-down flat. She didn't understand what I had accomplished. That I worked my way up from a plucky paperboy hawking papers in front of the *Times* to junior editor. It was unheard of, and I wasn't taking any chances. It required work and a lot of hours. I hardly saw Anna at all that first year."

"How did Rigan enter the picture?"

Mitch sighed. His chest shifted against her cheek. "He hated me from the get-go. Blaine Gallagher used to toss pound notes into my tin can whenever he stumbled into the paper, which wasn't often. He liked me, or at least my spunk. Used to say he wished Rigan had some of my gumption. I have a feeling he went home and told Rigan that, rubbed it in his face. When Blaine gave me a job with the paper, he enlisted Michael to mentor me. I think he did it partially to goad Rigan into developing an interest in the *Times*. Only it didn't work. The only interest Rigan had was in making me pay for winning the respect of his father."

Mitch shifted again, tightening his arms around her. "You okay out here? Not too cold?"

"I'm fine if you are."

He grunted and continued. "I didn't know Anna was seeing him until it was too late."

Charity jolted up, her eyes wide in the dark. "She cheated on you?"

He nodded, softly pressing her head back against his chest. He twined his fingers through the hair at the back of her neck, as if unaware of the motion. She held her breath and closed her eyes, his touch sending peaceful warmth through her body.

"He knew I was never home and took advantage. Knew Anna was my wife and decided to go in for the kill. She fell hard. And why not? He was charming, good-looking, and had more money at the age of twenty than I could dream of in a lifetime."

"Did she . . ."

The harsh timbre of Mitch's laugh vibrated against her cheek. "Yes, she was definitely sleeping with him. I think he got quite a thrill out of the fact that he could share my wife with me. Especially since I shared his father's attention."

"Mitch, I'm so sorry. It must have been awful. Anna sounds a bit like your mother . . ."

"She was, in a way. But mostly she was just young and naïve. Rigan promised her the moon, and she went for it."

"What happened?"

He released another heavy sigh. "She waited till I got home one night after a particularly grueling shift and told me she was leaving me."

"For Rigan?"

"She thought so. Claimed she loved him. Said he promised to marry her."

"How? Not divorce?"

"Annulment. A special dispensation, bought and paid for." His voice was savage.

"But the marriage was consummated . . ."

"Apparently he convinced her it didn't matter. Not if they didn't know."

Charity shivered. "How awful."

"I was eaten up by rage, not so much because I loved her, but because it was Rigan who had poisoned our marriage. I packed my things and left. I moved in temporarily with Bridie and her husband, Wesley, my best friend at the *Times*. I wanted to kill Rigan, but they got me through it. I owed them my life."

Charity hesitated, reluctant to put voice to her words. "How did . . . how did she die?"

He shivered, transferring a chill to her bones. "Suicide. Slit her wrists. And all because Rigan wouldn't marry her."

Charity jerked around to stare in his face. It was rock hard in the moonlight, a glimmer of wetness in his eyes. "Oh, Mitch, no."

He blinked, and his gaze seemed lost in the rolling waves. "She was pregnant and he wouldn't marry her. So she killed herself and her child instead of coming to me." He closed his eyes. "And every day I live with the same question. Was there something I could have done? Should have done? To save the life of my wife and her child." His voice strained to a rasp. "A child that could have very well been mine."

Charity pressed in close. "I'm so sorry. I wish there was something I could say . . . or do."

He lifted her chin. "You can. You can promise you'll stay away from Rigan Gallagher and any man like him. Someone as beautiful as you is bound to be a magnet for men like that. A magnet for men like I used to be, lusting after women to satisfy their own needs. That's why I fell in love with your sister. Because she had something pure inside, an honesty, a conviction that had nothing to do with her being better than you or more lovable. It had everything to do with her deep love for God and his precepts. Faith wasn't good by nature. None of us are, nor will we ever be. But Faith loved God, trusted him, relied on him, no matter what. That type of commitment won her the desire of her heart, just like God promised. It can do the same for you if you let it. If you let him."

Charity looked away, her eyes trained on the sliver of moon-light rippling across the water. "I understand you a lot better now. Anna and your mother are why trust is so important to you." She paused, her voice a bare whisper. "And Faith is how you found it." A sad smile pulled at her lips. "I never stood a chance, did I? After what I did?"

"You do with God. And that's all that really matters. Run to him, Charity. He can change your life like he changed Faith's . . . and mine." He sat up and stretched. "Ready to go in? We've had a long day and not much sleep before it."

She shuddered and nodded her head.

He picked her up and pressed a kiss to her cheek, a faint smile on his lips. "You're not going to be waking me up all hours of the night, are you?"

She jutted her chin toward the sky. "I'm afraid you're out of luck, Mr. Dennehy. It makes little difference. Wine or fresh sea air—both do it every time."

❦ ❦

He hadn't felt this close to a woman since Faith.

And it scared him silly. Suddenly they were friends. Honest-to-goodness friends. No embarrassment, no flirting, no thoughts of anything more.

Well, almost.

They spent every waking moment together, talking, laughing, moonlight chats on the deck or playing cards. Dining in or dining out, it didn't matter. Even the powerful attraction they'd shared seem tempered, quiet, not raging like before. He suspected it wasn't gone, only disarmed by the focus on friendship. Kind of like trying to touch someone through a pane of glass. You wanted to, but the connection was cold. He thought of Kathleen, probably praying her heart out for him, and smiled. The letter he'd left had asked for her prayers, and he was pretty sure they were in play. A smile flickered on his lips. *Good girl.*

Simply put, he couldn't remember when he'd enjoyed a woman more. Okay, he could. *Faith.* He ignored the niggling guilt in his gut. And this was the sister that had betrayed them both. A familiar tightening creased his jaw. As a woman, he didn't trust her a hair beyond her shadow. But as a friend? He was starting to cave. And that scared him silly too.

He positioned the cards in his hand and studied her, narrowing his eyes to assess the woman before him. She lounged on her bed, back propped against the headboard and legs stretched flat. She crossed delicate ankles beneath a blue muslin skirt while her bare feet twitched back and forth. She chewed on her lip, apparently trying to decide which card would bring him down.

"Do I have to impose a time limit?" he growled.

With lips kinked in thought, her lashes flipped up. "Don't threaten me, Dennehy. I'm the invalid here. I'll take as long as I please, and there isn't a thing you can do about it."

He bit back a grin, going for stern. "No, I suppose there isn't." He crossed his arms on the table and steeled his jaw. "Not unless you want to eat or go to the bathroom or anything else that your demanding little heart desires."

Her nose lifted in the air. "I have my crutches, thank you. I'll just use them. My arm is stronger every day. Besides, who needs a whining, condescending, ill-tempered nursemaid?"

He slid an arm along the back of his chair and gave her a veiled stare. "I swear that before this week is done, you little brat, I'm going to turn you over my knee."

She hurled a card down and looked up, her blue eyes glinting with challenge. "I believe I'd like to see you try. By the time I got done with you, you'd be huffing and puffing like the first day on the ship." She tilted her head and presented him with an angelic smile. "But then, I suppose that happens to men of your age."

He threw his cards on the table and jumped up. "All right, that's it." He lunged and scooped her up before she could even blink, then sat and carefully turned her over his knee. Her giggles bounced off the cabin walls as she thrashed in his arms, his laughter in harmony with her own. She squirmed like the little girl she was, sassing him with a salty tongue. He raised his hand and popped her lightly on the behind. At the moment of impact, her giggles died a quick death, and she froze in his arms. A pitiful cry wrenched from her lips.

His stomach lurched. "Charity, did I hurt you? Your leg? Your arm?" He carefully righted her, holding her on his lap. He scanned her body with anxious eyes. Her face was white and her lips parted. Short, shallow breaths escaped from her mouth.

"What did I do?" he breathed.

She started to shake, and he pulled her close, rocking her in his arms. "I'm so sorry. I didn't mean to hurt you."

"I'm okay. You just . . . scared me for a moment."

He lifted her face with his thumb, his eyes intense. "I would never hurt you on purpose. You do know that, don't you?"

She sniffed and pushed her hair from her eyes. "Yes, I know that, Mitch. It's just that for a moment . . . when I was over your knee . . . I had this strange feeling. An awful feeling, really, that I can't explain. And when you hit me . . ." She shivered. "I got sick inside. It brought back a memory."

"A bad one?"

She nodded, wringing her hands in her lap. "Of Uncle Paul, my father's brother. I hated him."

"Hated? Past tense?"

"He died, years ago in a factory accident." She swallowed hard. "And I was glad."

"Charity, I . . . I don't know what to say. I'm sorry. I was only teasing. I wouldn't have done it if I'd known." He rose and gently placed her on the bed. He fluffed the pillow behind her. "Do you want to talk about it, or do you want me to go? You need to be alone?"

Her head jerked up. She pressed a hand to her stomach. "No, I think I need to talk. I want to talk. Are there any crackers left from the other night? I feel queasy."

He searched the nightstand drawer and pulled out two. "Need more than this?"

She shook her head and reached for one, then nibbled on the edge. "It seems so odd . . ."

"What?"

"Remembering Uncle Paul. I've closed him out of my mind for so many years now." She looked up, her brows furrowed in confusion. "At least until the dream the other night."

He bumped her shoulder with his hand. "Move over."

She complied, shifting so he could sit beside her. He kicked his shoes off and stretched his legs out, then grabbed the blanket lying at the foot of the bed. He tucked it safely between them. Leaning back, he curled an arm around her shoulder and settled in. "He was in it?"

She nodded and sucked in a deep breath.

He tightened his hold. "Did he hurt you when you were young?"

She looked past him in a hard stare while her forehead strained in thought. "I don't really remember clearly, but I think . . . I think he may have."

Mitch took her hand in his. "The dream—tell me about it."

She closed her eyes as if to remember, and her face crimped in pain. "All I recall is Rigan slapping me, knocking me against a wall. There was blood on my face and I screamed, calling for my father."

"He was in the dream too?"

She nodded. "He and Uncle Paul were enjoying a smoke, watching the whole scene as if it were a day in the park. When I screamed, my father turned away. And the next thing I knew, Rigan had me on his lap, whispering in my ear, telling me that my daddy left. He kept saying that he would take care of me and what a beautiful girl I was." She looked up at Mitch, her eyes wide. "He smelled like smoke . . . like Uncle Paul."

She closed her eyes and began to fidget with her hands, rubbing hard between the fingers. "I remember how scared I was when he took his hand and . . ."

Mitch waited, the muscles in his stomach constricting. He could feel the tremor in her body. His voice was a whisper. "What, Charity? What did he do?"

Her hand flew to her mouth. Tears escaped from beneath her pressed lids. "His hand . . . in the dream . . . it went up my dress and . . . he hurt me." Her eyes suddenly opened, wide and wet. "Oh, Mitch, it was Uncle Paul—Rigan was Uncle Paul! I remember now!"

Her shiver chilled him to the bone, and fury thickened in his throat. He reached inside his pocket for his handkerchief and handed it to her. He drew in a deep breath. "He didn't . . ."

She shook her head violently, sobs choking her words. "Not in the dream, but . . . I don't remember. I was young, probably only five or six. I never allowed myself to think about it before. I . . . I couldn't."

He released a slow breath and pulled her close, stroking her hair with his hand. "You've had that buried inside of you a long, long time, little girl. Your uncle Paul—did he visit often?"

She shook her head against his chest. "Almost never. But when Hope died and Faith was in the hospital for a year, Mother and Father were desperate. He stayed for a month."

"I thought Bridget was there, taking care of you and the others while your mother and father spent time with Faith."

"She did, but every summer, she'd go back to Ireland to see Mima, and Father didn't want to deny her that. So he asked Uncle Paul to stay."

"And you think he . . . did that to you?" He forced his voice to remain calm.

She nodded.

"Did it . . . happen more than once?"

Her voice was almost inaudible. "I think so."

His jaw felt like a trap about to spring. "Did you tell anyone?"

A bitter laugh spewed from her lips. "No, of course not. Once, when I cried, he spanked me, threatening to tell my father. Said if I told on him, he would tell my daddy what a bad girl I'd been. And I didn't want that. I worshiped my father. I was 'Daddy's Girl,' or at least that's what he called me. And I was. Faith and Hope had each other. And I had my daddy. I didn't know it at the time, but I must have been painfully ashamed, because even after Uncle Paul died, I never said anything. By that time, Father was so immersed in Faith, I didn't think it would do much good anyway."

Mitch felt like putting a fist through a wall. He held her tighter. "You know something, Charity O'Connor? This explains a lot. Bitterness toward your father for leaving you in the clutches of that monster, your unwillingness to forgive him for his preoccupation with Faith, and your anger toward your sister." He lifted her chin with his finger and gazed long and hard into her swollen eyes. "Not to mention your propensity to use sensuality as a means to get love."

She blinked and her lips parted in surprise. "It does . . . doesn't it?"

He nodded. "I once told you that what you were selling, only the wrong guys would buy. I made you promise you would stop. Do you remember your response?"

She scrunched her nose. "No."

"You said that you didn't know how. That this all came so easily for you."

"I did?"

"You did. And maybe this is one of the reasons why."

She stared at him for several seconds, the wheels apparently turning in her brain. With a quiet sigh, she leaned her head against his chest. "I didn't realize."

"I know," he whispered. He closed his eyes. His jaw hardened as images of a wounded little girl seared his mind. His teeth clenched in silent rage. *God, why?* How can anyone forgive an injustice such as this? It was inconceivable. And yet he knew she must, lest her uncle's painful violation live and breathe forever. *God help her, please!* He drew in a ragged breath and released it slowly. But not today. No, today had seen the wounds of the past reopened, jagged and raw. A sense of protectiveness surged within as fierce as his fury. Right or wrong, forgiveness would wait for another day.

With a gentle squeeze, he kissed her head and slowly rose to his feet. She stared up at him with doleful eyes, lashes spiked and wet with grief, and he felt his resolve begin to crumble. His resolve to stay at arm's length, to be only a friend, to offer a shoulder and not his heart. He turned away to reach for the nightgown she had strewn across the other bed. He avoided her gaze as he gently tossed it in her lap. "It's late, little girl, and you've had a long day. You need your sleep. I'll be back in a while to take you to the bathroom." He moved toward his cabin.

"Mitch?"

He stopped, his shoulders slumped with fatigue. "Yes?"

"Thank you for listening . . . and for caring. You're a good friend. You make me feel safe."

His chest expanded and fell with the weight of his relief. He stared straight ahead, not willing to turn and glimpse that wounded little girl once again. It was too dangerous. And he needed his distance. "You're welcome, Charity." He reached for the door.

A catch in her voice stiffened his hand on the knob. "Can you . . . will you . . . pray for me? That I can get past . . . everything?"

He paused, then nodded. The faintest of smiles curved the edge of his mouth. "Already have, little girl," he whispered, and then closed the door without so much as a glance back.

12

Surface impressions. Never would he trust them again.

Mitch lay in the midget-sized bed and stared at the ceiling, feet exposed and chest too. But the chill of the room had no effect whatsoever. A warmth unlike anything he had ever experienced surrounded him like a cloud, straight from the threshold of heaven. He released a cleansing sigh and blinked, clearing the wetness from his eyes.

"Well, you did it. You told me to pray for her and I did. And tonight you showed us both the hurt she's been hiding. How can I ever thank you?"

He turned on his side. His king-sized yawn turned into a smile. "Wait, don't tell me—pray for her, right? Okay, I'm asking you to get ahold of her, deep in her heart. I don't want any shallow commitment here, just all out or nothing. Like Faith. Charity O'Connor needs you more than anybody I've ever met. Except maybe Rigan. And, yeah, I might as well throw him in too. I'm still not sorry for roughing him up, but I'll work on it. In the meantime, bless him and bring his sorry life to you. Thanks."

He closed his eyes and rotated his neck to dislodge a kink. Kathleen's gentle face came to mind. The smile faded on his lips. She was praying for him—for them—he knew it. He could feel it, the strength, the clarity. She loved him, but she loved God more. Like Faith. Two women who would make remarkable wives. One he could have. The other he couldn't.

He flipped on his stomach, and for the first time in weeks, his thoughts drifted to Faith. A malaise settled on his mind like a damp mist. He steeled his jaw. What would it be like to see her again? A year ago she'd been his world, the light of his life—the woman he would live with, sleep with, grow old with. Would it crush him? Knowing she was soon to be wed, in Collin's bed instead of his own? The thought stabbed his heart with pain he didn't expect, destroying the peace he'd felt just moments before. He jabbed his pillow and railed in his mind. Why? He was supposed to be past this. Hadn't he spent a year putting it behind? Why now when he was ready to move on?

A shudder forced its way down his spine. Why? Because soon he would face her again, those emerald eyes and red-gold hair. Her pure heart and her will of iron. He jerked to his side, like an animal trapped in a cage. What he wouldn't give to send Charity home in a taxi. To avoid Faith altogether. To get back on that ship and sail away, never to face the demons of his past. But that wasn't an option. Marcy and Patrick would expect him to come and beg him to stay. God help him, he had no will for the struggle, no desire to pretend all was well. He was trapped, held captive by two sisters. In love with one and impassioned by the other.

Three days. That's all he had. Three days until he saw her again, in the embrace of another man. A man he had willingly stepped aside for. Had, in fact, given her to. Without so much as a fight. He rolled on his back and blinked in the dark, sick with regret. It was a hard, cold fact. It was over. The woman he loved would never be his. And there was nothing he could do but tough it out. And leave. As quickly as possible.

Mitch closed his eyes. Not much of a plan. But it was all he had.

Charity snuggled into the warmth of the bed. She felt so safe. A feeling she hadn't had in a very long time. At least, not since she'd been small, when her father would rock her to sleep in his arms. She glanced at the door to Mitch's cabin. A shaft of moonlight cut through the crack, beaming across the floor like a light from heaven. He was there, just a few feet away, the man who calmed her soul and stirred her blood.

She sighed. The friendship was backfiring. She wanted more.

She turned on her side and closed her eyes, tucking her hands beneath her head on the pillow. Was it prayer or the man that gave her such peace? Mostly the man, she suspected. Although prayer had certainly elevated in her mind. Mitch had planted the seeds that night in the car, compelling her to speak to God on her own. And from the moment she'd agreed to become Rigan's wife, that communication with the Almighty had burgeoned into a daily occurrence. Whether she wanted to admit it or not, God had intervened on her behalf, despite her reckless actions. He'd sent an angel in the form of a bobby that night in the park, sparing her from Rigan's lustful intent. She may have broken bones and bruises, but even that had worked out for her good, just as she and Emma had prayed. She smiled in the dark. Very good, as a matter of fact. The man she loved was in the next room, and for three more days, he was all hers.

She closed her eyes and thought of Mitch, then released a gentle sigh. Her eyelids suddenly flipped open. Three days. A mere seventy-two hours until they arrived in Boston. And the euphoria would end. Her stomach constricted. She'd have to face them all: Faith, Father, Collin.

She jolted up in bed and pinched her hand to her chest. Mitch would be there, but how long would he stay? She thought of Kathleen, and her stomach began to cramp. Her breathing became irregular. She glanced at Mitch's door. Surely the last few days meant as much to him as they did to her? He had to be falling in love too, didn't he? Confused, just like her, happy victims of a beautiful friendship? She squeezed her eyes shut. Oh, Lord, let it be so!

But what if it wasn't? What if he planned on taking her home and then sailing away? Returning to Ireland to marry Kathleen? The sick feeling rose from her stomach to her throat, causing her to heave. No! She couldn't risk it. She needed him. He needed her.

Didn't he?

She felt dizzy. Her breathing accelerated and she reached for Mitch's handkerchief. She pressed it to her mouth, feeling the nausea rise. What could she do? How could she make him stay? The fear of losing him, never seeing him again nearly suffocated her. With a violent thrust, she retched into his handkerchief, filling it with the taste of worry that poisoned her tongue.

With shaking fingers, she wadded the cloth and dropped it on the nightstand. The smell of her fear was strong in the room. She lay back on the pillow and closed her eyes. She couldn't do this. Allow herself to worry like this. She would simply ask him. Find out tomorrow what his intentions were. Maybe, just maybe, they were one with hers.

The thought calmed her. She drew in a deep breath, desperate to steady her pulse and regain control. She needed sleep, escape from the what-ifs that clawed at her mind.

And she needed to pray. The thought surprised her somewhat, and she turned on her side to blink in the dark. A heavy sigh escaped her lips and she closed her eyes, ready to entreat the Almighty. *Dear God, please . . . can you let me just drift away . . .*

A sense of peace pervaded her soul and she finally slept, a prayer answered before barely uttered.

He stood over her, watching her sleep, her face more pale

than usual. He sniffed the air. The scent of lilacs was conspicuously absent, replaced by the sour smell of vomit. He glanced at his handkerchief on the nightstand and wrinkled his nose. Definitely unsalvageable. He pulled a clean one from his pocket and wrapped it around the mess, causing his stomach to heave. He tossed both in the trashcan, then went to his room to retrieve a hand towel. He dampened it with water from the pitcher and returned to her bed. He gently touched her shoulder.

She opened her eyes, blinking at the early-morning light.

He stroked her cheek with his finger. "You were sick last night. Why didn't you call?"

"It didn't last long, and I didn't want to bother you." Her lips curved into a sleepy smile. "Sorry, but you're one handkerchief short."

His own lips twitched with humor. "Two. I used a clean one to toss it in the can. Here's a wet towel. Wipe your face." He rested a hand to her head. "You don't feel too warm. Is your stomach still upset?"

She flushed. "A little, but I think it's just a touch of seasickness. What time is it?"

"Almost eight. I didn't want to wake you, but I need some food in my stomach. Maybe you should stay here, and I'll bring you some dry toast."

She sat up, holding the blanket to her chest. "No, I want to go with you." She yawned with a hand to her mouth, then suddenly focused on him. "You don't look so good yourself. Didn't you sleep well?"

"Not particularly. Maybe we both should blame the weather. The waves were a bit restless last night." He glanced out the porthole, then back at her face. "But this morning is nice, the best weather we've had so far. Cool, but no wind. I think we should try to get you walking with those crutches. After breakfast, I want to take you up on the deck so you can practice."

She nodded, slowly swinging her legs out of the bed. "I'll

dress warm. Can you hand me the plaid woolen skirt and the high-necked blouse? Oh, and the gray woolen stockings?"

He snatched the requested items from her suitcase and placed them on the bed. "Yell when you're ready, and we'll hit the loo and then eat."

She was particularly quiet through breakfast, refusing to eat anything but crackers and tea, claiming her stomach felt a touch nauseous. It worried him that she was getting sick. He made sure she was well bundled in her coat and blanket when he finally carried her to the top deck. Several couples strolled on the bow, so he headed to the back of the boat and set her on the last bench in the stern. He tugged the blanket around her and squatted down. "I'll go get the crutches. You feeling okay?"

She nodded. Her face was less pale in the cool morning air and her eyes as blue as the sky. They were soft as they searched his. "Thank you for taking such good care of me."

He smiled. "That's what friends are for."

She looked away, her eyes scanning the deep blue of the ocean as it merged with the sky. He followed her gaze. Streaks of yellow sun glittered over the water. "Yes. Good friends. Forever, I hope," she whispered.

He stood up, a twinge in his gut. "I'll be right back."

He returned quickly, forcing his mind to focus on the next three days and not those that would follow. He leaned the crutches against the wall and held out his hand. "We'll take it one crutch at a time. Can you stand on your good leg?"

She nodded and reached up to grasp his hand. He tugged her up and looped an arm around her waist. All at once she looked up beneath a sweep of heavy lashes and he swallowed, painfully aware of her body close against his. He stepped back and reached for the crutch. "Here, put it under your good arm and lean all your weight on your strong leg."

She took it and wobbled while struggling to wedge it beneath her arm. He stood behind her, steadying her with hands to waist. She gave him a shy smile over her shoulder, and her voice was soft and low. "Thanks."

Heat traveled his body. He yanked his hands away. What in the blazes was wrong with him today? They were friends, nothing more. They'd established that. "You're welcome," he muttered. He took another step back, silently vowing to put an ocean between him and the O'Connor sisters as soon as humanly possible.

In no time she was thumping up and down the deck with a satisfied grin on her lips. She was breathless when she finally halted in front of where he lounged on the bench. "Don't look now, Dennehy, but I think you've been replaced."

He studied her through half-lidded eyes, noting the rose on her cheeks from the cool sea air. "Good, now I can sleep in."

She nudged him over with the crutch and sat down. "Only if I let you. I still need help with the stairs, you know, on the ship and at home."

He stiffened. "Your father and brother will be there to help."

She gave him a sideways glance. "So will you, won't you, at least for a few days?"

He kept his eyes trained on the rolling waves, reluctant to gaze into those deadly eyes. "I don't think so, Charity. I need to get back."

She whirled to face him. Her hand clutched his arm. "You can't stay? Just for a while? It would be so fun to show you the sights of Boston."

His lips twisted in irony. "I've seen the sights of Boston, thank you. I'm still trying to forget them."

She blinked. "You mean Faith? I . . . I thought you were over her?"

"I am," he said, lifting a curl away from her eyes. "But I'm not looking forward to stirring any memories. Besides, I need to get back."

"For what? You don't have a job."

He arched a brow. "Thanks for your vote of confidence. We don't know that. Michael seems to think Old Man Gallagher will let me stay. But even if he doesn't, I need to find work."

"Father will hire you. He's always looking for good editors."

That one made him laugh. *Perfect.* A job at the *Herald* with the ex-fiancée who'd haunted his dreams. "I don't think so."

Charity plopped back against the wall and crossed her arms, a pout surfacing. "Give me one good reason why you can't stay, at least for a few weeks."

He hated to bring it up, but she would understand. He hoped. After all, they were friends. He glanced at her to gauge her reaction. "Kathleen."

The friendship died in her eyes, replaced by steely anger. "She can't spare you for a few measly weeks?"

He exhaled and scratched his brow with the blunt side of his thumb. "She already has, Charity. She's been very patient. More than anybody I know."

"So you're going through with it then? You're going to marry her?"

He gave her a pointed look. "Yes. I am. You know that. We've discussed it over and over again. That's why we're friends and nothing more, remember?"

She reached up and grabbed his chin, jerking his face toward her. "And friends stop friends from making mistakes. You can't marry Kathleen."

"Why not?"

She chewed on her lip, apparently preparing her strategy. "Because deep inside, I don't think you love her . . . do you?"

He huffed out a sigh and massaged his temple with the ball of his hand. "In my own way I do."

She was back in his face again, the blue eyes fairly sizzling with sarcasm. "A heartfelt declaration of love if I ever heard one. Please stop, Mitch, the passion is scalding me."

His jaw tightened. "Knock it off, Charity. There's more to passion than boiling your blood. And just for your information, we had that, too, in the past. We'll have it again."

"But why? You're settling for lukewarm when you can have more."

He leaned against the wall, his head back and eyes closed. His lips quirked into a faint smile. "I'm old, remember? I don't need more. Besides, I owe Kathleen. She was there years ago when I needed her, waiting in the wings. Soft, warm, a kind of ethereal beauty. Everything Anna wasn't. She got me through one of the worst times of my life."

"But that was then. This is now."

He gave her a slitted glance. "She's a good woman, Charity. She loves me and God."

"But you don't love her." Worry glistened in her eyes.

He expelled a heavy breath and reached to tuck her under his arm. "I do love her . . . not like I love Faith, but enough. Our love will grow."

He felt her stiffen. "What's wrong?" he asked.

"You said 'like you love Faith.'"

"What?"

She looked up with a challenge in her eyes. "You said 'like you love Faith.' Present tense."

He blinked, then sat back. "For pity's sake. *Loved* Faith, all right?"

She shifted on the bench to face him. "You're lying. You're still in love with my sister, aren't you?"

He closed his eyes. A scowl tainted his lips. "Of course I love your sister. I'll always love her. For pity's sake, she was going to be my wife. But it's different now. I'm over her."

"Swear it."

He blinked at her as if she'd said she was going for a swim. "What?"

"Swear that you're over my sister. I don't think you can. I think that's the reason you didn't sleep last night. And the reason you're grouchy this morning. And I'm pretty sure it's the reason you won't stay in Boston, either. Even for a few days."

He clamped his lips tight and ground his jaw. "I'm not staying in Boston because I need to get back and find a job. And I'm not grouchy."

"You are too. You're doing that thing with your jaw again. And the real reason you're not staying in Boston is because you're a coward. Why don't you just admit it?"

He glared, incensed all the more at the anger in her eyes. *She thinks I'm a coward?* "The only thing I'll admit is that both of us got up on the wrong side of the bed this morning. And you've got a lot of nerve calling me grouchy. I've seen better moods on a wounded Rottweiler."

She sat up straight, all color gone from her cheeks. "Suddenly I don't feel so well. I'm going back to the cabin." She snatched the crutch and pushed herself to a standing position.

He clamped a hand on her arm and stood. "You're not steady enough on those crutches yet. I'll carry you."

She jerked away. "I don't want you to carry me. I can do it."

He ignored the heat in her eyes and swooped her up in his arms, searing her with heat of his own. "I'm carrying you."

She tried to smack him with the crutch. "I don't need you. I can get along just fine."

He knocked the crutch from her hand. It hit the deck with a noisy clatter, causing several people to glance their way. He left it where it lay and strode toward the door. "So we're back to this, are we?" He kicked the door open and stormed up the stairs.

"You're a yellow-bellied bully and I hate you, Mitch Dennehy!"

"You'll get over it," he said with a grunt. He swung her cabin door open and heaved her on the bed, breathing hard from the effort.

She landed with a bounce. Wet anger glinted in her eyes. "Get out! You're a better coward than friend. I don't want to see you for the rest of the trip. Just bring me my crutches."

"That may work for the bathroom, but you may starve in the process."

Her face suddenly paled and she pressed a hand to her stomach, emitting a tiny burp. She lifted her chin. "I'm sure Mr. Graham Huntington would be glad to oblige."

A nerved popped in his cheek. "Take a nap, will you? Your disposition is downright ugly. I'll be the only one carting your sassy mouth around, not some smooth-talking dandy."

"What do you care? You're nothing but a pathetic coward, running home to Kathleen. Too afraid to face your past and put it behind."

He stared at her, seeing the hurt in her eyes for the first time. He sighed. "Get some rest, Charity. I'm worried about you. You look pale."

"Mitch . . ."

He stopped, hand on the knob. "What?"

"I . . . don't feel so good."

He turned. "Your stomach again?"

"I think so."

"Are you going to throw up?"

Her mouth opened and he lunged for the waste can. He shoved it in her hands. She heaved and buried her head, retching her little heart out. Mitch sat beside her and held her hair away from her face. When she finally came up for air, her lips were white and her face pinched. His heart twisted. "Are you okay? All done?"

She nodded.

He frowned and reached for the damp towel on the nightstand. He wiped her face. "You've been sick an awful lot, young lady. No appetite, upset stomach all the time."

She shivered. "I know. I don't know what's going on, but I feel like I can't breathe." She grappled for the high collar of her blouse and fumbled to open the first two buttons. She drew in some air and groaned. "I must be eating something, though, because my clothes feel so tight. This skirt feels like it's cutting me in two."

He pushed hair away from her eyes. "Maybe sailing doesn't agree with you. Something's not right. All those endless trips to the bathroom, up-and-down moods . . ." He kissed the top of her head, inflecting tease in his tone. "Nasty temper."

She didn't laugh and he pulled away, studying the haggard look on her face. His lips parted to speak, but in one wild beat of his heart, the air trapped in his throat.

No. It couldn't be.

She looked up, a hand to her mouth, barely concealing another belch. "Mitch, could you hand me that last cracker in the drawer? This nausea seems to be getting worse."

He swallowed hard. Crackers. Moods. Nausea. He'd seen it before. Twice with his own mother, before she'd eventually miscarried. Irascible moods, pale face, morning sickness.

And crackers.

He reached in the drawer and handed it to her, his gaze fixed on her face. "Charity, that night that Rigan beat you . . . did he . . . do anything else?"

Her eyes went wide and she began to cough.

He jumped up to pour a glass of water and handed it to her. "Take a drink."

She guzzled, then drew in a deep breath and handed the glass back with shaky fingers.

"Did he?"

She stared at him in horror, blood flooding her pale cheeks. Her lips quivered as if to speak, but nothing came out.

He grabbed her by the shoulders, panic rising in his chest. "Did he rape you? Is that it? All this nausea, up-and-down moods, trips to the bathroom—could you be pregnant?"

She blinked in shock, ready to tell the truth, but it lodged in her throat at the fury in his eyes. The blood drained from her face as she realized his train of thought. He was worried. Worried that Rigan had done to her what he'd done to Anna. She began to heave, a battle warring in her brain. Tell the truth. Or allow its absence to work in her favor.

He pushed the trash can back into her lap and stood. "I'm going to get more crackers and ginger ale to settle your stomach. But when I get back, we're going to talk."

The door slammed. She sagged on the bed while her pulse pounded in her brain. She shuddered at the awful opportunity that loomed before her. Tell the truth and lose him to Kathleen. Remain silent and let him believe a lie. A lie that could change the course of his heart.

And hers.

Charity stared at the ceiling, and her breathing shallowed as she lay flat on the bed. Her stomach persisted in a dull ache, but it was nothing compared to her heart. Fear of losing him sliced through her like the thin razor of deceit she now considered in her mind. *But Lord, I love him!*

Enough to let go?

For the first time in her life, the weight of that pure emotion slammed headlong into her desire to have him, roiling in her stomach like the foam on the sea.

Did she? Love him enough to let go? To put his wants before her own? She shuddered. To relinquish and bend to the will of God? She turned on her side and blinked, gentle revelation catching her unaware. When had the will of God become a factor? When had her vendetta against him softened and waned? Somewhere along the way, she supposed, between the pain of Rigan's beating and the utterance of prayer. Prayers she'd begun whispering in the dark of night, flooding her with something she'd never experienced before. His peace.

But where was his peace now? She jolted up, clutching at her throat. The thought of losing Mitch forced a groan from her lips. "Oh, God, I need him! And this is my chance. Just one small silence, that's all. Not even a lie uttered from my lips, only tears to bear the blame."

She pushed shaky fingers through her hair as she scanned the ceiling, hoping for some sense of divine approval. All she saw was Mitch's face in her mind, and her resolve hardened like the sin in her heart. Conviction pierced, but she shook it off, steeling her nerve. "I love him, Lord. You know that. And he loves me. Please. One small white lie. I can't afford to lose him."

Breathing hard, she reached for the half-eaten cracker and broke off a tiny piece. She glanced at the door, then quickly ground it with her thumb and placed a single crumb in her eye. Guilt shivered through her. She flinched a number of times. Her eye began to water. She repeated with the second, blinking until both felt red and scratchy. She reached for the water and dipped her fingers in. Patting her cheeks, she rubbed hard to produce a blotchy effect, then dampened her pillow. She felt faint and sucked in a gulp of air, undoing another button. Her fingers stilled as she stared down at her blouse.

No.

She chewed on her lip, wrestling with her conscience. Her fingers twitched in her lap, and her gaze darted to the door. She moistened her lips. With heart thumping wildly, she unlatched another button, allowing the blouse to flap open and hint at the soft swell of her breasts. She swallowed hard and made the sign of the cross before lying prostrate on the bed. Burying her head in the pillow, she squeezed her eyes shut to wait.

The doorknob turned, and fear heaved in her stomach.

"Charity?"

She glanced up through swollen eyes and choked back a sob. He loomed large in the cabin, ginger ale in hand and worry on his face. Pain squeezed in her heart. *Oh, Lord, I need him!*

He closed the door and moved toward the bed. He put her drink on the nightstand and squatted beside her, searching her eyes. "You've been crying."

She turned on her side and pressed a hand to her stomach.

He stood up and stared, his gaze fixed on her open blouse. She blushed and closed the gaping material with her hands. "Sorry, I felt like I was suffocating."

He dragged a chair over to sit, his lips pressed tight. "I suggest you latch the lowest button, if you don't mind."

She nodded and looped it closed.

He fished a napkin from his pocket and unfolded it to reveal the crackers. "Here."

She took one, barely nibbling on the edge.

He touched her hand. "Tell me the truth. Did Rigan rape you?"

The truth.

Guilt twisted in her chest. She began to cry uncontrollably, cracker tears spilling like rain. *God, please, I can see it in his eyes. He loves me.*

"Charity, answer me."

She wept harder, unwilling to lie . . . unwilling to tell the truth.

He pulled back and lifted her chin with his hand. "Are you late?"

She felt the blush to the roots of her hair.

"You are, aren't you?"

She was, by several days. She bit her lip and nodded, followed by a rush of pitiful heaves.

He wrenched her to his chest. "So help me, I'll kill him."

He rocked her and stroked her hair, guilt robbing her of the comfort of his arms. Her sobs had never come so easily.

He stood and lifted her up, then dragged the bedspread down. With gentle hands, he placed her on the far side and tucked the covers around her, leaving his side of the bed bare. Without a word, he sat down beside her and pulled her to him, resting her head against his chest. He wrapped his arms tightly around her. "You need to sleep, little girl. You look exhausted.

And when you wake up, I'll be right here. It's going to be okay. Trust me."

"I do, Mitch. More than anyone I know." She squeezed her eyes, trying to shut out the shame she felt. "Are you going to try and sleep too?"

"Yes."

She curled closer and shivered, her body shuddering with painful whimpers. Tears seeped from her eyes that had more to do with regret than crackers. *I'll tell him in Boston, Lord, I promise.* And with a quivering sigh, she cried herself to sleep, hopefully to a place of slumber far from her wretched soul.

❦ ❦

Sleep? He couldn't even blink. He just sat staring, his body stiff and his eyes dry sockets of shock. He could hear the even rhythm of her breathing as she slept, and it calmed him somewhat. He looked at her beautiful face, delicate lashes curved against soft skin and full lips parted. He felt a stab in his chest. She didn't deserve this.

He closed his eyes and forced himself to think. What was she going to do? She would be ostracized, not by her family, but by everyone else. Forced into hiding for six months or more, her body torn apart by the pain of pregnancy and labor, and for what? To give birth to the child of the man who brutalized her. Mitch's heart seized in his chest, pumping with fresh hate. He released a ragged breath. *God forgive me.*

He steeled his jaw. He wouldn't run again. Not a second time. This time he would stay and make sure Rigan's dirty work didn't take a life. Or two. He would marry her, if need be. They'd become good friends over the last week, able to talk about anything and laugh about everything, sharing hopes and dreams. He sucked in a deep breath, thinking about the chemise. And she stirred his blood more than any woman alive. He didn't completely trust her, but that would come in time.

Wouldn't it?

She jerked in his arms and he studied her. A beautiful little girl with a big ugly problem. One he could certainly solve. Would she marry him? Probably. His talk of Kathleen always upset her. And his slip of the tongue about loving Faith had put her over the top. Despite her attempts at nonchalance and friendship, every indication seemed to be there. She was a woman in love. And he was pretty sure it was with him.

But did he love her? He let his mind wander over the months he'd known her. She was a spoiled little brat who used her beauty to manipulate and coax. But she'd started to change, gotten under his skin in a big way. She could rouse his temper—or his passion—with a tilt of her head or a word from her lips. He looked down. Or a deadly undergarment.

When Bridget had asked him to take her to Boston, he hadn't been happy. But the idea had grown on him, settled in like a habit that was hard to break. In so many ways she was like a child constantly underfoot, trying one's patience. But when they were gone, you missed them something fierce. Did he love her? He swallowed hard, finally willing to admit it. He was pretty sure he did. He let that sink in, roll around in his brain for the very first time. Images flashed of the week they'd shared: a gloating competitor at Whist; a wildcat in his arms when she couldn't get her way; a little girl awed by a seagull in flight. He thought of her on deck, cocky and sure as she hobbled on a crutch, strutting with as much confidence as the Queen of England herself. He looked at her now, asleep in his arms, and his heart swelled with love. He glanced at the ring on her finger, then touched the one on his own. Somehow it felt right. She belonged to him.

She moaned and shifted away. The blanket scooted down to reveal a hint of lacey chemise inside the unbuttoned blouse. He let his eyes linger, enjoying the heat flooding his veins. She would be his, his very own wife, in his bed and sanctioned by God. He inhaled deeply and released it in one long, shaky breath. He jerked the blanket back up. Not near soon enough.

～❦ ❦～

The cabin was almost dark when she finally stirred to the sound of snoring. She propped up on her good arm and blinked, adjusting her eyes to the shadows of the room. Mitch lay sprawled in the chair beside her bed, arms folded loosely across his chest. A low grunt, similar to a growl, escaped his open mouth. She scanned the length of him and chewed on her lip. He looked ridiculously uncomfortable, like a giant in a schoolroom chair, slouched low and those long, powerful legs slanted stiff, halfway across the tiny cabin. His head rested on the back of the seat, forcing that formidable chin to jut in the air, and his broad chest rose and fell with every groan issued. She reached to wake him, and her fingers stilled on his arm. She swallowed hard. Even in sleep, his biceps were taut and firm. She released a quiet sigh. He was truly a beautiful man. The snoring continued, so she allowed her fingers to trail . . .

In one shocked breath, he jolted awake. "What are you doing?" he whispered.

Heat stung her cheeks. She quickly glanced out the porthole to deflect her embarrassment. "Nothing. I just turned to look out the window. Goodness, would you look how dark it is! It must be nigh past dinnertime."

"Uh-huh." He slowly stood and stretched his limbs with a dubious smile. "It sure felt like a caress to me," he said with a yawn, then paused long enough to reveal the flicker of a smile at the corners of his mouth. He fixed her with a penetrating gaze and angled a brow. "Was it?"

She was glad it was getting dark—her face was on fire. She looked away, taking great care to adjust the blanket and avoid his eyes. "Don't be silly, Mitch, you're imagining things. I didn't even touch your arm—"

He squatted and took her chin firmly in hand, forcing her to look him in the eye. "Don't, Charity. Don't start our marriage off with a lie. No more lies. Just truth. Do you understand?"

The air thinned in her throat. "Our . . . marriage?"

His eyes searched hers for a brief moment, then strayed to her lips. "If you say yes."

"M-marry you?" Her heart stopped, then commenced thudding in her chest.

His eyes locked on hers as he slowly brought her hand to his mouth and kissed it. He eased from his squatting position to his knees. "That's not an answer," he whispered. He pressed his lips to her palm, causing warmth to fan through her. "Will you marry me?"

She swallowed hard, guilt colliding with joy. "Oh, Mitch . . . are you . . . are you sure?"

A crooked smile tilted his mouth. "Still not an answer."

She sucked in a deep breath. Guilt won out. "But why? Why would you do this?"

His smile faded as he rose to his feet. "Because I'm not going to let you go through this alone."

She chewed on her thumbnail and glanced up. "Is . . . is that all?"

He studied her through narrow lids. "No, that's not all. We're good friends."

"Oh." She tilted her head and gave him a shy look, allowing for a slow sweep of lashes. "Only friends? Nothing more?"

He laughed and turned to grab a fresh dress from her suitcase. He threw it at her, heating her with a wicked grin. "Yeah, there's more. Because you're nothing but trouble, little girl, and somebody's got to take care of you. Here, put this on. That one looks like you slept in it." He started for the door.

"But wait . . . I mean, do you . . ."

He paused, not bothering to turn around. "Do I love you?"

Her heart constricted. "Yes," she whispered. "Do you?"

His shoulders slumped a fraction of an inch, and she saw his head dip, as if deep in thought. It seemed an eternity as she waited, daring not to breathe lest she miss his reply.

His back finally heaved with a quiet sigh. "God help me, I do," he whispered.

The relief rushed from her lungs and she closed her eyes. *Thank you, God.*

He opened his cabin door. "Get dressed. I'll be back in fifteen minutes."

"Mitch?"

He turned, hands slung low on his hips. "Yeah?"

She scrunched her nose. "I'll marry you, I guess."

He grinned. "Thanks."

"You're welcome."

❧ ❧

A ton of bricks. When had it fallen? Yesterday he wasn't sure he even liked her. Today he was hopelessly in love. When had the world shifted on its axis and become a better place?

Mitch yawned and tucked his shaving kit back in the drawer and stripped off his shirt, thinking about the woman in the next room. The woman who would be his wife. Breathtaking, exasperating, engaging, arousing. He grinned. Especially arousing. And she was all his—a little girl, a woman, a mother.

His glow faded. A mother. Bearing the child of a man he hated. If she was, in fact, pregnant. He supposed it could be a false alarm. But the symptoms were all there, and her tears had been more than real. Rigan had raped her. Her emotional response to his question had made that abundantly clear.

He flung his trousers over a chair. It didn't matter. He would raise it as his own. And Rigan Gallagher would never know that Mitch Dennehy's child was his. He slipped into his pajama bottoms and pulled the covers back, flopping into the bed.

Soon he would see Faith. In the same house he had said

goodbye to her over a year ago. And the woman who had destroyed them both would be on his arm, poised to share his life. He sighed. God certainly had a bizarre sense of humor, although Mitch didn't crack much of a smile. He glanced up, his mind exhausted with thought. *Am I doing the right thing? Am I making a mistake? This woman has laid claim to my soul. But what do you want, God?*

He closed his eyes and saw Kathleen, and the gloom of guilt was immediate. His heart ached in his chest. More hurt. By his hand. *Dear God, please protect her. Strengthen her spirit and prepare her. Please don't let her grieve. Bless her with a man who will cherish her and love her the way she deserves.*

Mitch turned on his side. *And help me, please, to do the right thing.*

❦ ❦

Charity turned on her side. *I'll do the right thing, Lord, I promise, once we're in Boston.* She pressed a hand to her chest as if to calm the rush of her heart. *I'm so close, and he's everything I've ever wanted. I didn't actually lie after all. I just didn't tell the truth.*

"Don't, Charity. Don't start our marriage off with a lie. No more lies. Just truth."

She swallowed hard, guilt souring her stomach. *Just this once, God. And never again.* She would turn over a new leaf. Mitch Dennehy's wife—pure as the driven snow. She bit her lip. And holier than Faith, if need be.

She tucked the pillow under her chin, wondering what her sister would think. She sighed. Did it really matter? She and Faith were strangers at best. Charity blinked in the dark. How very odd their lives had turned out. Strangers in love with the same men. Two sisters, like night and day. A sad smile shadowed her lips. And maybe more alike than they knew.

13

"Scared?"

She nodded against his chest. His woolen coat was solid and warm against her face, in stark contrast to the frigid air of the cab.

Mitch rubbed her arms and pressed a kiss to her head. "Don't be. You're not alone. We're a force of two now." Soft billows of steam drifted from his words, lingering.

Like her doubt.

She cupped her gloved hands to blow on them. "I know, but the whole thing is so surreal. Seeing Faith again. Her marrying my ex-fiancé, me marrying hers. Gives me cold chills."

He lifted her chin with his finger. The soft leather of his glove tickled her jaw. He had that smoky look he'd worn the last forty-eight hours. The kind that fixated on her lips instead of her eyes. He gave her a dangerous grin. "Well, then how about some warm ones?"

Her temperature rose even before his mouth met hers, firm and warm, staking his claim. Heat shot through her, making her dizzy in his arms. Her head languished back, hungry for more. He caressed her lips, gently nibbling, playful at first, then deeper and deeper. His urgency seemed to collide with her own, evident in the press of his mouth and the pull of his hands. And then, with a low groan, he pushed her away, his breathing as erratic as if he'd just run a mile. The glazed look in his eyes defied the words of his mouth. "This has got to stop, Charity."

She snuggled close, brushing her lips up his neck. She felt him shiver. "Why?"

He clamped his hands on her waist and lifted her to the other side of the seat. When she tried to lunge back, he blocked her with a massive hand to her shoulder. Sparks glinted in his eyes. "Give me a chance to cool down, will you?"

She grinned and draped her hands over his extended arm. "But I don't want you to cool down. I rather enjoy raising your blood pressure."

He scowled and peeled her hands from his. "Then I guarantee you'll be one happy woman." He nodded toward her window, his eyes peering past her. "Be good, we're here."

She whirled in the seat and scanned the street, her heart thumping in her chest. The cab jolted to a stop in front of her house. She thrust a hand to her stomach. "I'm going to be sick."

"Here?" He shoved his handkerchief in her hand. "For pity's sake, Charity, I thought it was called 'morning sickness.' It's the bloomin' afternoon."

She sucked in a deep breath and pressed the cloth to her mouth. "I'm okay." She reached for his hand and squeezed his glove. "You'll stay close?"

He squeezed back. "Like a shadow." He hopped out to help the cabbie unload the bags onto the sidewalk, then reached for his wallet. He handed him the fare and tip, then glanced up at the house. "Will everyone be home?"

She stared up at the house where she'd been born and raised, and felt a twinge in her chest. "No . . . Father and Faith will be at work, and I think Sean too." A wave of homesickness overpowered her. Tears pricked her eyes.

Home. She lifted her gaze, scanning every inch of the meticulous red-brick three-decker with its pretty wraparound porch. Crisp, white shutters, freshly painted by her father, no doubt, framed an abundance of windows, various shapes and sizes. In the front, perfectly manicured yews surrounded the porch, flanked by her mother's cherished lilac bushes on either side, little more than sticks this time of year. Charity glanced at the sight of her father's towering oak, trimmed within an inch of its life. She smiled. Another victory for Mother in her longstanding battle over light for her garden.

"Ready?" Mitch whispered.

She smiled nervously. "No. Are you?"

He grinned. "Doesn't matter." He hefted her up in his arms. "We're going in."

Halfway up the steps, the door flew open and Katie came bounding out, blond hair bouncing on her shoulders. Jubilant squeals harmonized with Blarney's barking, filling the air with a noisy welcome. "Charity, Mitch! I missed you soooo much." She threw her skinny little arms around Mitch's legs, and her blue eyes danced with excitement as she peered up.

"Katie Rose, you look so old," Charity teased, eliciting another high-pitched giggle from her youngest sister. "Are you dating boys yet?"

"Yuck. I'm only eight. Besides, I'm never gonna do that stuff. Can I see your cast? Does Mitch have to carry you everywhere? Even the bathroom?"

Mitch laughed, propping Charity with his knee so he could scrub Blarney's snout. "Hey there, big guy. Katie, you're way too inquisitive, you know that?"

"What's in-kwiz-a-tiv?"

"Katie Rose, leave them alone. They haven't even stepped foot in the house." Marcy stood on the porch, grinning and swiping her eyes.

Charity's heart squeezed in her chest as she looked up. Marcy held the door wide. "Welcome home, Charity. We missed you so much. And, Mitch—it's wonderful seeing you again."

"Oh, Mother, I missed you too." Charity lunged in Mitch's arms, wrapping her arms tightly around her mother's neck.

Mitch chuckled. "Whoa, girl, we have plenty of time for hugs once I put you down. It's great to see you, too, Mrs. O'Connor."

Charity looked past her mother to see Steven extending a hand. "Welcome home, sis."

"Steven, sweets saints above, you've grown two feet, at least." She pulled him into a hug. "A handshake for your long-lost sister? I don't think so." She grabbed him to her side and kissed him on the cheek.

He grinned and pulled away. "Hi ya, Mitch."

"Hi ya, Steven."

"Welcome home, Charity. We missed you." Beth stepped forward to hug her sister with a shy smile on her full lips.

Charity gaped. "Beth? Is that you? Goodness, you look like a woman!"

A deep blush shaded Beth's cheeks. She ducked her head. "I'm almost sixteen."

"She's in love," Katie taunted.

"That's enough, Katie Rose," Marcy warned, shooing everyone inside the door. "Mitch, put her in the parlor, on the sofa, if you will." She turned to Beth. "Beth, will you and Steven get the luggage please? And Katie, run upstairs and tell Faith they're here."

Charity's stomach tightened, along with Mitch's hold. She glanced up to see the smile stiffen on his face. She turned to her mother. "Faith's home? I thought she'd be working."

Marcy ushered them into the parlor with a wave of her hands. "Oh, she hounded your poor father for the afternoon off so she could be here when you arrived. She's upstairs putting the finishing touches on your room. She wanted it to be perfect."

Mitch laid Charity on the sofa. Their gazes locked. "It's going to be fine," he whispered.

She swallowed hard and nodded, squeezing his hand.

Katie tugged on his sleeve. "Come on, Mitch, carry me like I have a broken leg."

He laughed and took off his gloves, shoving them in a pocket before slinging his coat over the back of the loveseat. He picked her up and tickled her. "Oh, I like this. You're much lighter than your sister."

Charity gave him a smirk. "Thanks a bunch, Dennehy."

He grinned and sat down, tucking Katie into his arms.

Marcy plopped down beside Charity and cuddled her. "Oh, I can hardly believe you're finally here. Your father hasn't slept a wink this week, he's so excited. Do you realize it's been over two years since you've seen each other?"

Footsteps thundered down the staircase. Charity looked up, and the air locked in her lungs.

"Charity, you're here!" Faith flew across the room and bear-hugged her sister. "It's so good to have you home."

"It's good to be home," she whispered, shocked at the wetness that sprang to her eyes. She squeezed her sister back. "It's been a long time."

Faith laughed and pushed at a tear of her own. "Too long. Lots to catch up on." She stood and turned, as if suddenly aware that Mitch was in the room. Her smile softened to shy. "Hello, Mitch."

Katie was wiggling on his lap like an earthworm in soggy peat, but he barely noticed. He stared, his eyes drinking her in like a man in a drought. She'd always had a glow, but never more than now. She blinked, her smile tentative and tears glimmering in those beautiful green eyes.

He forced the words past wooden lips. "Hello, Faith. You're looking well."

She blushed and lowered her gaze, then nodded her head toward Charity. "Did she give you as much trouble as she used to give me?"

His grin broke the tension in his face. He fixed Charity with a telling look, steadied by the vulnerability in her eyes. "Worse. But I'm bigger than her. Of course, the broken leg and arm helped."

"He's a bona fide bully, Faith, as you probably already know."

Faith grinned and crossed her arms. "Oh, yes."

Marcy laughed and embraced Charity again. "I'll bet you two are thirsty. Faith, would you mind bringing the cider in from the kitchen? And Beth, can you help her with the cookies, please?" Marcy started tugging on Charity's gloves. "Here, let's get that heavy coat off. So, how was the trip? It's a long seven days, isn't—*Oh!*"

Marcy's feeble cry caught Mitch's attention. He stopped bouncing Katie on his knee long enough to look up. She held Charity's left hand in her trembling fingers, her cheeks burnished with a pink glow. "Charity . . . is this a wedding band?"

Mitch froze, arms wound around Katie as she straddled his knee. Marcy's eyes flicked over to him, expanding in shock at the ring he'd forgotten to take off. "Are you two married?"

He flipped Katie off his knee onto the sofa, where she landed with a giggle. "No, of course not, Mrs. O'Connor, it was just a precau—"

"Mitch, it's no use. They're going to find out sooner or later." Charity's eyes pleaded from across the room. She flashed him a nervous smile, then turned toward Marcy. "Oh, Mother, we were going to surprise you tonight at dinner, but I guess we forgot to take our rings off."

Mitch jumped to his feet as blood rushed up his neck. "Charity, no!"

Faith entered the parlor carrying the cider, with Beth right behind her. She stopped, her brows bunched in a frown. "What's wrong?"

Marcy put a hand to her mouth and squealed, sealing Charity

in a tearful hug. "Oh, my goodness, Faith, they're married! Charity and Mitch are married."

Mitch clenched his teeth and shot Charity a heated glare. "Charity?"

"Married?" Faith's voice was weak. The tray rattled as she set it on the table.

Mitch took a step toward the sofa, grinding his jaw. "Charity, tell them the truth."

Charity, locked in a tight hug, peeked over her mother's shoulder. "Well, the truth is that Mitch and I got engaged on the ship . . ."

He let out a slow breath, chancing a glimpse in Faith's direction. Her face was white.

Charity bit her lip and gave him a shaky smile. "But we were so much in love, we decided we couldn't wait. There was a priest aboard ship who married us."

"What?" Mitch's mouth dropped open.

Marcy jumped up to throw her arms around him with another loud squeal. "Oh, Mitch, I couldn't ask for better sons-in-law than you and Collin. I'm so happy!"

The muscles in his body were numb as he stood, Marcy hugging his waist. He carefully unlatched her arms to look in her face. "Mrs. O'Connor, you've got it all wrong. We are not—"

"Mother, Mitch is just worried that you and Father will be angry for cheating you out of a wedding, but I told him that Father would probably thank him for sparing the cost." She suddenly twisted on the sofa, clutching her stomach. "Oh!"

Marcy spun around. "Charity, what's wrong?"

She doubled over with a groan. "I think I may have another spell of seasickness coming. Mitch, can you carry me to the bathroom, please? *Now?*"

He clamped his lips and swooped her up in his arms, burning her with a look. He strode in the direction of the downstairs bathroom, aware of everyone's eyes on his back.

"Wait, Mitch, I think I'd better go upstairs instead and lie down a bit. Mother, everyone, can you come up in a few moments after I'm settled, so we can talk?"

"Absolutely." Marcy hurried toward the door.

Mitch grunted and tore up the steps two at a time. Charity seized in his arms with another painful groan and he halted, glancing over his shoulder at Faith, who followed on the steps below. "Which way?"

She scooted around and continued down the hall, leading them to her and Charity's bedroom. She pushed the door wide. "The bed on the left."

Mitch fought the urge to drop Charity like a sack of potatoes, but Faith stood at the door. He set her down carefully, then straightened, his fists clenched at his sides.

"I'll leave you two alone," Faith said. "We'll be back up in a few minutes. I know Mother is dying to talk to you." The door clicked closed behind her.

Mitch glared, thunder rumbling in his chest. "Just what the blazes was that all about?"

She pressed a hand to her stomach and scrunched her nose. "Oh, Mitch, let's not fight, please? My stomach is so queasy."

He began to pace, his eyes boring into hers at every turn. "A lot more than your stomach is going to be queasy if you don't start telling the truth. Now I'm going downstairs right now and give it to them straight since the truth obviously gives you indigestion."

She sat up with panic in her eyes. "Mitch, no! I don't want to be separated, please? We've spent the last week together and there are two beds in here. Can't we just stay together?"

He blinked, amazed at the way her mind tracked. "Lie to them? Deceive them into thinking we're married? Why are you doing this?"

"Because I don't want to be alone with Faith. I'm not ready. And I need you close. Please?" Her hand moved from her stomach to her throat, clutching as if she couldn't breathe.

He shook his head and started for the door. "No, I won't do

it. I told you before that we are not starting our marriage off with a lie."

"Mitch, wait!"

He stopped at the door, his back rigid. "What?"

"I know I don't appear to be thinking rationally . . ." She looked away with a gnawing of guilt. "But I am terrified that if a baby comes . . ."

He turned and waited.

"I'm afraid it could be early and reflect poorly on us."

He slacked a hip and groaned. "For pity's sake, babies come early all the time."

Her face went pale and she began to heave. He hurried to her side and sat, pushing his handkerchief in her hands.

She clutched it to her mouth. "No, Mitch, I don't want any-one to know. I'm so ashamed."

He sighed and pulled her in his arms. "Your family has a right to know. They love you."

"Later, yes. But not right now. I'm so scared and shaken, I couldn't bear it." She looked up, her eyes entreating his. "Please, Mitch, will you do this for me? Just this one time? One tiny, white lie? For my peace of mind?"

A muscle jerked in his jaw. "What about my peace of mind, Charity? I don't want to lie."

She leaned in to rest her head against his chest with a heavy sigh, then slowly lifted her face to his, her eyes pleading. "Just this once, Mitch. Please?" She reached to feather his neck with kisses. Barbs of heat waged battle against iron-cold will. She continued, her words disarming him as much as her lips. "Maybe we could get married this week, secretly. You know, before Faith and Collin's wedding?" Her hand fluttered to his leg. A flood of heat melted his resolve. She looked up, her lips parted and her eyes issuing an invitation. "Man and wife? In the same bed?"

He stared, his iron will liquefying into a puddle of metal.

He focused only on the lips he craved to taste. Dear Lord, he had to have her. Soon.

He jerked away, eyes glazed with desire. "Tomorrow. We get married tomorrow."

A smile eased the worry from her face. "Perfect," she whispered.

He frowned. "Is City Hall open on Saturdays?"

"I think so."

His legs felt shaky as he stood. A spasm twitched in his cheek. Desire or nerves? He wasn't sure. He poked a menacing finger in her direction. "So help me, Charity, after we're married, no more lies. Do you hear me?"

She nodded. "Whatever you say."

He exhaled loudly and headed for the door.

"Mitch?"

"What?"

"I love you."

"Yeah, I know." He jerked the door open.

"Do you love me?"

He turned to give her a sulking gaze, wondering which was stronger—the desire to make love to her or the desire to put her over his knee. He groaned inwardly. No contest.

"Yes, unfortunately."

She giggled and clasped her arms around her knees. "Good. Will you send Mother up? I can't wait to tell her everything that's happened."

He grunted and left the room, an uneasy feeling settling in his gut.

Yeah, neither could he.

Faith sighed. He stood before the fireplace staring into the flames, head bent and hand propped on the mantle. His shoulders sagged far too much for a man newly married. It had been over a year since she'd seen him, but she could still read him like the front page of the *Times*. And the news wasn't good.

"Congratulations."

He spun around, his blue eyes registering surprise. "What?"

She moved into the parlor, fiddling with her nails. She gave him a tentative smile. "Congratulations . . . on your marriage. It certainly shocked us."

He exhaled and dragged his fingers through his hair. "Yeah. Me too."

She felt like a schoolgirl as she lowered herself to the love-seat, more from the need to calm her nerves than to converse. Seeing him again was unsettling. She hadn't realized how much she'd missed him.

"How are you?" She stared at him with a pointed gaze, noting the absence of a smile on his handsome face. He cuffed the back of his neck with his hand, then dropped on the sofa with a grunt. The once-familiar action brought a smile to her lips.

He sat on the edge, arms cocked over his knees. "Okay, I guess."

"Just okay?"

He sighed and leaned back, a smile working its way to his lips. "Good. I'm good."

"You look good, that is when all those worry and frown lines disappear."

"You look good too, Faith. Collin must be treating you well."

Heat broiled her cheeks and she nodded. "He is." She looked up, a tease in her tone. "Except when he heard *you* were coming. Suddenly he started acting like a grizzly yanked out of bed." Her lips tilted up. "Reminds me of you."

He grinned, and his eyes softened. "Yeah. I can be a bear. At least I gave you practice."

"So. Charity got her man, after all. Must have been God's plan all along."

"Yeah, I guess. Even though I fought it tooth and nail."

She focused on her clasped fingers. "Do you love her?" Every breath and muscle stilled in her body as she awaited his reply. When he didn't answer, she glanced up.

He looked away and sighed, then returned his gaze to hers. "Yeah, I do."

Faith released the air from her throat, but it did little to clear the tension from her body. She chewed the edge of her lip and assessed him through narrowed eyes. "Then, what's wrong?"

He huffed out a loud breath and jumped to his feet. He turned to study the flames in the hearth. "Blast it, Faith, why are you able to do that? Delve in and see my soul?" He turned to look at her. There was a glimmer of pain in his eyes. "Do you have any idea how much I've missed you?"

She swallowed hard. "I've missed you too, Mitch. Just because I'm marrying Collin doesn't mean I don't love you." She glanced away. "You're a dear friend. Always will be."

"I love you too. Guess I always will. It was difficult getting over . . . us, but I think I have. At least, I hope I have."

She rose to her feet. "Look at me, sitting down on the job. Mother asked me to get you that glass of cider and maybe a sandwich if you wanted one. Are you hungry?"

"You have to ask?"

She laughed and headed to the door. "As if I could forget. The bottomless pit." She shot a playful smile over her shoulder. "Wanna keep me company while I feed you in the kitchen?"

She pushed through the swinging door and pulled a chair out from the table. "Sit. Ham sandwich okay? Milk or cider?"

His eyes followed her as she raided the icebox. "Ham's great. And milk."

She busied herself with the preparations, her cheeks warm from his piercing gaze. She looked up. "You're awfully quiet for a dear friend I haven't seen in over a year." She tried to concentrate on slicing two thick slabs of Marcy's homemade wheat bread. "Care to discuss what's bothering you?"

He leaned back in the chair. "No."

She paused, knife in hand. "Have you prayed about it?"

His jaw compressed, shifting back and forth the slightest bit. "Yes."

She slapped the ham on the bread, then wiped her hands on a towel. She crossed her arms and gave him a look that made him smile. "Well, then, did you *listen* for his answer?"

He kneaded his forehead with his fingers. "Yes. No. I'm not sure."

"Mustard or horseradish?"

He looked up. "Huh?"

She lifted her brows. "On your sandwich."

"Oh. Mustard."

She slathered the sandwich with care, then patted the bread on top. She put it on a plate and set it in front of him. Hesitating for just a moment, she put a shaky hand on his shoulder. "You're talking about Charity, aren't you? You're not sure?"

He reached up to put his hand over hers and clutched tightly, his head bent and his voice strained. "No."

She squeezed his shoulder and padded back to the icebox to pour him a glass of milk. She pushed it toward him and sank in the chair. "It doesn't matter, Mitch. God is faithful. You're married now. He'll help you make it work."

"No."

Faith blinked. "What do you mean 'no'? Of course he will."

"I mean we're not married."

The blood drained from her cheeks. "What?"

Mitch picked up the sandwich and took a bite, heaving a sigh as he did. "She lied. Something she has a true talent for, I'm discovering."

"You're not married?" Faith sagged in the chair, mouth gaping.

"Nope." He continued to chew, staring straight ahead.

"But she said you got engaged on the boat . . ."

He took a swig of milk. "That much is true."

"But why lie about being married? What's the point?"

He swallowed a big bite of the sandwich and glanced at her. "She's afraid."

"Of what?"

He studied her as if to gauge how much to divulge, his cheeks stuffed with food as he chewed. He swallowed and picked up his glass, then drained the milk.

She rose to get him a refill. He clamped his hand on her arm and pulled her back. "No. We don't have much time. I need to talk. And pray. Charity's in trouble."

Faith stared at his hand on her arm, then up at his face. Her chest tightened. "What do you mean 'in trouble'?"

He inhaled, then released it in one long, agonizing breath. "We think she's pregnant."

Her gasp echoed in the room "No . . . you didn't . . ."

A hurt look clouded his eyes. "No, not me. You know me better than that. How much did Bridget tell you?"

"That Charity was beaten by a man she was engaged to briefly, the man from your past, Rigan Gallagher."

A hard veneer settled on his face. "Yeah, otherwise known as scum of the earth. At any rate, she led Bridget and Mima to believe that he only beat her, but she was lying about that too."

Faith's eyes widened in shock. "He raped her?"

Mitch glanced up, his expression grim. "Apparently. She started throwing up on the boat the last few days, sick with nausea, especially in the morning. Said she was late, that her time of the month never came."

Heat scalded Faith's cheeks. "Dear Lord."

Mitch expelled a halting breath. "I started thinking about Anna, what Rigan had done to her and how it ended. I was afraid. Afraid that Charity might do something . . . hurt herself

. . . like Anna." He looked up. "I swear I had no intention of marrying her even though I love her. I can't trust her, Faith, and that scares me to death. So much so that I planned to return immediately to Ireland and make a go of it with Kathleen. Until this."

Tears stung Faith's eyes. She stood up and put her arms around Mitch's shoulders, clutching him tightly. "Oh, Mitch, I'm so sorry. For both you and Charity. And Kathleen. I know how much she's always cared for you."

He leaned against her and closed his eyes. "I had to tell you. Charity begged me not to say anything to anyone. She's ashamed and embarrassed. But I need your prayers. We both do."

Faith sniffed and sat back down, taking his hands in hers. "I'm glad you could confide in me. Prayer is the only thing that will chase the hurt and fear from your souls. God will work this out for good, you mark my words. He's so faithful."

His smile was gentle. "I know. I had a good teacher."

She closed her eyes and lifted her chin. An assurance flooded her senses that she hoped would transfer to Mitch. "Dear Lord, what would we do without you in our times of need? Charity and Mitch need you, now more than ever. Give them peace and wisdom in this situation. Show them exactly what to do. Help them to get through this, and Kathleen too. And if for some reason," Faith swallowed hard, "this marriage isn't what you want . . . we ask you to stop it. Amen."

Faith opened her eyes to see Mitch watching her. She smiled. "Feel any better?"

"Yeah. Until I have to go upstairs and sleep in that room with her."

Faith jolted upright. "No, you can't!"

"Yes, I can. Do I have to remind you that I learned restraint from the master? Besides, we're going to sneak away and get married in the morning." He hesitated, his brows puckering. "City Hall is open on Saturdays, right?"

Faith bit her lip, thinking. "I think so, till noon, but I'm not sure."

He groaned. "Well, either way, this is our secret. You can't tell your family." He squeezed her hand. "Sorry to kick you out of your room."

She bit her lip. "Maybe I should stay."

He grinned. "No. Your praying would keep me up."

He stood and tugged her to her feet, his expression tender. "You were absolute murder getting over, Faith O'Connor, but I'm in love with your sister now, against my better judgment. But I sure could use a hug from the best friend I ever had." He pulled her into his arms and squeezed her tightly, his head buried in her neck. "God knows how I've missed you."

She closed her eyes and smiled, hugging him back. "I've missed you too, Mitch."

"Not too much, I hope."

Her body went stiff at the sound of Collin's voice.

She jerked out of Mitch's arms as blood whooshed into her cheeks. She put a shaky hand to her face. "Collin! I didn't expect you this soon."

He stood with a hand on the door, one hip slacked. A muscle jerked in his cheek. "Apparently."

"Mitch and I were just praying."

"Is that what you call it?"

Mitch's jaw hardened. "It was perfectly innocent, McGuire. The woman's engaged to you, for pity's sake. What more do you want?"

Collin singed him with a look. "To stay out of the clutches of her former fiancé would be nice."

Mitch took a step forward. "You're a moron, McGuire. You don't deserve her."

Collin rushed across the room, his fists knuckled tight.

Faith threw herself against him with palms to his chest. "Stop it! Mitch is a guest in our home. I'll not have you terrorizing him because of your pig-headed jealousy. He's in love with Charity now."

Collin's chest heaved and his teeth clenched tight. "Yeah? He's got a strange way of showing it. Crammed against you so hard, you'd need a crowbar to pry him off."

Faith swung around to face Mitch, one hand still pressed against Collin's chest. "Mitch, would you mind excusing us, please? There's cider and cookies in the parlor. Help yourself."

Mitch glared at Collin and then glanced at Faith. "Sorry, Faith. I didn't mean to cause trouble." He strode to the door. "Some idiots don't know how good they have it."

Collin lunged as Mitch left the room, but Faith yanked him back. Her eyes burned hot. "You were way over the line."

He pushed her hand away. "Don't sling this on me. You're the one plastered against your old fiancé, doing only God knows what."

Shock stilled the blood in her veins. In a knee-jerk reaction, she slapped him hard across the face, the sound deafening in the silent kitchen. "Don't you dare accuse me or that man of anything tawdry. He's got more restraint in his little finger than you have in your entire body, Collin McGuire. And how dare you accuse either of us of any unseemly behavior when I've had to fend you off for the last month, your commitment to God or no."

She spun around. He grabbed her arm and jerked her back, his eyes crazed. "Don't you dare walk away from me." The anger in his eyes suddenly melted, and he crushed her to his chest, pressing his lips to her hair. "Faith, forgive me. I don't know what gets into me. You're right, I have no reason to suspect you of a thing other than Mitch Dennehy scares the living daylights out of me."

She relaxed in his arms, sinking against him with a frustrated sigh. "Collin, I love you. Don't you know that by now? Aren't you secure in that? I chose you over Mitch, and I'd do it again.

And that man walked away and let me." She pulled away and cradled his face with her hands. "Because he knew. Knew deep down that my heart belonged to you. Not him."

He pulled her back, burying his face in her neck. He gave her a gentle kiss. "I know. He's right. I am a moron. I'll apologize, I promise."

She wriggled out of his grasp. "Good. You owe him one."

He reached for her hand and brought it to his lips. "I owe you one too. For accusing you of something I know you would never do." He attempted a smile. "How well I know."

Her cheeks heated. She pulled her hand away.

He sighed and shifted, digging his hands in his pockets. She saw a rare blush of shame creep up his neck into his face. He avoided her eyes. "And I apologize for pushing you this last month. God forgive me, it was wrong." He looked up. "If you hadn't been strong, we could have gotten into serious trouble."

She folded her arms. "It wasn't easy."

"I know. But I'm grateful you're a forgiving woman. And I'm especially grateful it's a short-term problem. You have my word, Faith—I promise to be a good boy until the wedding." He hooked her waist to pull her back into his embrace, his breath hot against her face. "And after that, I just promise to be good. Very, very good."

❦ ❧

Charity stretched in the bed, feeling wonderful despite the cramps bubbling in her stomach. She sighed and tugged the cover up to her chin. The nap had done her a world of good. Her time of the month always made her so tired. She glanced up at a sound at the door.

Mitch poked his head in. "Finally—the princess has risen! Your mother's cooking up a storm. She said twenty minutes. Need anything?"

Charity flashed him a sleepy smile. "Yes. Everybody knows a princess doesn't wake up without a kiss."

His mouth twisted into a wry smile as he propped against the door. "Forget it. I intend to stay out of harm's way until we're safely married. I'm here to carry you downstairs and nothing more. Do you need to use the loo?"

"No," she said with a teasing pout, "but if you would be kind enough to hand me my skirt and blouse off the other bed, I'd be most grateful."

He strolled in and snatched the items, then handed them to her with a patient smile. "I'll be waiting outside. Call me when you're ready." He turned to go.

"And the hairbrush off the bureau, please, if you don't mind. The hand mirror would be lovely too." She fluttered her lashes.

He deposited both on the nightstand and turned toward the door.

"Oh, and I almost forgot . . . Faith has the most wonderful perfume she said I could use. It's right there on the bureau in the blue bottle. See it?"

He glanced at the bureau, then back. He squinted. "Are you going to be this much trouble after we're married?"

She grinned and sat up in bed, the blanket tucked tightly to her chin. "Oh, way more, I assure you! But, don't worry . . . I have every intention of making it well worth your while."

He grunted and retrieved the perfume, then set it on the nightstand. He cocked a brow. "You better," he mumbled, then gave her a dangerous grin before striding from the room.

The door clicked shut and she sighed. Goodness, but she was crazy about that man! Humming under her breath, she quickly dressed, then brushed her hair to a high sheen. She dabbed a touch of perfume to her neck and wrists and set the bottle back on the table. With a low groan, she swung her legs over the side of the bed and slipped on one shoe and then the other.

She swept her hair over her shoulders and folded her hands in her lap. "I'm rea . . .dy," she called in a singsong voice.

The door swung open and Mitch grinned. "That didn't take long. You look nice." He picked her up in his arms and sniffed. "Mmm . . . you smell nice too."

She tossed her head back and grinned, then fingered the back of his collar. "Thank you. And how do I taste?" she asked.

His gaze dropped to her lips, and she saw his throat shift. "Not willing to find out, little girl," he said with a twist of a smile. "While we're in this house, you're off limits . . . until tomorrow, when we become man and wife."

She started to grin, then caught her breath. *Tomorrow.* He wanted to get married tomorrow.

His brows dipped into a frown. "What's wrong?"

She drew in a deep breath, realizing that tomorrow night, nothing would keep him from her bed. She put a hand to her stomach, feeling the cramps.

"Charity, what's wrong?"

Her lips trembled into a smile. "Nothing. Mother just said something about a big brunch at Mrs. Gerson's, and we'll probably be there most of the day. I'm not sure we'll have time to get married tomorrow. It may have to wait."

He hefted her in his arms and headed to the door, his jaw stiff with intent. "We're getting married tomorrow, and nothing is going to stop us. I'm not going to sleep two nights in a room with you and lie to your family in the process. I'll buy you breakfast out. After." He gave her a quick kiss on the top of the head. "Come on, little girl, your father is anxious to see you."

She swallowed hard as he carried her from the room and down the hall. "Uh, Mitch, I better stop off in the bathroom after all. Sorry."

He halted on the top step and gave her a droll smile. "Yes, ma'am." He turned and deposited her in the bathroom. "I'll be right outside."

She nodded and watched as he closed the door. Her stomach cramped again, and she pressed her hand to her abdomen. She bit her lip and glanced in the mirror. Maybe it would work. Her time of the month would be almost over. And if not, she could tell him it had just come, mere hours after they were married. Nothing more than a false alarm. A smile flickered to her lips. And no baby to take care of. Just Mitch. She sucked in a deep breath and smiled. Yes, that could work—she was sure. The perfect scenario for the perfect life.

The smile faded from her lips and she closed her eyes. Except for one minor flaw. Her stomach tightened into a knot on top of another bout of cramps as she realized what waited at the bottom of the stairs.

Facing her father again.

Faith looked up as Collin stood and pushed in his chair. "Mrs. O'Connor, dinner was wonderful. But I have an early day tomorrow, so I'm going to head out."

Marcy blinked. "But we haven't even had dessert yet. And you'll miss trimming the tree. We waited all this time for Charity to be here before we decorated, and now you're leaving?"

He smiled and tugged Faith up from her chair. "If I want a honeymoon with your daughter the week after next, I have to get a lot done this week. Brady can only do so much."

Patrick leaned back in his chair and unbuttoned his vest. "Hate to see you work a Saturday, Collin, but at least your business is thriving. See you tomorrow night for dinner?"

Collin grinned. "Honestly, Mr. O'Connor, when's the last time I missed one of Mrs. O'Connor's Saturday night feasts? I'll be here." He shot Charity a smile and nodded at Mitch. "Congratulations, you two, and welcome home. Good night, everyone."

Faith followed him to the front door. "I hate to see you work so much."

He backed her against the wall and pressed in for a gentle kiss. "You're worth it, Little Bit. A week with you in New York—sheer heaven."

She kissed him back, clinging tightly to his waist. "Oh, Collin, I can't wait. And I'm not talking about New York."

He smiled and pushed her away. "Me too. Now get back in there and have some fun." He lifted her chin. "Just not too much without me, okay?"

She stifled a yawn and smiled. "Nope, I think I'll go upstairs and change my sheets for Mitch, since he's sleeping in my bed tonight. Then I'm going to turn in myself."

"Where? With Katie?"

Faith groaned and sagged against Collin's chest. "Yes, with Katie. Which is why I need to go to sleep early. Once she gets done trimming that tree, she'll probably keep me up all night."

Collin kissed her nose, then brushed her lips. "I love you, Faith."

"Me too, Collin. Good night."

She closed the door and leaned against it, listening to the laughter floating out from the dining room. She smiled a sad smile, her mood melancholy. It was hard to believe she'd be leaving this house soon, this family she loved, if only to move into Collin's flat a few blocks away. And now with Charity home, and Mitch, things seemed even stranger yet. No, she definitely needed a good night's sleep, if only to drive this edgy feeling from her soul.

She popped her head in the dining room where she caught the tail end of one of Mitch's stories. Marcy looked up. "Faith, are you all right? You look pale."

She smiled. "Yes, Mother, I'm fine. Just really tired. I think the wedding is taking its toll on both Collin and me. If you don't mind, I'm going to go up and change the sheets on my bed for Mitch, then turn in, in Katie's room."

"You're sleeping with me?" Katie jumped up in her chair, eyes wide with excitement.

Faith leveled her with a threatening look. "Yes, Katie Rose, but only if you don't kick me like you used to at Grandmother's."

"I promise, Faith, I'll be still as a mouse."

Faith smiled. "Then I'll be waiting for you after you trim the tree, okay?" She rounded the table to kiss her mother and father good night, then stopped to hug Charity and smile at Mitch. "Good night, you two lovebirds. I'm glad you're home, Charity. I'm looking forward to spending time with you before the wedding."

Charity smiled. "Good night, Faith. Thanks for giving up your bed."

She gave Mitch a smirk. "Well, I suppose it's for a good cause. Good night, everyone."

Faith felt like an old woman as she trudged up the steps, her exhaustion warring with an uneasy feeling inside. She dismissed it and entered her room, lighting the lamp on the bureau. In a near-numb state, she moved to the linen closet in the hall and pulled out a fresh set of sheets, then returned and tossed them on Charity's bed. With a huge yawn, she stripped the sheets off her own bed and replaced them, smoothing the comforter just right. She sighed and turned around, noting the rumpled covers on Charity's bed. She reached for the edge of the blanket and pulled it back, ready to tuck it in. She gasped.

Blood on the sheets.

Faith froze. The edge of the cover slipped from her hand. With shaky fingers, she pulled it back to stare. Either Charity was miscarrying . . . or she wasn't pregnant at all . . .

She dropped on the bed and closed her eyes, her thoughts buzzing in her brain. What was going on? Or more true to form, what was Charity up to? She thought of Mitch and groaned. He deserved so much more. A woman he could trust. A woman who wasn't tricking him to marry her, if that's what Charity was doing. She pressed her hand to her head, exhaustion overpowering her. "Dear Lord, what should I do? I need your help, please."

Faith stood to her feet. Resolve suddenly buoyed her energy. She flipped the covers back and marched downstairs, where her family was just finishing dessert.

Marcy looked up in surprise. "I thought you were going to bed?"

Faith forced a smile. "I am, but I'd like to talk to Charity first. In private, if I could." She glanced at Mitch. "Would you mind carrying her up to our bedroom? Just for a few moments?"

"Can't it wait?" Charity looked up in surprise.

"I'm sorry, but I wouldn't be able to sleep a wink until I get this off my chest. It won't take long."

Patrick's eyes reflected concern as he tapped his pipe. "It's a little late in the evening for resolving differences, Faith. Are you sure it can't wait until morning?"

Faith glanced at Mitch, and her heart twisted in her chest. "No, Father, it can't."

Mitch stood and gathered Charity in his arms. His eyes trained on Faith as she moved to the door. Charity peeked over his shoulder. "We'll be right back. Don't trim without us."

Mitch followed her up the stairs, his tone gruff while Charity sat mute in his arms. "What's this all about, Faith?"

"Just clearing the air so I can sleep. Nothing more." She held the bedroom door open.

He set Charity on the bed with a quick kiss to her cheek. "Call me when you're done."

She nodded. He closed the door, leaving an uneasy silence between them. Charity hiked a brow. "So. What's important enough that you have to drag me upstairs?"

Faith sat on the other bed. Her nerves were raw under her skin. She took a deep breath. "Mitch told me that you and he aren't married."

Charity paled. "Why would he tell you that?"

"Because he's worried about you. So am I." Faith lifted her chin. "And about him."

Charity's jaw hardened. "There's nothing to worry about."

"There is if you're lying to him."

Anger glinted in Charity's eyes. "Worrying about him is my job now, not yours."

"I loved him way before you did, and I still do. He's one of the dearest friends I've ever had. I don't want to see him hurt."

"You didn't worry about that a year ago when you walked out on him."

Faith stood to her feet. A spasm flickered her cheek. "At least I told him the truth."

Charity cocked her head. "And I'm not? Is that it? I love him. And he loves me. And that's the hard, cold truth, Faith. Get used to it."

"You aren't pregnant, are you, Charity?"

The blood drained from her sister's cheeks. "What?"

"And I have a suspicion the rape was a lie too."

Charity closed her eyes, pain streaking her face. "He told you? Why would he do that?"

"Because the man is worried! Worried he's marrying a woman he can't trust."

Charity's eyes shot open, blazing with anger. "He needs a woman like you, is that it, Faith? What, Collin and Father aren't enough? You want Mitch's heart too?"

"This has nothing to do with me, Charity. It has everything to do with Mitch and you. I want it to work between you, I do. But it never will if you lie to get him to marry you."

Charity shuddered and wrapped her arms around her stomach. "I'm not lying."

Faith's anger flared. She reached across the bed and jerked the blanket back to reveal the bloody sheet. "Either you're lying or you're losing your baby. Which is it?"

Charity stared at the sheet. She looked up, her eyes wet

with fear. "I didn't lie to him, I swear. He just jumped to his own conclusions."

"And you let him."

"Faith, I love him. I didn't intend to mislead him, but he assumed my nausea had to do with pregnancy. And I let him believe it. He asked if I was late, and I was!" She looked away. "And then my time of the month came the very next morning." She looked back up, her eyes frantic. "I panicked when he said he was going back to Ireland. I knew I would lose him to Kathleen. I couldn't let that happen."

Faith drew in a deep breath and sat down next to her sister. She took her hand. "You weren't raped, were you?"

Charity looked away. She shook her head.

"I'm glad. But you have to tell him. He loves you. He'll forgive you. But not if you lie."

Charity squeezed her eyes shut, tears spilling down her cheeks. "I can't, Faith. I'm afraid I'll lose him. I'll tell him tomorrow, after we're married, I promise."

Faith pressed her hand to Charity's cheek, smoothing away the tears. "No, tonight. I'm begging you—give him the choice. He's been betrayed by too many women he's loved. He will never trust you if you deceive him."

Charity began to sob, and Faith pulled her into her arms. She closed her eyes and stroked Charity's hair. "Lord, give my sister the courage and grace to do the right thing, please. Help her to tell the truth. And show her how much you love her." Faith ducked her head, giving Charity a tired smile. "It's going to work out. Just do the right thing and trust God. Mitch loves you. He told me so." Faith gave her a tight hug, then stood to her feet. "Should I call him?"

Charity wiped her face with her sleeve. "No, not yet. Would you mind getting me a wet washrag to blot my face?"

Faith smiled. "Sure." She headed for the door.

"And Faith?"

She turned.

"You won't say anything, will you? To Mitch or the family? It needs to come from me."

"No, not if you promise to tell him tonight."

Charity stared, her eyes steeped in fear. "I promise."

Faith smiled. "Good girl. I'll get that cold rag." She padded down the hall, stifling a yawn. Opening the linen closet, she grabbed a clean washcloth and soaked it good under the tap. She paused and stared in the mirror, barely seeing the exhaustion in her face for the barrage of thoughts in her head. So many lies: married but not; raped but not; pregnant but not. Faith sighed and twisted the wet rag in her hands. But at least she admitted the truth to her. Now she just had to tell Mitch.

Tonight.

Faith closed her eyes and leaned hard against the sink, the rag limp in her hands. "Oh, God, help her to do the right thing. Please." She sighed and wrung out the cloth one last time. Her lips tilted in a tired smile. Limp and wrung out. Funny. She felt exactly the same way.

14

"So? How do you think it went?"

Patrick looked up as he unbuttoned his shirt. "What, trimming the tree?"

Marcy pursed her lips in a wry smile. "No, you goose, the evening. You know—Charity, you, Faith. Having Mitch as a son-in-law, the whole thing. How do you feel it went?"

Patrick smiled and stepped out of his trousers. He hung them in the wardrobe, then peeled off his shirt and tossed it toward the hamper. It skimmed across the top and landed on the floor. "Fine, I suppose. It's good having her home, although I didn't get a chance to talk to her alone."

Marcy wiggled up against the headboard and bunched her knees to her chin. She tucked her flannel nightgown tightly around her feet, then pulled the covers up. There was a buzz of excitement in her manner. "Well, what about Mitch? You like him, don't you?"

He smiled and tugged his pajama bottoms up, then jerked the cord tight. "Of course I like him. He's a newspaper man, isn't he? And a smart one, judging from the little we talked." He reached for his pajama shirt and slipped it on. His mouth zagged into a droll smile. "He's perfect for Charity—no nonsense and too big to push around."

She giggled and slid down into the bed, a look of contentment on her face. "I know. I absolutely love him. He was such a god-send after the army said you were dead."

Patrick arched a brow. He leaned down and planted a kiss on her cheek. "I hope I've convinced you I'm very much alive, Mrs. O'Connor."

She rolled on her side and propped her head against her hand. She teased him with a smile and patted the bed. "I might need just a wee bit more convincing."

His hands settled loosely on his hips. "Must be all the romance in the air that's putting ideas in your head, woman. And I'll be more than glad to oblige. When I come back." He bent to brush his lips against hers, then headed for the door. "Keep the bed warm."

She sat up. "Where are you going?"

He snatched his robe off the hook on the door. He slipped it on and tied the sash. "To talk to Charity."

"Now?"

He scrounged around in the closet for his slippers. "Yes, now. She's alone."

"How do you know?"

He returned to the bed and sat, dropping his slippers on the floor with a thud. He put them on, one at a time, then turned to look Marcy in the eye. "Because that son-in-law of ours is still downstairs reading the paper. Claims he's a night owl. Tell me, does that strike you as odd?"

She blinked. "Well, maybe just a little."

He angled a brow. "A little? The man is on his honeymoon, married to a woman who has turned every male head since she was five. And he'd rather be downstairs reading the paper than in there with her?" He grunted, adjusting his shoe. "The *Boston Herald* is a good paper, if I say so myself, but no paper is that good. Something's not right."

Marcy wrinkled her brow. "What do you mean? Things seemed all right to me."

He turned to face her. "You were too busy with dinner and

decorating the tree to notice, but there's a tension in Mitch's manner, an unease. Charity's too, for that matter."

"That seems inevitable with Mitch seeing Faith again, and then Charity with Collin too."

He pressed his lips and shook his head. "No, I watched the interplay between Mitch and Faith tonight—it was warm and comfortable. The tension's with Mitch and Charity." He stood.

"You're not going to try and broach all that tonight, are you?"

He sighed and ran his hands over his face. "No, I don't have enough energy for both that and you." He grinned. "I'll reserve my strength and save that for another time. Right now I just want to tell her I love her. And that I'm glad she's home."

Marcy snuggled in the bed with a big yawn. "Hope I'm still up when you get back."

He flashed a grin over his shoulder on the way to the door. "Doesn't matter, darlin'. You're already committed."

Patrick moved down the hall, pausing at the top of the steps. A soft stream of lamplight still shone from the parlor. He shook his head. *Night owl, my foot.*

He stood in front of Charity's closed door and drew in a deep breath. He knocked, then pushed it ajar. "Charity?"

"Mitch? Is that you?"

"No, darlin', it's your father. May I come in?"

"Yes."

A shaft of moonlight lit the room, allowing him to see her form sitting up in the dark, blanket pressed to her chest. He moved close. "I noticed Mitch hasn't come up yet, so I thought I'd come in to say good night. Like I used to. Do you mind if I sit down?"

She shook her head and scooted over.

He reached to put his arm around her shoulder, then removed it when he felt her stiffen. He clasped his hands in his lap, suddenly feeling awkward. "Charity, I just wanted to tell you how glad I am that you're home."

"We probably won't stay, Father."

He shifted to stare at her, hurt by the indifference in her tone. "I know that, darlin', but I'm happy to see you, nonetheless. I missed you. We all did."

She turned away, and he saw a glimmer of wetness in her eyes. "I can't imagine Faith missed me all that much."

Her words weighted his head down. "Well, she did. She loves you. And so do I."

She blinked quickly, and her smile seemed to harden in the moonlight. "That's difficult to believe, Father, after what I did . . ."

He released a heavy breath. "Faith isn't one to hold a grudge, Charity, you know that. She's forgiven you long ago."

Her chin trembled. "Have you?"

He stared at this fragile daughter of his, and his heart clutched in his chest. "No need, darlin'. I've done nothing but fiercely love you since the day you were born."

"I wish I could believe that." She turned away, but not before he saw a trail of tears.

He drew in a deep breath and reached out to pull her close, collecting her in his arms. Her body was stiff, but he clutched her anyway, squeezing his eyes tight. "I wish you could too, darlin'. My heart's not the same without your love."

Her laugh was muffled and harsh. "There's always Faith."

He groaned and held her away, his eyes searching her face. "It's time to forgive your sister, Charity. It wasn't her fault that Hope died nor that she developed polio and needed our attention. Faith has forgiven you and moved on. I suggest you do the same."

She jerked away and shielded herself with the blanket. "Yes, she has. But then I've never been as good as Faith, have I, Father?"

He expelled a frustrated sigh. "Stop it, Charity. Now! I won't have lies uttered to my face, and that's all they are. Lies you've believed your whole life. You are my daughter, and I love you deeply. But all that love doesn't mean a thing if you won't accept it."

"Lies? Was it a lie when you deserted our family for a year to attend to Faith?"

Heat fused up the back of his neck. "She was sick. I know you were only six at the time, but you have to understand. A parent's heart is crushed when they lose a child, and I was close to losing another. Faith needed me. A true father doesn't desert a child in their time of need."

She shivered, the curve of her chin rigid as she lifted her head. "Yes, I know."

Her telling whisper sucked the life out of him. His shoulders slumped as he put a hand to his eyes. "I'm sorry, darlin'. Sorry for all the hurt I obviously caused. I want to make it up to you, I do. I want to make it right, but I can't until you forgive me. And Faith." He stood to his feet, suddenly overwhelmed with fatigue. "I'll leave you be for now, but this is not over, because I need your forgiveness and I need your love. Good night, darlin'."

He turned and left the room, his exhaustion complete.

She sat, still as a statue, covers still clutched to her throat. She blinked at the door, the blood rushing in her ears. Pressing a hand to her mouth, she stifled a sob that threatened the silence. Why had she done that? Why had she turned him away? She loved him! What was wrong with her heart that made it withdraw whenever her father reached out?

She slid down into the cool sheets, shivering from the absence of his love. She needed him to hold her, to love her, to tell her she was his girl. But he couldn't.

Her heart wouldn't let him.

A creak sounded at the door, and she froze in the bed. She held her breath as a large form eclipsed against the light in the hall. It faded into shadows when the door closed with a click.

"Mitch?"

The shadow stilled. "Charity? What are you doing up?"

She glanced at the clock on the nightstand, lit by a stream of moonlight. Midnight. She shuddered. "I couldn't sleep."

He moved toward her bed. "Are you all right? Do you need to use the bathroom?"

She shook her head and sniffed.

He sat down and bent to study her face. "Are you crying?"

She nodded and leaned into him with a sob.

His arms swallowed her up. "What's wrong? Are you sick again?"

"No. It's my father. He came to see me."

Mitch pulled away to look in her eyes. "What? Why?"

"To tell me he loved me, that he was glad I was home."

"That's good news, isn't it?"

"Not if I turned him away."

"Did you?"

She nodded, wiping her cheeks with the sleeve of her night-gown.

"Why?"

She put her hand over her mouth as a shiver traveled her body. "I don't know. Something's wrong with me. I need his love so badly, but I can't seem to accept it." She collapsed against his chest with a broken sob. "Oh, Mitch, I need to be held and loved. It's like I'm starved inside, empty. The feeling . . . it's so awful."

He stroked her hair with his hand, and his voice was tender. "Charity, I love you. Your father loves you, and most importantly, God loves you. The more you draw close to God, the more you will realize that and be free from this emptiness."

She clutched at his shirt. "Will you hold me? Lay beside me till I fall asleep?"

He hesitated for a long time, then slowly laid her back on

the bed. He reached down to take off his shoes, then tucked the covers tightly around her. He stretched out his legs as he sat back against the headboard and scooped her close to his side.

She released a soft sigh and snuggled close. The heat from his body seeped into hers, and she closed her eyes, melting against him. She felt the urge to be closer yet and stretched her arm around his waist. She needed his love, his touch. Just enough to push the hurt away. She trailed her hand across the broad expanse of his chest, then lifted up to kiss the crook of his neck. She could feel his pulse as her lips explored.

"Charity, what are you doing?" His voice was a strangled mix of harsh and husky. He fisted her hand. "Don't start this."

She pressed in closer. "Mitch, I need your affection tonight. There's this frightening loneliness inside of me. I need your kisses, your love, to chase it away." She heard the catch of his breath as she skimmed her hand down the side of his leg.

He pushed her away and lunged from the bed. His voice was a hiss. "Charity, no! If we start, I won't be able to stop. And this is wrong."

"Please, just hold me and kiss me, nothing more. We'll be man and wife in the morning, eight or nine hours, at the most. God would understand. He knows I need to be close to you tonight. Please!"

He stared at her in shock, his chest heaving as the heat of his anger warred with the heat of his passion. Dear God, he wanted her, but not this way. Not in the throes of lust, where sin could taint a love already too fragile.

He closed his eyes. But she needed him. And he needed her. They wouldn't make love, his mind argued. But he knew better. Every touch, every kiss would set his body ashiver and his soul ashamed. His passion was intense, pent up and bottled far too long. But in the light of day—or the dark of night—when his fervor finally cooled, there would be nothing left but the burden of sin.

His. And hers.

He opened his eyes and watched as she pushed the covers aside, the pull of her invitation melting his resolve.

"Mitch, please . . . ," she whispered, and his gaze trailed from the deadly source of that plea to the soft curve of her nightgown as it clung to her body. Lust invaded his mind, bidden by thoughts of what lay beneath, and against his will, he found himself moving toward the bed.

All at once, he thought of her sister in a room down the hall, and his ragged breathing stilled. Faith had given him a glimpse of something holy and rare, a passion most pure. And despite the raging desire pumping through his veins at the moment, he meant to have it as well. With—or without—the woman before him.

He turned and ripped the cover off the other bed and retrieved his shoes. "I can't do this, Charity. I'm sleeping downstairs."

She sat up. "Mitch, wait, please . . . don't go!"

He ignored her and stormed toward the door, his anger resurging as his desire died down. He heaved it open with a whoosh of cold air, then closed it quietly, padding through the hall to wend his way down the steps. Blarney met him at the bottom with a wet nose to his hand. He absently scratched him under his chin and moved into the dark parlor to drop on the sofa. The glow of the waning fire did little to warm the chill within. He tugged the blanket closer and stared in the dark, his mind muddled with confusion and his stomach roiling.

He'd made love to scores of women, but never encountered this sick feeling inside at the mere temptation of it, the regret of passion so strong, his body had craved to relent. And this was a woman he loved, a woman who would be his wife in a handful of hours. Not even consummated, no matter how close. Why?

He closed his eyes, and grief pierced his heart.

Because he knew the truth. It had set him free despite the

chains of conviction that now tethered his soul. There'd been no guilt before, but no freedom either. He had been chained to sin, ignorant of the goodness of God or the blessing of obedience.

He pressed his hands to his face and closed his eyes, a low groan issuing from his lips. "God, forgive me for all the times I gave in to my lust."

For the hundredth time he searched his heart, wondering if he was making a mistake. He'd committed himself to marrying a woman with a heart for God, a woman he could trust. Charity was neither. Yet she needed him. And so did her baby.

He sucked in a deep breath, feeling closed in and desperate for air. His eyes flicked open, and his heart pounded in his chest. He swallowed hard, licking his dry lips. His eyes scanned the ceiling. *Am I making a mistake? Please, God . . . show me.*

He closed his eyes and sagged into the sofa, hours of fatigue finally having their way. Sleep hovered at the edge of his mind, and he felt a release. Tension slowly siphoned from his body. "Thank you," he whispered. And with gratitude yet warm on his lips, he sank into the folds of the couch and slept.

∾ ∾

"Trouble in paradise?"

Mitch's eyelids barely peeled open. A blur of navy serge towered over him. He blinked. Patrick O'Connor stared, newspaper tucked under his arm and a compressed smile on his lips.

Mitch's brain kicked into gear. He lurched up on the sofa. The bedspread slithered to the floor in a heap. "Mr. O'Connor, I must have fallen asleep."

Patrick stooped to retrieve the blanket, letting it dangle in his hand. His brow jagged up in blatant curiosity, the faintest glimmer of a smile threatening.

Mitch tunneled his fingers through his hair and cleared his throat. "It's not what you think, Mr. O'Connor. I have a snoring problem."

Patrick nodded and tossed the cover back on the sofa. "Marcy wants to know if you'd like a cup of coffee."

Mitch shifted his legs to the floor and began kneading the back of his neck. "That sounds wonderful. What time is it?"

"Eight. We leave for Mrs. Gerson's at ten. I'll get that coffee."

"Mr. O'Connor?"

Patrick turned.

Mitch rose, quickly tucking in his wrinkled shirt. "Charity and I have plans . . . I'd hoped to buy her breakfast out." Heat singed the back of his neck. "Errands to run, you know."

Patrick nodded, eyeing him with a narrowed gaze. "No problem. I'll tell Marcy." Patrick headed toward the kitchen, then stopped to face him at the door.

"You know, Mitch, Charity is what I've always lovingly referred to as a handful. More than any of my children, with the exception of Katie, she's always needed more attention. You know, a firm hand coupled with a firm heart. I've struggled over twenty years to understand her, and I haven't mastered it yet. Don't let a marriage of a few days derail you."

Mitch swallowed. "Yes, sir. Thank you."

"You're welcome." Patrick's eyes traveled the length of him. "It might be good to clean up and get into some fresh clothes. Those look like you've been wrestling with the devil all night."

Heat bloodied his cheeks. "Yes, sir."

"Hot coffee will be waiting when you come down." Patrick smiled and left the room.

Mitch released a shuddering breath. Wrestling with the devil. And then some.

ᘗ ᘖ

A soft moan of contentment drifted from her lips as she dreamed, snuggling against her husband-to-be. Her hand dropped to the emptiness beside her, and she jolted up. Her gaze shifted to Faith's empty bed, bereft of its bedspread, and she chewed on her lip. He'd actually done it—slept downstairs, just as he said. Riddled with guilt, no doubt.

Over nothing.

She leaned back on her pillow and tugged the covers to her chin. She bit the nail of her thumb as her lips curved into a shy smile. She thought of the way he'd looked at her last night, his eyes glazed like a man possessed. Delicious heat braised her cheeks. If it weren't for her own nagging guilt over tempting him—and his refusal to give in—today, the day of her wedding, would be perfect. She sighed. But her condemnation—and his—would be gone once the vows were said, she reminded herself.

Tingles of excitement raced through her. They would be man and wife today. She bit her lip as she thought of her promise to Faith. No, telling him now was way too risky. She would tell him tonight. She slid deep under the covers, the warmth in her cheeks traveling to the tips of her toes. Right after he made mad, passionate love to her. A giggle rose in her throat, the sound of it muffled from the weight of the spread. Preferably enough times to seal his fate. She grinned. And his heart.

ᏌᏫ ᏃᎳ

Mitch reread the headline for the umpteenth time, not comprehending any better than the first. He dropped the newspaper to his chest and closed his eyes, shifting to adjust his cramped legs on the sofa. The scent of pine needles drifted in the air along with a hint of cinnamon from Marcy's Christmas pinecones, soaked for days and then dried with care. They now graced the tree, along with a wealth of homemade ornaments and cranberries on a string, a subtle reminder that Christmas was less than a week away. The fire in the hearth cracked and popped, the only sound in a house where everyone had long since gone to bed.

A key rattled in the front door.

Mitch scowled. Well, almost everyone.

He snatched the paper back up and gave the headline another go. He heard Faith's gentle laugh followed by Collin's low rumble. And then nothing. Mitch scowled again, staring at the headline longer than he cared to.

"Hey, what are you still doing up? We thought you'd be in bed at dusk."

Mitch dipped the paper enough to peer over the top, his eyes narrowed in annoyance at Faith's teasing tone. "It was closed."

She blinked. The smile faded on her face. "City Hall?"

The paper rustled back up, accompanied by a grunt. "Nope, that was open. The marriage license window. Closed up tighter than a wedding band on a chubby girl's hand. Seems they pick and choose their hours at random."

Faith moved to his side and stared down at him with sympathetic eyes. "I'm sorry, Mitch. But you only have to wait till Monday, right?"

He sighed and rubbed a hand over his face. "So they tell me."

Faith bent and kissed him on the cheek. "The wait is almost over, my friend. Besides, you should be happy. This was a big step for Charity. I'm proud of her. And you too." She stood and stretched. "Well, I'd tell you to sleep well, but I don't think it would do much good. Good night, Mitch."

He squinted over the top of the paper, confused by her comments. He opened his mouth to say something, then stopped when she stood on tiptoe to give Collin a quick kiss on the lips. "Good night, Collin. See you tomorrow."

"Good night, Little Bit. Love you."

"Me too."

Mitch heard the sound of her steps retreating up the stairs. He returned to his paper.

"I'm going to get a drink of water before I go. You want anything?"

Mitch didn't bother to glance up. "No, thanks."

Collin headed for the kitchen and then returned a few moments later, apparently standing at the entrance of the parlor. Mitch buried himself behind the *Herald*. He was in no mood to chat, but the silence ate at his gut. He exhaled and lowered the paper. "Is there something you want?"

"Yeah, there is." Collin shifted a hip and pushed his hands deep in his pockets. He ambled into the room and straddled the edge of the loveseat, arms folded across his chest. He avoided Mitch's eyes and stared at the tree as if seeing it for the first time.

Mitch gritted his teeth. "Yeah?"

"Sorry about City Hall."

"Yeah, well, they can't work around me, I guess."

"Nope."

Irritation twitched in Mitch's jaw as he studied him. "You got something on your mind, Collin?"

Collin drew in a deep breath and finally looked at him. "Yeah, I do. I wanted to apologize. For being such a jerk."

"Okay."

"I had no right to be jealous. I trust Faith. And you've never done me any harm."

A scowled tainted Mitch's lips. "Practically threw her in your lap. Been kicking myself ever since."

"I know. Can't say I would have done the same."

Mitch tossed the paper aside and sighed. He rubbed his eyes with his fingers. "Seemed like the right thing to do at the time."

Collin stood up. "It was. We were meant for each other."

He looked up with regret in his eyes. "Yeah, I know."

"So are you and Charity. I didn't think so at first, but I've changed my mind."

"Why?"

Collin pulled his gloves from his coat pocket and shoved them on, tugging them tight. "Because you're strong. She needs that."

"Yeah, right. My 220 pounds could take her 120 anytime."

"I meant spiritually."

His laugh was hollow. "Don't bet on it."

"Not many men would do what you're doing, forgive and forget. I'm not sure I could."

The muscles in Mitch's stomach tensed. "Yeah, that's me. An atypical guy." He swung his feet to the floor and stretched his arms high over his head. His heart pounded in his chest. "So, Faith told you, then?"

"Yeah. She said Charity promised to drop the bomb last night. I was pretty shocked."

"Not as much as me."

Collin laughed. "No, I guess not. I admire you, though. I know you love her, but honestly, if she'd lied to me about being raped and pregnant, I'd be long gone."

Mitch felt like he'd been gut-punched. He forced himself to breathe. "Yeah, I'm a real sucker for punishment."

"You okay?"

He looked up, the air thick in his throat. "How did Faith find out? Do you know?"

Collin shook his head. "Female issues, from what I gather. I think Faith confronted her and Charity confessed. Made her promise to tell you the truth before you got married." Collin headed for the door. "Of course, I guess you could look at it that she loved you enough to lie."

Mitch stared. "Yeah. Just not enough to tell the truth."

Collin turned. "What?"

"Good night, Collin. Thanks for the apology."

"You're welcome. Get some sleep. You look like you just lost your best friend."

Mitch dropped back against the sofa and closed his eyes. "Yeah, I will."

A sick feeling clogged in his throat. *And I have.*

❧ ❧

She stretched in her sleep, the curved steel headboard cool to the touch as she grazed it with her hand. The sound of movement stirred behind her, and she rolled over. She yawned with a sleepy smile on her face. "Good morning."

He ignored her, his broad back bent over the bed.

"Mitch?"

Silence.

She rubbed her eyes and sat up, noticing the suitcase. "What are you doing?"

He adjusted a few things, then snapped it closed. He jerked it off the bed and turned, his face as hard and cold as her cast-iron bed. "Leaving."

All air suspended in her throat, and the blood rushed from her face, making her dizzy. She put a hand to her head. "Leaving? But, why? What happened?"

He stared, eyes slitted and void of all warmth. "You've lied to me for the last time. It's over." He started for the door.

She cried out and lurched from the bed, attempting to stand on both legs. "Mitch, no! At least talk to me. Don't leave like this. Please!"

He spun around. "Get back in that bed; you're going to strain your silly leg."

She hobbled forward, a fiery sting shooting the length of her cast. She grimaced and blinked. His face floated before her in a wash of tears. "Not unless we talk. You owe me that."

He hurled the suitcase against the door and charged toward her, swearing under his breath. He heaved her up and tossed

❧ 346 ❧

her back on the bed, his eyes dark with fury. Towering over her, he clenched his fists at his sides. "I don't owe you a blasted thing, you little liar, but the back of my hand."

"Who told you . . . ," she whispered. Her fingers shook as she pushed hair from her eyes.

The cords of his neck pulsed as he glared. "You mean instead of you? The woman I gave my trust . . . poured my heart out to?"

She closed her eyes. Tears glazed her cheeks. "How could she? Faith promised—"

His laugh was savage. "And we both know Faith doesn't lie, now don't we? Unlike you. No, don't hang this one on her, Charity. Collin tripped you up."

She looked up at him, fear shivering through her. "I did it because I love you. I didn't want to lose you."

His face was hard. "Big mistake, little girl. You didn't just lose me as a husband and a lover. You lost me as a friend." He strode toward the door.

"Mitch, no! You love me, I know you do."

He stooped to pick up his suitcase and paused, his back rigid as ice. "You're right, I do." He slowly turned. "But I'll get over it. Out of sight, out of mind. You'll be here and I'll be there. With Kathleen. She's seen me through more than one heartache; I suspect she'll see me through this. Only this time, she'll do it as my wife." He jerked the door open and flung it against the wall with a loud crack. He hurried down the hall.

She screamed. A horrendous ache seared inside. "Please, God, no! Faith! Mother!" She started from the bed and collapsed on the floor, her body wracked with sobs. She heard footsteps running and screamed again, keening in pain.

"Charity, what's wrong?" Faith hurried to her side. She knelt to hold her in her arms.

She could barely get the words out for weeping. "Mitch . . . he . . . left me. Collin told him . . . and he's leaving. Faith, stop him, please."

Faith grabbed Charity's shoulders, her eyes wide with shock. "You mean you didn't tell him? He didn't know?"

"I w-was afraid. A-afraid of this. And now he's gone." She clutched her sister's hand. "He trusts you, Faith, stop him. I love him and I need him. Please?"

Faith stared, then jumped to her feet. Charity shuddered as her sister fled the room. With a moan, she crumpled to the floor in a heap. A piercing wail escaped her throat. *Dear God, what have I done?*

꿏 ꙙ

Mitch dropped his suitcase with a resounding clunk and butted the kitchen door open with his fist. The swinging door squealed on its hinges, banging against the wall with an ominous thud.

Patrick jumped up from the table while Marcy stood at the stove, eyes round with shock.

"What the devil's going on up there?" Patrick demanded.

Anger pumped in Mitch's chest. "Charity's upset."

Patrick threw his newspaper on the table. "What the blazes for?"

"I'm leaving."

Marcy's face turned white. "Mitch, what are you saying?"

"I'm sorry, Mrs. O'Connor, but Charity and I are through."

The veins in Patrick's temple were pronounced. He slammed his chair against the table and glared at Mitch. "What? You're running out on your marriage? You're going to bolt every time there's a fair-weather storm?"

Mitch clenched his fists. His veins kept pace with Patrick's. "Yeah, well, this is more like a hurricane making landfall, Mr. O'Connor. And just for the record? There is no marriage."

Marcy's cheeks went ashen. "What?"

He tore his glare from Patrick's to look at Marcy. His heart twisted at the grief in her eyes. "I'm sorry, Mrs. O'Connor, but Charity lied. I tried to tell you the day we arrived, but she railroaded me into lying along with her. Please forgive me for that. I never meant to hurt you."

Patrick stormed over to jab his finger into Mitch's chest. "You mean to tell me you've been sleeping with my daughter without the benefit of marriage . . . right under my own roof?"

Mitch clamped his lips tight. "Not in the biblical sense, sir."

"What the blazes is that supposed to mean?" Patrick bellowed.

Marcy slumped in a chair. "Oh, God help us."

Heat seared the back of Mitch's neck. "It means I didn't make love to her."

"Mama, what's going on?" Katie demanded, barreling into the kitchen with Miss Buford in her arms. "Charity's crying."

The door slammed open again, and everyone looked up. Faith stood, hand pressed to the door and green eyes shooting fire. "Mitch Dennehy, what do you think you're doing?"

Mitch spied a bleary-eyed Sean and Beth making their way to the kitchen. He hung his head and groaned. "I just came to say goodbye to your parents, but apparently the whole family is here to see me off."

Faith let the door swing shut. She crossed her arms and jutted her chin in his face. "My sister is upstairs crying her heart out because you're too pig-headed to forgive her. You're making a big mistake."

He ground his teeth. Muscles jerked everywhere in his body. "Correction. I made a big mistake. Now I'm rectifying it." He tried to move toward the door.

Faith blocked his way, her jaw set just like his. "You're a coward, you know that, Mitch Dennehy?"

"That seems to be the general consensus. And you're blinkin' right I am. I've had my heart bashed in one too many times by you O'Connor women. Get out of my way, Faith." He tried to bulldoze past.

Sean blocked his path. "Settle down, Mitch. Can't we just cool down and talk this out?"

Mitch thumped Sean on the chest, his patience exhausted. "No, we can't, Sean. When I cool down, I have a tendency to get bamboozled by you O'Connors. Well, I'm done. With your sister and this family." He shoved Sean back and blasted through the door, snatching his suitcase on the way to the front porch.

A noisy parade followed, led by Patrick, whose face was as red as the cranberries looping the tree. He pushed the storm door wide, glaring at Mitch on the porch. "See here, Dennehy, you are not going to come into my house and cause this uproar, then waltz out of here scot-free, leaving nothing but problems."

Mitch spun around. "Don't threaten me, Mr. O'Connor. Your daughter has bigger problems than me. And if you're looking to solve them, I'd suggest you look in the mirror."

Patrick's face blanched white. "What are you talking about?"

"Let's just say ol' Uncle Paul left a lasting impression. I'll let Charity fill you in on the gory details. It's about time you heard the whole story."

Patrick clamped his arm. His eyes were glazed with shock. "What are you saying?"

Mitch's gaze swept past Patrick. Katie's eyes were wide as she huddled in her mother's arms. Sean burrowed Beth close to his side, then slid an arm around Faith's shoulder. Steven was making his way down the steps, a puzzled look on his face.

Mitch looked back at Patrick, sick at the sorrow he saw. He exhaled a heavy breath. "I can't say, Mr. O'Connor, not in front of your children."

Patrick closed his eyes. His fingers gouged white on the door. "Sean, take the others into the kitchen and get them something to eat. Faith, go check on Charity, please. *Now.*"

They silently dispersed, each to their assigned duty, leaving

Marcy in a near stupor and Patrick leaning limp against the wall. He hung his head and gripped the door for support. His voice was barely a whisper. "I'll ask you again. What are you saying?"

Mitch drew in a deep breath and shifted his valise from one hand to the other, avoiding Patrick's eyes. "On the ship, Charity had a nightmare. It triggered memories. She claims your brother sexually abused her . . . apparently a number of times . . . when he stayed that summer."

Patrick sagged against the door with a low groan. "Please, God, no . . ."

Marcy clutched him from behind with a feeble cry, her shoulders heaving into a sob.

"Did he . . ." Patrick couldn't go on.

"She doesn't remember the details, just that it hurt."

Patrick turned and slumped into Marcy's arms with a violent sob.

Mitch stared for several seconds, a wave of compassion dousing his anger. He finally spoke. "Mr. O'Connor, Charity is desperate for your love. She needs to heal. And only your love and God's can accomplish that."

Patrick nodded, trying to compose himself. He wiped his face with his sleeve. When he looked up, his eyes were raw. "Is there more?"

"Only the reason I'm leaving."

Patrick lifted his chin and straightened his shoulders, then clutched Marcy tightly to his side. He pushed the storm door open. "Care to come in and discuss it?"

Mitch switched the suitcase to his other hand. "I don't think so, Mr. O'Connor. I need to be away from Charity. If I go inside, I'm afraid the warmth and love of your family will wear me down. Charity's a lucky girl, you know. She just doesn't realize it."

Patrick nodded. "All right. Why are you leaving, then?"

Mitch released a deep breath. "Because your daughter lied to me. Over and over. But this time was the worst. Before Bridget asked me to bring her home, I was practically engaged back in Ireland. But Charity's convinced that she loves me—"

"And you love her?" Marcy's eyes were hopeful.

Mitch set the suitcase on the floor. He plunged his hands deep in his pockets and bent his head. "I do, Mrs. O'Connor, but I can't marry a woman I don't trust."

Patrick cleared his throat. "How did she lie to you?"

"She led me to believe Rigan Gallagher had raped her and that she was pregnant."

Marcy blinked and turned her face into Patrick's shoulder. "Oh, Charity . . ."

Patrick absently rubbed Marcy's back. "You mean the man who attacked her?"

Mitch nodded.

"How do you know he didn't?"

"Because Faith confronted her and she confessed. On the ship, when she realized I was intent on returning to Ireland to marry someone else, she started getting sick toward the end of the sailing. Throwing up and leading me to believe she was pregnant." Mitch rubbed his fingers to the side of his head. "I was worried. I thought she might try to harm herself." He sighed. "So I proposed."

"And the rings?" Marcy looked at him expectantly.

"Bridget thought it would be a good idea. One, because she knew Charity didn't want to leave Ireland and would fight it, which she did. Bridget said it would give me leeway if people thought I was Charity's husband. And two, because it would protect Charity's reputation while we traveled together. The weather was nasty when we left the ship, so with our gloves on, we simply forgot to take the rings off before we arrived here."

Marcy shook her head. "Mother and Charity—they're a lot alike, you know."

He attempted a half smile. "They're very close, Mrs. O'Connor. It about tore Bridget's heart out to send Charity home."

Patrick looked up. "How did Faith find out in the first place, to confront her?"

"When we arrived, I confided in her that Charity and I weren't married, telling her about the rape and pregnancy." Mitch looked down at his feet, suddenly conscious of Marcy's gaze. His cheeks grew warm. "Apparently Charity was having her time of the month, and Faith put two and two together. She made Charity promise to tell me the truth before we went to City Hall."

"City Hall?" Marcy repeated.

He nodded. "Yesterday, to get married. Only we found out they don't perform marriages on the second and fourth weekends. At any rate, Charity was supposed to tell me before we went. Only she didn't. It was Collin who dropped the bomb. By accident."

Patrick rubbed his hand over his face. "God, forgive us."

"I swear to you, Mr. O'Connor, I slept on the couch both nights."

Patrick eyed him. "So nothing happened?"

Blood flooded Mitch's cheeks. He looked away. "No."

"Thank you for your honesty. It appears we've got our work cut out with this wayward daughter of ours." He sighed. "I'm sorry for the grief she's caused you."

He picked up his luggage. "I love her a lot, Mr. O'Connor. I'd give anything if she were like Faith, a woman with deep faith. But she's not. She's Charity. And because of my own problems, I can't get past the distrust and her lack of regard for God."

"I understand." Patrick opened the storm door and held out his hand.

Mitch shook it and then nodded at Marcy. "Mrs. O'Connor, I'm sorry I lied. I never should have allowed it. I thought I was stronger than that, but your daughter can be a very persuasive woman."

Marcy pushed past her husband and put her arms around Mitch, hugging him fiercely. "You're quite a loss for us, Mitch Dennehy. My heart grieves for my daughter and all of us."

Mitch cleared his throat. "Me too, Mrs. O'Connor." He turned to go.

Patrick stepped out on the porch and put a hand on his shoulder. "Where are you headed? Can I call you a cab?"

Mitch shook his head. "No, thanks, I'll call for one at the confectionary on the corner. I'll get a room in town and then take the first ship that sails."

"Mitch?"

Patrick and Marcy turned to see Faith at the door, her face wet with tears. "Father, may I speak with Mitch before he leaves? Please?"

Patrick patted Marcy's shoulder and steered her inside, rubbing her arms to ward off the cold. "Don't be long, Faith. Mitch needs to go, and we need to get ready for church."

Faith tugged a jacket from the coatrack and eased past her parents to stand beside Mitch on the porch.

Mitch set his suitcase down and helped her on with her coat. "Thanks again, Mr. and Mrs. O'Connor, for your hospitality. And your understanding."

They nodded and closed the door, leaving him alone with Faith. He blew out a weary breath and picked up his valise, continuing down the steps to the front gate. They walked in silence down the sidewalk for several yards. The cool air was a welcome change from the tension at the house. He gave her a sideways glance. "It's cold. Why don't you go back?"

She looked up at him, and her face was swollen from crying. With a small heave, she launched herself against his chest, squeezing tightly. "Oh, Mitch, I'm so sorry. My heart is sick. For you and for Charity."

He set his bag down and embraced her, pressing his head to her hair. "I'm going to miss you, Faith O'Connor." He swallowed hard. "For the rest of my life."

She pulled away and sniffed, swabbing her face with the back of her hand. "I love you, Mitch. I always will. I pray that God blesses you more than you ever dreamed possible."

He grazed her chin with his thumb. "He already did. With you. Wife or friend, you're the best there is."

"Charity has potential too. As a wife and a friend. She begged me to ask you for a second chance."

His smile was sad. "A very wise woman once told me that the man she married would have to love God with the same intensity as she did. In fact, she told me she turned away the man she loved because he cared more for his own lust than for her. More for himself than her God. You were right then, Faith, and your words are right now."

She shivered. "I know."

He hugged her one last time. "Go home and love on your sister. She's starved for it."

Faith nodded and pulled away. "I'll never forget you, Mitch."

"Nor I, you, my friend." He hoisted his suitcase in his hand. "Now, Collin McGuire?" He grinned. "Him I'd like to forget."

სდ ჵ

The glow of Christmas Eve was everywhere except in the gloom of Charity's room. The distant sound of clatter from the kitchen and Katie's giggles filtered in beneath her closed door, along with the smell of roast turkey and fresh-baked pies. Charity rolled over and curled one leg into a ball, the other still hard in the cast. She stared aimlessly across the room, oblivious to the beauty of dusk as it streamed across Faith's bed in pale lavender hues.

With great effort, she lifted her head to glance at the clock. When she did, a fresh wash of tears invaded her eyes. There on the nightstand stood a miniature balsam tree, snipped from the top of one of her father's fir trees. A strand of cranberries draped it with care, along with shimmering strands of tinsel. Tiny lace snowflake doilies, the kind Faith and Hope used to soak in Marcy's sugar solution to make them stiff, perched on the branches like stars in a verdant sky.

Charity's hand flew to her mouth to stifle a sob. She remembered—Faith remembered! She touched the tip of her finger to one of the snowflakes, and forgotten memories flooded her mind. From the age of two until six, she had awakened to her own personal tree, provided by twin sisters who'd shamelessly doted on her. Whether Hope's idea or Faith's, she didn't know. But they'd found a way to make sure she'd sleep in her own bed and not under the tree, with nary a tear shed in the process. A sad smile curved her lips.

Precious memories.

She laid back on the pillow, knowing they'd be coming for her soon. It was almost five, the time when the doorbell would ring and Collin and their neighbor, Mrs. Gerson, would arrive, joining in on the laughter and love. Her father or Sean would carry her to the table where her mother and Faith would display a feast for the senses. Wassail would be poured and candles lit while heads bowed and her father prayed, rejoicing in the celebration of Christ.

Charity squeezed her eyes shut, forcing rivulets of tears to soak her face. Dear Lord, when would the weeping stop? Ten days had passed since Mitch walked out that door, and the waterworks showed no sign of relenting. Nor the lonely pain of missing him.

Not that she'd been alone. No, her family hadn't allowed that. Especially her father and Faith. Sitting by her bed whenever she was awake, reading to her, talking to her, loving her. Once, when she'd jolted with a nightmare in the middle of the night, Faith had crawled in beside her and rocked her in her arms. It was sustenance to her battered soul. She cried and they soothed. She hurt and they loved.

The door creaked open and a shaft of light split the room.

The smell of musk soap and pipe tobacco drifted in along with it, stirring her heart. Her father loomed large in the light, reminding her of Mitch, and she was struck at how much she craved both men's love.

He closed the door to a crack, reducing his form to a shadow as he moved to her bed. He sat in the chair and leaned forward, his eyes searching hers in the dark. "You awake, darlin'?"

She rolled on her side to look up. "Is it time?"

His chuckle echoed rich and husky in the small room, filling it with his presence. "It's Christmas Eve, darlin', not a funeral. It will do you good. Get your mind off things."

She sniffed. "I won't be much fun."

He stroked her hair. "Broken hearts have a way of doing that, I'm afraid. But they always heal."

His touch brought tears to her eyes. "I don't know if I'll ever heal. Mitch is a part of my soul, my heart. When he left, it felt like something inside of me died."

He sat beside her and cradled her in his arms. His voice was thick with emotion and tinged with resolve. "You'll heal, darlin', if it takes the rest of my life to see to it. My heart grieves with you, Charity, broken just like yours for the loss you've sustained. But there's a part of me that's glad I can hold you and comfort you, love you like I've wanted to for so many years."

Charity laid her head on his chest, the salt of her tears mixing with the scent of her childhood. She wound her fingers tightly around his neck, soaking in his love. She shuddered in his arms, her voice a broken whisper. "I need you, Daddy."

A hoarse moan rasped against her ear as he squeezed her tightly in his arms, bending low to tuck his head against hers. "I need you too, darlin', more than you know. You've been the missing piece of the puzzle all these years. The piece of my heart I couldn't find. I love you, Charity. I always have."

Something wet slid down her neck, and when his chest heaved against her face, she knew he was crying too. They huddled like that for several moments, her tears soaking his shirt, while his dampened her neck. And when their weeping finally stilled, the silence was warm and safe and full of promise.

"Charity . . ." Her father's voice was gruff with emotion.

She stroked a hand across his shoulder. "Yes, Father?"

He shuddered before he cleared his throat. "I . . . need your forgiveness."

She pulled away to look up at him and touched her hand to his cheek. "Father, I forgive you. I know Faith was sick and needed you . . ."

"No . . . not about Faith." He paused, then looked away, his eyes glossy with wetness. "About my brother. Uncle Paul."

She sucked in a harsh breath, the sound drawing his gaze. "You knew?"

"No . . . not until Mitch told me." He closed his eyes and pressed a palm to his forehead, gouging his skin with the pressure. He exhaled and opened his eyes once again. "I had no idea. And when I found out, I wished . . . I wished Paul were alive . . . so I could hurt him."

There was no way to stop it. The sobs escaped from her throat and wracked her body against his. "Oh, Daddy, he hurt me . . . he made me feel so ashamed."

"Darlin', why didn't you tell me? Why?"

She clutched him with all her might. "Because he said he would tell . . . tell you I was bad. And I didn't want that. I loved you, Daddy. I was your girl."

He crushed her to him with a groan while his hand kneaded her shoulder. "You'll always be my girl, Charity. Daddy's girl. Please forgive me for not being there to protect you."

Something inside of her opened up, filling her with joy. "I forgive you, Daddy, always. Forgive me for turning you away all these years. I need your love. Now, more than ever."

His raspy chuckle vibrated against her cheek, the sound buoying her with hope. "You have it, darlin'. Now, more than ever."

15

Mitch stared out the window of his office, his eyes glued to the red glow of dusk staining the city skyline, lingering with its varying shades of gloom. He sighed. Another day behind. One step closer to getting on with his life. He crossed his arms and leaned back, resting his head on the chair, letting his mind go numb. Not that it took any effort.

Numb was what he did best these days, at least since he'd sailed from Boston. The trip had been excruciating. Seven days of tossing and turning, both in his mind and in the ship, leaving him with a sickness in his gut that rivaled the flu. He closed his eyes. He was sick, all right. Sick with despair, loneliness, hurt. And the only remedy his body and soul craved was a lost little girl who was sheer poison to his system. A poor antidote to love betrayed.

He sucked in a deep breath and opened his eyes. It was time to move on. He'd done it before; he'd do it again. Only this time Kathleen would be there to soften the blow. She hadn't said a word about Charity since he returned, other than welcoming him back like all the others. After a few minutes of ribbing over the way he had left, Michael had been ecstatic and Bridie, belligerently beaming. According to Michael, Rigan Gallagher had disappeared from the face of the earth, his father apparently none the wiser as to the reason why. Even Jamie had been ready to turn the reins back over, preferring the comfort of his old job to the demands of management. A faint smile crossed Mitch's lips. It was good to be loved. Even if it wasn't the kind he was looking for at the moment.

"Mitch?"

He spun around in the chair, heat slinking up the back of his neck. "Kathleen, I was just thinking of you."

It was her turn to blush, albeit much prettier than his. She dipped her head and smiled, bonded to the side of the door like epoxy. "I finished your report. Is there anything else you need before I go?" She uttered the words, then looked down at her feet with a fresh whoosh of red at the way it had sounded.

He grinned. "Thanks for staying. That's one less headache for Michael in the morning."

She nodded and backed away. "Well, then, good night."

"Wait."

She startled.

He laughed. "I mean, why don't you stay? Talk a while."

Her chest rose and fell with a deep breath before she made her way to the chair in front of his desk. With a timid smile, she sat on the edge.

He smiled and leaned an elbow on his desk to prop his chin in his hand. "I'm not going to bite, you know. I don't believe I ever did."

She glanced up, a definite smile on her lips. "No, not that I recall. Thanks for leaving the letter of encouragement. I read it almost every night."

"Thanks for your prayers. I felt them."

Her eyes glowed. "I'm glad. I pretty much kept a constant vigil." She focused on her hands, knotted in her lap. "Especially when I knew you were on the ship."

He scratched his head and leaned back. "Yeah, well, the ship was fine. It was nearing Boston where the problems began."

She looked up. "What do you mean?"

"It's a long story, but the sum of it is that I asked Charity to marry me."

He heard her catch her breath, the shock evident in her eyes. "Oh . . ."

"Because I thought Rigan raped her and she was pregnant."

"Oh."

"But she lied."

Kathleen swallowed hard. "Oh?"

"Yeah. So I hightailed it out of there. But I wanted you to know that it was a close call."

She seemed to teeter on the edge of the chair. "How close?" she whispered.

Heat collared his neck. "Very."

"You're still in love with her, then?"

He stared at her. "Yes, but I have no intention of doing anything about it. Other than falling in love with you."

She looked down again and began picking at her nails. "And how do you propose to do that?"

"By courting you like I should have years ago. If you'll let me."

She continued to fidget, her eyes fixed on her fingers, but a semblance of a smile flickered across her lips. "As if I could stop you once you've made up your mind."

"I have."

Her gaze locked with his. "I won't marry a man in love with someone else. But I can try to help you get over her."

"That's all I'm asking. That and to be my wife when the time is right."

She rose to her feet and moved toward the door, giving him a shy smile over her shoulder. "Well, then, I suppose I could use a ride home."

❧ ❦

"So, how's the invalid today?" Faith poked her head in the kitchen with a smile.

Charity continued to peel the potato in hand. "One week and counting until the cast comes off, and the doctor says I'll be good as new." She flashed a wry grin. "I guess there's no need to ask how you're doing with that sparkle in your eye."

Faith chuckled as she sauntered to the sink to get a drink. She shot a grin over her shoulder. "Marriage is even better than I thought." She sighed and leaned against the counter, filling a glass with water. "That man is amazing."

"Yeah, we O'Connor women have great taste in men." Charity's eyes glinted as she leaned forward. "So, tell me . . . how was it?"

Faith blushed and gulped a large swallow of water. "I told you, marriage is good."

Charity quirked a brow. "Not marriage, 'it.' Come on, Faith, give. I have no one else to ask, and I'm dying to know. Is sleeping with Collin wonderful?"

Faith chugged the rest of her water and set the glass down. She pulled a knife from the drawer and hurried over to sit. Her face was bright red. "Charity, hush! Keep your voice down." She plucked a potato from the bowl and began peeling, her eyes suddenly serious. "That's a very private thing, you know—between a husband and wife. And something that you will find out for yourself someday." Her eyes took on a faraway look as she stared at the potato in her hand. A soft smile curved on her lips. "But take my word for it, when the Bible says two shall become one flesh, it's a bonding of human souls unlike anything in this world. Not only physically, but when you truly love someone and God's in the middle, spiritually and emotionally too." She looked up and grinned. "What can I say? Collin's amazing. I'm crazy about the man." She sliced a long peel of skin from the potato, then cleared her throat to quickly change the subject. "So, enough about me . . . how are *you* doing today?"

Charity scrunched her nose and sliced a long curl. "Today's

better than most. Maybe because I know I'm getting this albatross off my leg." She smiled. "But probably because I've cleared the air with you and Father."

Faith grimaced and stuck her thumb in her mouth. "Ouch! Stupid knife."

Charity grinned. "Yeah, I got the good one."

Faith's lips creased into a tolerant smile. "Guess the air's not completely cleared."

"Nope. Some things will never change. The good knife is mine."

Faith hesitated, then flicked a peel into the bowl. "Have you thought . . . about dating?"

Charity laughed. "No."

"I mean it. It would do you good to get out there again. Wouldn't take long. Never did."

Charity glanced up. "Maybe not, but you're the one who got her man."

"You will too." She assessed her through narrowed lids. "Care to pray about it?"

Charity stabbed a large potato to cut it in half. "Just because I cleared the air with you and Father doesn't mean I cleared it with God. I know it's basically my fault, but I'm a bit mad at him for Mitch leaving in the first place." The knife sliced cleanly through, meeting the cutting board with a loud clack. She looked up. "Him *and* Collin."

Faith cocked her head, apparently measuring her response. "You can't blame Collin. He thought you told him, and so did I. Besides, he feels awful."

"Good."

"I think you would have learned by now that nothing good comes from holding a grudge."

Charity stuck her nose in the air. "Yes, I have, but I reserve the right to give Collin a piece of my mind before I forgive him. *If* I forgive him."

Faith shook her head. "What about God? You gonna

continue to hold a grudge against him too? He only wants the best for you."

Charity gave Faith a thin stare. "Really? Well, he had the perfect opportunity with Mitch."

Faith sighed. "You are one of the most stubborn people I know."

Charity reached for the crutch that was leaning against the table. "Thank you. It's a trait that I hope will serve me well in the next month."

Faith looked up. "What do you mean by that?"

"Simply that mule-headed Dennehy has met his match." Charity stood, leaned on the crutch, and toddled to the sink to wash her hands. She nodded toward a pot on the counter. "Mind putting those potatoes in there for me?"

Faith reached for the pot, then clutched it to her chest. "What are you going to do?"

Charity lifted her chin. "Get him back. In the same way I got him in the first place."

"What, by lying?"

"Nope, I'm done with that. He can't abide women who lie."

Faith shook her head. "Then how?"

Charity arched a brow. "Seduction, pure and simple. The man is putty in my hands. Once I get him there, that is."

"There's nothing pure about seduction. And Mitch isn't looking for a woman like that."

"No, he isn't. But somehow he forgets that every time he kisses me. Which, by the way, he does in the most amazing manner."

Faith frowned. "Yes, I remember. But you'll lose him with tactics like that."

She shrugged her shoulders. "I've already lost him, Faith. What more do I have to lose?"

"Oh, I don't know. Your self-respect, maybe? God's approval?"

Charity laughed. "Haven't had God's approval before; why start now?"

"I'm telling you, you're making a big mistake trying to win him like that."

She cocked her head. "But not in trying to win him back, is that what you're saying?"

Faith chewed on her lip, apparently mulling it over. "No, you're not making a mistake going after him. Just in how you plan to do it."

"Well, at least we agree on something. I never thought I'd see the day. So you'll help me convince Father to let me go back?"

Faith stared, then finally sighed. "Okay, I'll help you. On one condition."

Her eyes narrowed. "What?"

"No seduction. Just plain, God-fearing honesty."

Charity crossed her arms. "No way. That man plans on marrying another woman, and soon. I need all the weapons in my arsenal."

"Then I can't help you convince Father . . ."

Her lips skewed in thought as she stared at her sister. She finally plopped into the chair with a resigned smile. "Okay, deal. No seduction. I suppose it's hard to argue with a success story."

Faith grinned. "It is, isn't it? But you can have success too, you know."

"Well, I certainly intend to. Maybe not by seducing him, but I'm sure not going to let him get away scot-free." She gave Faith a pointed look. "I want to make sure that man understands what he's giving up."

Her sister's eyes were tender as they searched her face. "Just keep it on the up and up, Charity, please. I don't want to see you get hurt."

Charity released a heavy sigh and gave her a bittersweet

smile. "Me, neither, sis. But I can tell you one thing. It sure can't feel any worse."

⤳ ⤶

Charity squinted through the pane of glass in the door, then backed up to double-check the sign overhead. McGuire & Brady Printing Company. She took a deep breath and straightened her shoulders. She'd promised Faith she'd clear the air with Collin, but not before she gave him a piece of her mind. She pushed the door open and glanced up at the sound of a tinkling bell. She scanned the tiny shop, impressed with its neatness even though it was crowded with furniture, equipment, and stacks of paper everywhere. And no Collin.

A tall man with a thatch of brown hair tumbling over his eyes peered out from the back, telltale smudges of ink spanning his face. He blinked. "Can I help you?"

She crossed her arms. "Yes, I'd like to speak with Collin McGuire, please."

He smiled. "He's out making deliveries right now. Is there something I can do for you?"

Her eyes narrowed. "Not unless you want an earful, Mr. . . . ."

"Brady, John Brady." He reached out an ink-stained hand, shirtsleeves rolled up to expose a hard line of muscles knotting his arm.

She stared.

He quickly wiped his hand on his work apron, which looked suspiciously like he'd cleaned every machine in the place with it. "Sorry, tends to get a little messy in the back room."

She nodded, taking in the way his brown eyes twinkled despite the seriousness of his hard-chiseled face. "When do you expect him back?" She moved about, surveying the shop.

"Who?"

She turned and lifted a brow.

"Oh, you mean Collin. Not for a while, I'm afraid. He just left."

Her eyes widened. "Wait, you're Brady! Collin's trench mate during the war, right?"

He grinned, revealing perfectly straight, white teeth. "One and the same. And you?"

She smiled and extended a hand. "Charity O'Connor, Collin's former fiancée."

With a wide grin, he pumped it with a firmness that made her wince. He immediately pulled away. "Yeah, now I remember seeing you briefly at the wedding. You missed the reception, as I recall. Collin said you weren't feeling well. Sorry about the handshake. Sometimes I don't know my own strength. It just feels so good to finally put a face to a name."

"Not one used in vain, I hope?"

The sound of his laughter lifted her spirits. "I don't believe I'm at liberty to say."

She looked at the ink smudge on her hand and wrinkled her nose. "You wouldn't happen to have a spare rag, would you?"

Leaning over a box, he fished out a towel that was even dirtier than his apron. "It's not exactly pristine, but it should do the job."

"Thanks." She wiped her hand and tossed it back.

He caught it in the air and grinned. "So what do you think of our boy, married at last?"

She smiled and folded her arms. "Well, 'our boy' is not my boy anymore, so I guess I can say I'm pretty happy for the both of them. Actually, they're perfect for each other, although I have to admit, I never thought I'd see the likes of Collin McGuire enamored with God."

Brady shook his head and leaned against the doorframe, a boyish grin on his face. "I can tell ya, there were many a moment

I had my doubts. But God got him in the end." He shifted, his eyes boring into hers. "He usually does."

She cocked her head. "Oh, I forgot. You're the one who preached at him day and night till he was blue in the face. I'd love to know what you said that turned him around."

His grin softened into a smile. "Why, you interested?"

She blinked. He was attractive, but not her usual type. Too clean, too honest to suit her, none of the bad-boy gleam that always turned her head. And yet, there was something . . .

She gave him the benefit of her sweeping lashes and dazzling smile. "Maybe."

He stood up straight, shocking her with his towering height. "Good. Come by anytime for Bible study with Beth during lunch hour. She's here three days a week about this time." He glanced out the front window and smiled. "In fact, she's here right now, if you care to join us."

Charity looked up to see her sister running down the street. She swallowed hard and glanced back at Brady. "Bible study? You want me to come to Bible study? That's it?"

The smile faded on his face. "Yeah, of course. What did you think I meant?"

A blush heated her cheeks. A rare occurrence, except when it came to Mitch Dennehy. The bell over the door jangled, sounding like an alarm in her mind.

Beth was huffing when she finally rushed in. Her hand all but froze to the knob as she stared at Charity, mouth and door gaping. "Charity . . . what are you doing here?"

"I came to have it out with Collin."

Beth's face relaxed. Her gaze darted to Brady. A shy smile creased her lips. "Hi, Brady."

He grinned and walked over to loop an arm around her shoulders. He gave her a big-brother squeeze. "Hi, buddy, how was school today?"

Beth gazed up, her face positively glowing. "Good, Brady. I did what you said."

He planted a kiss on her head and grinned at Charity. "She's a quick study."

Charity cleared her throat. "Well, I guess I'll be going. I don't want to intrude."

Brady smiled. "Okay. Nice meeting you. Come by anytime." He turned and ushered her sister to the back room. Beth smiled and gave Charity a quick wave, then focused her attention on Brady as he reached for a Bible and plopped it on the table. He eased back in a battered cane-back chair, annoyingly oblivious to the fact that Charity was still in the room.

She blinked. What just happened? The cold shoulder? From a grown man? One preferring time spent with her waifish fifteen-year-old sister than her? She gaped at his back, irritated by the muscled span of it as he leaned over the table, head propped against one hand while flipping pages with the other. She lifted her chin. Who in the devil did he think he was, anyway? Mr. Holier-than-Thou?

She spun on her heel and charged toward the door, her pride stinging as much as the heat in her cheeks. She yanked it open with a loud clang of the bells, then slammed it closed to vent her frustration. Two men whistled as she passed, helping to temper her mood. She pressed her lips tight and ignored their smiles, jutting her chin in the air.

Bible study, her foot. When pigs—or Mr. John Brady—could fly.

The door banged closed, sending shivers through the small shop. Brady looked up with a grin. "So that's your big sister, Charity? Didn't get a chance to meet her at the wedding."

Beth bit her lip and nodded. "Do you think she's pretty? Everyone else does."

He studied the fragile hope in her eyes as she awaited his answer. He smiled and chucked her on the chin. "Not as pretty as you, Beth."

She blushed near scarlet and looked down at her open

notebook. "Don't lie to me, Brady. Everyone says Charity's one of the prettiest girls they've seen. At least every boy in my class."

He lifted her chin with his thumb, his eyes serious. "I'm not lying, Beth. Charity is beautiful, there's no doubt about that. But you've got a gentle beauty inside and out, which makes you twice as pretty, to my way of thinking."

She giggled and grabbed his hand, squeezing it tight. "You always know the right thing to say, John Brady." She picked up her pencil and began to doodle, working the edge of her lip with her teeth. "So . . . tell me, why have you never married?"

He looked up with a chuckle. "What?"

She lowered her gaze, quickly sketching on the paper. "You heard me. You're nice-looking and good, and you always say the right thing." She looked up and tilted her head. "How old are you, anyway? Haven't you ever fallen in love?"

This time he laughed out loud and pushed the Bible toward her. "Come on, Beth, you've been reading too many romance novels and not enough of this."

"I think you're stalling."

He leaned back in his chair and ran his hand over his emerging shadow of beard. He expended a weary sigh. "I'm twenty-six and I'll marry when God wants me to."

"That's no answer, and you know it. Tell the truth. Have you ever been in love?"

He looked up, softening at the innocence in her eyes. He smiled. "Yes, a long time ago."

She thudded her elbow on the table and leaned in, resting her jaw on her hand. Her eyes widened in expectation, accentuating their unusual violet hue. "So, what happened?"

"She sent me a letter during the war."

"A letter?"

His lips slanted into a droll smile. "She broke the engagement."

"Why?"

He sat up and started rustling through the pages of the Bible, his jaw set. "None of your business, young lady. We're here to discuss the Word of God, not my social life."

"Do you think you'll ever fall in love again?"

He glanced up. "Don't know. It's up to God."

She paused, rolling the pencil between two fingers. "Charity's free. Do you think you could fall in love with her?"

"Do you want to study or not?"

"It's just a harmless question. Do you?"

"One last answer, then no more, agreed?"

She nodded.

"I'll fall in love with a woman if and when God wants me to, but I can guarantee you one thing right off the bat. If I do, it will be someone with a heart for God and his Word. Now. Do you want to study or should I send you packing?"

She grinned and picked up her pencil. "Nope. That's all I needed to know. Studying would be lovely."

※ ⁂

"No? What do you mean, no?" Charity sat up straight in the chair, then leaned over the table to give Brady the benefit of her incriminating gaze.

He glanced up from the Bible. "You know what no means." His lips quirked. "Or maybe you don't."

She crossed her arms. "You're refusing to pray?"

He exhaled and closed the Bible, unwinding his long legs from around the chair. He stood and stretched. "About that, yes."

"But why? For a solid month now, you've been railing at me to get closer to God, badgering me with Scripture, and now you tell me you won't even pray?"

He extended his arms high overhead, his tight muscles straining with the effort. One of his thick, dark brows jagged up. "Railing? Badgering?"

"Oh, all right, I came here willingly, but only because I needed your help."

He strolled over to a pot-bellied stove and poured thick coffee into an ink-stained cup. He lifted the pot in the air. "Want some?"

She shivered and made a face. "That swill? No, thank you. Last time, it felt like I had tar in my throat for days."

He chuckled and sat back down, eyeing her over the rim. "God's help, not mine."

"What?"

He put the cup down and sloped back in the chair. "You came because you needed God's help. To win Mitch back, remember?"

She sank back in the chair with a sigh. "And now you won't even help me pray about it."

"I will help you pray about it, Charity. But God's way, not yours."

She worked at her lip as she studied him. John Brady was a true enigma. A quiet man with a strength of heart she had seldom encountered. A towering mystery, more enamored with the spirit than the flesh and totally indifferent to his own attraction. And certainly hers. His indifference had stung at first, provoking a challenge to turn his head. But instead he had turned hers . . . to the God she long denied.

She released her frustration in one telling breath. "Okay, you win. I'll do it God's way, not mine. Satisfied?"

"Nope. You can't. You're not capable."

"What do you mean I can't?" She rose up in her chair, ready to take him on.

He grinned. "I mean you haven't made him Lord of your life. Oh, you've danced around it plenty this last month, digging into the Bible, praying more, and talking about doing things his way, but the truth of the matter is, you've never invited him in."

"What are you talking about, 'invited him in'?"

He leaned back and studied her for a moment, then took a deep breath and planted his arms on the table. "I mean you've never given your life to him, Charity. Not completely. Never made the decision to live for him instead of yourself. You know, no more doing things your way, out of selfish motivation?" He hiked a brow while a smile fidgeted on his lips. "You want God's blessings in your life? You have to obey him. Deuteronomy 30 in the flesh, my good friend. And there's only one way any human being can even hope to make an attempt at obeying him. And that's to make him Lord of their life."

"But how?"

"Invite him in, Jesus Christ, the Son of the Living God, to live in your heart and be the Savior of your soul. But there's a catch."

The breath stilled in her lungs. "What?" she whispered.

"You do things his way, not yours. You pray, you listen, and then you pray some more. You take one step at a time, with his Word as a lamp unto your feet. In everything you say, think, or do, you look to honor him, not yourself. You become a new creature in Christ Jesus, one who can finally say no to sin and yes to God." He leaned back and folded his arms, a grin surfacing on his lips. "And then, if I were you, I'd duck my head and look out."

She blinked. "Why?"

"Because the blessings of God are going to overtake you, Charity O'Connor, and you're going to find yourself overloaded with the desires of your heart."

She released a long, quivering breath, unaware she'd even been holding it. She leaned in and extended her hands. "I want it, Brady. I want everything you just said. Pray with me?"

A sheen of wetness glimmered in his eyes as he took her hands. "My pleasure." He bowed his head. "Lord, Charity has something to ask you. The gospel of John says that a godly Pharisee named Nicodemus once came to you in secret during the night. He wanted more, Lord, more of you. You told him that no one can see the kingdom of God unless he is born again. Lord, Charity wants to see your kingdom in her life. She wants you to change her, mold her, make her the woman you want her to be. Help her in her journey and please open her heart to you." He looked up and nodded.

Charity sucked in a deep breath and closed her eyes. "Okay, Lord. This is it, I guess, the official beginning of my walk with you. Come into my heart, Jesus, and be Lord of my life. Forgive me for my sins and help me to follow your precepts all the days of my life. Amen."

She opened her eyes and grinned. "Satisfied now?"

He squeezed her hand. "Almost, but not completely."

"Why not?" She dropped his hand on the table with a thud.

He grinned. "Your plan to win Mitch back. I want details. A plan of action."

She folded her hands on the table and looked up at the ceiling, plotting her strategy. "Well, once I manage to convince Father to let me go back," her eyes flicked to Brady's face to emphasize her point, "which will require heavy prayer since he's already said no, then I will simply go see Mitch and explain that I've turned over a new leaf. That I'm doing things God's way now and that he can trust me enough to marry me."

"What if he's already married?"

Nervousness bobbed in her throat. "He's not. Grandmother's letter contains the most recent information from Mrs. Lynch."

"What if he's engaged?"

She bit her lip. "Then, with the help of God, I'll try to convince him that he's marrying the wrong woman."

Brady assessed her through narrowed eyes. "What if he says no?"

She drew in a thick breath and lifted her chin. "Well, then I'll just continue with my plan to purchase a shop and pour myself into a career."

He guzzled more coffee, eyes fixed on hers. "No plan B? No attempt to seduce him?"

She looked away, avoiding his gaze. "No."

"Charity?"

Her tongue glided across her teeth in nervous habit. She looked up.

"Promise me."

She could feel her pulse pounding in her throat. "Don't make me do that, Brady."

He reached to take her hand, smothering it in his rough, calloused palm. "Charity, if you've learned anything this last month, I hope you've learned that the kind of love you crave comes from God. Sensual love entices—the taste of honey for the moment. But sin will turn it to ashes in your mouth. It will never make you happy, never sustain you."

"I know." Her voice was a whisper.

He squeezed her hand. "Promise me."

She hesitated, then lifted her chin. "I promise I'll try."

He smiled. "Okay, then I'll pray with you." He closed his eyes and calm assurance settled over his hard-sculpted features. "Father, this woman's given her heart to you. She's pursued your Word with a fervor beyond anything I ever expected. And your Word says you honor those who honor you. Lord, I'm asking that you honor Charity with favor, first with her parents, and then with Mitch. I pray that you strengthen her to do your will and not her own, and that you would bless her with the desire of her heart. But if Mitch isn't right for her, help her to realize that and let him go. And give her peace in the process. Thank you."

Charity opened her eyes and grinned. "Nobody prays like you, Brady. I swear your words travel straight to the ear of God on the wisp of an angel wing. Whenever you're done, my heart is flooded with peace." She cocked her head. "Why in the world aren't you married?"

He shook his head. "What is it with you O'Connor sisters? Preoccupied with my marital status. First Beth, then you."

Charity laughed, then paused. "She has a crush on you, you know."

He looked up, a faint tinge of color staining his cheeks. "Yeah, I know. It'll pass."

"I don't know. I fell in love with Collin at sixteen and would have married him if it hadn't been for Faith."

He quickly rose to his feet and snatched the coffee cup in his hand. He dumped the black slime into the sink. "She's the little sister I never had, Charity. She'll grow up, fall in love with the son of a banker, and get married." He turned. "And I'll be Uncle Brady to her kids."

She stood up and smoothed her skirt. "And what about you? Any kids in your future?"

He chuckled and leaned against the counter, one leg casually cocked against the other. "Yeah, spiritual ones. You, Collin, and Beth."

She walked over to where he stood and smiled up at his hulking frame. "I'd hate to see you go to waste, John Brady. You'd make some lucky girl a very happy woman." She reached up to give him a tight hug. "I'm grateful for your friendship."

She felt his tentative embrace, then a powerful hug. "Not as grateful as I am, Charity. Your turnaround has brought me—and God—a lot of joy."

"Excuse me . . . am I interrupting something?" Collin stood motionless in the back door, not bothering to hide the scowl on his face. "I hope."

Charity spun around. A hand fluttered to her chest. "Goodness, Collin, you scared me! When did you get back?"

He strolled over and tossed a stack of papers on the table. "Apparently not soon enough."

Heat rushed into Charity's cheeks. She matched his glare with one of her own. "What is that supposed to mean?"

Giving her shoulder a quick squeeze, Brady sidled in front of her. "Rough day, Collin?"

Collin grunted, then postured his hands on his hips. "Not until now."

Charity peeked around Brady with her chin hiked up. "Why? Your mouth get you in trouble again?"

"Charity . . ." Brady's tone held a warning.

"It's true, and he knows it. He shot his mouth off and ruined my chances with Mitch."

The gray of Collin's eyes cooled to pewter. "No, I think you get credit for that all by yourself."

"Collin, back off." He glanced over his shoulder. "Charity, go home. And study Matthew 18:22, forgiving seventy times seven. We'll discuss it later."

She huffed and backed out of the room, her lips bent in a stubborn crease. "Why don't you have him memorize it? Not that it would do any good. Good night, Brady." Her eyes flicked to Collin. "And good night, you mule." She slammed the front door.

Brady faced Collin, squaring off. "What exactly is your problem?"

"She's my problem, Brady, and yours. She was wrapped around you like a python."

"It was a hug, Collin. Between friends. Nothing more."

Collin jerked out a chair and sat down, resting an arm on the table. "Look, Brady, it's none of my business, I know, but I care what happens to you. When's the last time you've even been with a woman? I'm not saying you don't attract them, 'cause I know better. I've seen the stream of females in and out of this office, batting their eyes, hoping you'll give 'em a second look. But you've had no interest since I've known you, so you can't have much experience with how they think. Especially a woman like Charity. She's way out of your league, my friend. She'll rip your heart out like she did Mitch Dennehy."

Brady wheeled around to wash his cup in the sink. "She

may be out of my league, Collin, but she's not out of God's. She's given her heart to him."

Collin grunted and hiked his boot up on a chair. "Yeah, if you can believe her."

With a clipped sigh, Brady dried the cup and put it back in the cabinet. He turned around slowly. "I do."

Collin studied him for a moment. "Did you know she intends to go after Dennehy? Return to Ireland as soon as she can?"

"I know. She told me. We prayed about it."

"She told you?"

"Yeah, Collin, she did. Because we're friends. Nothing more."

Exhaling, Collin rubbed the back of his neck. "I'm sorry, Brady, Charity just makes me nervous. I don't want you wasting your time."

"I'm not wasting my time, or God's. My feelings for Charity are purely platonic."

Collin shook his head. "There's not another man alive that I would believe if he said that. But if I've learned anything, it's that you mean what you say. I trust you, my friend."

Brady reached for his apron and slipped it over his head. He tied it in back and smiled. "Don't trust me, Collin, trust God. For some reason, he's given me immunity when it comes to Charity. The state of her soul is my only concern." He headed to the front of the shop to clean a press.

"Don't disappoint me," Collin called after him.

Brady glanced at the soft beam of sunlight streaming across the room. Specks of dust swirled like the doubts in his brain. He shifted his gaze to the sky. His prayer exactly.

16

"Oh, my dear, let me look. Is it really you?" Bridget clasped Charity's arms as if to make sure she were real. Her blue eyes were misty with tears. "Saints above, I couldn't believe it when Marcy wrote you were coming. It's nothing short of a miracle that Patrick let you go."

Charity grinned and dropped her valise in the foyer, giving her grandmother a powerful squeeze. "I know. Father and I have gotten really close, Grandmother, so he was reluctant. But, in the end, he knew what I had to do, so he gave me his blessing." She inhaled the sweet scent of home, then released it with a satisfied sigh. "Providing, of course, that I visit each Christmas."

Bridget chuckled. "I knew there would be a catch."

Charity tugged on the sleeve of her sweater to pull it off. She flipped it on the rack by the door. "And speaking of what I have to do, any word from Mrs. Lynch?"

The tip of Bridget's tongue glazed her teeth. "Not much. Margaret says she hears him come in late every night."

"Is he still working long hours?"

"No, I don't think so." Bridget hesitated, as if measuring her words. "Margaret seems to think he's been seeing a lot of Kathleen."

Several lines creased Charity's brow. "They're not engaged, are they?"

"No. Or at least Margaret doesn't know about it. And although she hasn't seen much of him lately, they're close enough that she thinks she'd be the first to know."

Charity straightened her shoulders. "Good. Then he's fair game." She glanced in the parlor, then down the hall. "Emma's at work, I guess. How's Mima?"

"Well, if you had asked me that last week, I would have told you 'not so good.' But ever since she heard you were coming back, I do believe she's taken a turn for the better. Almost spry, I'd say."

Hurrying down the hall, Charity grinned over her shoulder. "So I'm good medicine, am I? Well, let's hope we can get Mr. Dennehy to take a hefty dose."

She peeked into the dim room. "Mima? Are you awake?"

Mima's translucent lids popped open and a grin crinkled her pale face. "As if I could sleep with all that racket. It's been somber as a tomb since you left, young lady. Three months is a long time. Get over here and give this old woman a hug."

Charity laughed and pressed herself against Mima's frail body, stroking her soft cheek with her hand. "You're feeling better, I understand."

"She most certainly is," Bridget said, pushing the curtains back to let in some light. "Why, just look in her eyes. You'll see a bit of the devil in there for sure."

"Must be the intrigue of having this one back." A hoarse chuckle sputtered from Mima's cracked lips. "Mitch Dennehy has no earthly idea the trouble in store, does he, young lady?"

Charity giggled and brushed a kiss to Mima's cheek. "No, ma'am, and that's how I intend to keep it—for now. I've found the element of surprise to be a most strategic advantage. Especially with a man like Mitch Dennehy." She reached across the bed to grasp Bridget's hand while cupping Mima's shoulder with the other. "But right now, I'd like to exercise my most valuable advantage."

Bridget's eyes widened in surprise. "And what might that be, pray tell?"

Charity cocked her head and angled a brow. An impish grin hovered on her lips. "Close, Grandmother. Praying is definitely involved and telling too. That is, when God tells me what his answer will be. Until then, I intend to leave nothing to chance. Mitch Dennehy is the desire of my heart, and I'm taking my request to the top."

Mima and Bridget blinked, their mouths slacking in unison.

Charity smiled and hugged Mima's shoulder. With a tilt of her chin, she squeezed Bridget's hand. "Shall we pray?"

❧ ❧

Mitch coasted to a stop in front of Kathleen's house and disengaged the drive gears. The engine sputtered to a stop as he shifted in the seat. "It was a wonderful evening, Kathleen."

She turned to him, her face backlit by the glow of the street lamp. "It was, wasn't it? They get better and better."

He reached to take her hand and caressed her palm with his thumb. "Yeah, they do. Come here." He pulled her toward him on the seat and wrapped his arms around her waist. He buried his lips in her hair, burrowing through to find the soft skin of her neck. He made contact with his mouth and heard her faint moan as she weakened in his arms. "Marry me, Kathleen," he whispered. "Don't make me wait any longer."

She pulled away, but her breathing was soft and rapid. "Mitch, please. You're not ready."

He stroked the curve of her chin with the back of his hand, then caressed her lips with his thumb. "I'm ready," he whispered and leaned in to fondle her mouth with his. He felt her catch her breath and pressed in. "Marry me, Kathleen. I need you."

She pulled away, breathless. "What about Charity?"

His jaw stiffened. "What about her?"

"Do you still love her?"

He groaned and trailed her throat with urgent kisses. "I love you. I want you. As my wife, in my bed. Now!"

"But you're not over her, Mitch, I can feel it."

He sighed and pressed his mouth to the soft fold of her ear. "I'll get over her with you by my side, night after night. Trust me."

She cupped his face in her hands. "I do trust you, Mitch. I just feel unsettled in my spirit."

He went in for the kill, gliding his fingers along the delicate crease of her collarbone before dipping low to graze his lips at the hollow of her throat.

"Mitch, stop," she moaned. "What are you doing?"

He answered her with a tug of his teeth on her lips, culminating in a hungry kiss. "I need you, Kathleen. Every time I'm with you, I have less and less control. Marry me, please, or I can't be responsible for what I do."

She pushed him back to stare for several seconds, her chest rising and falling. "All right, I'll marry you."

He pressed his mouth to her ear, filling it with a husky chuckle. "Better to marry than to burn, 1 Corinthians 7:9."

She laughed in his arms. "So you win me with Scripture, do you? You're a devil, Mitch Dennehy."

He kissed her on the cheek and pulled something out of his pocket. "Maybe, but a devil who wants you for his wife, Kathleen Meyer." He held up a ring that glittered in the lamplight.

She uttered a soft cry and grasped it in her hand. "Oh, Mitch, it's beautiful! Will you put it on me? Please?"

He laughed and took her hand, slipping it on her finger.

She grinned and held it out to admire, a hand pressed to her mouth. "Oh, I love you, Mitch Dennehy!"

"And I you, Kathleen Meyer, till death do us part." He gripped her in his arms and squeezed his eyes shut, blocking every other thought from his mind. She would be his wife. The mother of his children. And with time, the love of his life.

And nothing was left but the vows.

"I smell smoke. Are you burning the candle at both ends again, Mitch Dennehy?"

Mitch startled, spinning around to face a nighttime Mrs. Lynch, who assessed him through a crack in her door. She opened it wider, revealing her faded lavender robe cinched tight at the waist, littered with the most garish pink and purple flowers he'd ever seen. She wrinkled her nose and adjusted the matching kerchief on her head. Her lips pinched in a comical way. One that usually brought a smile to his lips. If he were in the mood.

He blew out a heavy breath and groaned. "Mrs. Lynch, don't you ever sleep?"

A silver brow jutted up. "Don't you?"

He rubbed his face with his hand and bit back a growl. "Right now, as a matter of fact. Good night."

"Not so fast, young man. I don't wait up all hours of the night for my health, you know. What have you been up to?"

He was too tired to scowl. "I'm thirty-six, Mrs. Lynch. My need for a mother expired twenty-five years ago. I'm going to bed." He shoved the key in the keyhole and hoped this wouldn't be one of its temperamental nights. It ground in the lock—not unlike the teeth in his mouth.

"I haven't seen hide nor hair of you for the last month, young man. Are you going to give me some information, or am I going to have to badger you for it?"

He jimmied the lock with more force, which only made it more bullheaded—not unlike the silver-haired bloodhound breathing down his neck.

"Mitchell? Are you going to answer me?"

He slammed a fist against the door and rattled the knob with renewed fury.

"Oh, stop that banging." She shot out from her apartment, lavender robe swishing around fluffy slippers. She butted him aside to flick the key in the lock with all the ease and precision of a safecracker. She pushed the door with an impatient prod. With a pitiful squeak, it wheeled open in complete submission.

Mitch gritted his teeth. "Thank you, Mrs. Lynch. Good night."

A lavender-clad arm thrust against the door, yanking it closed. "Not so fast. Are you getting serious with that young woman?"

He huffed out a sigh and sagged against the wall, feeling a lot like he was thirteen and caught smoking in the bathroom. He heard Runt whining on the other side of the door. "Yes, Mrs. Lynch, I am." He clamped his lips shut, unwilling to go any further. He had pressed the engagement because he was desperate to get on with his life. But not desperate enough to disclose it to Mrs. Lynch. Yet.

"And?"

He gently lifted her hand from the door, trying to muster a patient smile. "And, you will be among the first to know, all right?"

She crossed her arms and lifted her chin. He must be tired. He imagined a glint of steel in her jaw. "Well, I'd better be, young man, or your name is mud. Is that clear?"

"Yes, ma'am. Can I go to bed now? Please?"

"I suppose. Lean down."

He bent over.

She perched on tiptoe to brush a kiss to his cheek. "Get

some sleep, will you? You look terrible." She whirled around and disappeared with a slam of the door, leaving him in a stupor.

He hung his head and lumbered into his dark apartment, too tired and numb to greet Runt with more than a rub of his ears. Seeming to sense his mood, Runt trotted into the bedroom and curled up in front of the bed, his eyes following Mitch's every move. Mitch hung up his jacket in the closet, then loosened his tie and slung it over a chair. He stripped off his shirt and undershirt and flung them across the room, missing the hamper by a mile. He trudged to the bathroom with a yawn, then plucked his pajama bottoms off the back of the door and slipped them on. Assessing his image in the mirror by the light of the full moon, he looked tired and spent, like a man with a lot on his mind.

Out of sight, out of mind. Yeah, right. So much for fantasy. She was there every night. In his dreams, haunting him with her smile and her laughter and her beautiful memory. He turned on the water and reached for his toothbrush, closing his eyes while he scoured his teeth. Maybe they weren't dreams. Maybe they were just thoughts that refused to go away. He spit in the sink and reached for a towel, wiping his mouth with a sigh. This was normal, wasn't it? He'd felt it before. First with Faith, and now with her. The terrible longing, the dull aching, the missing that throbbed like a deep-seated nerve. All the more reason to marry Kathleen. He'd gotten over Faith with time. He'd get over Charity with passion.

He stumbled to his bed, collapsing on the springs with a weight that far exceeded that of his frame. He lay, legs spread and arms limp at his sides, no energy left to even tug at the blanket to cover his chest. He closed his eyes. At least she was an ocean away.

Out of sight, out of mind.

Lord, please, one down and one to go . . .

"No!" Emma sat up on the bed and blinked, her mouth gaping open. She pressed a hand to the collar of her silk blouse.

"Yes!" Charity giggled and twirled around, propping her hands on her hips.

"But you never breathed a word in your letters."

"Of course not, silly, it's a surprise. So what do you think?"

The hand at Emma's collar flew to her mouth, muffling a giggle that rolled from her lips. "Oh, my goodness. You . . . a merchant with your own store. And not just any store—one of the finest in the city." She bounded from the bed and squeezed Charity in a peal of laughter. "So, no more Mrs. Shaw? I'm working for you now?"

Charity laughed, knees bent as she squealed at the top of her lungs. "Yes!"

"God bless Mr. Hargrove. He came through? How?"

Charity took a deep breath and flopped on the bed, adrenaline twitching under her skin. She tucked one leg under her skirt, fairly quivering with excitement. "Well, shortly after Mitch left, I knew I had to do something, so I wrote Mr. Hargrove. Told him I planned to return to Ireland and wanted to know if his offer was still good. He responded right away with a plan of action that made me giddy. He sent me a proposal, which Father looked over and approved. Most of the proceeds, of course, will go back to Mr. Hargrove initially, but I'll have a tidy sum to live on until the debt is fully paid. And so, with a stroke of my signature and a good-faith deposit from my savings, Mr. Hargrove and I will soon be the proud owners of Shaw's Emporium."

Emma sighed and sat on the edge of the bed, a dreamy look in her eyes. "Does this mean that we might actually have wood heat in the back room and maybe even an icebox?"

Charity laughed. "That and much more, my good friend. Because you—my new assistant manager—and I are going to dream up ways to make Shaw's Emporium the most prosperous store in all of Dublin."

She squealed again and looped her arms around Emma's neck, toppling them in an outbreak of giggles. All at once, she jolted up from the bed to glance at the clock. "We have to go. You need to get to work, and I need to meet Mr. Hargrove at the bank. I've got a busy day."

Charity bounded to the closet to hunt for an outfit. She spotted the pale pink double-breasted satin blouse and smiled. Perhaps "snug" in Grandmother's estimation, but completely alluring in hers, and certainly professional. She snatched it from the hanger, along with the matching burgundy and gray plaid skirt.

"Will you be coming into the store after?"

Charity glanced over her shoulder before lifting the tight hobble skirt over her head. "For a little bit. But then I have an engagement."

"An engagement?"

She slipped on the blouse and latched the pearl button, turning to admire the sheen of the satin as it hugged the curve of her breast. She smiled and reached for the brush, a glimmer of mischief in her eyes. "Well, actually an encounter . . ." She grinned at Emma in the mirror. "That I hope will turn into an 'engagement.'"

Emma's eyes widened. "You're going to see Mitch?"

"I am." Charity bent over and brushed her hair with hard, determined strokes.

"Does he know you're coming?"

She peeked out through the honeyed folds of her hair. "Nope."

"You haven't seen him in almost four months. What are you going to say?"

"The truth. That I've been a fool—both about him and about God. And that I've changed." She stood and flipped her hair over her head. It rippled down her back in waves of gold. "The old manipulative Charity is gone and a new, improved model has taken her place. Honest, trustworthy, no longer bent on seduction."

Emma's lips twitched as she eyed Charity's blouse. She tilted her head and cocked a brow. "I think the old Charity left her blouse here."

She looked down at her sateen breasts and bit her lip, smoothing her hands at her waist. "Well, I can't leave everything to chance, can I?"

"I thought you were leaving it to God, not chance," Emma said with a hint of a smile.

Charity jutted her jaw. "I am, but he and I are in this together. I'm just doing my part."

"And then some."

Charity whirled around to apply a touch of rouge to her cheeks. "I never claimed to be Faith, did I? Besides, I'm new at this."

Her friend chuckled. "I suppose we should be grateful it's not more . . . revealing."

She touched some rouge to her lips, then pursed them into a pout. "Yes, we should. I happen to know that Mitch Dennehy has a particular fondness for 'revealing,' so God knows I'm conceding advantage." She sighed and shoved several hairpins into her mouth, twisting her hair into a loose chignon. She rammed the pins in with a grunt, then patted her head to test the hold. She turned. "How do I look?"

"Like a woman with business on her mind." Emma picked her purse up off the dresser and strolled toward the door, turning to flash a grin. "But I won't say what kind."

Charity gave her a smirk. "You're working for me now, so behave. And don't forget to pray. I need all the help I can get if the old Charity's taboo."

Emma shook her head and opened the door. "Somehow I find that hard to believe."

Charity stared up at the *Irish Times* and put a shaky hand to her mouth. A belch bubbled in her throat and her stomach churned with acid. She took a deep breath and straightened her shoulders to steel her resolve. This was no time for nausea. She had a job to do and a heart to win. And by God—literally— she would succeed.

She sucked in a breath of air thick with the smells of the city, then released it again, shaking off the barbs of fear that nettled her nerves. With a thrust of her chin, she entered the door, ignoring the obvious disdain of a certain Miss Boyle.

"Excuse me, miss, may I help you?"

Charity smiled, then continued toward the double doors, her chin leading the way. "No thank you, Miss Boyle, I've been here before." She ignored the receptionist's objections and glided into the newsroom, scanning the area for some sign of Mitch. She spotted Bridie hunched over her desk, immersed in a stack of galley sheets while Kathleen typed away, ramrod straight and fingers flying.

Charity stiffened her spine and moved across the room, head high and gaze fixed on Mitch's office. Heads turned as she passed, but she ignored them, her lips compressed as she made her way to his door.

He sat sprawled in his chair facing the window, one leg braced on the sill while he talked on the phone. A burly arm reached up to scratch the back of his head. It finally rested on top of shaggy curls in dire need of a trim. Her stomach squeezed at the sight of him, and her heart picked up pace.

"Charity?"

She spun around.

Bridie rose to her feet, all color draining from her face. "What are you doing here?"

Kathleen looked up. Her fingers stilled on the keys while her cheeks faded to chalk.

Charity glanced at Mitch, still on the phone, then back at Bridie. She forced a smile. "I'm back with my grandmother."

Bridie blinked. "For how long?"

"For good. I'm the new owner of Shaw's Emporium."

Kathleen listed to the side, looking faint.

"Does Mitch know?"

Charity chanced a peek at his broad back. "No."

"Dear Mother of Job."

Charity bit her lip. "I wanted to surprise him."

Bridie sank into her chair. "Oh, you will."

Charity avoided Kathleen's face. "May I go in?"

Bridie nodded, her gaze flicking to Kathleen's. "Leave the door open. We'll need to know if he has a stroke."

"Thanks." Charity turned and tiptoed in, parking herself in one of the chairs at the front of his desk.

"The devil with McGettigan, Lucas, I want names and I want 'em now. Tell them that if they don't comply, we're going to press with what we have. Five o'clock edition. Front page."

Silence ensued while Mitch dropped his head in his hand, massaging his forehead. His fist heaved down on the arm of his chair. "No way! I'm done pussyfooting. Let's see how much bluster they have when we expose 'em."

He glanced at his watch. "Fine. Tell them they have till four o'clock. No names, no mercy. Ya got it? Yeah, thanks."

Mitch wheeled around and slammed the phone on the receiver. The earpiece fused to his hand as if embedded in his palm. He tried to breathe. He couldn't.

"Hello, Mitch."

His mouth opened to speak, but nothing came out but shallow air. Ice-cold prickles of heat traveled from the crown of his head to the soles of his feat. He swallowed.

Still no air.

She shifted in the chair, a shimmer of pink satin straining against full breasts while she adjusted her form-fitting skirt.

Several seconds passed and his hand was still one with the phone. With a rash of heat up his neck, he slowly removed it, sagging back in the chair.

She smiled. "I knew I'd surprise you, but I didn't expect to render you speechless."

He stared, vaguely aware of Bridie hovering at the door. Air finally returned to his throat. He licked his lips, aware his heart was pumping at an alarming rate. "What are you doing here?"

She seemed nervous and shy, although she undoubtedly had the upper hand. Her front teeth absently tugged at her lower lip while her fingers fidgeted in her lap. With a soft sigh, she looked up, not a hint of seduction in her wide, blue eyes. "I came to apologize. To ask you to forgive me for what I did. It was wrong to lie and deceive, especially to someone I love."

He shook his head. "No, I mean what are you doing here . . . in Ireland?"

Those deadly lips curved into an innocent smile. "I moved back . . . with my grandmother. In fact, I'm the new owner of Shaw's Emporium."

Air left his lungs again and he wheezed, jumping up to catch his breath. "You're what?"

She lifted her chin with a proud smile. "Yes, part owner and operating manager in partnership with Mr. Horace Hargrove, a dear friend of mine. He bought the store from Mrs. Shaw, and I make the payments."

"You're staying? In Ireland?"

She blinked, her smile fading a hair. "Well, of course. I can't run the store from Boston."

He turned and leaned his palms on the window ledge, wilting into a cold stare. "Congratulations. Was that all you wanted?"

"What?"

He lifted his head, his back to her. "To apologize and tell me your news?"

He heard the scrape of the chair as she rose. He stiffened when she stood beside him.

"No, that's not all. I also wanted to tell you that I love you—"

He jerked away. "No, Charity, don't."

She took a step forward, her eyes glossy with tears. "I wanted you to know I made amends with Faith and Father, and then with God. I serve him now, Mitch. I honor him with my life."

His heart clutched in his chest. He could barely breathe.

She rubbed a tear away. "Don't you see? He meant for us to be together all along—"

"It's too late." His whisper sliced through her like the cut of a barb, twitching her face.

Her pale lips parted. "What do you mean?"

He looked out the window, unwilling to witness her pain. "Kathleen and I are engaged."

He felt her shiver from five feet away.

"But you said that before and you weren't, and Mrs. Lynch never said anything . . ."

He stared at his feet. "She doesn't know. I just gave the ring to Kathleen last night."

He heard her gasp and looked up, his gut twisting at the shock in her face. She turned and braced her hand on the ledge, body trembling. "Why, Mitch? When you love me, why?"

He glanced at the door, his nerves raw. "Bridie?"

Her head popped around the corner. "Yeah, Boss?"

"Close the door."

She pressed her lips tight and did as he said, slamming it shut. He turned back to Charity. "Because you lied. And I was afraid. I wanted a woman I could trust, one who loved God."

She whirled around, her eyes full of fury. "And you have it—in me!"

He hung his head, guilt flooding his soul. "No, I have it in Kathleen."

"Even though you love me?"

He met her gaze, his voice barely a whisper. "Yes."

Her chest heaved with ragged breaths, and then she lunged with a pitiful cry, her fists bludgeoning his chest. "I hate you! I wish I could hurt you as much as you've hurt me."

He gripped her hands and pinned them to her sides. His eyes burned into hers. "You have, Charity. I'm bleeding inside. I love you so much it aches. But it's too late. I won't do that to Kathleen. Not again. She's a good woman, and in my own way, I love her."

Tears streamed her face. "Not the way you love me."

"It doesn't matter. I've given her my word, my ring. I won't go back on that."

She moaned and collapsed against his chest, her sobs echoing through the office. He held her in his arms and closed his eyes.

Dear God, what have I done?

He picked her up in his arms and carried her to the chair to set her down. He squatted in front of her and searched her face. "Charity, listen to me. What we had wasn't meant to be. It wasn't God's plan. It started off illicitly two years ago and ended the same way. Believe me, I've prayed about it, and if God intended us for each other, I wouldn't be marrying Kathleen. But I am. And both of us will get over this. We'll move on. And eventually be friends, like Faith and me." He lifted her chin with his finger. "God has someone for you, Charity. Someone wonderful and God-ordained. It's just not me."

She looked up, her thick lashes spiky from tears. Her chin trembled. "I love you, Mitch, and I will never stop, no matter whom you marry."

"Yes, you will. And it won't take long." He forced a smile. "You'll probably marry before me."

She sniffed. "And when is that going to be?"

He stood up. "We haven't set a date." He sat on the edge of his desk. "You okay?"

She nodded and swiped at her face with her sleeve.

He pulled a handkerchief out of his pocket and handed it to her. "Here, keep it. I bought extra when I met you."

She didn't smile. "May I congratulate the bride?"

"That would be nice. Kathleen would appreciate that. She worries about you."

Her laugh was brittle. "At least one of you does."

His heart was sick. He ducked his head to look at her. "Come on, now. You know I care about you, worry about you. I'm proud of you with the store and the strides you've made with your family. You've grown into a good woman, Charity."

She glanced up. "For all the good it does."

He tried to smile, but failed miserably. He walked to the door and opened it, sticking his head out. "Kathleen? Can I see you a moment?"

He waited until she approached, then guided her in. He looped an arm around her waist, then slowly slipped it away at the look in Charity's eyes. Heaven help him, he was an idiot.

Charity lifted her chin. "Kathleen, I wanted to congratulate you on your engagement. You're a lucky woman."

Kathleen's eyes were soft with compassion. "Thank you, Charity." She glanced up at Mitch. "I think so."

"Well, I'd better go. I've got a shop to run." Charity stood to her feet.

Kathleen touched a hand to Charity's arm. "Can we give you a ride?"

She stared, a flicker of pain shadowing her face at the diamond on Kathleen's hand. She swallowed and shook her head. "No, I'll be fine. But thank you."

She moved to the door and turned, a sad smile lining her lips. "Goodbye, Mitch, Kathleen. I wish you the best."

He swallowed hard, gazing at the face he saw every night in his dreams. "Goodbye, Charity. Stay in touch."

She nodded and slipped through the door.

Kathleen glanced up and twined his fingers with her own. "Are you all right?"

He pulled her into his arms and rested his head against hers. "Yeah."

"Is she?"

He hesitated, his gaze traveling to the door. He exhaled. "God help her, I hope so."

❦ ❧

The front door flew open with a resounding thwack. Charity blew in and vaulted up the stairs, the sound of the door banging behind her. Bridget's knitting needles froze in the air. Another door slammed upstairs. She looked at Mima. "Dear me, what on earth happened? Did you see her face? Blotchy and swollen, eyes red and raw."

"Well, don't just stand there, Bridget, put those blasted needles down and find out."

Bridget nodded and jumped up, tossing the needles on the sofa before running from the room. Her heart pounded as she raced up the steps. "Charity?"

She hurried down the hall and knocked, opening Charity's door to peek in. Her granddaughter lay on her bed, her form still as death.

"Charity? What happened? Are you all right?"

She heard a muffled cry from the bed and ran to her granddaughter's side. She sat and touched her shoulder. "Charity?"

With a moan, Charity turned and caved in her arms, sobs wrenching from her throat. "Oh, Grandmother, I . . . l-love him so, and he's . . . marrying Kathleen. Even though he loves me."

Bridget stared in shock. "He told you that?"

She nodded, heaving uncontrollably.

"Did he tell you why?"

"Be . . . cause he com . . . mitted to her, g-gave her a ring, just last n-night. He says w-we're not right for each other."

"Why, that's balderdash. If the man's in love with you, he needs to get his head on straight and marry you, not some other woman."

Charity continued to sob, wiping her nose with her arm. Bridget yanked a handkerchief from her sleeve and handed it to her. A dangerous frown hardened on her face. "So help me, I have a good mind to unleash Margaret on that boy. She would set him straight."

"No, sh-she wouldn't. H-he's made up his m-mind, Grandmother, and that's how he is. Too stubborn and th-thickheaded to see we belong together."

Bridget held her close, doing her best to soothe. "Then you don't want to marry him anyway. He'd be nothing but grief, a bullhead like that, always demanding his own way."

Another jag of weeping swelled in Charity's chest. She jerked away and languished on the bed, her sobs breaking Bridget's heart.

"Oh, Grandmother, w-what am I g-going to do?"

"I'll tell you what you're going to do, young lady. You're going to cry your heart out and get it all out of your system. Then you're going to say good riddance to a man who doesn't have the sense that God gave a goat to know that he's just turned away the best thing he's ever had. Then you're going to blow your nose, wash your face and stand up tall, and never look back. You've got the store, you've got us, and you've got God. To the devil with Mitch Dennehy!"

Charity sat up and sniffed, her eyes wide and wet. Her mouth formed a soft "oh." "D-did you say 'to the devil with Mitch Dennehy'?"

Bridget hiked her chin and pursed her lips. "I most certainly did, and I'll say it again."

"Grandmother, you'd wash my mouth out with soap if I said that."

She huffed and folded her arms across her chest. "Not today I wouldn't. The man's obviously an idiot when it comes to love. When you tamper with the feelings of my favorite granddaughter, you tamper with me."

. A soft chuckle bubbled from Charity's lips, followed by another wrenching sob. She hurtled herself into her grandmother's arms. "Oh, Grandmother, I love you so much. What would I do without you?"

She stroked Charity's head, her eyes welling with tears. "You would survive, granddaughter of my heart, because that's what you are. A fighter, a survivor. Not a coward in love like Mitch Dennehy."

Charity's lips trembled into a smile. "Really, Grandmother, he's not a coward, just pig-headed and a bit obnoxious. I suppose we should pray for him. And the poor woman he's marrying. Brady says prayers are more powerful when they're attached to our obedience."

Bridget pulled back and angled a brow. "And who, pray tell, is Brady?"

Charity sat up and leaned against the headboard, scrunching her knees to her chest. She wrapped her arms around her legs and gave Bridget a wobbly smile. "You remember, Grandmother, Collin's friend, from the war?"

Bridget squinted. "You mean the religious soldier Collin always complained about?"

Charity nodded. "He's Collin's partner now in Boston. They have a printing business."

"Oh, that Brady." She cocked her head, giving Charity a curious smile. "Is he handsome?"

"Oh, Grandmother, for pity's sake, he's in Boston and I'm here."

"But if you weren't, here I mean, if you were in Boston instead, would he be handsome?"

Charity hesitated, giving it thought. "Yes, I suppose so, although not in an obvious way like Collin or Mitch. Brady doesn't have their roguish good looks, or maybe it's just he's not aware of it so he doesn't exude it. His attraction is more understated, quiet, almost as if it sneaks up on you. I suspect it's because he's more concerned with things of the spirit than the flesh. There's definitely something very appealing about him, something very gentle and kind." She looked up. "And very, very strong."

"All wonderful qualities, my dear."

"Yes, they are. But more than anything, Grandmother, Brady's a wonderful friend. I have to say I was a bit put off in the beginning because he didn't swoon over me like men often do. He was actually rather detached. But the more he talked about the Bible and prayed—"

"You talked about the Bible together? And prayed?"

Charity laughed and nodded. "For several months. The fact that he had no romantic interest in me sort of freed me up, helped me to let down my barriers and really listen. Brady's the one who finally opened my eyes to God. He says when you pray for someone who's hurt you, you unleash powerful blessings. Not only in that person's life, but in yours as well. Brady's convinced that if two people are praying for the same person, and one's been hurt by them and the other hasn't, well, Brady thinks the prayers of the person who's been hurt are more powerful."

Bridget nodded slowly. "Because they're attached to obedience—saying no to your flesh and yes to God. I think I would agree with that."

"He claims it has something to do with two Scriptures, in particular—'pray for those who persecute you' and 'the prayers of the righteous availeth much.'"

"Well, your Brady certainly sounds like an amazing young man."

Charity smiled. "Well, he's not 'my' Brady, Grandmother, but he is amazing. I miss him a lot. I guess I miss his friendship."

"Perhaps you better write him a letter and tell him so. Just channel that grief over Mitch into gratitude for Brady."

"I will, Grandmother. But first, I'd like to apply his advice and pray for that pitiful excuse of a man."

Bridget hiked her chin. "If you insist, but don't expect me to like it."

With a plaintive sigh, Charity took her grandmother's hand. "That's okay, Grandmother, I don't like it either. Right now I'd rather spit in his eye. But the irony is that Mitch once told me that obedience is a decision, not a feeling. And it's all that God requires."

Bridget gummed her lips. "That's good, because it's all he's going to get. You go ahead and start because I have a few more names I'd like to call him in my mind."

A smile flickered on Charity's lips as she closed her eyes. "Well get 'em out, Grandmother, because the heavens are about to open and we're going in."

֍ ֎

"Goodness, I'm betting Mr. Quinlan will be love-struck in no time." Emma stepped back from pinning Charity's last curl in place. She smoothed the folds from her friend's new dress.

Charity laughed and spun around in front of the mirror, her cheeks aglow for the first time in three months. "It does feel rather good to dress up and go out once again. Even if Ryan doesn't put a skip in my pulse."

"Nobody would put a skip in your pulse right now except for he who shall remain nameless." Emma settled back on her bed and tucked her legs to her chest.

"You can say his name, Emma. I do—every time I pray." She folded her hands and reverently gazed at the ceiling. "Dear God, please bless that mule of a man, Mitch Dennehy, and help me to forget he ever existed. Amen."

Emma giggled. "Has it worked yet?"

Charity sighed and adjusted the feathery silk of her new ice-blue dress. "A little. But with the shop doing as well as it has, and the flurry of new customers flocking to our store, I don't have much time to think about him. Except the nights. Those are the worst."

"Well, you're on the mend, and that's all that really matters. Did you know that Mr. Hargrove said the store did almost twice as much business this month as the same time last year?"

Charity put on her matching pumps. "So he says. I think he's quite pleased with his return on his investment, especially the new merchandise we've brought in. Particularly the knickerbockers and felt fedoras." She grinned as she swept her hair over her shoulders, admiring Emma's handiwork. She felt pretty again, rather chic with her hair pulled up on the sides, pinned into loose curls at the back of her head. She turned, pleased with the way the rest tumbled down her back in soft, gleaming waves. "He actually bought a dozen before I even put them out."

"So that's where our profits are coming from. I thought Mr. Ryan Quinlan might be responsible for the surge. Did he even miss a day last week?"

Charity rolled her eyes and applied some pink to her cheeks. "Not that I know. Honestly, the man couldn't be more obvious."

"He is smitten. Do you like him?"

Eyes pensive, Charity reached for her silk evening wrap and fingered the soft material while she thought about Emma's question. "I do. He treats me like a goddess, of course. But he's a bit overeager, which bothers me. I guess I like a challenge."

Emma laughed. "Well, think of his money as the challenge. Straining your brain over all the wonderful ways to spend it once you become Mrs. Ryan Quinlan."

"I'm not interested in marriage right now, no matter how handsome or wealthy the suitor. I just want to heal and move on."

"Well, this is a step in the right direction. Your first date since you know who. What are you seeing at the theater tonight?"

"A new play by George Bernard Shaw called *Heartbreak House*."

"How appropriate."

She grinned. "It is, rather, isn't it?"

"Charity? Mr. Quinlan is here." Grandmother's voice drifted up from the foyer.

She stole one final glance in the mirror, then turned to Emma. "Tell me again, Emma. I need to hear it."

"You look beautiful, my friend. Ryan Quinlan is a dead man."

Charity gave her a droll smile. "Well, that would certainly tone him down a bit. Good night. Love you."

"Love you, too. Have fun, okay?"

Charity nodded and sailed out the bedroom door, excitement in her step for the first time in months. She scampered down the stairs to greet Ryan in the parlor and watched from the door as he chatted with Bridget and Mima. She smiled. He appeared as comfortable as if he'd known them all of his life. He was so different from Mitch, for which she was grateful. Not nearly as tall, he was a comfortable height at close to six feet, with thick, dark hair as straight as Mitch's was blond and cropped. He turned, suddenly aware she was in the room. His dark eyes seemed to glaze as he stared.

She grinned. "Hello, Ryan."

He swallowed hard. "Hello, Charity. You look incredible tonight." A faint ruddiness colored his cheeks. "Of course, you look incredible all the time, but especially tonight." He held out his arm. "Ready?"

She nodded and leaned to kiss Mima good night and then Bridget, who patted her on the cheek. "Have a good time, and don't be too late."

"I'll have her home at a decent hour, Mrs. Murphy. Good meeting you both. Good night."

The drive to the theater seemed to settle her nerves. Charity glanced at Ryan as he talked about his family, noting the warmth in his tone. She sighed. It would be a good evening, she hoped. She desperately needed one.

The theater was crowded and Ryan ushered her to the door, his hand firm at the small of her back. She looked up with a smile, which locked on her lips. Her heart sank as she stared.

Kathleen was making her way through the crowd. "Charity? Is that you?"

Charity managed a tenuous smile. "Kathleen, hello! Are you here with Mitch?"

Kathleen looked over her shoulder to scan the crowd. "Yes, he's purchasing a program."

Charity tried to swallow, but her throat was too dry. She glanced at Kathleen's hand. "And are you . . ."

"No, not yet. The wedding's July twelfth." She searched again and then waved.

Everything in Charity's body ceased for a split second—air, pulse, reason. She had no problem picking him out of the crowd. He stood a head taller than every man there, the slight scowl giving him away as he maneuvered the throng. Her pulse started racing and her hands began to sweat as she drank in the sight of him, this man who owned her heart.

His scowl eased into a smile as he spied Kathleen, then froze on his face when his eyes fixed on her. Charity turned to Ryan, her breathing shallow. "I'd love a program, Ryan, if you don't mind, shall we? Kathleen, so good to see you. Please say hello to Mitch." She latched onto Ryan's arm and tried to tug him away.

"Dennehy? Is that really you?" Ryan's face broke into a smile and he extended an arm. "I haven't seen you in years. What, a big-shot editor doesn't rub shoulders with the common folk anymore, is that it?"

Charity spun around, shock glazing her skin. *Good Lord, they're friends?*

Mitch grinned and pumped Ryan's hand, his handsome smile harpooning straight through her heart. "Hello, Ryan, it's good to see you again. And you'd hardly qualify as 'common folk' with your bank account."

Ryan laughed and slapped Mitch on the shoulder. He cupped an arm around Charity's waist. "Mitch, this is Charity O'Connor, the woman who just may be the love of my life."

Mitch's searing blue eyes scanned the length of her from head to foot, causing heat to blister her cheeks. A stony smile sculpted his lips. "We've met."

She pressed a hand to the filmy bodice of her scooped-neck dress, praying she wouldn't faint. She leaned into Ryan's arm. "Hello, Mitch. Nice to see you again."

Ryan grinned. "You two know each other? That's wonderful. How about a late supper after the theater?"

"No!"

Their voices resounded in unison, raising Ryan's brows to the level of curiosity. "Why not? It will be fun, catching up on old times."

Charity began to hyperventilate. Mitch intervened, draping an arm over Kathleen's shoulder. "Can't tonight, Ryan. My fiancée has to be home by eleven." He squeezed Kathleen to his side with an obstinate press of his lips. "Ryan, this is Kathleen Meyer, my fiancée."

"Well, congratulations. And good job, Kathleen. I thought this one would end up a confirmed old bachelor for sure. Well, maybe another time, Mitch. Good to see you." The lights flicked several times and Ryan looked up, absently massaging the back of Charity's neck before steering her toward the door. "I'll take you to our seats, Charity, and then get your program."

Charity waved. "Good night, Kathleen, Mitch. Enjoy the show." She breathed a sigh of relief when Ryan braced the back of her waist with his hands and guided her through the crowd.

She glanced over her shoulder to see Mitch watching with a frown on his face. *Good. Let him stew.* She suddenly felt a tiny bit evil and leaned her head back against Ryan's chest, looking up to give him a saucy smile. He bent to press a kiss to her cheek and whispered in her ear. She giggled for full effect, hoping that Mr. Dennehy enjoyed the show. She glanced back one more time and smiled. Success! The frown was a definite scowl.

Mitch shoved the tickets at the doorman and hoped for a dark corner where he could disappear. No such luck. But then he'd known his luck had run out the moment he'd seen her face. One look into those almond-shaped eyes, and his evening had been doomed. What did it matter that their seats were dead-center like Ryan's, a mere two rows behind? The perfect vantage point to see a play entitled *Heartbreak House*, nicely complemented by a bit of his own.

Kathleen reached for his hand, and he smiled, hoping to dispel the stiffness he felt. He squeezed back and tried to relax, willing his eyes to fix on the stage. But they had a mind of their own and strayed at will, searing the back of a golden-haired girl. She leaned to whisper in Ryan's ear and he drew her close, brushing her cheek with a kiss. Then he lifted her chin and brought her lips full to his, merging into a silhouette that tightened Mitch's gut. She tucked her head on Ryan's shoulder, allowing her silky curls to spill down his back. Mitch clenched his hand.

Kathleen touched his arm. He jolted. "Are you okay? You seem tense."

He nodded and drew in a deep breath, forcing his body to unwind. "I'm okay, just tired."

Her forehead puckered. "Do you want to leave?"

Yes.

"No, I'm fine." He returned his gaze to the stage, never seeing it for the girl in his view. He felt Kathleen's eyes on him for a long moment, before she finally eased back into her seat, leaving him alone with his thoughts. A dangerous thing to do.

Charity thrust herself against the front door and waited. She heard the sputter of Ryan's engine before it faded away, leaving her alone in the dark. She turned and bolted the door, her exhaustion evident in the slump of her shoulders and the heaviness of her heart. She glanced at the stairs and moved into the parlor, no energy to even scale the steps. Dropping onto the sofa, she flung herself over the arm, unleashing tears forbidden by hours of restraint.

Why, God? Why did you let me see him again? After months of agony and then finally some hope. Why dash it all with just a glimpse of his smile? Why?

Trust in the Lord with all thine heart . . .

"No!" She sat up on the couch, her eyes stinging with tears and her heart breaking. "I did t-trust you. I gave you my h-heart, but you didn't follow through. I trusted you with Mitch, God. And where is he? In the arms of someone else, while I sit here, empty and alone. With nothing but a c-cold prayer on my lips."

She stumbled to her feet. "I love him, God, and I can't live without him, I can't!"

Something sinister settled on her spirit, bleeding the air from her lungs. She staggered against the sofa, then sank in its depths while nausea welled in her throat.

Pray.

She closed her eyes, feeling his pull but warring against it. In her mind's eye she saw Mitch—that night in her room and the look in his eyes—and a dangerous warmth suffocated all reason. She gave in to the thought, sending heat licking through her. She wanted him. And he wanted her. And she would have him.

Sensual love entices—the taste of honey for the moment. But sin will turn it to ashes in your mouth.

"No, Brady, you're wrong." Her whisper violated the still of the house.

It will never make you happy, never sustain you.

"It will! I've felt it. Mitch loves me, and I love him. I've seduced him more than once. I can do it again." She rose from the sofa with the strength of sin in her bones, moving to the door with unholy purpose.

Love doth not behave itself unseemly . . . seeketh not her own . . . thinketh no evil . . .

She froze, the memory of Brady's Scriptures echoing in her brain. She sagged against the parlor entryway, a feeble sob wrenching from her throat. "Noooo . . ."

She doubled over, revelation impacting her with the force of a blow. If she loved him—really loved him—would she force her own way? Disregard his wishes? Exploit his weakness for her gain? She wept, her body heaving with silent sobs. *Love suffereth long . . . vaunteth not itself . . . beareth all things . . . endureth all things . . .*

A painful groan rose from her spirit. No. She would not.

If she loved him.

She slid down the wall and collapsed to her knees in a pool of pain, sobbing until nothing was left. "All right, you win," she whispered, her voice little more than a rasp. "No more seduction. No more lies." She lifted her gaze to the ceiling. "But I have to see him, God, please . . . just one more time. Without Kathleen near to sway his heart. One more time to win him with honesty . . . or to say goodbye. And whatever you decide, I'll endure."

She rose to her feet and wiped the tears from her face. Brady had once quoted that "love never fails." She lifted her head to heaven and closed her eyes, her thoughts directed in prayer. "Please, God, I'm asking from the depth of my soul—don't let it fail me."

17

Charity closed the front door quietly and hurried down the steps. She glanced at her watch, then exhaled. 5:10 p.m. Thank God she could walk by the light of day for another hour at least. She glanced back at Grandmother's cottage, tinged pink by the first glimmer of dusk, and fought off a wave of guilt. She'd left a note that she would be out. She chewed on her lip. It was better they didn't know where.

By the time she reached the city, rush hour was in full sway, bringing a bustle and excitement that invaded her mood. People milled and autos sputtered, harmonizing with the shouts of vendors and the music of pubs. Evening settled in, shadowing buildings with a rosy glow that would soon fade into night.

Charity stared at the *Irish Times* as it loomed overhead, twinklings of light peeking from its windows. She thought of Mitch, and adrenaline flowed like a wellspring. Her eyes scanned the street, taking note of his car. She merged with the crowd and made her way to where it sat. Nearby, a toothless vendor hawked papers to the crowd. She glanced around, biding her time until he was engaged in a sale, then slipped in the backseat of Mitch's car and slid to the floor.

The sounds and smells of the city whirled outside, but here she was cocooned in the warmth of Mitch's scent. Soap and leather and the smell of Bay Rum filled her senses, clutching at her heart. She drew in a shaky breath. She had to see him alone, not in an office full of people. And away from Kathleen. One last chance to convince him he was marrying the wrong girl.

Snippets of conversation floated in the air, laced with laughter and teasing and occasional song. She lay on her back on the hard floorboard, stretching her legs to dislodge a cramp. How long had she been here? An hour? Two? She could see a sliver of the full moon through the window, wedged between two murky buildings. Stars winked in the sky, as if privy to her plan. She closed her eyes and shuddered. *Maybe she should go . . .*

"How's it going, Jimmy?"

Her eyes popped open and her heart started to pound.

"Fine, Mitch. How are you two tonight?"

You two?

"Hi, Jimmy, no firepot, I see." A woman's muted tone faded on the breeze.

Charity's stomach rolled.

"Not tonight, Kathleen. It's so balmy, I'm thinking of going for a moonlight swim."

Mitch laughed, the deep timbre of his voice blending with the soft melody of Kathleen's. "You just may get yourself a moon burn, Jimmy. Give Mary my love."

"Will do, Mitch."

She held her breath as the passenger door opened and Kathleen slid in. The springs squeaked in her ear. She heard Mitch walk to the front and rattle the crank, causing the engine to rumble to life. The strong smell of gasoline drifted up as the chassis vibrated beneath her. She released a heavy breath, taking advantage of the noise.

Mitch got in and slammed his door, jerking the gears to maneuver into traffic.

"You sure you have to go home? We could get a late supper." His voice sounded lonely.

"I wish I could. There's nothing I'd rather do than be with

you." She paused. "Although that can be dangerous lately." There was a hint of tease in her tone.

"Sorry. Guess I'm low on restraint these days. That'll change after we're married."

"You mean you'll have more?" There was a smile in the question.

"No, ma'am, I won't need any." He shifted in the seat, as if reaching for her hand. "I wish we could get married tomorrow. I'm tired of waiting."

"Only one more month, Mitch."

He shifted to pick up speed. "I should have never let you talk me into putting it off."

She sighed. "I think it was best. You needed time."

"No, I need you," he growled.

They rode in silence until the car slowed to a stop. He pulled the lever back and turned the engine off. His voice was gruff. "Come here." The front seat creaked as he pulled her close.

Charity held her breath, her mouth dry as dust. Soft breathing and the press of the springs were the only sounds she could hear. Her stomach twisted into painful knots.

"Mitch . . . I need to go in and you need to go home."

He sighed and opened his door, getting out and jolting it closed. He opened Kathleen's and helped her from the car, muttering something Charity couldn't hear. The door slammed, and their footsteps faded.

Charity's breathing was ragged as she fumbled for her purse. She bit her lip and fished out a bottle of lilac water to dab on her throat. A surge of guilt heated her cheeks and she shivered, glancing up at the sky. "This is not seduction, Lord, I promise. Just pure common sense. I need all his senses in play when he makes his final decision."

She pushed the bottle back in her purse and returned to the floorboards, her muscles quivering. She squeezed her eyes shut and started to pray. All at once, Kathleen's sweet face came to mind, and Charity's stomach churned. Her hand flew to her mouth to compress a queasy burp. She opened her eyes to dispel the image, but it burned in her sight nonetheless. Sweet and loving Kathleen—she loved Mitch too. A low groan issued forth from Charity's throat, her regret as painful as her guilt. "Oh, Kathleen, I'm sorry—please forgive me! But I love him too, and I don't know what else to do . . ." Her words fused to her lips at the sound of his footsteps. She closed her eyes and prayed.

Mitch lumbered down the steps and rubbed the side of his head. He felt a headache coming on. He rounded the car to grind the crank with more force than needed. The growl of the engine matched that of his mood. He got in and heaved the door closed with a grunt, then shifted the car into gear and headed home.

He'd needed Kathleen . . . tonight, more than ever. The touch of her lips, the heat of her body, anything to take his mind off Charity. Seeing her last night had stabbed him through the heart, undoing months of healing with a single glance. He drew in a deep breath and sagged over the wheel as he drove. Five minutes in her presence, and now even the air carried her scent.

Why was he doing this? Pushing her away?

Trust. It had been the issue in the beginning and the issue in the end. But she had changed, so she said. Given her heart to God. Then why was he marrying Kathleen?

He sighed. Because he'd hurt Kathleen more than once. He wouldn't do it again. He'd given his word, in the form of a ring, and in his mind, there was no turning back. He thought of all the reasons Charity was wrong for him. Fourteen years younger, as stubborn as he, and an affinity for deception that would boggle the mind. He needed more. A stable woman with a compliant heart. And lips that warmed his without the burn of a lie.

Not a woman who could only heat his blood as well as his temper.

He coasted to a stop in front of his apartment and disengaged the drive gears with a weary thrust. The engine sputtered to a slow death. Like his hope. He would marry Kathleen.

He glanced at Mrs. Lynch's lit window, then exhaled and leaned back against the seat, reluctant to chance a repeat encounter. He slammed his fist against the door and groaned. "Why, God?"

"Let me know if you get an answer. I haven't heard a peep."

Mitch jerked around, bumping his head on the roof. He put a hand to his head and swore.

"I thought you gave that up," she said, climbing over the back of the seat. She plopped into the passenger side as casually as if she'd been there all night, giving him a sweet smile. Two perfectly manicured brows wiggled in a playful tease. "Alone at last."

He stared, unable to compose a coherent thought, never mind a coherent sentence. There she sat, the haunt of his dreams, mere inches away, and in full flesh and blood. His gaze traveled from the hypnotic eyes to the full lips, quickening his pulse with a nervous sweep of her tongue. She studied him through shy eyes while she fidgeted with her nails. Her lips suddenly twitched with a near smile. "You don't do well with the element of surprise, do you, Mitch?"

"What are you doing here?"

"I came to talk."

"Yeah, right." He hissed under his breath and jerked the handle of the door, kicking it open with an angry thud. He leapt out and hurtled the crank, then jumped back in and gunned the car from the curve. "Never in my unfortunate life have I ever met a woman like you. I swear, you will drive some poor slob right over the edge."

"Actually, Mitch, I was hoping that would be you."

He squealed around a corner on two wheels, burning the air. "Not on your life, little girl. I'm too old, remember? My heart couldn't take it."

She crossed her arms. "You might as well park the car. We *are* going to talk."

He gave her a sideways glance. "No, Charity, we're *not*. I'm taking you home."

"No! We're going to talk this out, Mitch Dennehy, or die trying." She grabbed his arm, forcing the car to swerve.

He slammed on the brakes and jounced the advance lever up. The vehicle skidded to a screeching stop as he whirled in the seat. "Get out. You can walk from here." He couldn't risk talking to her, not for one blinkin' minute. He wanted her out of his life. Gone.

She stared in disbelief, the fire in her eyes burning away any good intent. He wouldn't even hear her out? Give her five minutes of his time? After all they'd been to each other? She groaned and pounced, pummeling his arm as hard as she could. "You can go to the devil, Mitch Dennehy, for all I care, but first we're going to talk."

He shoved her back on the seat. "Get out of my car, *now*."

She propped up on her elbows, her jaw quivering with anger. "Make me."

He lunged to open her door, and she battered his chest as tears blurred her eyes. He deflected her blows, forcing her wrists to the seat. A choked sob broke from her lips, and the anger faded from his face.

And then she saw it. Pain, regret, longing. Her conscience stilled and her pulse quickened. As if against her will, her own longing took control. He wanted her—still. He loved her!

He loosed his hold and backed away. His tone was pleading. "Charity, please do us both a favor and go home."

Hope surged and she grabbed his shirt, wrenching him close until their lips met. He moaned and finished the job, devouring her mouth with his own. She pressed in, clutching him with all her might. "You love me, I knew it!"

He launched back to his side of the car, his breathing out of control. "So help me, I will hurt you if you come at me again."

She sat up with fire in her eyes. "You've already ripped out my heart, Mitch, what more can you do?"

He stared at her and rubbed his mouth with the back of his hand.

She returned his petulant gaze. "I'm the woman you should be marrying, why can't you just admit it?"

His tone hardened. "How many times do I have to tell you? I'm marrying Kathleen. Stay away from me."

She crossed her arms. "Stay away? At the theater, you said 'don't be a stranger.'"

He glared. "It's a bloomin' figure of speech, code for 'stay out of my life'!"

Her chin jutted up. "Well, I can't. I've tried, and yes, I've prayed about it too. I know it deep down in my bones, Mitch—we belong together." Her voice lowered to a whisper. "After that week in Boston, when my family thought we were married, I felt as if we were. Tell me you didn't feel it too."

He ground his teeth. "I don't feel anything but profound frustration and anger, two things that seem to go hand-in-hand with you."

"You're lying. I know you still think about me . . . our engagement, our kisses—"

He swore under his breath and started the car, veering away from the curb. "You're the one who's lying, Charity, *again*. It's a pattern with you. You lied and ruined my life two years ago, lied to win my heart, and then lied to become my wife. Now you tell me you've turned over a new leaf, given yourself to God." He shot her a hard look, raking her with his eyes. "Then you have the gall to sneak into my car and try and seduce me—"

"No! I didn't come to seduce you, I swear! I came to talk, and that's the truth."

He gunned down Ambrose Lane and squealed to a stop, keeping the engine running. He gave her a cold stare. "The truth. As if you have any earthly idea what that even is. Lies or truth, it's all the same to you, isn't it, Charity? As long as you get what you want."

Fear thickened in her mouth and she put a hand to her throat. "No, Mitch. Maybe before, but I've changed, I promise. My faith in God has changed me."

"Yeah, I see how you've changed. Hiding in my car, lying in wait like some tart ready to throw yourself at me, with no regard for my fiancée, me, or God. Your so-called faith is nothing more than stubble and chaff. Always has been, little girl. Psalm 83. Read it sometime."

Her voice shook. "Please, just one more chance, Mitch. You have to believe me."

"Sorry. Lying seems to be a fatal flaw in your personality. Get out."

She blinked, anger fueling her desperation. She lifted her chin. "Well, I may be a liar and a tart, but you're a liar and a fake. Lying to yourself that you'll ever be happy with Kathleen, pretending you love her when I'll wager it's me in your thoughts at night."

Her words barbed him with the truth, and heat stung the back of his neck.

She appeared to sense their effect and moved closer, gently touching his arm. Her face seemed so innocent in the lamplight, her eyes so wide with hope. "You love me and want me, Mitch, I know it. That's why you're really angry, isn't it?"

Heat engulfed him. He wanted to push her away, but he was afraid to touch her, afraid he'd give in. To the feel of her skin, the curve of her body, the taste of her lips.

God, help me.

He thought of Kathleen, and anger swept through him like a cleansing fire, burning away the lust from his soul. He stared at the woman before him and knew what he had to do. His heart was bleeding, but he had no choice. She would never let go, never let him be. Always gauging love by her standard of lust rather than God's measure of obedience. He longed to hold her and teach her, but she would never receive. His heart squeezed in his chest. Hers was a lesson only pain would impart.

He switched the ignition off and turned in the seat, hand gripped to the steering wheel and his jaw hardened for battle.

She lifted her face to his. Longing shimmered in her eyes. "Marry me, Mitch. I love you and I know you love me. We belong together."

Tension quivered his cheek, but his will was as steady and unyielding as the steel beneath his hand. His voice was cold and calm. "No, Charity, it's over. Your lies have destroyed any chance we may have had. I don't want to hurt you, truly I don't. But you need to understand that any love I felt has been damaged beyond hope. I'm in love with Kathleen now."

Even in the dark, he could see the color drain from her face. Her lips trembled open and tears welled in her eyes. She touched a quivering hand to his arm. "You can't mean that. You love me and you want me. I saw it in your eyes and felt it in your kiss."

He was not a man prone to reining in his emotions. A lifetime of explosive temper and unbridled passions had marked him as such. But he knew if change were to come, the moment would be now, when his life—and Charity's—hung in the balance. From the moment he'd met her, she had read him so easily, his reaction to her, his attraction. And she had used it against him time after time, measuring his love by the desire she provoked.

He had no choice but to end it all now. And so, in his mind's eye, he shut her out with a veneer of indifference so cold that he felt her shiver. His face was a mask of iron and his will a wall she would never scale. Slowly, deliberately, he removed her hand from his arm. "Love you?" His smile was not kind. "As always, you're confusing love with lust. You know, all take and no give? All heat and no heart? And, yes, I suppose in the past I have lusted after you, or at least my body has. But not anymore."

"No! I felt it! You love me!"

He raked her with a cool gaze. "Not love, Charity, lust . . . as surely as if you had peddled your charms on Mountgomery Street."

The breath hitched in her throat. Her eyes bled tears as she clutched at her sides. "Why are you doing this?"

"To make you understand once and for all, little girl—the price of your 'love' is more than I'm willing to pay."

She flinched as if he had slapped her. She shrank back, shock and fury glistening in her eyes. "You snake, how dare you treat me like this, no better than a common—"

He arched a brow while his lips clamped into a hard smile. "Whore?"

She caught her breath, the force of the word pressing her hard against the door. Wetness pooled in her eyes and began to spill, slicing through his heart.

He forced himself to go on. "I told you once that what you sell, only the wrong men would buy. You came here tonight to sell your body for my love. But you've sold your soul instead. Sorry, I need a wife with both." He leaned and slammed a fist hard against her door handle. She cowered against the seat as the door wheeled open. "Go home, little girl, and leave me alone."

She shuddered and wiped her face with her sleeve, avoiding his eyes. "My purse . . . it's in the back."

He reached over to fist it in his hands and flung it in her lap.

The set of her jaw was hard and cold, chiseled in ice. "I despise you," she whispered.

Her words burned like acid. "Good. Let's keep it that way."

She clutched her purse and struggled with the door, her fingers shaking. She swung out from the car and managed to stand, teetering the slightest bit. He saw her shoulders straighten as she engaged that familiar lift of her head. Without a backward glance, she left the door wide open and moved to the porch, her back as rigid as the nerves in his neck.

In a ragged beat of his heart, she slipped inside, leaving him alone with a gloom in his soul darker than anything he'd ever known. He touched his hand to the ignition, then collapsed on the wheel, putting his hand to his eyes.

He'd had no choice. Not against her will of iron. No recourse but shame. And God willing, conviction. Tears stung his lids. God help her. He squeezed his eyes shut. God help him.

18

"Charity, please, come home with me." Emma stood in the door of the back room, purse in hand and her face strained with worry.

Charity glanced up, her tone lifeless. "No, Emma, I want to stay awhile and work on these books. Tell Grandmother not to wait supper."

Emma took a tentative step forward, wringing her coat in her hands. "You can't work late every night, Charity. You're not eating well and you're losing weight. You can't keep up with a thriving business if you don't take care of yourself."

She flipped a page over in the ledger and forced a smile. "You know, Emma, you become more of a mother every day. Go home. I'll be fine."

Her friend moved to the table and sat down, her fingers pinched tight on her wrap. "No, you're not fine. I don't know what's happened, but you've shut us all out. We're all sick with worry. You spend all your waking hours here, never talking to us, laughing with us. It's like you're dead inside. You can't go on like this, Charity. Talk to me, please!"

Charity sighed and sagged back in the chair. She put the pen down and closed her eyes to massage the bridge of her nose. "Okay, Emma, what do you want to talk about?"

"You. Why you've lost the spark in your eye, the bounce in

your step. And why I've lost the only real friend I have ever had."

Charity opened her eyes, stunned to see tears in Emma's. Her heart squeezed in her chest. She leaned forward and pressed a hand to her arm. "You haven't lost me, Emma. I'm right here. Maybe in a bit of a funk, but always your friend."

"No, you're not here, that's just it. You go through the motions, but you're gone, empty inside. I want to know why, Charity, why you're closing out the people who love you the most."

Charity looked down at the table, her eyes drifting into a dead stare. She saw Mitch's face, rigid and cold, heard his voice, filled with disdain. She closed her eyes and felt the hard grip of his disgust for the way that he saw her. A whore. Not worth his respect, his love, his commitment. Only his lust. Pain slashed through her and she shivered. And all this time she'd thought he loved her.

She squeezed her eyes shut, and tears spilled down her face. She felt Emma's arms wrap around her, and she leaned into her embrace, sobs wrenching from her lips. Emma's voice was soft in her ear. "This is about Mitch, isn't it?"

Charity heaved against her chest and nodded.

Emma stroked her hair. "Did something happen?"

She nodded again. Her voice carried on a broken sob. "H-he . . . d-doesn't love me. He's never l-loved me."

Emma pulled away with shock in her eyes. "No, I don't believe that. I know better."

Charity sniffed and blew her nose on a handkerchief. "It's true. He as much as told me."

"When?"

"Last week."

"The night you left and didn't tell us where you were going? You went to see Mitch?"

Charity looked away, her chin trembling. "I hid in his car and waited for him."

Emma moaned. "But why? To seduce him? You promised Brady. You promised God."

Charity put her hand to her eyes. Her voice was barely audible. "I know, but I didn't go to seduce him, Emma, I'm telling the truth. I just went to talk. But things got out of hand and . . ." Her voice cracked on a sob. "Mitch was right. I am a liar . . . and a whore."

Emma gasped. "He said that?"

She nodded, the shame thick in her throat.

"But that's not true. We all lie . . ."

"Don't defend me, Emma, I don't deserve it. I do lie, when-ever it suits my purpose. And I have used my . . . affections . . . to get what I want. First with Rigan, then with Mitch." She faded off into another hard stare. "Let's face it, I'm a miserable human being."

"We're all miserable, Charity, that's why we need God's love and forgiveness."

"No! I especially don't deserve that. I turned on him, Emma. I told him I'd live for him, and then I went my own way. I lied—to him, to Brady, and to Mitch." A brittle laugh escaped her lips. "The fatal flaw in my personality, I'm afraid, as Mitch so brutally pointed out."

"You're being too hard. You forgave your father and Faith. It's time to forgive yourself."

Charity sighed and reached for her ledger. "I will, Emma, in time. But right now I'd like to get into these books. You better go. Grandmother will be worried."

"Can we pray first, before I go? Please?"

Charity shook her head, then looked away. "I'm not ready, Emma, but I will, I promise."

"Don't wait too long, Charity. You need God's love and grace. We all do."

Charity nodded. "See you tonight. Bolt the door, will you?"

She waited until she heard the click of the lock, then sighed and refocused on the books at hand. In the last week, she'd found that the store and the books were the only things that kept her mind from straying. At least days and early evenings. Nighttime was another matter. Those were the hours when her broken heart would fester with the realization she was in love with a man who would never love her back.

She dipped her pen in the inkwell and entered another figure, pushing the thought from her mind. The felt fedoras were selling nicely. She would have to reorder. She calculated the column and bit her lip. All of her inventories, as a matter of fact, were dwindling faster than she could tally. They'd have to hire another clerk soon, maybe two.

She looked up and cocked her head, listening. "Emma? Did you forget something?" Charity rose and walked to the curtain, pushing it aside to glance at the door. The shop was still and dark, lit only by the soft wash of the streetlamp. She moved to the front door to jostle the knob. Securely locked. She exhaled and returned to the back room, sweeping the curtain aside.

A cry lodged in her throat as someone grabbed her from behind and spun her around, plundering her mouth with his. Nausea curdled in her stomach as her eyes went wide.

Rigan!

He laughed and pushed her toward the table, a wicked grin distorting his face. "Burning the midnight oil, my dear? That's what I like to see in an employee."

She butted up against a chair. Her heart hammered in her throat. "How did you get in?"

He leaned close and hiked a boot up on the table, effectively blocking her in. The flash of white teeth chilled her. "Why, I have my own personal key, of course."

"You're not welcome here. It's no longer Mrs. Shaw's store, it's mine. Leave at once or I'll call the police."

His laughter echoed off the walls of the tiny back room. "And tell them what? That I broke into my own store?"

Shards of ice prickled her spine. "This is my store, mine and Mr. Horace Hargrove's."

Rigan traced a finger along the curve of her jaw, and she shivered. "You know, I've always liked Mr. Hargrove. Did you know that his wife used to teach my mother in school before she married Horace? It's true. Horace always liked me, you know. Of course, he was quite dismayed when he learned you broke our engagement. So you can imagine his relief when I told him it was back on again."

"What?"

His finger stroked along her collarbone. "Yes, he was bowled over too. So naturally when I told him I wanted to surprise you with the store as a wedding gift, well, he just couldn't resist. So there you have it—he sold it to me, lock, stock, and Charity."

She had trouble breathing. "You're lying."

"No, I assure you I'm not." He reached into his vest and pulled out a folded paper. He flipped it open, displaying his deed of trust.

She sagged against the table while the blood drained from her cheeks.

He smiled and returned the paper to his pocket. "So you see, darling, you now work for me. But don't worry. I have no qualms whatsoever about letting my wife work."

Revulsion clotted in her throat. She tried to move away. He jerked her back to the table, shoving her on top. "But before we get married and you begin paying your debt on the store, there is another wage I'm afraid you owe."

Fear glazed in her stomach. "Rigan, can we talk about this tomorrow, perhaps at dinner? I'm very tired tonight and need to go home."

He laughed, feathering her cheek with his thumb. "No, darling, I'm afraid this needs to be settled right here and now. As your future husband, I have a responsibility to keep you honest. After all, if you told Mitch Dennehy that I raped you, well, naturally I have an obligation to make it right."

She screamed and lunged to the other side. He gripped her ankle and jerked her back, slamming her hard on the table. An unholy grin spread across his face as he pinned her arms and straddled her. "Go ahead and scream, darling, no one can hear. It's just you and me . . . and a debt long overdue."

He crushed his mouth against hers and strangled her cry, cutting the breath from her throat. She gasped for air and lashed against him, but he only laughed and locked her in his hold. His lips plunged again and again, brutalizing her mouth. She coughed from lack of air. Her vision dimmed to a sickening blur. His hands gripped her shoulders and jerked, ripping her blouse down her arms. She gagged on the bile in her throat.

Whore.

Liar.

She moaned and darkness swept her away.

The wages of sin is death.

꿍 꿍

Her eyelids fluttered open. Comprehension strangled like a fist to her throat. She gasped for air, eyes unblinking as she stared at the stained ceiling of the back room, laced with cobwebs and jaundiced with age. She attempted to draw a full breath and felt a stab of pain. Shock droned in her brain, merging with her own shallow breathing to create a surreal symphony, violated only by the creak of the door as it banged in the wind.

She felt a chill and realized she still lay flat on the table, legs bare and clothing torn. Her limbs felt like deadweight as she tried to rise, her body stiff from the force of the wood beneath her. All at once, the memory flushed the bile from her throat and she heaved, spewing her revulsion onto the pitted floor.

She gagged until nothing remained but the shame in her throat. If only she could dispel that as easily.

But she could not. She doubled over, clenching her sides.

Shame. Her face was branded by it. The painful legacy of Psalm 83, prophesied by Mitch that night in the car.

Make them like a whirling thing, like stubble before the wind. As fire burneth a forest, and as the flame setteth the mountains on fire, so pursue them with thy tempest, and terrify them with thy whirlwind. Fill their faces with shame, that they may seek thy name . . .

She covered her eyes with her hand. Oh, God, he'd been right! Her faith had been nothing but chaff, whipped about by her own passions and desires, with little or no regard for others. Or God. And tonight, she had paid the price.

She shivered and tried to stand, seeing it clearly for the very first time. Her lust for Mitch had been a consuming fire, infecting her with sin, setting her passion ablaze. Misguided passion that had callously wounded her sister and Mitch and Rigan. And in the end, the very men she had strived to enflame had rejected her, despised her, degraded her. Until nothing was left. A raging fire to burn away the dross, a tempest to blow away the chaff. And a storm of shame so she would seek his name . . .

With a wrenching cry, she collapsed into a chair, arms strewn across the table and her body wracked by sobs. "Oh, God, forgive me. I've been so blind. So lost." She thought of what Rigan had done and wanted to hate him, but knew she could not. Her dance with sin was over. The choice was clear. Forgive or hate. Life or death. Peace or shame.

In the shudder of a single breath, she knew what her decision would be. A decision that would set her free from a life adrift. Bind her wounds and save her soul.

She looked up with swollen eyes and pushed the hair from her face. Tears of pain made way for tears of hope. Her heart surged with a rush of adrenaline as she bowed her head and committed her life. Totally. Completely. Devoid of ulterior motives.

The time had come. She would finally belong to him.

Not to Mitch. Not to Father. Not to herself.

To him. The apple of his eye.

Charity leaned over the railing of the *Cambria* and closed her eyes, reveling in the sting of the sea breeze in her face. She could smell Boston in the spring, the earthy scent mingling with the pungent smell of the harbor and its fishing dinghies and shrimp boats. A sigh drifted from her lips and she opened her eyes, drinking in the welcome sight of home.

Emma's chuckle sounded behind her, wisping on a breeze. "So this is where you've been hiding. I should have known. You're even more anxious than me to see dry land again."

Charity looked over her shoulder and smiled. "I came up at dawn and didn't want to waken you." She turned back to the harbor and felt the rush of tears in her eyes. "I never thought Boston would look so good." She sniffed and pointed to a squat-looking cast-iron lighthouse, half on a sandbar, half in water. "That's the Deer Island Lighthouse. Four years ago, Keeper Joseph McCabe met his fiancée on Deer Island to fill out wedding invitations. When he returned to the lighthouse, ice trapped his boat and he drowned."

Emma shivered. "That's awful."

Charity glanced at her friend. "Sorry, Emma, I don't mean to be morbid. Blame it on the harbinger of gloom over my head, especially these last few weeks." She looked out over the water, scanning the city's skyline with longing in her eyes. "But the winds of change are coming. I can feel them blowing." She pointed again, this time with a smile. "And to prove it, I'll show you a part of Boston Harbor that's full of hope—a boatload, to be exact. See that ship against the seawall, the one with a flag on either end?"

Emma squinted and nodded.

"Well, that, my friend, is the Boston Floating Hospital for Children. Begun by Reverend Rufus B. Tobey. He was a minister who wanted to help indigent women and their sick children. In the summer, you can actually see naked babies and toddlers playing on the sundeck, therapy for vitamin D deficiency."

Emma giggled. "I bet that's a sight."

Charity laughed, the sensation welling her with hope. Her laughter had been scarce the last few weeks. She sucked in a fishy breath. Weeks? Try months. And too many to count. Her fingers lightly traced along the steel bar of the railing while her gaze gently traced the line of the shore. But this was a new day and a new place. And thanks to the many prayers of her family, Brady, and Emma, a new heart.

She glanced up at the sky, puffs of clouds billowing in the breeze like her spirit in the gentle wind of God. Tears pricked her eyes and a lump thickened in her throat. He was real and alive! The Light of the World, flooding her with hope when darkness tried to snuff hers out. For the first time in her life, she understood her sister, Faith, and her fervor for God. She closed her eyes and exhaled a cleansing sigh, thinking of Mitch, and then of Rigan. In the past, she would have blamed God. But in her darkest hour, his mercy had illuminated her life, revealing a painful path twisted by sin.

She felt Emma's arm encircle her waist and looked up, tears streaking her face. "Oh, Emma, God is so good."

Emma leaned her head against Charity's. "He is for a fact."

They stood there, arm in arm, until the ship docked at the shore where crowds milled at the gangplank. Charity's heart began to race. Her gaze anxiously probed the throng, searching for the one face that could heal her heart. And when she spotted a zoot hat waving wildly above the crowd, she laughed, the sound winging in the air.

"Father," she screamed. She jumped and waved and cried till she laughed, hugging Emma with more joy bubbling inside than she'd known in a lifetime. Her father stood tall on the shore, dressed in his best suit and a grin, pressed in on all sides by people he probably didn't even see. She'd forgotten how handsome he was, and her heart swelled with love. *Daddy, oh Daddy, I missed you so much.* She wiped a sleeve to her eyes and stifled a sob. One of the last, she hoped, for a while. He blew her a kiss, and she caught it, holding the fragile gift in her hand. She pressed her lips to her palm and held it to her heart, then swooned. The giggle of a little girl took flight from her throat.

She spun around. "Oh, Emma, the bags!"

Emma chuckled and motioned her head to the side. Charity looked down and laughed. She hefted her bag and made a beeline for the gangplank. "Come on, Emma, we're home!"

She streamed down the passageway with a flood of people, her nerves itching under her skin like a bad case of the measles. She jumped and stood on tiptoe, hoping to catch a glimpse of her father. She grinned when she saw his dark cropped hair, salted with gray, stubbornly resisting the slick style of the day.

"Charity, darlin'!" He wagged his hat in the air, then put it on as she ran for him.

She squealed and dropped her suitcase, launching into his arms. He swept her up, high above the crowd, twirling her in the air. The rumble of his deep laughter tickled her stomach, and she squeezed him hard, tears puddling her face. "Daddy, oh Daddy, I love you so much."

He put her down with a chuckle. Wetness glimmered in his gray eyes. "I love you, too, darlin', and don't be looking to stray too far from home again, because I'll be keeping you close." He clutched her again, his voice hoarse in her ear. "My heart grieves for what you went through, Charity. But you're home now, where we can love on you." He kissed her cheek and hugged her again, eyeing Emma over her shoulder. He swiped a hand at the tears in his eyes. "And who's this pretty young thing staring at us like we've taken leave of our senses?"

Charity giggled and spun around, grinning at Emma. She grabbed her arm and pulled her close. "This is Emma Malloy, my best friend in the whole world, and the only one who would put up with me."

Emma's look was shy as she peeked up beneath dark lashes. She extended a hand. "It's a pleasure to meet you, Mr. O'Connor. And thank you for allowing me to stay with Charity for a while. At least until I find a job."

Patrick propped thick palms on his hips. He jutted a brow and nudged the brim of his hat, then stared at her hand. "I think we need to do better than a handshake, don't you, Emma? From what I understand, you're one of the family." He swooped in and gave her a voracious hug, taking her airborne while she held on to her cloche hat. When he put her down again, her cheeks were as red as the scar on her face. "And as far as staying with Charity, Faith has a habit of sleeping with her husband in their home a few blocks away, so I doubt she'll be needing her bed anytime soon. It's yours as long as you like."

"Father!" Charity tilted her head, giving him a shocked smile.

He laughed and picked up their bags. "Nothing wrong with two people in love, darlin', when the good Lord joins them as one." He glanced at his watch. "Now let's get you two home so your mother and I can fawn over you before the horde descends after work and school. Marcy's been cooking up a storm all day, so everyone will be chomping at the bit to see you again." He winked as he opened the car door. "And the heavenly smells will be drifting, no doubt, so you can bet Collin and Brady will show up early to eat me out of house and home."

Charity looked up, her eyes wide. "Brady will be there tonight?"

Patrick grinned and helped her and Emma into the car.

He closed the door and leaned in the open window. "Unless I can figure a way to change the locks before dinner. He eats more than Collin, and you know that's saying something." He whistled as he rounded the car to the front, churning the crank with a grunt.

Emma pursed her lips into a curious smile. "So . . . I get to meet your Brady, do I?"

Charity tilted her head and arched a brow. "I suppose you do, but he's not 'my' Brady."

Emma folded her hands in her lap and looked out the window. A hint of a smile shadowed her lips. "No, I don't suppose so. At least not yet."

෴ ෴

Collin wrapped a stack of forms in brown paper, then slapped an invoice label on top. He turned and tossed it on a table stacked high with packages of completed jobs. "That's it, Brady, we're done for the day. Close down the presses."

Brady looked up, then checked his watch. He squinted. "It's only four o'clock."

Collin wiped his hands on a towel and grinned. "Marcy's cooking a special dinner."

A broad smile inched across Brady's face. He wiped his forehead with a rag, certain it would leave a trail of ink. He tossed it in the laundry box and rolled his neck, groaning as he worked out the kinks. "So, what's the occasion? You and Faith have news to share?"

Collin sauntered to the back of the shop to wash his hands in the sink. He glanced over his shoulder. "Not yet." He turned around and leaned against the counter, drying his hands with a clean towel. "Although it's not from lack of trying, ol' buddy, I can tell you that."

Brady scratched his throat and gave Collin a droll smile. "A six-month honeymoon. I'm real happy for you, Collin. Now stop rubbing it in."

Collin chuckled and picked up a rag to help Brady clean the press. "I wouldn't have to if you would get married and curl up with something other than your Bible every night. Not that the Good Book isn't sustenance for our souls, but right now, it's your body I'm worried about."

Brady dropped on a flat wooden dolly with a grunt and rolled beneath their Bullock press, checking the rotors for nicks. "Worry about your own body, Collin, not mine. When Faith figures out that you're trying to get her pregnant so you can make her quit her job, your body's going to be sleeping on the couch."

Collin chuckled. "Not a chance, Brady. The woman can't keep her hands off me."

Brady extended an arm. "You sure it's not the other way around? Hand me a wrench."

Collin squatted to snatch a wrench from a tool chest on the floor. He shoved it in Brady's hand. "Yeah, that too." He paused. "Brady?"

"Yeah?"

"About dinner tonight . . ."

Brady groaned. "Spit it out, Collin."

"There is a celebration."

"I figured as much. What is it?"

Collin rolled his chair back, bracing himself for Brady's reaction. "Charity's home."

The wrench clattered to the floor. Brady rolled out, his pale face accentuating the ink on his forehead. "What did you say?"

Collin smiled and leaned back in the chair, crossing his arms. "She's at the house right now. Arrived today."

Brady swallowed, a lump shifting in his throat. "With Mitch?"

"Nope. He's marrying someone else."

He swallowed again, the lump growing. "Why didn't you tell me?"

"Because I knew this is how you would act, love-struck and staring off into space like a zombie. We're too busy for that."

Brady stared, then quickly shifted to a frown. "Give me a little credit, will you, Collin? Charity's my friend. You should have told me she was coming home."

"And go through a week with you pale as death? No way, ol' buddy. And she may be your friend, but it doesn't take a mental giant to see you wish it were more."

Brady scowled, flinging the towel toward the laundry box. He missed. "Where are you getting half-baked ideas like that? I told you we're friends, pure and simple."

"With you, the 'pure' I believe. With Charity? Nothing's 'simple.' Every letter she sent you cost us a half day of your time."

Brady glared, rare prickles of irritation wrinkling his brow. "You're crazy."

Collin grinned. "Ah-hah! The tables are turned, aren't they, Brady? How does it feel to have someone scratching beneath the surface, delving into your mind?"

Brady sighed and lumbered to his feet. "Look, Collin, you're ruining my appetite. Charity's letters meant a lot to me because I was concerned about her spiritual progress, nothing more. And I thought she bought a store. Why is she coming home?"

The smile faded on Collin's face, and Brady's stomach tensed. He watched his friend's jaw harden. "Tell me what's wrong, Collin—now!"

Collin huffed out a sigh and looked up, his eyes dark with anger. "Same reason as before, only a different twist. She was raped."

Brady caught his breath and slowly slumped in a chair. He felt like he'd been kicked in the gut. "By the same scum who beat her last time?"

Collin nodded.

"Did he beat her again?"

Collin shook his head. "No, the lowlife just took what he wanted and left. Thinks he can force her to marry him because he bought the store out from under her. As soon as Faith's grandmother heard that, she put Charity on the next ship home."

Brady sagged and put his face in his hands. "Dear God, no."

"Yeah, and on top of all of that, Mitch treated her like dirt."

"I can't believe it." He groaned and ran a hand over his face. "God bless her."

"He already has." Collin stood and massaged the back of his neck. "He's given her a friend like you."

Brady looked up, a nerve pulsing in his cheek. "Thanks, Collin. I only hope and pray I can be the friend she needs."

Collin smiled and made his way to the door. He plucked his coat from the rack. "Don't waste good air on that prayer, my friend, it's a done deal." He gave Brady a quick once-over and grinned. "And that, ol' buddy, is why we quit early. 'Cause my money says you'll be wantin' a bath."

19

Charity hovered close to her father as he carved the turkey, waiting for him to turn and talk to her mother before stealing another piece. A luscious hunk of dark meat was halfway to her lips when he snatched it from her hand. He popped it in his mouth and arched a brow. "So you're wanting special treatment, are you now? Long-lost daughter or no, you'll wait like everyone else or you won't get the wishbone."

She reached up and kissed him on the cheek. "We both know I'll get the wishbone, now don't we, Father? Turkey thievery or no."

He grinned and tossed a piece to her, then one to Blarney, who lay at his feet. "Enjoy the attention, young lady. It ends at the stroke of midnight when you turn back into just another O'Connor sibling."

Katie hopped up on the table and began picking at the turkey. "Why are we having turkey and dressing? It's not Thanksgiving; it's almost Fourth of July."

Patrick swatted her hand and handed her a consolation piece. "Stop fingering the food, Katie Rose. Only God knows where your hands have been. And we're having turkey and dressing because it's Charity's favorite. Get off the table."

Katie rolled her eyes and jumped to the floor. "*My* favorite is chocolate cream pie; are we having that?"

Marcy turned at the sink. "No, ma'am, we're having peach pie because—"

"It's Charity's favorite," Katie mimicked. She crossed her arms, a petite eight-year-old with the air of a matriarch. "You have other children, you know."

Charity grabbed Katie and swung her up in her arms, nose to nose. "You got a problem with peach pie, little girl?"

Katie squealed and squirmed. "Nooooo! It's my favorite."

"I thought chocolate cream pie was your favorite," Charity teased, tickling her sister.

"After peach," Katie shrieked before sliding to the floor.

Charity squatted to hug her, then stood. She touched her own ear. "Oh-oh, ear kiss."

Katie cocked her head. "What's an ear kiss?"

Charity leaned back down and hugged her again, pressing her head to Katie's. She pulled back, catching Katie's tiny ear on hers. It sprang back. Katie giggled. "Oooo, I can't wait to give one to Collin! Mama, when are they gonna be here?"

Marcy glanced at the clock over the stove. "Anytime now. Beth, is the table all set?"

"Yes, Mother, everything's ready."

Marcy paused, ladle in hand. "You look very pretty tonight, Beth. Very grown up."

"Too grown up to suit me," Patrick muttered.

"Thanks, Mother. Charity helped me."

Marcy blinked at Charity. "Did you use all the rouge on Beth, dear? You look a bit pale."

Charity smiled. "No, I haven't been fixing my face for a while. No interest."

Her parents exchanged a look. Marcy pushed a limp strand of hair from her eyes. Her face glistened from the steam of the mashed potatoes. "Well, you're pretty with or without makeup, Charity. And Beth too. You're all growing up into beautiful women. I'm afraid if your father had his way, you'd still be in pinafores and playing with dolls."

"I hate dolls," Katie announced, filching more turkey. "Except for Miss Buford."

"Katie Rose, are you eating all that turkey before I even get a taste?"

Katie whirled around to see Collin propped in the door. She threw her hands up and bolted toward him. He doubled over, groaning with her force, then hiked her up over his shoulder and tickled unmercifully. Her squeals rang through the house.

Faith butted him out of the way with a smile and barged into the kitchen. She made a beeline for Charity, squeezing her with a happy moan. "Oh, Charity, we missed you something fierce, didn't we, Collin? I am so glad you're back for good."

Collin flipped Katie over his other shoulder and grinned. "Yeah, even I missed you, kid. Almost as much as Brady."

Charity felt a dusting of heat in her cheeks. "He is coming, isn't he? Tonight, I mean?"

Collin dropped Katie into a chair with a thump and hooked an arm around Faith's waist. "You bet. Wild horses—or in Brady's case, tame ponies—couldn't keep him away. He went home to clean up first."

The doorbell rang. Katie shrieked and Blarney barked. Beth jumped up and knocked over a chair. She jerked it up and ran for the door. "I'll get it."

Charity put a hand to her chest and grinned at Emma. "I'm afraid this is going to take some getting used to, isn't it, Emma? After living with Grandmother and Mima?"

Emma nodded and smiled.

Charity laughed and yanked her up from the table, slinging an arm over her shoulder. "Faith, Collin, this is my dear friend, Emma Malloy. She's going to be staying awhile. Emma, this is my sister, Faith, about whom I have given you many an earful."

Faith smirked. "I'm sure that's safe to say."

Collin reached out a hand. "Welcome, Emma. I have great

admiration for anybody who can put up with my sister-in-law."

Emma shook it with a timid grin. "She is a handful, I'm afraid."

Charity stuck out her tongue. "The saints be praised for Faith taking you off my hands, Collin McGuire."

Faith laughed and gave Emma a hug, then leaned to buss her father's cheek before sidling up next to her mother. "The natives are restless, Mother. Can I help you get food on the table?"

Marcy sighed. "That would be lovely. Patrick, Charity, Katie—make yourselves useful and grab a platter or bowl."

Charity snatched the tray of turkey from her father's hands and headed for the door, almost toppling it when Beth and Brady pushed through.

Brady steadied Charity's hands. "Whoa, girl, that's my dinner you're messing with."

Charity squealed and handed the tray off to her father. She laughed and threw her arms around Brady's neck. "John Morrison Brady, as I live and breathe. Did you come here tonight to see me or get a free dinner?"

Brady lifted her off her feet in a voracious hug. "No lie shall cross these lips. No comment." He put her back down with a thud.

Charity laughed and tried to throttle him. He grabbed her wrist with a playful gleam in his eye. "Don't mess with me, woman, I'm hungry."

"Charity, Brady, if you two don't settle down, I'll make you eat in the kitchen." Marcy pushed past with a steaming bowl of mashed potatoes. "Beth, don't stand there gawking, darling, get that dressing in on the table, please."

"Yes, ma'am," Beth muttered, her face pink as she jostled past Charity.

Charity quirked a brow at Brady. Her gaze followed her sister through the door. "She's still smitten, I see," she whispered.

Brady grinned and shrugged his shoulders. "Puppy love. She'll get over it." He grabbed a basket of rolls. "Although I have been known to have that effect on women."

Charity swiped the gravy boat from the table and shoved him through the kitchen door. "You mean little girls, don't you, Brady?"

Patrick stood at the head of the table. "Everyone, take your seats." He looked around. "Where's Steven and Sean?"

"Sean's running a bit late," Marcy said. "Rough day at the store."

"And Steven's asleep in the parlor," Katie said with a smirk.

"Katie, wake him, please."

"Steeeeeeeeeeeevennnnnn!" Katie's screech could have curdled the gravy.

Patrick gummed his lips and singed her with a menacing stare. "Thank you, Katie Rose, for that delightful display of table etiquette. Marcy, your daughter needs fine-tuning."

Marcy bit back a smile. "Yes, dear."

Charity giggled and snatched a piece of turkey, pitching one in her mouth and sailing the other across the table to Emma's plate.

Patrick gave her the eye. "Make that two, Marcy." He sighed. "Steeeeeeeeven!"

Steven stumbled into the dining room, sofa prints embedded in his cheek. "I'm coming, Father. I'm not deaf . . . or at least I wasn't." He plopped down next to Brady and scratched his head, mussing his red hair even more than it already was.

Patrick stood and closed his eyes, palms pressed to Marcy's lace tablecloth. Candlelight flickered on bowed faces as a hush fell over the table. "Heavenly Father, thank you for your incredible blessings, not only for the bounty of this table, but for the bounty of our lives, evident in this woman beside me and the children we have borne. And for bringing a precious one of our own back home to us, Lord, and a special bonus, too, in Emma. Amen."

Katie's lips twisted. "You forgot to bless the food, Father. *Again.*"

Patrick sat down and gouged a piece of turkey with his fork. He gave Katie a caustic gaze that prompted another round of giggles around the table. "And bless this food, Lord, both in the nourishment of our bodies and in the peace of its partaking." He held the tray of turkey for Marcy. "Emma, dig in and start passing to the left or you're likely to go to bed hungry tonight."

The front door flew open, and Sean blew in, his cheeks ruddy from the night air. "Sorry I'm late. Kelly's was a madhouse." He spotted Brady and Collin and groaned. "If I'd known you two were going to be here, I would have hustled a bit more. There's still food left, I hope?"

Collin stuffed a roll in his mouth. "Not much."

Marcy smiled. "We just said grace and I made plenty, Sean. But before you sit your weary bones down, isn't there something you're forgetting?"

He hurled his coat on the rack by the door and grinned, rounding the table to pluck Charity up out of her chair. He crushed her in a bear hug. "Welcome home, you little brat. I guess Katie's got some competition now."

"Thanks, Sean. Any interesting things—or people—in your life these days besides Kelly's Hardware?" She pushed haphazard strands of straw-colored hair from his blue eyes.

He ruffled his hair with his hand and plopped down beside her, reaching for the potatoes. "Nope. No time. Pass the turkey, McGuire, if you can bear to part with it."

Marcy smiled and handed Sean the rolls. "Charity brought her good friend home to stay. Emma, this is Sean, my oldest."

Sean stood and extended his hand across the table, his smile as broad as his reach. "Welcome. Anyone who can put up with this sister of mine has to be the genuine article."

Charity smacked him.

"Nice to meet you, Sean," Emma said with a blush.

"So, Charity tells me you and she met at Shaw's and that you've worked there forever." Faith dolloped potatoes on her plate, then handed them off to Collin.

Emma gave her a crooked smile. "Yes, I was actually Mrs. Shaw's top sales clerk before Charity came on the scene. Dublin's gentry took one look at her and pushed me aside."

"Oh, pshaw. Don't believe her. It took me a solid six months to catch up." Charity removed a roll from the basket, eyed the lighter one on Brady's plate and switched it with hers. He stared her down, but she ignored him.

"What happened to your face?" Katie asked.

"Katie Rose!" Marcy, Faith, and Charity's voices rang in shock.

Emma smiled. "No, it's a natural question and one I don't mind answering. I got in the way of a pan of hot grease, I'm afraid."

Katie's eyes bugged. "How did you do that?"

"Katie, hush," Charity warned.

"Someone accidentally threw it in my face."

Forks, knives, and spoons stilled as all eyes focused on Emma.

Charity cleared her throat and elbowed Sean, who stared as if Emma had just announced she was from the moon. "So, Sean, Mother tells me you finally wrangled a promotion."

He chewed slowly, his eyes still fixed on Emma. He swallowed and turned to his sister. "Yeah, I did. Don't look now, sis, but you're rubbing shoulders with the assistant manager of the largest hardware mercantile in south Boston. Not to mention future manager of a new store."

One of her brows slanted up. "Well, well. Must be those

dangerous good looks drawing all the ladies in to buy nuts and bolts."

He grinned and chomped on a roll. "Must be."

The conversations steered in various directions as the family ate, their laughter as warm as the soft glow from Marcy's silver candlesticks, dancing high with flame. Charity glanced across the table and winked at Emma, then looked up at Brady who was immersed in an intense discussion with Collin and Patrick. She sighed. How could she have believed this place was not home? Her thoughts wandered to Bridget and Mima, and a bit of melancholy tempered her mood. *Oh, Lord, if only they were here.*

When pies had been cut and eaten, and the candles waxed to near gone, Patrick stood from the table and stretched. "Any takers on chess? I need to work off that second piece of pie."

Marcy rose and began stacking plates. A smile twitched on her lips. "You might want to consider a five-mile jog instead, my love. I counted three."

Patrick chuckled and pushed his chair in. He hooked an arm around her waist and kissed the top of her head. "Or I could just chase you around the house, Marceline, if you prefer."

"Patrick, stop. We have company."

He laughed and winked at Emma. "Not company, Marcy, family. Emma will get the lay of the land soon enough, eh? Sean, Collin, Brady—to the parlor. One of you lucky boys is about to learn a valuable lesson in chess."

Faith jumped up. She wrestled a stack of dirty plates from Marcy's hands. "Oh, no, you're going into that parlor and put your feet up. We can handle the dishes. Go on, get in there and keep Father honest."

Marcy sighed and gave her a grateful smile. "Thanks, Faith."

Charity hefted two bowls in her hands, and Faith promptly stole them away. She motioned her head toward Brady, who was laughing as he followed the others from the room. "It's your first night home; no dishes. Why don't you see if Brady wants to take a walk?" She wriggled her brows, giving Charity a telling look.

Charity laughed and gave her a kiss on the cheek. "Thanks, Faith. I could use a good talk with that man right about now. He makes a wonderful sounding board."

Faith grinned over her shoulder as she moved toward the door. "Among other things, if you would open your eyes."

Charity smiled. "They're open, Faith. It's the heart that's still a bit closed."

Faith stopped at the door, her eyes soft. "I know. It'll get better, I promise. Now go grab him before Father robs him of his pride."

Charity found him on the sofa, talking politics with Sean. She tapped him on the shoulder. "Good, I see it's Collin who's to be fleeced tonight. I was worried about you."

"What about me?" Sean asked, his tone wounded.

"You could use the humility." She propped her hands on her hips. "But I do have a favor to ask. Emma's in there trying to help with dishes, despite Faith's best efforts to shoo her away. Would you mind dragging her out and keeping her company while Brady and I take a walk?"

Sean smiled and stood, pushing his shirtsleeves up. "With pleasure. She seems like a gentle soul, Charity. I like her."

"She is, Sean, one of the best. She's been wounded more than any human being I know, but it never seems to touch her or harden her. She's a true gift from God." She clamped a hand on Brady's arm and yanked him up. "And speaking of 'true gifts from God,' get a move on, Brady; you're taking me for a walk."

"I don't suppose I have a choice?" He lumbered toward the hall to get her sweater.

Charity snatched it off the rack first. "Nope. I need a shoulder to cry on."

Sean sailed by. "Better wear a raincoat, Brady."

Charity stepped outside and clutched her sweater tightly around her, lifting her face to the cool of the night. She sucked in a deep breath and let it out again, grateful for her family and the love they supplied. And the diversion.

"Where to?" he asked, his voice suddenly soft and low.

She nodded toward the swing on the porch.

He cocked a hip. "Not much of a walk."

She tugged him over. "All of a sudden I'm too tired to walk. Do you mind?"

Did he mind? Sitting with her in the shadows, the scent of her hair as fresh and inviting as the smell of summer rain? Not likely.

He sat down beside her, giving her plenty of room. She edged closer and put her head on his shoulder, warming him more than he liked. With a sigh of resignation, he slipped an arm around her and pulled her close. "So how are you? Really?"

Her sigh was heavy, and he tightened his hold. "Fine, now that I'm home. Or almost fine."

"Almost?"

"Yeah. Coming home again has been like balm to my battered soul, Brady. Thanks to you and your prayers, I'm a different person inside."

He shifted, uncomfortable with her praise. "I just finished the job that Mitch started. He got you thinking about God, pursuing him. I just tied up the loose ends."

She listed against him a bit more. "I need you to do it again."

He looked down at her with a sideways glance. "What?"

She closed her eyes, pain etched in her features. "Tie up the loose ends that Mitch left unraveled. He wounded me, Brady, to the core. Not that I didn't deserve it. I did. But he plucked my heart out and stomped on it for good measure." She grunted a hollow laugh. "Then Rigan finished me off."

His muscles tensed. "Charity, Collin told me. God help me, if I could, I would kill him."

She looked up, her eyes wet in the moonlight. "That's the miracle in all of this, Brady. God did help me. He opened my eyes to the sin in my heart like nothing has ever been able to do. Rigan stole my virtue on a kitchen table in Shaw's back room, but God gave me his in its place. In the midst of Rigan's sin, I saw my own as clearly as the depravity in his eyes. When he left that night, for the first time in my life, I repented. Really and truly repented. Not only for all the lies and deceptions, but for all the people I've hurt. You once told me that people are attached to our obedience. You were right. And because of my lifelong rebellion against God, I have hurt the people I love most in life, as surely as Rigan hurt me. I love Mitch with all of my heart, but I didn't act like it. I lied, I deceived, and I seduced him until he had no choice but to turn me away. In the process, I discovered that sin is a cold blade that slices to the heart, wounding all in its grasp. But my God has delivered me."

Her voice cracked on a sob and Brady pulled her into his embrace, resting his cheek against her hair. "Charity O'Connor, angels are leaping before the throne of God over you." *Like my heart.* He closed his eyes, drinking in the heady scent of her.

She sniffed and he handed her his handkerchief. She wiped her nose and leaned back against his arm, her face somber. "But the wages of sin is death, Brady, and I now have a terrifying knowledge of exactly what that means."

He stiffened. "Why do you say that?"

She closed her eyes. "Because when Rigan . . . did what he did . . . something inside of me died. Trust and confidence, replaced by fear and loathing. Loathing of who I am, what I did."

"We're all sinners, Charity."

She shook her head vehemently, dispelling the pool of tears in her eyes till they streamed down her face. "No, Brady, don't soften what I did. What Rigan did was wrong, but I had a hand in it. From the moment I met him, I used him and led him on for my own purposes with no regard for him or his feelings. He was in love with me and I knew it, and I played it for all it was worth." She pressed a shaky hand to her mouth. "I struck a deal with him as surely as I did with the devil himself. I sold my body and my soul, just like Mitch said."

Brady's heart pounded in his chest. "You mean . . . you slept with Rigan before the rape?"

"No, nothing like that, but I gave him my lips freely, whenever and wherever, letting him believe he could have more down the road. I used him to make Mitch jealous, never caring that every kiss stoked the fire inside of him. I led him on, Brady, tempting him with my body. Until he finally took it . . ." She turned her face away, her throat working in the moonlight. "And my womanhood along with it."

Brady touched her cheek with his finger, softly turning her to face him. "I don't understand. What are you saying, Charity?"

She shivered and looked away, refusing to meet his gaze. "I'm saying I have no desire to . . . be with a man, to be pretty for one or let one touch me. I just feel afraid . . . inside."

He held her face in his hand and gently stroked her chin with his thumb. His voice was tender. "I'm touching you, Charity. Does this make you afraid?"

She looked up, her eyes wide and wet. "Oh, no, Brady. You're my friend. I trust you."

He smiled. "It will be the same with the man you fall in love with."

She shuddered. "Do you really think so?"

"With God's help, I do. You just have to heal and learn to trust again."

She pressed her cheek to his chest, clutching him with shaky fingers. "But the old Charity, the tease and the temptress, is gone, Brady. I have no desire to fix my face or my hair or dress up and be pretty. I feel so . . . dead inside. So worthless. God opened my eyes and gave me his forgiveness, but as a woman, I feel so lost, so imperfect."

Brady held her tightly, resting his head on top of hers. "We don't have to be perfect, Charity, because God is. In time, he'll heal the woman in you as surely as he healed your soul."

She shuddered and wept against his chest, every quiver of her body wrenching his. After a few moments, she pulled away to blow her nose with his handkerchief, then gave him a shaky smile.

He cupped her chin with the palm of his hand. "I'll say it again, Charity O'Connor, the heavens are rejoicing over you. You bring a smile to God's face . . . and mine."

She blew her nose again and laughed at the same time. "I'm sure both you and God thought nothing would ever get through this thick head of mine." She sighed. "And speaking of thick heads . . ."

Brady's heart stopped.

"That's where the rest of 'almost fine' comes in."

He pulled away and took a deep breath. "Mitch?"

She nodded and plunked back down on his shoulder. "I can't get him out of my head, Brady, much less my heart. I pray and I plead and seem to make strides, and then, boom! I turn a corner or blink an eye and I see his face . . . his smile . . . his unbelievably annoying stubbornness." She glanced up. "What am I gonna do?"

He swallowed hard, wondering the very same thing. "You just need time, time to heal and move on. You will, you know, with God's help and your family's."

She crooked a brow. "And yours?"

He smiled. "That goes without saying. But it's going to entail a strict regimen of Bible study and prayer. None of this fly in, fly out on a whim, asking me questions and looking for prayer when you need it the most. You up to that?"

She flung her arms around his neck. "O Brady, try me!"

Lord, help me. He peeled her arms off his neck. "Good, then we start Monday. You can either come to the shop early or with Beth after school. Your choice."

She scrunched her nose in thought. "I think I'll come early. That way I'll have you all to myself and Beth doesn't have to know, okay?"

Lord, help me. He stood and rolled his neck. "Ready to go in? I think there was pie left."

Her mouth gaped open. "You can't possibly be hungry!"

He grinned and latched a gentle hand behind her neck and firmly steered her to the door. *Charity O'Connor, you have no idea.*

ক্ষ ঈ৹

Marcy eyed her husband stretched out on their bed, eyes closed and arms propped behind his head. "Patrick, you're not going to sleep without me, are you? I still have a hundred strokes to do."

A semblance of a smile shadowed his lips. "No, Marcy, take your time. I'll be right here when you're done."

She turned in shock, brush in hand. "Take my time? You want me to take my time? Are you talking in your sleep?"

A low chuckle rumbled from the bed. One eyelid lifted, along with the curve of his lips. "No, darlin', I'm just lying here, enjoying the memory of the evening."

She sighed, laid the brush on her wardrobe, and blew out the lamp. She padded over to the bed and crept in beside him, wrapping an arm around his waist.

"So, what happened to the hundred strokes?"

"I'd rather be next to you." She snuggled close. "It's good having Charity home, isn't it?"

His arm scooped her to him, tucking her head against his chest. "More than I can say. I've missed that girl."

"Me too. I want her right here, where we can love on her and protect her. She's been through a lot in the last year."

"Some of it her own doing, I'm afraid, but I sense a change. I think she's growing up."

Marcy shivered. "Has she said anything to you . . . about . . ."

"No."

"Me, either. I'm worried, Patrick. Worried about the long-term effect . . ."

He shifted to face her. "You mean pregnancy?"

She nodded. "And her feelings about men, her trust. She has a lot of wounds to heal."

Patrick sighed and closed his eyes. "We all do, Marcy. When one of us is wounded, we all hurt. But God has seen us through more than one crisis, as you've reminded me many a time."

"He has at that." She touched a hand to his cheek, skimming across the serious set of his jaw. "I've gone and robbed you of your good mood, now haven't I?"

"No. Nothing can daunt the joy of having my girl home." He leaned to brush his mouth to hers. "And you by my side."

She responded with a force that opened his eyes. He chuckled and tugged her closer. "You can, however, make it up if you like."

She clutched him fiercely, squeezing her eyes tight. "Oh, Patrick, why is it that when trouble comes, I need you close to me more than ever?"

He stroked her hair and pressed a kiss to her cheek. "Because we're one, my love. Man and wife reveling in that wonderful and warm, incredibly safe place that God has given us. Where we can be one with him and one with each other, shutting out all the hurt and the pain."

Tears stung her eyes. "I love you, Patrick. So much."

His lips caressed hers for several seconds before his mouth strayed to the curve of her jaw, nibbling her ear. His low laughter vibrated against her cheek. "I believe I'd like to see some proof."

She giggled and ran a hand down the length of his thigh. "Gladly."

"Mother? Father? Are you asleep?"

Marcy's hand froze on Patrick's leg. The heat of his embrace suddenly rushed to her cheeks. She sat up, blinking in the dark. "Charity? Is that you?"

Charity stood in the doorway of the darkened room, feeling the pull of her parents' love. "Yes. I couldn't sleep. Would it be all right if I snuggled with you for a while? Emma's long gone, I'm afraid, and I . . . well, I'm feeling a bit lonely."

"Of course you can. Get over here and hop in." Marcy pushed the covers aside and scooted over to make room.

"I didn't waken you, did I?"

"No, your father and I were just talking."

Relief flooded as she slipped in the bed and turned on her side. Her mother cuddled close, wrapping an arm around her waist. Her father hooked his arm around them both, spooning. "Why so lonely, darlin'? You couldn't be surrounded by more love than you are here."

Charity swallowed hard, fighting a tremor in her voice. "I know, Father. And that's what's getting me through. That and God."

Marcy squeezed her. "You miss Mima and Mother, don't you?"

Wetness stung her eyes. "Terribly."

"And Mitch?" Marcy's tone was hesitant.

Charity shivered. "With all my heart."

"Darlin', I know this is hard to believe," Patrick whispered, "but you will get over him. We'll all see to that."

"I believe that, Father, but right now, it seems so impossible. My heart is sick with grief, and not just over missing Mitch, Mima, and Grandmother. Over the shame I've caused.

To myself, to you . . . and to God. I know he's forgiven me, but I'm not sure I can forgive myself."

"Have you prayed about it?" Marcy's tone was quiet.

Charity hesitated. Had she? Her lips parted in surprise. "No, I don't think I have."

Marcy stroked her hair. "Well, then, I'd say that's a good place to start, wouldn't you?"

Charity smiled. How in the world had she been blessed with such parents? "Yes."

"Good. Then we'll do that. But first, I want you to know something. Never in one breath of your life have we ever been ashamed of you, Charity O'Connor. Befuddled, perhaps, sometimes angry, and occasionally frustrated, but never—I repeat, never—have you brought shame to your father's heart or mine. You have been a joy to our souls, and I don't think that deep down you ever really knew that. Know it now, daughter, and know it well. God isn't the only one who loves you with a depth beyond your comprehension."

Charity clutched her mother in a joyous sob. She felt Marcy's gentle stroking while her father's strong hand kneaded her back.

"Please forgive me for all the hurt I've caused. I don't deserve you."

"We forgive you, darlin', but it's time you forgive yourself."

Charity sniffed and wiped her nose with the sleeve of her gown. "I know. Will you pray, Father? Pray that I can?"

"No, darlin', that prayer belongs to your mother. She's the woman who taught me, and quite frankly, I never thought I deserved her either. But then none of us really deserve the blessings of God, do we? But he gives them nonetheless . . . to those who seek him."

Charity felt joy rise within her spirit. Yes! To those who seek him! She drew in a deep breath and lay back on the pillow, reaching for her mother's hand. She squeezed it and smiled.

"To those who seek him. Well, Mother, we better give it a go, because there's no doubt in my mind—that would be me."

⁘

Collin put his sack lunch under his arm and butted the door with his knee, turning the key in the lock at the same time. It wheeled open with a high-pitched squeak that harmonized with his off-key whistling. He tossed his lunch on the delivery table and glanced toward the back of the shop. "You here?"

Brady rolled into the doorway on a low-wheeled dolly, his face already streaked with ink. "Yeah."

"Good Lord, Brady, it's barely six in the morning. How in the sweet name of heaven did you get ink on your face already? What d'ya do, roll around in that stuff?"

He wheeled back out of sight. "Yeah, Collin, it makes me feel like a man."

Collin chuckled and sauntered into the back room. He snatched the pot off the stove and poured himself a cup of coffee, then turned to lean against the counter while he sipped. "So . . . anything else making you feel like a man this morning?"

No answer.

Collin grinned. Nothing tight-lipped about John Brady unless you wanted to talk about Charity. Sweet justice after all those times during the war when Brady had grilled him about Faith. "So . . . where do you two stand?" He cleared his throat. "Faith's dying to know."

Brady rolled out to give Collin the benefit of a scowl. "Friends, Collin, just like before. Nothing more."

Collin took another sip. "Your decision . . . or hers?"

Brady leapt to his feet, dusting off his work pants to no avail. He grabbed his coffee and took a swig. "God's. She's not ready." His scowl deepened. "This coffee is awful."

⁘ 450 ⁘

"You made it." Collin shrugged and took another drink. "I just thought it was me."

Brady strode to the sink to make a new pot. His voice sounded annoyed. "Don't you have business to attend to?"

Collin gave him a sideways glance. "I am. You're my partner and best friend. Your happiness or lack thereof *is* my business."

Brady muscled him out of the way to fill the pot with water. "Well, my happiness or lack thereof doesn't bother me, so why should it bother you? I can assure you Mrs. Tabor needs her daughter's wedding invitations far more than I need your help."

Collin faced him, his smile fading. "I'm worried about you, Brady. So sue me."

Brady sighed and closed his eyes. The pot hung limp in his hands. He clunked it on the boil plate and turned. "Sorry, Collin, I know you only want what's best for me. I'm just not sure what that is right now."

Collin studied him with concern. The bad coffee started to curdle in his gut. "You're falling for her, aren't you?"

Brady looked up, the answer in his eyes as plain as the ink on his face. He shuffled to the table and slumped in a chair.

Collin followed him. "So? What's the big deal? She could use your love right now. And hard as it might be for me to believe, she could be the woman God has for you."

Brady seemed lost in a stare, his eyes fixed on the floor. He stayed that way, hand limp upon the table.

"Brady?"

He looked up, and Collin's stomach constricted. No, this wasn't right. Brady was always the strong one, the one gripped tightly to the hand of God.

Brady exhaled slowly, his tall frame sinking deeper into the chair. "I'm worried, Collin. Before she left, I was fine. God protected my heart. We were friends. She was going to marry Mitch and live happily ever after and raise a houseful of kids.

Suddenly she's back, free as a bird, and God's called me to be her friend." He clenched his hand on the table, flexing several times. "And only a friend . . . at least for the moment."

"So, be her friend."

His put his head in his hand. "I don't know if I can."

Collin took a deep breath and stretched out in the chair, scratching his head. "Yeah, I see your dilemma. Charity's a beautiful woman with a powerful pull. Loving her can be like playing with fire. But I can do for you what you did for me many a night. All those times when I was passed out in my bunk, drunk with grief over Faith marrying Mitch . . ." Collin looked up, giving him a sheepish grin. "Never did like that guy. Now you know what I mean."

A half smile flickered on Brady's lips. "Yeah, I guess I do."

"You prayed me through. I plan to do the same. Especially if I find you drunk in bed."

Brady smiled. "Thanks, Collin. I'm going to need all the prayers I can get."

Collin stood and moved to sit beside him, clamping a hand to his shoulder. "Well, you have them, my friend. Now, and for the rest of your life." He leaned in and closed his eyes while Brady did the same. And in the sacred confines of a ramshackle back room, they bowed their heads and prayed, invoking God to do what he does best: pull their feet from the fire.

20

Charity lay there with eyes weighted closed, wondering why she had no desire to get up. She squinted at Emma in the other bed, fast asleep despite shafts of winter sunlight filtering across her face. With a low groan, Charity slumped back on her pillow, suddenly remembering.

December 12. Mitch and Kathleen's six-month wedding anniversary.

A sharp pain sliced through her as intense as the day he had called her a whore. She caught her breath and turned on her side, her eyes welling with tears. *No, God, why?*

She shoved the covers aside and slipped out of bed, careful not to waken Emma. She needed to see Brady—now. She bit her lip and glanced at the clock. 7:30. They'd leave for church at ten. If she hurried and dressed, she'd have almost two hours for him to talk with her, pray with her. *Hold her.*

She tiptoed to the closet and pulled out her favorite blue dress, hooking the hanger on the knob. With a soft grunt, she stripped off her nightgown and put on her chemise, then bent to shimmy into her stockings. In a split second, she had the dress lifted over her head. Her fingers shook as she fumbled with the buttons. Holding her breath, she glanced at Emma and smiled. That woman could sleep through a cyclone if it whirled her away, bed and all. Charity slipped her shoes on and made her way to the door. She stopped in the bathroom to brush her teeth and wash her face, barely running a comb through her hair. She blinked in the mirror, wondering if she should take the time to apply some makeup, then decided against it. This was Brady. He didn't care. And neither did she. She hesitated, then touched a bit of lilac water to her temple and sighed. He was a man, after all.

The house was quiet as she hurried down the steps, her parents' muted conversation drifting from the kitchen. She started for the front door, then stopped with her hand on the knob. As much as she didn't want to, they needed to know where she was going. She sighed and walked toward the kitchen, pushing through the swinging door.

Her father looked up from the table with the paper propped in his lap. His brows lifted in surprise. "Was there a blue moon last night, darlin'? I haven't seen you up this early in a while."

Marcy turned at the sink. "Are you all right, Charity? You look . . . anxious."

Charity rolled her tongue over her teeth and suddenly thought of Bridget. Her mind leap-frogged to Mitch, and the pain was immediate. Her mouth parted to release shallow breaths.

Patrick put the paper down. "Charity, what's wrong?"

She glanced up and lifted her chin. "Nothing. I just need to see Brady, that's all."

"At this hour?" Patrick checked his watch.

She nodded and looked to Marcy, her eyes appealing for help.

Marcy took a step forward. "Are you down again, Charity? Is that it? Thinking about . . ."

Charity nodded quickly, blinking her eyes to keep them clear. "I just need to talk to Brady, to pray with him."

Marcy put her hand on Patrick's shoulder. "Of course, darling. You've got plenty of time before we leave. Just be back by ten, okay?"

"I will." She whirled around and rushed out the door, barely slowing as she snatched her coat from the rack. Once outside, she sprinted down the sidewalk as if the devil himself were on her heels. Several blocks away, she vaulted the steps of Brady's apartment, her heart hammering in her chest. She leaned against his door and pounded hard. Her breath came in jagged gasps.

The door swung wide and there he stood, clad only in a sleeveless undershirt and a pair of trousers with bare feet. She would have smiled at the shock on his face if not for his hard-muscled chest straining his scoop-neck T-shirt. Her eyes traveled the thick line of his arms, sculpted with muscles and propped loose on his hips.

She swallowed hard and looked away, a warm flush creeping up her face. "Sorry, Brady, I didn't mean to barge in."

He didn't seem the least bit concerned about his attire, but pulled her inside and took off her coat, tossing it on the table. He pushed her into a chair and squatted beside her, searching her face. "What is it, Charity? Is something wrong?"

Her eyes roamed the tiny apartment, desperate to avoid looking at him, then widened in surprise at how neat and clean it was. She had never been inside before. Though sparse with décor, it exuded a definite masculine air with heavy but simple wood pieces arranged in a practical manner. A mahogany desk was laden with books wedged between brass book ends, leaving just enough room for a wood and brass lamp in the shape of a sailing vessel. Her eyes scanned a dark burgundy sofa where his Bible lay open, splayed in a sea of papers. Overhead, framed prints of ships added a decidedly nautical feel. She smiled and looked up, noting for the first time the cinnamon color of his hair and how it curled at the back of his neck. Before she knew it, her eyes lighted on his powerfully built arms as he hunkered beside her. She swallowed.

He followed her gaze and glanced down at his T-shirt, as if suddenly aware of his state of undress. With a haze of color up the back of his neck, he jumped up and strode into another room, returning with a shirt in his hand. He slipped it on, then sat in the chair beside her and leaned forward, forgetting to button it up. "Okay, Charity. Why are you here?"

She drew in a deep breath, suddenly remembering the reason she came. The painful realization sapped her strength once again, and tears sprang to her eyes. "Brady, I've been fine, haven't I? Wonderful even, for the last six months?"

He nodded.

"Yes, I've had my moments when I was blue and thought I'd never get past this, but they've been fewer and fewer." She searched his eyes. "Haven't they?"

He nodded again.

"And then this morning, before I even open my eyes, I feel this gloom, this malaise crawling on me like a hundred thousand spiders." She shivered and pushed the hair from her eyes. "And then it came to me—Mitch's six-month anniversary, and Brady, so help me God, it sucked the air right out of my throat. This awful pain ripped right across my chest till I couldn't breathe." She grabbed ahold of his arms. "Brady, this has got to stop. God has got to do something, anything, to get me over this."

She felt tears stinging her eyes and began to weep. He stared at her for several seconds, then slowly stood and led her to the sofa. He sat her down and bundled her in his arms, shooshing her with a soft, rocking motion. "He will, Charity, he will. Our God is faithful. I don't know why it's taking so long, but he's going to set you free. I just know it."

She pulled back, her vision blurred. "When, Brady? Tomorrow? Next month? Next year? I can't keep on like this, missing him, aching for him. I want to be done with it."

His heart wrenched with pain, both for her and for himself. He took her face in his hands and leaned to gently kiss her forehead and then closed his eyes, the touch of her skin soft and warm. "God's timing is not always ours, but it's perfect, Charity. He *will* get you through this." His lips moved to her cheek, the scent of lilacs triggering his pulse. He opened his eyes to see her watching him, her full lips parted in surprise.

No, my son . . .

He jerked away, his breathing suddenly accelerated.

Pray . . .

His eyes strayed to the fullness of her lips, and heat engulfed him, choking his air. Suddenly he was aware of every curve of her body as she sat beside him. He jolted back. She grabbed his hand, her eyes confused. "No, Brady, please. Just hold me?"

He swallowed hard and pulled her close, the press of her body inflaming his senses.

Pray.

No, God, please, I want her . . .

She lifted her face. "Brady?"

He stared, all reason fleeing his mind. She needed his comfort, not his passion. In his spirit, he knew she wasn't ready, but his need blinded him to hers. In slow motion, he bent toward her, grazing her mouth with his own. The touch of her lips unleashed a roll of heat that jarred his senses. He groaned and drew her close, tasting her lips like a man starved for sustenance only she could supply.

He jerked away and stood, panic pounding in his chest. "Charity, forgive me . . . I'm so sorry . . ."

She blinked. "There's nothing to forgive, Brady. It was just a kiss."

Heat rushed into his cheeks. He plunged his hands in his pockets and stared at his bare feet. "I did more than just kiss you. I lusted after you with a passion I didn't know I had. It scares me."

She looked away. "Goodness, you're the only man I've ever spent time with who didn't try to kiss me. I always thought you weren't interested."

He exhaled softly. "A testament to the power of prayer."

She laughed, and the sound warmed his heart. A grin pulled at her lips. "Well, I guess I should go . . ."

He tugged her up and to the door, opening it wide, then pushed her against the jamb. He stepped back to lean on the other side and folded his arms. "Not until we pray. But this apartment is off-limits."

She peeked inside. "Maybe we could just sit at the table, on opposite sides? I hate to pray in the hall."

He sighed. He took her hand and gently pushed her down in a chair. He rounded the table and sat across from her, leaving the door wide open.

She grinned. "If you and I were to ever get involved, you'd be a real stickler about this, wouldn't you?"

He stretched back in the chair and eyed her, his arms cocked behind his head. "You bet. *If* we got involved."

She arched a brow. "If?"

"You're not ready, Charity. I can sense it in my spirit." He shifted in the chair, painful memories from his past shuddering through him. He looked away. "And I'm not sure I'm ready either. I have things . . . things from my past." He looked up, his face tight with resolve. "You deserve more."

She leaned forward to take his hand. Her expression was intense. "There couldn't be more than you. You're the best there is . . . a good man and an amazing friend." She leaned back and took a deep breath. "I think I could fall in love with you, John Brady . . . if I could purge Mitch from my heart."

He shook his head. "Maybe, but I don't think I'm ready for that, and I know you're not. There's something deep in my spirit, Charity, a check . . . a still, small voice saying 'not yet.'"

"God?"

He sighed. "I'm guessing. It's seldom wrong. As much as part of me wants to forge ahead, I don't think we're ready."

She smiled and reached to squeeze his hand. "That's okay. I love our friendship, just the way it is. I'd be lost without it. Can we pray?"

He smiled and leaned forward, crossing his arms on the table. "Try and leave without it." He bent his head and closed his eyes. "Lord, we're in a pickle here. This is the most amazing woman I have ever met, and it would be easy to fall in love with her. But I've learned the hard way that unless you're behind it, we can get burned. And I don't want that for either of us. So give us wisdom and restraint. Show us your will in this situation and show us soon. Forgive me for not heeding your still, small voice. Never have I understood the Scripture 'The spirit is willing, but the flesh is weak' quite like I have today. Strengthen me, Lord, so it doesn't happen again. And get this woman past the heartbreak of Mitch Dennehy. Give her peace instead of pain, joy instead of mourning. And bless our friendship to the depths of our souls. Amen."

She opened her eyes and smiled. "And that, my friend, is why I came here today."

He scratched his head and grinned. "Yeah, I know. Sorry for the detour."

She rose. Wetness shimmered in her eyes. "Thank you, John Brady. And God bless you."

He stood and walked her to the door. "Yeah, I'm counting on it."

He watched as she waved and skittered down the steps, then closed the door behind her. He put a hand to his eyes and sagged into the nearest chair. He thought of the kiss he had given her, and sweat beaded on the back of his neck. No! He wasn't going there. Not again. He slumped over the table and buried his head in his arms. He couldn't do this. He couldn't love her.

Ever.

"Please, no more attraction. I want to be her friend. Only her friend."

Hot tears scalded his eyes as he silently wept. "I beg you, God, heal her, please." The memory of his own sordid past prickled his spine and shivered his soul. A wrenching sob broke free from his lips. "And heal me."

❦ ❧

"Father, I keep telling you, I'm not interested."

Patrick folded his arms in a manner that indicated it was settled. "Darlin', I refuse to go on seeing you torn up with grief every time you have a dream about Mitch Dennehy or a painful anniversary pops up on the calendar. What you need is a strapping young man to take your mind off of him. And since you refuse to do anything about it, then I will."

Charity moaned. "But I'm not interested. You're only wasting your time and theirs. Like the copywriter you brought home last week? Harold?" She rolled her eyes. "Honestly, Father, he may have been twenty-four, but he looked all of sixteen."

"Nonsense, you've just always had an eye for older men. First Collin, then Mitch. And Dillon *is* older. He's twenty-eight and hails from the *New York Daily News*. For pity's sake, he's a cum laude graduate of the Columbia University Graduate School of Journalism. And I haven't even told you the best part." He grinned, rolling back on his heels. "He's Collin's second cousin on his mother's side."

She groaned again and put a hand to her head. "He's related to McGuire? No possible good can come of that."

Patrick pulled her into a tight hug. "Ah, come on now, darlin', humor your old father, will you? Collin says he's a decent bloke even if he doesn't know him all that well. And after the interview I had with him today for the assistant editor position, I have a feeling you're going to like him."

She crossed her arms and gave him a pout. "I can't believe you put these poor men through the paces. This is the seventh one in six months, you know. When are you going to learn to let nature take its course?"

He grinned and gave her a peck on her cheek. "I am letting

❦ 460 ❧

nature take its course—I'm just helping it along a bit. I can't have a daughter of mine turning into an old maid, now can I?"

"Who are you calling an old maid? I just turned twenty-one last month. That hardly qualifies as a spinster. I think you just want some other man to support me."

"Twenty-one, pushing twenty-two, young lady, and yes, that thought has crossed my mind." He tugged on a stray lock of her hair with a chuckle and headed toward the steps, a newspaper tucked under his arm. "Dillon will be here at six. You've got exactly an hour and fifteen minutes. I suggest you see if your mother needs any help and then hustle upstairs to make yourself pretty."

She slapped her hands on her hips, a ghost of a smile on her lips. "Make myself pretty? Now on top of being old, I suppose I'm also unattractive?"

He turned on the landing. "Not at all, darlin', but I have noticed a scarcity of rouge on your cheeks these days." He scowled, waving his hand behind his head. "And since you've been home, you've been shoving your pretty hair up in that clump at the back of your neck. Why don't you wear it down like you used to before you lost your interest in men?" He grinned and blew her a kiss, then disappeared around the corner.

She shook her head and pushed her way into the kitchen. Marcy was at the sink peeling potatoes while Emma shelled peas. Katie was reading a book to Miss Buford.

Charity plopped in the chair. "Well, I guess I'm the sacrificial lamb again tonight. Mother, can't you stop him from this abuse?"

Marcy smiled over her shoulder. "Me? Stop Patrick O'Connor? Did the Irish air make you daft? This is your stubborn, bull-headed father we're talking about, bent on a suitable match for the daughter he loves. I can do nothing but cook."

Charity plucked a pea from Emma's bowl and squinted,

aiming it at the door. "You could poison them just a little bit, you know, so they wouldn't come back."

Her mother arched a brow. "We don't throw peas across the room, young lady, even if they are aimed at your father. Besides, I don't have to poison anybody. When you're done with them, we never see them again."

Emma grinned.

Charity narrowed her eyes. "What are you smirking at, Emma? How would you like to be sold off to the highest bidder?"

"I think it's wonderful you have a father who loves you so much."

Charity rolled her eyes. "Okay, Mother, what can I do to help? Brew the hemlock?"

Marcy glanced at the clock. "Well, Beth promised to be home by five fifteen to set the table, and Emma and I have everything else under control, I think." She smiled and tossed the peeled potatoes in the pot. "Why don't you go upstairs and make yourself pretty. I hear Collin's cousin is quite attractive."

Charity scowled and pushed herself up from the table. "What is it with me making myself pretty? Have I grown a wart overnight or something? Besides, attractive or no, if Collin's cousin treats me like Collin does, I suspect we'll come to blows."

Marcy smiled and wiped her hands on her apron. "Probably, but that's okay, darling. Love conquers all."

Charity groaned and headed for the door, then whirled around with a hopeful look on her face. "Hey, maybe he won't show! You know, like the one a month ago who came on the wrong night?"

Emma giggled. "Oh, this one'll show. He's spent the last few days at a hotel, according to your father. He'll be looking for a home-cooked meal, if not the editor's daughter."

Charity lifted a brow. "Well, I can pray, can't I?"

Emma grinned and flipped a pod of peas into the bowl. "Please do. Might do you good."

Charity sighed and slapped through the kitchen door, plodding through the dining room and up the steps with as little enthusiasm as possible. She trudged into her bedroom and flopped on the bed, staring at the ceiling with a moan.

"Lord, I don't want to be on this merry-go-round. I'd rather spend my time with Brady as a friend, hoping for more, than entertain the notion of falling in love with anyone else. I already did that twice and got nothing but heartbreak." She thought of Mitch, and the old familiar ache returned. She scowled at the ceiling. "Speaking of which, I think it's about time I moved on, don't you? What about Brady? I could sure use a little romance in my life."

She sighed and lumbered up from the bed. She grabbed her robe off the hook and traipsed to the bathroom to get a bath. Going through the motions, she bathed and primped and powdered until she almost felt like her old self again. Getting into the spirit of things, she dabbed lilac water along her neck. She reached for her rouge and patted a bit to her cheeks, rubbing it in to a rosy glow. Applying just a touch to her lips, she puckered in the mirror and smiled. Father was right. She felt almost pretty again.

Humming under her breath, she strolled back to her room and padded to her closet, deciding it was time to wear her most becoming frock. She shimmied into her chemise, then slithered on her silk stockings and clipped them to her garter. She pulled out the ice blue dress she had worn with both Rigan and Mitch. The memories flooded back with a vengeance. She shivered and shoved it to the back of her closet, opting instead for her favorite lemon yellow silk blouse with pale blue hobble skirt. She remembered the way Mitch's eyes had popped when she'd worn it, although he'd worked hard not to show it. She pressed the cool silk to her cheek and closed her eyes, allowing herself to remember him one last time.

"This is it, Lord, I'm ready to move on. Who knows, maybe Brady is the one. I'm praying that you will show me if he is, and soon. But first, please set me free from the pain of losing Mitch, and bless him and Kathleen with a rich, full life. Amen."

She drew in a deep breath and slowly released it, tears pricking her eyes. Yes, she still loved Mitch. Probably always would. But along with it, God had deposited something new—glimmers of hope and peace and joy. A single tear trailed down her cheek to settle in the crook of her mouth, salty on her tongue. She smiled. The taste of it released a surge of joy like an adrenaline rush. How had she gone a lifetime without knowing God's love? Feeling it to the depth of her soul, like now? With it, everything in life—her family's love, her friendships, her dreams—felt so much deeper, more intensified, as if everything were three-dimensional. She swiped at a tear and chuckled. It was, she supposed. Just like she hoped her marriage would be someday, God willing. A three-dimensional romance: the woman, the man, and the God who brings them together.

She bowed her head. "Lord, thank you for being so patient with me, for loving me despite the sin in my life, and for saving me. Help me to be the woman you want me to be—the daughter, the sister, the friend, and eventually, I hope, the wife. I know there's still a lot of work to be done—my temper, my strong will—but I have faith you can do it. I trust you and I love you with all of my heart. Amen."

She opened her eyes and sighed, feeling much lighter. With a sparkle in her eye, she slipped on the blouse and skirt, pleased with the way it accentuated her figure. Mr. Dillon Whatever-His-Name would have trouble keeping the conversation on journalism tonight, if she had anything to say about it. And if he left her as cold as the last six men that had darkened her door, well then, she would just march right over to Mr. John Morrison Brady's apartment and give him an eyeful, whether he was "ready" for it or not. She chuckled. If he was fighting falling in love with her now, just wait until she put her mind to it! She grinned at the ceiling. "Just give me the word, God, that's all I need."

She unpinned her hair and grabbed the hairbrush, bending over to stroke until her scalp tingled. She flipped her hair back over her head and watched it tumble over her shoulders like pale gold. With a hand to her hip and a lift to her brow, she gave the mirror a come-hither smile.

John Morrison Brady, you don't have a prayer.

Emma knocked and peeked in the door. Her eyes went wide. "Lord have mercy, Charity, you look amazing."

Charity giggled. "Thank you, Emma. I have to admit, it feels good to take an interest again. I think I may be turning a corner."

Emma grinned. "Me too. I just got a look at Mr. Dillon C. Harris of New York. He's almost as pretty as you."

Charity scrunched her nose. "Doesn't matter. I'm thinking of setting my cap for Brady."

Emma laughed. "After all this time? I thought you two were just friends."

Charity spun in the mirror, taking one last look. "We are, but that may be about to change. I'm praying about it." She wriggled into her pumps and gave Emma a nervous twirl. "So, do I really look okay?"

"Gorgeous, my friend. And I'm sure Mr. Harris of New York will be spellbound. See you downstairs. He's in the parlor with your father."

Charity put a hand to her chest and glanced at the clock. "Already? It's not even six."

Emma giggled. "I think he may be the eager type. Wait till he gets a load of you, my friend. He hasn't experienced 'eager' until tonight." She turned to go, then whirled around. "Oh, almost forgot. Your mother asked me to have you bring her silver candlesticks down when you come. She said you knew where they were."

Charity shook her head and followed Emma out the door. "As much as she uses them, you'd think she'd keep them downstairs. But she has this notion that someone might steal them, so she buries them at the back of her closet."

Emma turned on the stairs. "No!"

Charity grinned. "Yes! My trusting mother."

Emma laughed and continued down. "A healthy distrust, probably developed after the birth of her third daughter."

"Very funny. You're starting to fit right in, which is not necessarily a good thing."

Charity hummed on her way to her parents' room and dug the box of candlesticks out of her mother's closet, lugging them against her chest. She cocked her head to the side so she could see where she was going and took one step at a time, then set the box on the foyer table. She drew in a deep breath, pushed her shoulders back, and strode into the parlor.

A tall, dark-haired man with penetrating gray eyes stood to his feet. A dimple appeared on either side of his smile, reminding her of Collin.

"Charity, you made it down, I see. This is Collin's cousin from New York, Mr. Dillon C. Harris. Dillon, this is my daughter, Charity O'Connor."

Dillon C. Harris grinned and extended a hand, which Charity shook, noting the firm hold. "It's a real pleasure to finally meet you, Charity. Your father has told me a lot about you. Unfortunately, none of it prepared me for this."

She smiled and tilted her head, enjoying the flirtation. "What's that, Mr. Harris?"

His gaze was bold, and his lips formed a smile that told her he was a man of experience. "Call me Dillon, please. Why, the depth of your beauty, of course."

A blush heated her cheeks and she looked away, feeling off her game for the first time in her life. Being with Brady had required none of this, and she feared she was woefully out of practice. "Why, thank you, Dillon. You're very kind."

"I'm afraid kindness has nothing to do with it whatsoever, Miss O'Connor."

She blushed again and glanced at her father. "I'd better get Mother's candlesticks to her or we may starve. See you in a bit."

She whirled around and made a beeline for the box on the foyer table, then released a shaky breath. Dear Lord, she certainly hoped Mr. Dillon C. Harris didn't throw a wrench into her plans. Maybe he was a bore. She smiled and picked up the box, thrusting it to her chest. With a bounce in her stride, she hefted it high against the kitchen door and pushed through, cocking her head sideways to watch her step. "Well, he did it, Mother. Brought another prospect home for his pitiful daughter."

"Two," he said, his tone casual as he rose from the table. His tall frame unfolded to fill the kitchen, obliterating anything in her vision but him. "He brought two."

The door swung closed behind her in a swish of cool air. The box in her hands crashed to the floor. Everything stopped—her breathing, her heart, her brain—until she finally blinked. Then her hand flew to her mouth with a faint cry.

"Excuse me, Mitch," Marcy said with a giddy whisper, "but I think Emma and I will see to our other guest." They hurried from the room, retrieving the candlesticks, but leaving the box scattered on the floor.

A faint smile hovered on his lips as he took a step forward, as if waiting for her reaction. "You don't do well with the element of surprise, do you, Charity?"

She backed up against the counter, stumbling over the empty box. "What are you doing here?" she breathed. Her pulse was skyrocketing.

He took another step. "Applying for a job. Assistant editor for the *Boston Herald*. Ever hear of it?"

She rubbed her skirt to wipe the sweat from her hands. Her voice was a mere rasp. "B-but I . . . thought Dillon . . ." She waved a trembling hand toward the door.

He cocked a brow and kept moving, closing the distance

between them. The clean line of his jaw was firm—a man on a mission, barely six feet away. "Nah. I think I may have the edge. I'm going to marry the editor's daughter."

The blood drained from her face and she braced a hand to the counter. "But I thought . . . six months ago . . . you . . . Kathleen. Where is she?" With a nervous thrust, she rammed her thumb to her mouth and bit hard on the nail.

He glanced at his watch, his towering frame a mere five feet away. "Well, right about now, I'd say she's tucking her little girl into bed."

She blinked. Her chest heaved as he took another step. "What?"

The blue eyes locked on hers with all the precision of a man who knew what he wanted. "She broke the engagement. A day before the wedding. Said I should marry the woman I love."

She chewed on another nail. Somewhere inside a little bubble of joy floated to her throat, pushing a shaky grin to her lips. "She has a little girl?"

"Yep."

Four feet away.

"Ended up marrying a pressman at the *Times* whose wife died of the Spanish flu three years ago. Seems he's had a crush on Kathleen for a while, but was too shy to act on it. After she broke our engagement, he didn't waste any time. His four-year-old is crazy about her."

Three feet.

Charity started to hyperventilate, her breathing as ragged as her nails. She butted hard against the counter, gouging her spine. "That's wonderful."

Two feet.

"No," Mitch whispered, caging her in, "*this* is wonderful." With a heated look, he held her face in his hands and took his time with slow, deliberate kisses. Her forehead. Her cheek. The curve of her chin.

The breath in her throat refused to comply, dispelling in hoarse, jagged breaths.

"I love you, Charity," he whispered. "I was a fool."

She closed her eyes and felt the warmth of his lips on her lids. They moved to the soft lobe of her ear, and heat shivered through her. A faint moan escaped her, and he captured it with his mouth, caressing her lips with his own until the heat began to build.

She lunged away, her breathing erratic. "Six months? You think you can just waltz in here, Mitch Dennehy, and I'll swoon in your arms? Is that it? The last time I saw you, you were dead-set on marrying another woman." She shoved him hard with both hands, fury rising within. "You spurned me, you called me a whore!" She darted away, moving across the room to distance herself. Her insides quivered as she backed against the sink, hands gripped white on the counter. The heat in her eyes collided with the heat in her body, filling her with confusion. Dear God, she wanted to pop him . . . as much as she wanted to kiss him! How dare he presume he could have her back, scot-free?

He turned. The smile faded on his face. "Charity, I'm sorry. At the time, it was the only thing I could do to keep you away. I was committed to Kathleen." He swallowed hard. "I hurt her before. I vowed I wouldn't hurt her again."

His words barbed her, chasing all reason from her mind. "So you chose to wound me instead, cutting me to the core?"

The muscles in his throat shifted. "I didn't mean it. I love you."

Her brows jutted high. "You love me? And I'm supposed to believe that? You wouldn't even be here now if Kathleen hadn't thrown you over."

Ruddiness bled up the back of his neck. "No, I wouldn't. But God intervened." His lips pressed white as he took a step forward. "Let me make it up to you, please. I want to take care of you, protect you. Always. You were right, Charity. We belong together."

The nerve of him! Putting her off for years, when she'd known they were meant for each other all along. Oh, she wanted to throttle him! Her hand shot up in the air. "Hold it right there, buster. I have a full life without you. I have my family, an endless stream of suitors hand-picked by my father, and an amazing friend named Brady, with whom," she emphasized with steel in her tone, "I just may fall in love."

Mitch's jaw shifted, and the color drained from his face. He strode toward her with fire in his eyes. "You're not falling in love with anybody. You're already in love with me."

"Don't you dare come any closer!" Her hand flailed behind for something to throw. She gripped the edge of a small bowl and hurled it. He grunted in shock as it ricocheted off his chest and crashed to his feet. She stared in horror. So did he—down at his crisp, white shirt where a trail of Marcy's cranberry sauce oozed and plopped to the floor.

His gaze slowly rose. The muscles in his face were sculpted tight. "Feel better?"

The door flew open. "What in sweet saints is going on?" Marcy stood on the threshold, hand plastered against the door. Her eyes went wide. "Dear Lord, what happened?"

Mitch's searing stare never left Charity's face. "Mrs. O'Connor, your daughter is a spoiled brat who needs a strong hand."

Charity slammed her hands on her hips and glared. "Oh, and I suppose you think you're just the man for the job?"

He gave her a look that burned. "I might be. In fact, you can count on it."

Marcy grabbed the dishrag. "Oh, stop it, you two! You're acting like children, and I'll not have you ruin dinner." She marched over to Mitch and slapped the soggy rag against his shirt, brushing away pieces of cranberry pulp. She shoved him toward the door. "Now you get into that parlor, Mitch Dennehy, and herd everyone into the dining room, do you hear? And tell Emma and Beth I need them both—now! We all could do with a bit of food in our stomachs."

Mitch mumbled something under his breath and stalked from the room. The door whooshed hard behind him.

Marcy whirled around. "Charity Katherine O'Connor! Have you lost your mind? What has gotten into you?"

Charity put a hand to her mouth and sagged against the sink. The knot of anger in her stomach slowly dissolved into fear. "I don't know, Mother."

"You've been pining over that man for well over a year, and worrying your father and I sick in the process. For pity's sake, I thought you were in love!"

"I am," she whispered.

Marcy folded her arms. "You're in for a lifetime of heartache, young lady, if this is how you intend to show it."

Charity closed her eyes. A sick feeling bubbled in her stomach. "Heaven help me, Mother, I didn't even know I had any anger toward the man. It must have been buried deep. All that grief and loss and missing he put me through." Her eyes flickered open. "And then suddenly here he is, and I'm supposed to collapse into his arms? Well, it's not that easy."

Marcy moved to Charity's side. "Charity, you have to forgive him. As stubborn as both of you are, if you two are going to make a life together, mercy will have to be a key staple in your pantry."

Charity rested her head on her mother's shoulder and sighed. "I know. And I will. He just took me by surprise, that's all. All that pain and hurt just came welling up." She pulled away to retrieve the broom. Her lips twisted as she swept the sticky glass and goo into a pile. "But the man has no tact whatsoever. He actually admitted he's only here now because Kathleen threw him over."

Marcy chuckled. "Well, he's not a man to mince words, that's for sure. Thank God Kathleen had the sense to see what he was too stubborn to admit." She rinsed the stained dishrag and bent to wipe up the mess. She cocked her head and glanced up. "So when are you going to put him out of his misery?"

Charity tossed the contents of the dustpan into the trash. "Not until after dinner. I'm hoping Mr. Dillon C. Harris can teach him a lesson or two about taking me for granted."

"Mama, I'm hungry—wow, what happened?" Katie barged through the door and screeched to a stop. Emma and Beth collided behind her like stacked-up railcars.

Charity turned at the sink. "Nothing, darlin'. Mitch accidentally broke Mother's bowl of cranberry sauce, that's all."

"Oooooo, so that's why his shirt is all wet and pink." Katie crossed her arms. "Well, I certainly hope you intend to punish him."

Marcy and Charity exchanged glances, prompting Marcy to chuckle. She stood to her feet and winked at Charity. "I don't think you need to worry about that."

❧ ☙

Mitch buttered his roll with a vengeance. What was he doing here? She obviously still held a grudge—a monumental one, judging from the size of the purple blotch glued to the hairs of his chest. He shoved the roll in his mouth and glared across the table, irritated at the way this Harris character fawned over her. For pity's sake, she belonged to him, not some would-be editor with New York airs. Mitch's lips flattened into a hard line. And certainly not some would-be friend named Brady who probably had designs on the woman Mitch intended to make his wife. He just needed to convince her, get her alone so they could talk, tell her how sorry he was . . .

Mitch rubbed the sticky wet spot on his shirt. Yeah, he'd seen how far he'd gotten with that. The truth was, she hated him, and he didn't blame her. What he did, how he treated her, well, he wasn't sure he could forgive it himself. He shot a furtive glance across the table where she sat, conversing with the New York dandy. He'd been so blinded by his own fear, he hadn't realized that she was the woman God had given him to love. But love her he did, enough to work at stemming his pride and controlling his temper, if that's what he needed to do. He popped the roll in his mouth. He supposed it was time. Time to change his ways, time to grow up. He swallowed hard. Time to be the man God intended him to be.

"I understand you're a department editor for a small newspaper in Ireland," Mr. Harris said, taking his eyes off Charity long enough to address Mitch with a cool gaze.

"I'd hardly call Ireland's largest press 'a small newspaper,' Mr. Harris, but yes, I am."

"Seems rather curious to transfer from a European paper to an American one, such a difficult transition, leaving family and friends."

"Not at all. I've been to Boston in the past and have wanted to return for a while now." His gaze locked on Charity. "You might say my heart is in Boston."

"How so?" Harris asked, buttering a roll of his own.

Mitch was tired of pussyfooting. "It's simple, really. Charity and I are going to be married."

Charity's fork clattered to the floor.

"Oh, my, Mitch . . . ," Marcy stuttered, shooting a tentative glance at her daughter.

"Congratulations, son," Patrick boomed, reaching across the table to pump Mitch's hand. "That's great news!"

Charity jumped up to retrieve her fork. "Mother, I'll start the coffee." She bolted into the kitchen, her ire rising faster than the lump in her throat. The nerve! That man had all the romanticism of that wet stain on his shirt. How dare he just blurt it out like that, as if she had no say in the matter whatsoever?

The door creaked behind her. She spun around and singed him with a glare. "Just who do you think you are, announcing to the world that we're going to be married?"

Mitch stared her down. "Your future husband, that's who."

"Ha! And I suppose I don't have anything to say about it?"

He began to grind his jaw and took several steps forward. "You can say yes."

She moved back to lean against the sink, rankled by his attitude. "Maybe. And just maybe I'll say yes to Brady."

His cheek pulsed as he started toward her. "You'll say yes to me."

"Don't you dare think you can tell me what to do, you thick-headed bully!" She reached behind and scooped up the dishrag from the rinse water in the sink. Before he could clamp a hand on her arm, she pelted it at his face. It bounced against his rock-hard cheek with a noisy splat. Dirty water slopped into his eyes before sluicing down his neck. She stared in shock.

His water-slicked face accentuated the nerve twitching in his jaw. Little plops of water dribbled on his shoe while the dishrag dangled from his shoulder, soaking his tweed Norfolk jacket.

A hand flew to her mouth as she fought the urge to laugh.

He moved in to grip her arms, ignoring the dripping rag on his coat. "Who's Brady?"

She tried to twist free. "Let me go! You're getting me wet."

He pressed her to the counter. "Answer me! Who the devil is Brady?"

"A man who treats me with a lot more respect than you ever did."

He released his hold. "Do you love him?"

She glared at him, angry at the time they'd lost, the pain he'd inflicted. "Yes."

He stared hard for several seconds. Hurt replaced the shock in his eyes. He turned away.

Her heart shot to her throat. "As a friend . . . ," she whispered in a rush.

He slowly shifted to face her, one brow cocked. With a questioning gaze, he latched a thumb onto the pocket of his trousers.

She swallowed hard and crossed her arms. "Do you have any idea the torture you've put me through, Mitch Dennehy?"

His lips twisted. "I went through the same torture, you know, not to mention all the months you put me through the wringer with your charm."

She sucked in a deep breath. "But six months? It took you six long months? Why didn't Mrs. Lynch tell my grandmother?"

He sighed and slacked a hip, closing his eyes to massage the bridge of his nose. "I had a lot of issues to work through, Charity. With my mother, Anna, you. After Kathleen broke the engagement, I asked Mrs. Lynch not to say anything. I needed to stew for a couple of months, pray about a few things."

"A couple of months?" She propped her hands on her hips.

He looked up with sorrow in his eyes. "I felt compelled to pray about us, to be sure I was doing the right thing." He took a deep breath. "And I didn't know. About the rape. When Mrs. Lynch mentioned it in passing a few weeks ago, I thought I was going to lose my mind." He took a step forward, his eyes glistening. "That's when I knew. Knew I wanted to be with you. To protect you, take care of you." He hung his head, and the grief was evident in his face. "Forgive me, little girl, for wounding you like I did, for ever implying you were a . . ." He swallowed hard and lifted his gaze. "I was angry and desperate to push you away. I . . . I didn't realize . . . realize that I had been wrong all along."

"Thickheaded?"

He took a deep breath and another step. "Yes, thickheaded. Too much to see that although I'd forgiven my mother, Anna, and finally you, I had never dealt with my fear and deep lack of trust. It drove me away from you, Charity, and I was too blind to see it."

"You mean thickheaded."

He smiled and moved close, tugging her into his arms.

"Don't you dare try and sweet-talk me, Mitch Denne—"

He kissed her gently on the mouth, effectively silencing her as he intensified the kiss. He pulled away. "Yes, thickheaded, but desperately in love with an equally obstinate little girl. How are we going to make this work, Charity O'Connor? Two bullheads, but only one of us can win."

She stared, her anger momentarily doused by the heat throbbing within. She lunged to kiss him back, releasing years of pent-up passion. Mitch groaned and finished it off with a kiss that tingled all the way to her toes. She jerked away with her chest heaving. "Maybe we both can win. It would take a lot of compromise and even more prayer, but what do you think?"

He gave her a half-lidded look that made her mouth go dry, then leaned in and nestled his lips along her throat. The blood pumped in her veins. She felt the shadow of his late-day beard, and the realization of what was happening prompted a chuckle of joy from her throat. She shivered. "I love you, Mitch Dennehy, so much that even prayer couldn't get you out of my heart. Sweet saints above, I can't wait to marry you!" Her gaze narrowed. "You are asking, aren't you?"

He grinned. "Oh, I'm asking all right. And you won't have to wait. I don't intend to."

She blinked. "But, Mitch, it takes time. We've got a wedding to plan."

He leaned in close. "Take all the time you need, little girl. Pick the church and plan the wedding, but tomorrow you'll be my wife."

"What?"

"City Hall. You and me. Married at last."

"Oh, no you don't, Dennehy, we're going to—"

He cut her off with a kiss that weakened her knees, deepening it until her bones felt like warm oatmeal. He pulled away and she sagged against the sink with a hand to her stomach. She swallowed hard. "All right," she whispered with a catch of her breath. "But the hours, they change, remember? The window might not even be open."

He pulled her close to smother her throat with kisses, then trailed his mouth to hers. "Oh, it's open," he said, his voice husky against her lips. "And you can bet I made bloomin' sure."

Acknowledgments

To Charlotte Vernaci, for her invaluable support and insight on Books 1, 2, and 3 and to the rest of the "gang," Judy Jackson, Linda Tate, and Ruth Volk for brainstorming sessions at Donohue's. Your friendship means more than you will ever know.

To the great team at Revell, thank you for your patience and support—particularly Cheryl Van Andel and Dan Thornberg for another great cover and more patience than the law allows.

To my dear friends and former co-workers Carol Ann, Tammy, Cynthia, Sandy, Anna, Betty, and Jenny for their invaluable feedback and support on all three books. I miss you guys terribly!

To my precious prayer partners and best friends, Karen, Pat, and Diane—what a touch from God you are in my life!

To my Aunt Julie, my mother-in-law Leona, and my sisters, Dee Dee, Mary, Pat, Rosie, Susie, and especially Ellie and Katie, for your continued love and support. I am blessed to call you family.

To my daughter Amy, my son Matt, and my daughter-in-law Katie—true examples of God doing abundantly, exceedingly more than I ever hoped, thought, or prayed. I love you guys!

To my husband and best friend, Keith, who gives me more joy than I ever dreamed possible in this lifetime—I would be lost without you.

And to Jesus—without you, there would be no peace, joy, or hope . . . and definitely no books!

Julie Lessman is a new author who has already garnered writing acclaim, including ten Romance Writers of America awards. She resides in Missouri with her husband and their golden retriever, and has two grown children and a daughter-in-law. Her first book in the Daughters of Boston series, *A Passion Most Pure*, was released January 2008. You can visit Julie or contact her through her website at www.julielessman.com.